THE ENEMIES OF MY COUNTRY

JASON KASPER

Srishti
PUBLISHERS & DISTRIBUTORS

Srishti Publishers & Distributors
A unit of AJR Publishing LLP
212A, Peacock Lane
Shahpur Jat, New Delhi – 110 049

editorial@srishtipublishers.com

First published in India by
Srishti Publishers & Distributors in 2024

First published by Severn River Publishing, 2021

10 9 8 7 6 5 4 3 2 1

Printed and bound in India.

ABOUT THE AUTHOR

Jason Kasper is the USA Today bestselling author of the Spider Heist, American Mercenary, and Shadow Strike thriller series. Before his writing career, he served in the US Army, beginning as a Ranger private and ending as a Green Beret captain. Jason is a West Point graduate and a veteran of the Afghanistan and Iraq wars, and was an avid ultra marathon runner, skydiver, and BASE jumper, all of which inspire his fiction.

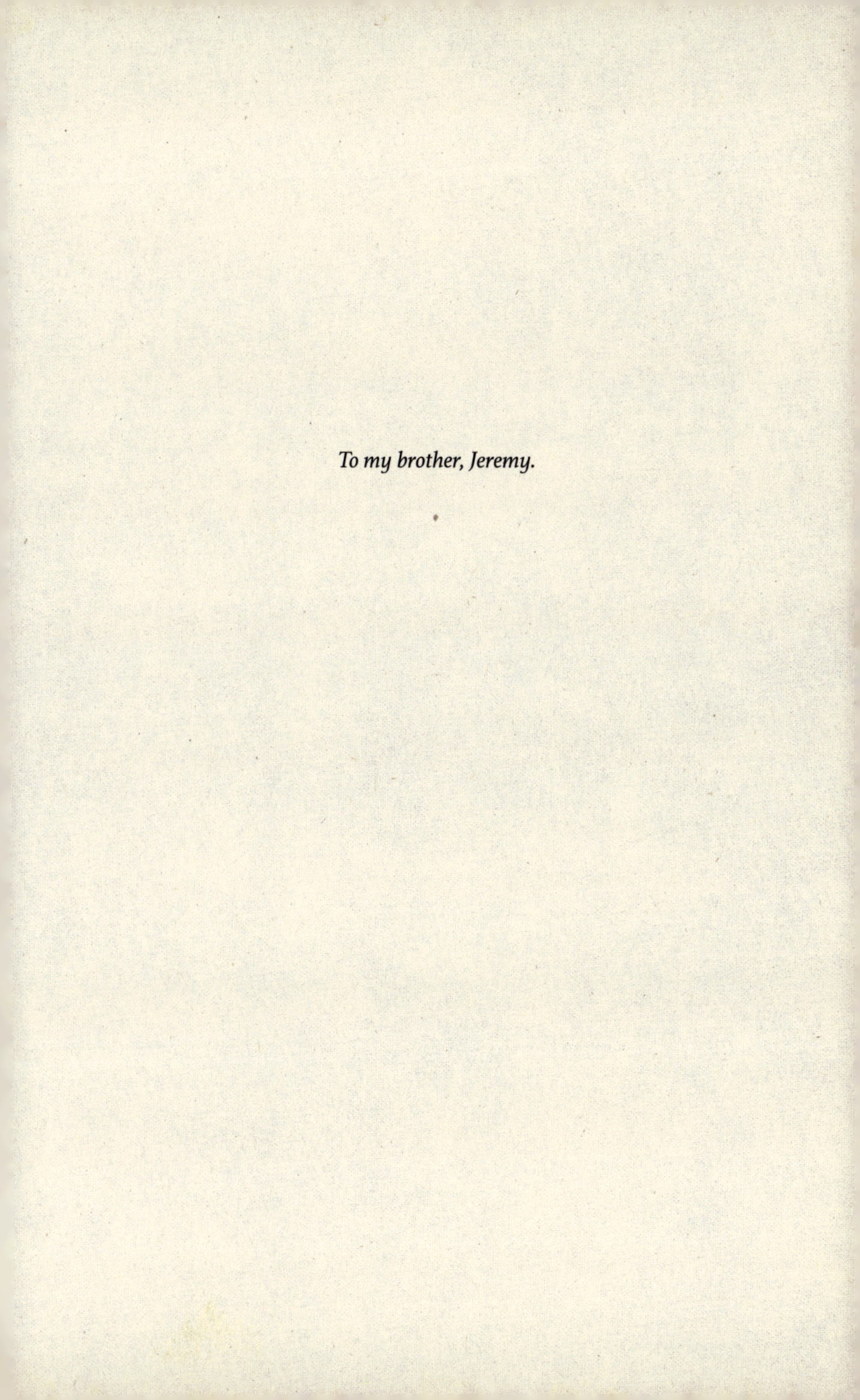

To my brother, Jeremy.

Out of every one hundred men, ten shouldn't even be there, eighty are just targets, nine are the real fighters, and we are lucky to have them, for they make the battle. Ah, but the one, one is a warrior, and he will bring the others back.

—Heraclitus

Some people just need to get shot in the fucking face.

—David Rivers

1

Northwestern Syria

The Syrian horizon had gone from black to coral with the onset of daybreak, and now that the sun was beginning to lift skyward, it settled on a flame-orange glow.

I stowed my night vision device, rubbing away the phosphorescent green hues to see my surroundings through my own eyes—and as was all too common in my previous incursions into foreign countries, the land was staggeringly beautiful.

Windswept hills of rock and sand undulated as far as the eye could see. From my vantage point under a stone outcropping, the ground fell away to a dirt road slicing through the ancient stream bed below, the rocky cliffs lit with the sun's first rays. The air was brisk with the fading night, fresh with the smell of a new day ahead. This was a sunrise I would've liked to share with my daughter, with my wife, save one small detail.

I was in Syria, and neither my family nor any sanctioned military force knew I was here.

Ian spoke quietly beside me.

"We've got a ping."

I turned to look at him, his face softly lit by the screen of his tablet.

He continued, "This is it—BK is on the move."

I released one hand from the grip of my HK417, a heavy assault rifle chambered in 7.62mm. Normally I preferred working up close with a smaller caliber, but today's target called for longer range, greater penetration, and increased stopping power.

Keying my radio switch, I transmitted to the rest of my team.

"Net call, net call. BK has departed. ETA to kill zone six minutes. Cancer, stand by for visual."

Cancer watched the world beyond his crosshairs, a crystal image of the village in the foothills to the west, and offset his reticle from a building just under two kilometers from his position. He wouldn't be shooting that far today—not that he couldn't.

The sniper rifle tucked against his shoulder was the Barrett M107, a thirty-pound beast of a weapon that had been beyond cumbersome to haul up the rocky slopes to his current position. But now that he'd reached his perch, and was currently sweltering inside his ghillie suit, he had the ability to deliver a .50 caliber round into anything within a one-mile radius.

Cancer focused on a faraway single-story building, letting his eyes tick to the dirt road emerging from behind it. For now, all he needed to do was report the make and model of any vehicles headed outbound on the road that snaked through the rocky canyons. Then, when Ian had positively matched the trace of their target's cell phone to the vehicle in question, Cancer would have a few minutes to reposition himself with a line-of-sight to the kill zone.

And once the vehicle entered that kill zone, Cancer thought with a grin, he'd be able to unleash torrential hellfire. Auto glass, human torsos, engine blocks—nothing was a fair match for the Barrett.

Cancer's grin faded with his first glance of a vehicle leaving the village. He watched for a split second of disbelief before keying his radio to transmit in his Jersey accent.

"I've got eyes-on, ETA five minutes to kill zone, and...we've got a problem."

The apprehension in Cancer's voice made me uneasy.

"What's the problem?"

"*It's not one vehicle, it's three. All pickups, and they're moving in a tight convoy. Looks like five to eight armed fighters in the back of each truck.*"

I looked to Ian.

"Any chance that's not our guy?"

Ian shook his head, the veins in his balding temples standing out in stark relief. "Tracker is on the move—it's him. Probably in the center truck."

Cancer's voice came over the radio again.

"*What do you wanna do, boss?*"

I weighed the options. None were good.

We'd already burned an extensive Agency ratline to move our five-man team into position along this ambush point, awaiting what was supposed to be one vehicle carrying our target. The sudden presence of two additional vehicles and ten to sixteen enemy fighters wouldn't matter much in Hollywood, where every bullet found its mark and the bad guys all died when they were supposed to.

But if we carried out our ambush here in the Syrian desert, we'd better kill them all on the first go. If they managed to disperse on foot, they'd be able to kill us in a counterassault either immediately or as we tried to reach the vehicles staged for our escape. Letting them pass in the hopes of getting a better opportunity later would increase our exposure time amid extremely dangerous terrain swarming with too many armed militias to count.

I transmitted, "Worthy, hit the first truck when it reaches the chokepoint. Cancer, you've got engine block of the trail vehicle, followed by the center truck in the convoy. Ian and I will engage the center truck. Reilly and Worthy, you work front to rear. Questions?"

"*Got it*," Cancer replied. "*Relocating to get eyes-on the kill zone*."

A moment later, and with a touch of hesitation in his Southern lilt, Worthy replied, "*Racegun copies all*."

Beside me, Ian muttered, "David, you sure about this?"

"Not even a little bit," I admitted, "but we're going to do it anyway."

From his vantage point on the eastern flank of the firing line, Worthy readied his M72 LAW with nervous anticipation.

The weapon felt light and powerful in his hands; it was a portable, one-shot rocket launcher designed for taking out a tank. Against an unarmored vehicle, the effects would be devastating.

At least, he thought, that's how it *should* have worked.

With weeks of intelligence indicating that BK traveled in a single vehicle, this was supposed to be a very short ambush indeed—one rocket explosion doing the job, with a machinegun, sniper, and two assault rifles raking the debris just to be sure. Then it would be a speedy exfil for the team, who would vanish before anyone else arrived. And when they did, the kill zone would appear as little more than another factional dispute in a country where such attacks were a daily occurrence.

But two additional trucks changed everything. Worthy's job would be largely the same: take out the lead vehicle at the geographic chokepoint in the canyon below. But now, the team was severely outgunned. They'd lose the element of surprise the instant he fired his rocket, and after that...well, the enemy would get a vote.

Worthy asked, "You think this is a good call, or a bad one?"

To his right, Reilly shifted his position, rocking his massive weapon forward on its bipod. A medic by trade, Reilly had a muscled build that made him a natural pick for wielding the team's sole machinegun.

He replied in a boyish voice, "With David calling the shots, definitely a bad idea. But so far he's always come out alive. Against all odds, sure. But alive."

Worthy nodded and cast a glance at the rifle at his side. As soon as his rocket was fired, that rifle would be his only weapon. He adjusted its position a final time, then stopped moving abruptly.

"You hear that?" he asked.

Reilly glanced right, picking up on the same sound—a vehicle engine churning its way across the winding road below.

There was just one problem: it was coming from the wrong direction.

Reilly pushed himself up on his hands to get a better look, then dropped back down and transmitted.

"Doc has visual on one vehicle inbound from the east. Looks like a civilian sedan."

David replied, "*Is it going to be a problem?*"

"Don't think so. Should pass by a couple minutes ahead of the convoy."

"*Copy*," David transmitted, "*we are weapons hold until that sedan is out of the kill zone.*"

"Copy," Reilly answered.

After a moment of silence, David transmitted again.

"*Cancer, we are weapons hold, how copy?*"

Begrudgingly, Cancer responded, "*Yeah, yeah. I got it.*"

Worthy smiled. Cancer didn't have the most polished personality on the team, but when it came time for combat, you wanted him on your side of the fight.

He caught a glimpse of the sedan, a battered white vehicle limping over the rough dirt road below.

To Worthy's unease, the sedan began braking before it rolled to a stop in the worst place imaginable—the chokepoint of two canyon walls, a point so narrow that only one vehicle could pass. It was the exact point that Worthy planned to deliver his first rocket.

"He's stopping," Worthy transmitted. "The sedan has stopped right at my chokepoint."

I cursed under my breath.

"Did he see us?" I asked.

"*Negative. Must have engine trouble—he's opening the hood.*"

Beside me, Ian transmitted for everyone to hear, "ETA two minutes."

Cancer responded quickly. "*Perfect. We wanted a chokepoint, now it's guaranteed.*"

"Negative," I replied. "We are weapons hold."

"*If that convoy stops at the chokepoint, the guys in the back will pull security and spot us. Then we're fucked.*"

"We're not getting a civilian killed in the crossfire. If we're compromised, we break contact and exfil."

Cancer made no effort to conceal his irritation. "*Think about this, man. It's gonna be self-defense, and we don't have the manpower to fight them off.*"

"We're weapons hold. That's final."

I released the radio switch, a sense of foreboding taking hold in my gut. As was too often the case in combat, there were no good options—anything you did or failed to do could pair with some absurdity of chance in the ensuing chaos, and turn out to be either your destruction or your salvation.

To my eternal relief, Reilly transmitted, "*Sedan driver has closed his hood and is continuing movement. Clear of the kill zone.*"

Ian followed this up with, "One minute out."

Keying my radio, I spoke quickly.

"Copy all—ambush is a go. We are weapons hot; Racegun, you have control to initiate."

Worthy and Cancer confirmed the order, and I nodded to Ian. "Let's go."

Grabbing our rifles, we high-crawled over the exposed rock to take up firing positions on the dirt road below.

The kill zone was selected for its location between curves—thus ensuring the slowest possible rate of travel—and for the chokepoint in the canyon walls, where any coherent defense from an elevated attack would be difficult if not impossible.

Drawing the rifle stock against my shoulder, I leveled my aim toward the kill zone and listened to the rumble of the approaching convoy. I whispered to Ian, "You good?"

"Yeah." He sounded assured, though what he actually felt in that moment, I had no idea. Ian's specialty was intelligence, not gunslinging, and while I was glad to have him around when his electronic gadgets were required, in the back of my mind he was a tactical liability.

I dismissed the thought as the first pickup came into view, bearing black Islamic State flags. Half a dozen armed men sat in the back. The second truck was just barely visible as the first approached the chokepoint, and with a sense of dread I heard the men begin shouting to each other.

Someone had seen something, and the men were struggling to hoist their weapons upward when I heard a loud explosion—Worthy's rocket firing from the high ground to my right.

I opened fire on the center vehicle, trying to hit the driver through the roof. My gunfire was dwarfed by Reilly's machinegun unleashing a rapid staccato burst, punctuated by the deep booming of Cancer's sniper rifle. Amid the melee, Worthy's rocket found its mark.

The deafening thunderclap of the lead vehicle exploding brought with it an enormous sand cloud that momentarily erased all three trucks from view. I continued pumping rounds into the cloud as fast as I could fire, hearing that all of my teammates were doing the same. In the ideal situation, the lead truck would be immobilized at the chokepoint, but suddenly I saw it bowling forward from the dust and smoke, propelled by the center vehicle now ramming it out of the way.

I desperately adjusted my point of aim to open fire, knowing that my teammates were likewise trying to disable the truck before it could escape. But the canyon road's tight turns resulted in limited sectors of fire, and the lone surviving truck soon careened out of sight.

"Ian," I shouted, "what do we got?"

He was already consulting his tablet to see if the signal from our target's cell phone was stationary or, better yet, destroyed completely. After a few moments, his eyes met mine.

"It's on the move—BK made it out."

I keyed my radio.

"Cease fire, cease fire, cease fire." The chatter of assault rifle and machinegun fire went quiet, and I continued, "BK is on the move. Haul ass to our trucks—we're going to interdict him on the road."

Cancer ran down the hillside, his footfalls displacing crumbling chunks of shale. He felt ridiculous in his ghillie suit, the sand-colored strips of burlap trapping his body heat while giving the appearance of a highly flammable human bush scrambling downhill.

Then there was his sniper rifle, which had been fantastic for destroying the rear vehicle's engine block before Worthy's rocket turned the kill zone into a whitewash of smoke and sand. Now, the Barrett .50 cal in his grasp was little more than a five-foot-long, thirty-pound burden threatening to topple him over as he ran toward his team's two vehicles at the bottom of the hill.

Once they'd gotten into position for the ambush, those vehicles were to serve one, and only one, purpose: to speed the men to their pickup point along the Agency ratline, where they'd be whisked out of the country before any coherent search effort could mobilize to find them.

There was nothing in the mission description about tear-assing around Syria, however briefly, in the hunt for an escaped vehicle with their target inside. Still, he could see the logic—there was an overland route by which they could intercept the curving canyon road as it emerged onto flat ground, and perhaps a brief diversion was in order to make it there. If the team arrived quickly enough, they could smoke the target vehicle in a hasty ambush.

The question was whether they could make it there before their target slipped away for good.

Nearing the bottom of the hill, Cancer caught sight of one of his team vehicles ripping east across the desert. Not until he'd threaded his way between boulders at the base of the hill did he see the second—a sand-covered SUV idling with Ian at the wheel.

Cancer yanked the rear door open, angling his massive sniper rifle inside without banging the scope out of alignment. He'd barely felt the seat beneath him before Ian floored the gas, causing the door to slam shut as they gained speed over the desert.

David turned around in the passenger seat and fixed Cancer with an accusatory glare. "What took you so long?"

Reilly braced himself in the pickup bed, doing his best to remain standing.

Trying to hold his machinegun stationary on the roof of the cab was like trying to use chopsticks while riding a rodeo bull. The truck pitched and bounced over the rolling terrain, causing the machinegun bipod to carve across the roof in ear-piercing metallic screeches as Reilly fought to stay upright, much less keep the big gun pointed forward.

The ammo presented an additional complication—for the ambush, Reilly had been able to neatly S-fold his ammunition belt in advance. Now, he had to control an ammo bag while keeping the belt angled evenly into the gun, all while trying not to die as Worthy sped them forward.

Ian transmitted, "*Looks like BK is exiting the canyon—we should have eyes-on any second now.*"

Reilly scanned the foothills to their front, catching sight of the target vehicle as it emerged a moment later. It was already speeding out of the canyon, perhaps three hundred meters distant and gaining ground fast on the mostly level dirt road. He couldn't tell at a glance if any men—any living men, at least—were in the back, but the pickup itself looked like it had just driven smoking out of some fresh hell. Its front half was coated in black ash and marked by shattered windows; its Islamic State flags flapped in tatters.

Astonishingly, there were survivors in the truck bed—Reilly knew this from the sparking muzzle flashes opening fire toward him.

Grabbing one leg of the bipod to steady it on the roof of the cab, Reilly took aim and loosed a long burst at the truck.

The orange streaks of his tracer rounds interspersed with ball ammunition arced toward the pickup, his first burst landing short as Reilly struggled to adjust his fire. By the third burst he was dropping rounds with general accuracy, the bullets kicking up clouds of sand around the pickup and sparking off the cab as enemy fire continued. Between machinegun bursts, Reilly registered the crack of incoming bullets slicing through the air overhead.

Worthy cut a hard right as they met the dirt road, causing Reilly to nearly fly out of the truck bed.

He slammed a fist on the roof of the cab. "Easy, will you? Trying to shoot here!"

"Sorry about that," Worthy yelled back.

Now, at least, Reilly had a straightforward shot to the target vehicle, which had black smoke billowing in its wake as it struggled to maintain speed. Lining up his iron sights on the fleeing truck, Reilly prepared to fire his next burst—then halted abruptly with two muttered words.

"Well, shit."

Civilian vehicles were pulling off the road, scrambling out of the way to make room for the war-ravaged pickup bowling toward them. It was as if a convoy of innocent bystanders had suddenly appeared at the most inopportune time, and a split second later, Reilly realized why: they were approaching a village, the flat roofs carving a swatch out of the morning horizon.

No matter how well he attempted to aim from the moving vehicle, he could no longer shoot without indiscriminately sending bullets into the civilian populace. He held his fire, fearing that his target was about to escape for good.

But then he saw that it may not matter anyway—the target vehicle was starting to fishtail across the road, the damage to it finally taking hold. As it careened into the outskirts of the village, the rear end pivoted violently to the left. The enemy driver tried to steer out of the turn, but overcorrected and sent his truck into a barreling roll.

Flooring the accelerator, Worthy watched the enemy pickup flip sideways three times before crashing to a halt in the village.

He pulled on his seatbelt and shouted to Reilly.

"Hold onto something, bud, I'm going to ram 'em."

Reilly screamed an exasperated response over the roaring engine.

"Well that's just *super*!"

Worthy smiled to himself, thinking that Reilly would do the same if he were behind the wheel. Their jobs had all the potential for physical injury that professional football players faced—minus, of course, the paycheck and fame and cheerleaders. Add in the threat of imminent death at any moment, however, and the two careers were virtually indistinguishable.

He transmitted to the other truck, referring to David by his callsign.

"Suicide, what's your ETA?"

No response.

Could have been a simple radio issue, or could have been David's truck getting tangled up with some enemy force along the way, but in any case, there was no time to consider it.

He was closing with the enemy truck, now inverted on the main road leading into the village. Worthy couldn't tell if there were any survivors, though he made out a few black-clad bodies of ISIS fighters strewn across the dirt.

With the enemy truck's engine block serving as its center of gravity, striking the rear quarter panel should cause the truck to spin and shake up any survivors in the cab. All Worthy needed was a few seconds to dismount and light up his target in the passenger seat, gaining his team a confirmed "jackpot" and getting the hell out of Dodge before enemy reinforcements could arrive.

He was seconds away from impact, barreling into the village at fifty miles per hour, when one of the enemy fighters on the ground recovered his weapon. Worthy scarcely registered the movement, hearing instead the long burst from an AK-47 as bullets pockmarked his windshield and rattled into the engine block.

Worthy cut the steering wheel to the right, keeping his head low as the gunfire continued, growing in volume until his truck ran over the enemy fighter with a lurching *thump*. Then he steered left, aligning his bumper with the enemy truck's rear quarter panel and smashing into it. The impact threw him forward against his seatbelt.

Braking to a sudden stop that brought with it a crashing sound from the truck bed—Reilly and his machinegun coming safely to rest, he presumed—Worthy glanced in his side-view mirror to see the enemy pickup completing a full rotation on its roof. He found his rifle half-wedged in the passenger seat footwell and snatched it up before shouldering his door open.

Worthy absorbed the chaos all around him: women screaming, civilians running for cover, the choking stench of gasoline and smoke from both his own wounded truck and the upended pickup.

He didn't bother checking on his teammate—Reilly could fend for himself, and the best thing Worthy could do for him now was to punch BK's ticket for good, allowing the entire team to escape with mission success intact. Now that they were compromised, every passing second in the Syrian village increased the danger to their lives. With David calling the shots, that danger wasn't likely to end until BK was dead.

Worthy raced to close the distance to the enemy vehicle, skidding to a halt beside the engine block before kneeling to take aim within the cab. Gunfire had carved long scrapes along the cab before ricocheting or boring into the truck, whose windshield was shattered by the triple roll that had crippled it for good.

But the truck was empty.

Before Worthy could fully process the implications of this discovery, he heard Reilly's belt of machinegun ammo jangling as his teammate ran toward him.

"I'm fine, in case you were wondering."

Worthy rose to a crouch, scanning the surrounding buildings in a desperate attempt to determine BK's location. They would have to get off the street in a matter of seconds—he and Reilly were completely exposed to view from countless buildings, any one of which could hold enemy combatants ready to deal themselves into a gunfight.

Just as this thought occurred to him, sparking muzzle flashes erupted from a darkened window across the street, and the first bullets impacted the truck to his front.

Ian sped toward the village, catching his first glimpse of Worthy and Reilly: they were pinned down behind the wreckage of the enemy truck, rounds kicking up sand around them. He couldn't tell where the enemy fire was coming from, but apparently the men in his truck could.

From the passenger seat, David asked, "Cancer, where do you want to set up?"

"Park next to that gray building."

Ian squinted through the windshield. Half the buildings in the village were gray. He steered toward the nearest one on the left.

"Not *that* gray building," Cancer reprimanded him, "the one to the right! How am I supposed to engage from over there?"

Ian adjusted course, suddenly far out of his depth. These men were all seasoned fighters; by contrast, he was an intelligence operative, more suited to analysis than combat. Sure, he could shoot and move when he had to, but he lacked his teammates' reptilian reflexes. If he could have somehow manned his surveillance equipment from a remote location, he knew that David would have kept him off the firing line.

He slowed as they approached the building, and Cancer spoke again.

"Park with the bumper facing our two o'clock."

Ian cut the wheel and braked to a halt, expecting some shouted order or criticism, but instead, David said calmly, "Ian, on me."

That was it, he thought; three words, no further explanation of where they were going or why.

Then the two men were out of the vehicle, David circling behind it and Cancer setting the bipod of his sniper rifle on the hood.

Ian was prepared to run straight toward the row of buildings opposite the enemy truck, and instead saw David cut left and begin a semicircle route.

Ian stutter-stepped and changed course to follow, hearing Cancer's voice over his earpiece.

"*Get outta the way, asshole.*"

He suddenly realized David's circuitous route was to clear a line of fire for Cancer, and he'd barely made it four steps when the sniper rifle blasted behind him.

It was a monumental sound, a .50 caliber gunshot heard at close range that was followed by several more at two-second intervals. Ian saw gaping holes being bored below the window of a building directly ahead of him. That was exactly where David was heading.

Guess that's where the bad guys are, Ian thought. David never moved this quickly unless there was some risk of death to be taunted.

Ian struggled to keep up, bursting through the doorway and moving to the corner opposite David. He visually cleared one corner, then the next, coming to a halt in preparation for David's announcement that the room was clear.

But David was already moving into the next room, not knowing or caring that Ian could barely keep pace.

Apparently Cancer had seen them enter, because his voice crackled over Ian's earpiece.

"*Shifting fire.*"

By now Ian was in the next room, trying to clear his corners but instead cracking his knee against a side table that crashed into a couch. Then Worthy transmitted, "*Racegun and Doc consolidating on target building.*"

"*Copy,*" David replied. Ian only heard the response over his earpiece, not in person—David had already moved into the next room. Ian rushed to follow, entering a kitchen with an open door leading into an alley.

David stood beside the doorway, his barrel angled outside. Ian started to move to him, then noted with surprise that two young women were in the room, both tucked into the corner.

Ian raced to David's back, giving his shoulder a squeeze to indicate he was ready to move.

But instead of flowing outside to continue the hunt for BK, David kept his eyes forward and asked, "They here yet?"

Ian blinked. "Who?"

As if on cue, Worthy and Reilly charged into the room.

They'd just been pinned down and very nearly shot, yet both men looked calmer than Ian felt in that moment. Worthy gently pushed Ian out of the way, assuming the number two position behind David. "My truck's down, engine is shot out," he said quietly.

Reilly nodded to the two women and said, "Hello, ladies," before jostling into the number three position, relegating Ian to the rear of the stack and muttering, "Pick up rear security."

Then David flowed into the alley, with his team following behind.

I moved quickly, scanning for any indication of BK's path. It was impossible to discern his footprints from the countless marks on the dirt path, and I threaded my way around clotheslines and children's bicycles that had been abandoned after shooting had begun.

There wouldn't be much to see—a door left ajar, if I was lucky—but I continued with the grim determination that this was our last opportunity, and the clock was ticking down to BK escaping forever.

Granted, the wheels had already come off this mission. But if we were going to get BK, now was our chance. He was on the run with at least one additional fighter—probably his driver—after Cancer's .50 caliber rounds had sufficiently dissuaded them from remaining in place. We had a very momentary advantage in numbers and firepower, but it wouldn't last. BK's trip hadn't been a social call; he was on his way to meet with some very bad people, who would be arriving any moment to rescue him.

The alley took a sharp turn, paralleling the village's main road. Cancer would have just lost his line of sight to our progress, and I suppose it didn't matter much—any fighting at this point was going to occur up close and personal.

Turning the corner with my rifle raised, I took aim at a figure tucked into the corner junction of two walls—an unarmed man, looking at me not with defiance but eager opportunity. He urgently pointed to the door of the building beside him, and I gave him a nod of understanding before running toward it.

The man didn't know who we were, only that we weren't ISIS, and that seemed to be motivation enough for him to help.

I threw the door open and flowed inside, cutting left to clear a blind corner and hearing my teammates' footsteps spilling inside the building behind me. We began clearing the ground floor, splitting into two-man elements. Worthy and Ian moved into a doorway, and I gave Reilly a moment to sling his heavy machinegun and draw his pistol before I proceeded into the next room.

But it was empty, with only a pair of windows providing a view of the dusty street extending northeast through the village.

And it was through those windows that I saw we were too late.

A convoy of ISIS vehicles was speeding down the main road, black flags waving as fighters jockeyed to take aim from the truck beds. They were two hundred meters distant and closing fast.

I called out, "Reilly, hit them!"

He obliged at once, holstering his pistol and readying his machinegun as I slid a table up the wall beneath the left window. Taking his ammo bag, I waited for him to set his bipod atop the table before linking the short, free-hanging belt of ammunition in his machinegun to the S-folded ammo belt inside the bag.

As soon as I said the word "linked," Reilly opened fire.

His opening salvo decimated the windowpane, with his successive bursts lacing into the convoy's lead vehicle.

The trucks screeched to a halt, the second and third vehicles flanking the first as men scrambled out to return fire. Our radio earpieces had a decibel cutoff to serve as hearing protection, but the tremendous blasts of the machinegun cycling inside a confined space were jaw-rattling nonetheless.

Reilly took hold of the ammo belt with one hand, continuing to fire in short bursts to conserve his dwindling supply.

I transmitted, "Cavalry has arrived—set up local support by fire to hold them off. Cancer, get the truck ready and stand by for an emergency exfil."

"*Copy*," Cancer replied.

Moving to the opposite window, I assessed the situation. My first glimpse told me everything I needed to know: the enemy fighters weren't the most highly trained opponents, but with their numerical advantage, that didn't matter much.

There were five trucks that I could see, and the ISIS fighters were firing indiscriminately into the village. They didn't know exactly where we were, not advancing and not needing to. They weren't coming for us, not yet. They were instead laying down a wall of lead to allow BK to make his way to them.

I took aim and found my first target, a rifleman shooting from behind an open truck door. Before I could squeeze off my first shots, a trio of rounds stitched across his collarbone and face. Judging by the accuracy, Worthy had just wiped him off the battlefield.

Swinging my rifle to the right, I fired four bullets at another fighter, tagging him with at least one round that caused him to drop out of sight. I aimed at the next visible ISIS combatant, who was standing in the open and paid for it with two bullets to the chest.

There was little we could do now but hold our positions and keep the enemy at bay until Cancer was ready to speed us to safety. Maybe—if we were lucky—we could get a clean shot at BK as he made his way to the trucks.

A shrill scream outside the window cut my thoughts short, and I adjusted my position to locate the source.

She was a girl of eight or nine, now crouched behind the insubstantial cover provided by a pile of mud bricks on the opposite side of the street, remnants of some half-remembered repair project that had probably been abandoned at the start of the civil war.

Now the bullets were kicking up sand around her, impacting the bricks to her front and the wall to her side. It was a matter of time before she got struck by a direct hit or a ricochet.

The sight of her seemed to suck all the oxygen from my surroundings; whether I liked it or not, the tactical situation faded completely from my mind. Here was a girl not much older than my own daughter, and I'd placed her in danger. If I didn't do something fast, she'd die because of me.

I was moving for the door before I consciously realized what I was doing, priming for the fastest run of my life. The morning sunshine beyond the doorway was dim behind the sandy clouds kicked up by bullet impacts, and with a final breath, I charged into the open.

There is a certain surreal quality imparted by racing through a hail of enemy gunfire. As my legs pumped in an adrenaline-fueled sprint, my peripheral vision registered the bullet impacts on the dirt road, on the brick and cinder block buildings around me.

The little girl watched my approach, screaming words I couldn't register above the noise and sobbing with terror. I heard the sharp paper-tearing sounds of bullets passing by, released my rifle with one hand, and fell backward into a baseball slide for the remaining few feet between us.

Skidding to a stop on my back, I wrapped my open arm around her chest, hoisted her tight against my side, and rose to a crouch.

The remaining distance to the nearest building corner was only four meters or so, but the few footfalls it took me to get there seemed to take an eternity. I darted for the corner and a narrow alleyway beyond it; the last thing I saw before reaching it was a bullet strike the tan wall, an impact that fired a spray of sand and debris into my eyes.

Then my vision was gone, eyes stinging as I proceeded into the alley by memory alone. I threw my back against the wall, hearing the staccato pops of gunfire continuing beside me. The girl was safe now. I tried to set her down, but it was no use—she clung to my side with animal ferocity, refusing to let go.

I wiped the back of my hand across my eyes until I could make out the foggy, unfocused expanse of alley before me, then found the nearest door and kicked it open.

She was still sobbing as I carried her inside to safety, perhaps uncertain whether she'd been rescued or kidnapped, and in the war-torn hellhole this nation had become, I couldn't blame her.

"It's okay," I said, aiming for a reassuring tone only to be met with a sense of sheer absurdity. There were no good guys or bad guys in this fight, and regardless of our intention—or the greater evils BK could inflict upon civilian masses if left unchecked—we'd nonetheless brought danger into this village, into her home. If I was looking for gratitude, I wasn't going to get it from her.

I tried to set her down again, to get back into the fight unencumbered. But she continued clinging to me with savage intensity, apparently deciding that in this moment I represented the lesser of two evils. I couldn't blame her for that assumption, and struggled to the nearest window to appraise the situation.

The convoy hadn't moved, though the fighters had dispersed to the surrounding structures to hold their line. I scanned the buildings across the street, trying to determine whether the fighters had begun advancing on us, when I caught a sudden flash of movement. I was prepared to duck behind the wall—with the girl clinging to my side, I wasn't about to get the jump on any determined enemy.

But something stopped me from hiding completely. It was a sense of disbelief, the jarring thought that I couldn't possibly be seeing what I was seeing.

I only observed him for a second, a momentary alignment of angles that caused me to catch a glimpse of the man's face in the window across the street.

For a fleeting moment, we locked eyes—here was my target, the man I'd been sent to kill. We referred to him as BK, but his real name was Bari

Khan, and the face that met mine was not Arab but Chinese. A Uyghur dissident, he'd found not-so-strange bedfellows in ISIS, with many of the same goals and enemies.

Bari Khan's face was covered in dust and glistening blood.

But his eyes were strangely unemotional, coolly in control. He seemed to be appraising me with disinterest, making no attempt to take aim.

I wasn't about to return the favor. Maneuvering my rifle around the girl, I struggled to bring my sights to bear on him.

It was too late. He was gone.

That was it, I knew at once. My team was stretched too thin to pursue any further—had, in fact, been stretched too thin to begin pursuing after the ambush failed to kill him. Our survival streak would end if we pushed our luck any further.

Moments later, the incoming gunfire abated almost completely as a group of enemy trucks whipped wild U-turns in the street, accelerating out of the village as my team continued firing at them. Two trucks remained abandoned, their engine blocks shot out by Reilly's machinegun.

Bari Khan was gone, this time for good, and his departure spelled something worse for our team. ISIS wasn't going to let our presence remain uncontested, and regardless of where they were taking the terrorist leader we'd been sent to kill, I knew at once that a larger opposition force was on its way to kill us.

I transmitted, "Cancer, they're gone. Need you to bring up the truck ASAP to get us out of here. Come up the main road until you see us."

He responded with one word: "*Moving.*"

Before I could attempt to pry the little girl off my side, Reilly transmitted, "*Suicide, you need support?*"

"Negative. Just flag down Cancer and I'll meet you at the truck."

Then I heard running footsteps approaching and immediately regretted my declaration to move alone. Whoever was coming toward me was doing so in a hurry, and it was too late to request help without him hearing me—and with confrontation imminent and the little girl still clinging to me like a spider monkey, my only advantage was the element of surprise.

I darted to the corner beside the doorway and knelt to keep the girl tucked behind my body. Then I aimed my rifle.

A man burst into the room so quickly that I almost fired out of blind reaction. His hands were empty, shirt taut against his torso, leaving no room for a suicide vest. This was no enemy fighter, but a panic-stricken man with tears staining his face.

Her father.

The man's eyes were wide, uncomprehending of the terror around him. He'd probably struggled to survive amid the endless bloodshed of the Syrian Civil War, only to find a group of armed men doing battle at his doorstep through no fault of his own.

He was just trying to safeguard his family the best he could, the same as I would have in his situation. The difference between us was little more than our place of birth.

I lowered my rifle and stood to hand him the child. She immediately clung to him, and as the man's eyes met mine with impossible gratitude, I gave him a silent nod—Arabic wasn't my specialty.

To my surprise, he addressed me in English.

"Thank you."

I felt a goofy half-grin spread across my face as the dim euphoria of recognition set in—if I'd been born elsewhere, this could just as easily have been my own daughter being saved. Then, I gave the only response I could think to muster.

"You're welcome."

I only had a moment to study his long, thin face and well-trimmed beard. Then he turned, keeping his daughter in his grasp as he moved not outside but rather up the stairs to the second floor. I realized in that moment that this wasn't some random structure I'd been occupying, but the girl's home.

Their departure jarred me to reality—my team was compromised in Syria, and the enemy surely didn't intend on letting us leave if they could prevent it.

The sound of an engine approached outside, and I knew Cancer was almost at my position. Then all hell broke loose as an automatic weapon began firing in wild bursts from just up the street.

I looked outside to find the source, and saw that the only possible location was from behind a partially finished cinder block wall jutting out from a building. Whoever this remaining enemy was, he was blasting rounds in our direction, shooting up the sides of buildings and shattering windows.

I transmitted, "Doc, can you drop that wall?"

"*Negative, I'm black on ammo.*"

"Anyone else got a shot?"

Worthy answered, "*No, we can't see him from here.*"

The remaining fighter was firing wildly while screaming in Arabic. He'd either not heard the order to withdraw, decided to ignore it, or had been sent to cover BK's withdrawal. The circumstances mattered precious little to us at present—he was shooting at us, and we couldn't flee the scene until he was dealt with. A single errant bullet at this point could disable our lone remaining truck, and I didn't want to test our odds with a commandeered local vehicle.

I also didn't want to take the time to maneuver forward until we could get a clear shot—not when there was a much quicker option available.

"Cancer," I transmitted, "we need you to get him. We'll cover you. He's behind the cinder block wall to your front."

He didn't respond; instead, I saw his tan SUV roll to a stop at the side of the road before he got out, hoisting his heavy sniper rifle and shaking his head in irritation. He marched angrily toward the cinder block wall, where the single entrenched fighter was still firing upward. Cancer's massive sniper rifle was intended for mile-long shots, not working up close and personal; but in the current situation, it was the best tool for the job.

Cancer moved along the wall, following the sound of gunfire on the other side. When he came abreast of the noise, he stopped, knelt, and strained to lift the enormous Barrett until its muzzle was level with the cinder block surface.

Then he fired a single shot, a deafening *boom* whose blast sent an enormous cloud of sand dust washing over him. The bullet ejected a spray of concrete out of the other side of the wall, bowling the enemy fighter over in a whirling froth of blood and bone fragments that painted the ground red.

I transmitted, "You got him."

Cancer's voice shot back over my earpiece.

"*No shit.*"

I shrugged and keyed my radio again.

"Consolidate on the truck. Let's get out of here while we can."

I ran toward the SUV, now idling with Ian at the wheel. Sliding onto the passenger seat, I turned to my team as Ian wheeled around and accelerated out of the village.

Worthy had piled into the storage space in the back of the SUV, and Reilly and Cancer fought to maneuver their giant weapons in the backseat. Combat always looked so cool in the movies, but the current dogpile reflected the reality we'd all experienced before: real war was an unglamorous, messy process of improvisation, and it would either claim your life or leave scars both physical and psychological.

I transmitted over my command frequency, "Paradise Seven One, this is Suicide Actual."

"*Send your traffic*."

"We are no-joy. Require emergency exfiltration, time now."

Long seconds elapsed before the response, the pause serving as an audible reminder of the collective disappointment from our mission failure.

"*Copy, assets are standing by at the link-up point*."

I moved my hand away from the radio switch, suddenly feeling like I'd run the hundred-yard dash while holding my breath. As soon as the adrenaline of battle faded, the body prioritized everything denied to it during the fight: water, oxygen, rest.

Ian looked over at me from the driver's seat.

"David, you think we'll ever get another shot at this guy?"

I adjusted the rifle between my legs, barrel pointed down to the floor.

Swallowing against a dry throat, I replied, "I don't know."

It was a good question, of course—the CIA had sent us after Bari Khan for a reason, and now he was on the loose with the full knowledge that he'd been located by men who were trying to kill him. He was about to go into hiding, and there was no telling if he'd surface again before an untold number of civilians paid the ultimate price.

But I knew one thing for certain: if the Agency succeeded in locating Bari Khan again, then my team sure as hell wasn't going to fail a second time.

2

Charlottesville, Virginia, USA

I let myself into the house quietly, trying not to jangle the keys in the lock.

Gently closing and locking the door behind me, I turned toward the entryway and living room, lit by the soft glow of various lamps that Laila had left on. I set down my bag and walked forward, tracing my hand atop a long white side table adorned with potted plants and family pictures.

Passing through my living room on the way to the kitchen, I paused to take in my surroundings. They should have felt familiar: a suburban oasis, a beautiful home by anyone's standards made more so by Laila's decorative touch, and warmed further by the toys and stuffed animals scattered about faster than they could be picked up.

How often had I passed through these surroundings, barely recognizing the splendor around me? Nearly every day for the past year, and yet it felt like I was seeing it all for the first time. On an average day, I took my home for granted. Having just returned from the frantic chaos of Syria, it seemed like I was passing through some alien wonderland that I didn't deserve.

I made my way to the cabinet, retrieving the trusty bottle of Woodford Reserve and pouring three fingers over ice. Then I sat at the dining room table, taking the first warming sips of bourbon. By my third pull from the glass, I was back on the high ground, waiting for Bari Khan's convoy to enter the kill zone, and by the fourth I was trying to pry the Syrian girl from my side so I could resume fighting alongside my team in the village. Those memories seemed real, concrete; by contrast, the normal home, the all-American life I had re-entered seemed to be some foggy, half-remembered dream. I took another sip.

A creak from the top of the stairs alerted me that I'd failed to enter quietly enough, and I approached the bottom of the staircase to see Laila descending toward me.

Even having been awakened by my return, she was stunning.

She wore sweatpants and a thin top without a bra, her blonde hair cascading over her shoulders in disarray, face puffy with sleep but radiant with all the beauty that had caused me to fall for her in college.

"Hey, babe," she whispered.

"Hey," I said quietly, receiving her into my embrace and kissing her lips. "I tried not to wake you."

"It's okay," she murmured, hugging me tightly before pulling back to appraise me with lucid green eyes. "You're having a drink?"

"Yeah, but I'll come to bed. Let's go."

"No, I'll join you."

"Don't you have to be at work early?"

"Yeah. It's okay."

I poured her a glass of red wine and carried it to the table, where she took a seat beside me. We raised our glasses and clinked them softly together.

She asked, "How was Jordan?"

"Hot," I said. "But everything went well."

"No issues starting up the contract?"

I shook my head. "The host nation instructors were really receptive, good rapport right off the bat. They're starting the marksmanship instruction today. We'll see how it goes, but I shouldn't have to go back over until my team lead needs some assistance."

"What unit are you guys training, again?"

She asked the question like a wife trying to verify her husband's whereabouts, and half the time I felt like I was keeping an extramarital affair from her. In a way, I was.

"101st SB," I replied automatically. "Jordan's Special Battalion within their Special Forces Group. Kind of like our Rangers. They're good, really motivated and capable. That makes things more interesting for my instructors, because they can teach higher-level stuff. Should be a great contract."

She said nothing, taking another sip as I asked, "Enough about me. How have you and Langley been?"

"Langley's so good, half the time I feel like she could raise herself."

"Guess she'd have to be that way to survive my parenting. I can't believe how smart she is, though."

"It's scary, right?"

"Yeah, I get the creeping suspicion we aren't going to need her college fund. How has residency been going?"

Laila took another sip of wine, closing her eyes halfway. "Can't be over soon enough. Most of my attending physicians are good, a couple have a God complex."

"I thought that was reserved for surgeons."

"I know, right?" She shrugged. "Things the movies never tell you, I guess. Pediatricians with God complexes—the threat is real. The kids are great, though. A few crazy parents here and there. Mostly it's the long hours and studying on top of everything else that makes it hard."

"Two more weeks?"

"Seventeen days, but who's counting? Let's just say I'm glad you're home. By the time I pick up Langley from day care, I'm ready for bed. And after my parents begged me to move here, I should sue them for false advertising."

I smiled, swirling the ice in my glass. Half the reason she'd jostled for a pediatric residency at the University of Virginia Children's Hospital was because her mother and stepfather lived in Charlottesville, where they'd spent years running a successful metalworking business.

But they'd recently received an acquisition offer from a corporate chain. After selling the business, they decided to use the substantial proceeds to buy a brown brick townhouse in Alexandria, just over two hours away.

Now, when I was gone for training or operations—two so far, the first in the Philippines—Laila was forced to juggle her job requirements with summer day care and babysitter schedules to ensure Langley was looked after.

Nodding, I said, "Well, I'll be able to help out there. Why don't I take her out this weekend? I'll make a day of it, and you can have some time to yourself."

"No, I'll go—I haven't seen you in a week. Last thing I need is time to myself."

That much suddenly seemed obvious. But I was new to being a parent and even newer to being a husband, and still felt like I was in a constant cycle of trying to figure out where and how to draw the lines.

"Right," I agreed, "it's a date, then. We can take her to Bumble Brews in the morning, then go walking downtown. Find a nice place for lunch and get her ice cream at Chaps."

"We're going to Chaps?"

I pushed back my chair and stood, locating my daughter standing in the shadows by the stairs. I could always hear Laila moving throughout the house; Langley, however, was still small enough at age six to creep around undetected.

"Hey, sweetie!" I approached and knelt before her, pulling her into a tight embrace. "Have you been good for Mommy?"

"Uh-huh," Langley replied. "I missed you."

"I missed you too. Want to see what Daddy got you?"

I felt her nodding against my shoulder, and carried her over to the front door where I'd set down my bag. Unzipping it, I procured a stuffed pink rabbit and handed it to her. She accepted it and pulled it into a hug between us.

"Is this from Jordan?" she murmured sleepily.

"Yes, from the Amman Airport."

"I love it."

I rubbed her back, feeling a mild sense of self-disgust. As much as I hated lying to my wife, I hated lying to Langley even more. The truth was, I'd picked up the toy at a truck stop on the way home, my one and only chance to procure a souvenir for her.

Setting her down, I remained kneeling and looked into her tired face.

Her curly brunette hair and brown eyes were in stark contrast to Laila and me—which was just as well, because she wasn't biologically related to either of us.

I looked up to see Laila standing in the lamplight, her expression sterner than I ever seemed to manage in front of our daughter. Langley had me wrapped around her finger, and she knew it better than anyone.

Laila said, "Sweetie, you're supposed to be asleep."

"I know," Langley replied. "I just heard you guys talking and wanted to see Daddy."

Laila shot me a raised eyebrow, and I hoisted Langley against my side to carry her upstairs.

Laila and I put her back to bed, her face going slack as she fell back asleep. Leaving her room and quietly closing the door, I turned to Laila.

"So, how tired are you?"

"Not *that* tired," she answered. "Let's go."

Taking my hand, she led me to our room.

3

CIA Headquarters
Special Activities Center

Kimberly Bannister deposited the teabag in the trash and added a double measure of honey to her steaming mug. After stirring the contents, she tapped the spoon against the rim and placed it back in its porcelain holder.

Then she returned to her leather chair with the mug, letting her gaze slip across the photographs on her desk.

She'd long ago stopped hanging pictures on her office walls. The first reason was privacy—yes, she was a very successful black woman in the Agency, but she'd built her career long before affirmative action and incentivized diversity were a consideration for anyone selecting the next generation of leadership. But she had simply tired of watching analysts' eyes darting to her walls when they thought she wasn't looking, trying to discern some secret for her success beyond simply being good at her job. By the time she'd been promoted to station chief, no one even called her Kimberly anymore. Instead, they used her old callsign as a term of respect: Duchess.

The second reason she didn't hang photos was that she'd kept being promoted too damn fast to maintain one office for long.

She kept her most treasured pictures in frames that faced her alone—

and they were, without exception, photographs of children. Mostly her grandbabies, one third-grade photograph of her son. That was taken around the time he'd begun to resent her frequent absences from his life, a shift that occurred right around the time her now ex-husband came to the same conclusion.

The personal sacrifices had been steep over her decades of service, and long after the excitement of the job wore off, she was left with the brutal bureaucratic grind. Duchess was feeling her age in this game, close to the pinnacle of her career as she worked to get the current program off the ground.

A double knock on her office door.

"Enter," she called.

The door swung open to reveal Jo Ann Brown, a white woman in her early forties. She was tall, solidly built, and looked like she'd grown up on a dairy farm, because she had. Duchess looked to the file folder in Jo Ann's grasp before making eye contact with her colleague.

Jo Ann Brown stepped forward, handing the file to Duchess before helping herself to an open chair.

"DIA got another hit." She spoke with a lilt that most would consider Canadian, but was in truth reminiscent of all true northerners in the Western Hemisphere: Jo Ann, bless her heart, was from Almond, Wisconsin. Duchess had looked it up once, out of sheer morbid curiosity, and found it lived up to every possible stereotype that the town name suggested. The population was 334 people, and their claim to fame was existing within spitting distance of the killing grounds for a murderer-slash-gravedigger whose exploits served as fodder for Alfred Hitchcock's villain in the movie *Psycho*.

Accepting the folder, Duchess flipped it open as Jo Ann continued, "This gives us independent corroboration between SIGINT, ELINT, and two HUMINT sources."

Duchess tried not to scoff as Jo Ann rattled off the number and type of intelligence indicators as if they meant something. But this wasn't some military operation with clearly delineated thresholds for mission execution, and while the nebulous boundaries should have been liberating for people trying to dispose of their nation's enemies, they were anything but.

The truth was, there were no defined protocols because this was all new and, perhaps just as importantly, they had no idea what they were doing. There was no existing playbook for Agency targeted killing operations—instead, Duchess was writing it one page at a time, and her efficacy or lack thereof bore dire consequences for everyone concerned, herself least among them.

Duchess scanned the first page, then the second, before her eyes halted abruptly on a single grid location. Then she began flipping the pages more quickly, analyzing the key points with increasing speed. In the end it was the target's location that concerned her the most, the one glaring inconsistency in otherwise logical intelligence reporting, and Duchess realized with a growing sense of unease that she was on a tighter timeline than she thought.

She snapped the file shut, setting it on her desk.

"This is enough to move on."

"Concur." Jo Ann hesitated a moment. "Universal consensus on my end is a drone strike, and I concur with that, too."

Duchess shook her head. "While the Agency would like to move forward as quickly as possible, we consider on-the-ground intelligence of sufficient value to rule out a drone strike in favor of a ground raid."

"Exactly what intelligence are you expecting to find?"

Now it was Duchess's turn to hesitate, to choose her words carefully.

"The Agency considers a Chinese dissident with full ISIS support a matter of grave concern. Since he's reacting how he is—or should I say, how he *isn't*—it's doubly concerning."

"How so?"

Duchess raised the mug to her lips, breathing the scent of lemon, ginger, and honey as she played a memory in her mind.

Then she set the mug down without taking a sip and pushed it away from her. "I've seen something like this once before, when I was station chief in Yemen."

"Well, what was the explanation in that case?"

"A story for another time." Duchess gave a mirthless grin that faded as she said, "All that matters at the moment is that we move at the soonest opportunity, and we use a ground team to do it. My people are ready to move on this if yours are."

Jo Ann's eyes narrowed. "Don't you have to ask your man?"

Duchess almost cringed at the use of that phrase. Jo Ann's left hand still bore a wedding ring—yellow gold, battered through decades of wear, with a small chip of a diamond that represented the best her husband could afford in their small-town youth.

Her right hand bore a class ring, a detail that Duchess found only slightly less irritating.

But Duchess replied softly, "I chose the type of people who don't say no to an opportunity like this. I can have the team wheels-up to Incirlik within seventy-two hours. But I'll need help with the route."

"Infil or exfil?"

"After the last attempt, the Agency is out of ratlines into that AO. We can provide the 'out,' but that's it. We'll need military infil, and it's going to have to be the air option."

Jo Ann gave a soft grunt. "Deferring on a drone strike is going to tax my connections at JSOC. Playing the air option will be far worse, especially after the last attempt failed. If your team doesn't deliver results this time, it's going to expend what credibility I've got left."

"If they don't deliver results this time," Duchess replied, "Gossweiler is going to shitcan our entire program. Can you get it done?"

A silence ensued, broken when Jo Ann swept both hands down her thighs and rose from the chair, speaking a single word that confirmed both her understanding and her departure.

"Duchess."

"Jo Ann."

Then she was gone, leaving the file and closing the door behind her.

Duchess lifted her phone from the receiver, waiting to hear a man's voice before she said, "Get me David Rivers on the secure relay."

She hung up the phone, and then lapsed into a deep and focused stream of concentration. Her thoughts danced across the memories of Yemen, the failed operation to kill a target and the subsequent confusion about his location after they picked up his trail again.

Her desk phone chimed twice.

She lifted the receiver to her ear, pivoting her chair toward the wall. "Duchess here."

David's voice was calm, level.

"Hello, Duchess. To what do I owe the pleasure?"

"We've located our mutual friend."

He sounded excited. "Really—has he left the country yet?"

"Not in the least." She gripped the receiver a bit more tightly. "He's in the same town as before."

A long silence followed.

Then David said, "I'm sorry, our connection must have broken up. It sounded like you said, 'he's in the same town as before.'"

"He is."

"Your information must be wrong."

"My information isn't."

Another pause, shorter this time, before David replied, "Why would that be?"

"I have my suspicions. And if I'm right, it's doubly important that we move ASAP. Do you want the op?"

No hesitation. "We'll finish the job this time."

"I'll be in touch with the particulars. Please notify your team."

"I will. Now if you'll excuse me, I have to get back to a tea party with my daughter."

Duchess felt a sad smile cross her face, her eyes drifting across the dated picture of her son. "David?"

"Yes," he replied, with a touch of irritation in his voice.

"Can I give you some free advice on raising your daughter?"

"Sure." David sounded mildly confused. "I'll take all the help I can get."

"There's really only one thing you need to know about parenting."

"I'm listening."

Duchess felt her breath hitch in her throat, then she swallowed and said, "Two words: don't blink."

She returned the phone to its cradle before he could respond.

Then, pivoting her chair to face the computer, she began constructing her next mission brief.

4

Charlottesville, Virginia

I pushed open the glass door, holding it for Laila and Langley to leave Chaps Ice Cream and join me in the late June sunshine.

The historic Charlottesville downtown was packed today, the weather warm but not oppressively so. Laila was in a sundress, Langley in a princess dress with sneakers, holding my hand while using her other to devour an ice cream cone that I knew from experience would begin melting long before she finished it.

We merged with the crowds strolling the walkway, continuing our relaxed afternoon together.

Langley looked up at me and asked, "Daddy, is it beer-thirty yet?"

I solemnly checked my watch.

"You know what? We're getting close. Maybe we can stop in at Jack Brown's up ahead. What do you say, Mom?"

Laila gave me a smile. "Sounds good. I'm just happy to have some time off with my two favorite people."

This was very often our weekend routine—lazily walk the downtown strip, get ice cream for Langley, and follow Laila as she ducked into various boutiques. And, of course, periodic beers for Dad. That part was key.

Any number of historic American downtown areas boasted restaurants, breweries, shopping, and local flavor. But the Downtown Mall in Charlottesville was special—one of the longest pedestrian malls in the country, with over a hundred venues lining a brick-paved walkway teeming with trees, flowers, and fountains.

Walking Charlottesville's historic Downtown Mall was the living embodiment of everything I wanted for my family. All around us, outdoor cafes were filled with families, couples, and groups of university students.

This was the American dream, indeed the dream of all civilized people no matter where they lived. To spend time with their family and friends in peace and abundance, absent the fear of a bomb going off or gunfire erupting at any moment. Preventing internal threats was the purview of law enforcement, and preventing external threats the job of the military—as well as the vast national intelligence complex and its attendant paramilitary assets, of which my team was now a part. I'd seen some horrific things overseas and would, if my current career continued, see many more —but no price was too high to keep those dangers eliminated or confined to foreign shores, to keep my family and countrymen safe.

I'd initially found Charlottesville far too yuppie for my tastes—it was difficult to come from my background and immediately adjust to the peaceful normality of eco-conscious local stores and hybrid vehicles.

And yet I'd come to embrace that yuppiness, at least somewhat. I knew this change had occurred in me when Laila asked me to get the milk out of the fridge and I cheerfully responded, "Almond or soy?"

I glanced over at my wife, her sundress swishing as she walked, her face content.

Then I looked down at Langley, who was growing unbelievably fast—each morning she seemed an inch taller than when we'd put her to bed. I always assumed that parenting would require some monumental effort on my part; instead, Langley had her own distinct personality that seemed to have been in place from her birth, and all I could—or should—do was be a constant supporting presence.

Licking her cone, Langley asked, "When can we go hiking again? I still need to see a bear."

Considering the timing, I replied, "How about we go camping in a few weeks? No better way to celebrate Mom finishing residency than hiking and continuing the search for black bears."

Laila offered, "Just what every girl dreams of. Count me in."

Langley nodded with delight—her memory was razor sharp, and she'd later recite this conversation down to the word in the event Laila and I forgot we ever agreed to the excursion.

I pointed to the ice cream dripping down her hand and said, "You don't have to finish that whole thing, you know. At this point the sidewalk is getting more ice cream than you are."

"I know. I'm done."

"Go put it in the trash over there."

She jogged to the trash can and deposited it, then ran back to take my hand again as we continued walking. When we came abreast of a water fountain, Langley tugged at my hand.

"Can I have some change?"

"Sure," I said, reaching into my pocket for the coins I always brought for this purpose. "If you can tell me how much is here."

I deposited a small handful of coins into her sticky palm, and watched her move them around with one finger.

She looked up and said, "One dollar and fifty-two cents."

Then she turned to the fountain until I stopped her. "Whoa, whoa. Hold it right there, hotshot—that was way too fast. Let's have Mom confirm, because Dad's math is...well, suspect at best."

My wife looked down at the coins.

"She's right. Two quarters, seven dimes, four nickels, and twelve pennies. Buck fifty-two."

I squinted at Langley.

"Lucky guess."

"No, it wasn't," Langley said, skipping off to the fountain before I could react.

Laila slid her arm around my waist. "I don't know why you're still surprised."

"I'm still surprised," I said, draping an arm over Laila's shoulders, "because at age six she's already smarter than I am as an adult."

We watched her tossing the coins into the fountain one at a time, then pausing to watch them sink. This was the good life, I thought. The family was together on a perfect summer day, and Laila was in a fine mood. My personal stock as a husband and father was at a dizzying high.

The moment wasn't going to get much better than this.

"Oh," I said casually, "I got a call from my team lead yesterday. There's been a bit of a hitch with the Jordan contract."

I felt Laila's body go rigid. Her arm fell from my waist, and she stepped back.

"Define 'a hitch.'"

I quickly explained, "A Jordanian captain got into a somewhat vocal disagreement with one of my instructors. He was in the wrong, but the Arabs treat their officers like royalty, so there was—"

She cut me off, her eyes boring a hole through mine.

"You have to go back already."

I nodded. "Just for a few days, to meet with my counterpart at the group headquarters and show my face at the training site. Just to get the contract back on the rails. It won't take long."

"When do you leave?"

"Day after tomorrow."

"When were you planning on telling me about this?"

I hesitated. "When? I mean, now, I suppose. I just found out yesterday, and you were busy with work so—"

"So you decided to wait until we're finally spending time together as a family?"

"You're right," I said automatically. "I should have told you as soon as I heard. I'll do that next time."

She looked away, fixing her gaze at some indiscernible point across the street.

"Because it's going to happen again."

Implying a future recurrence had been a bad call, I decided.

"I mean, I'm sure there will *eventually* be complications. But this will be a quick trip, I promise. I'll be back by next weekend, and we can—"

"Spend time together as a family?"

"Yes," I said. "That's right."

Laila said nothing, which was infinitely worse and more ominous than any response.

I asked, "What's going through your mind? You're scaring me."

"Oh, I don't know. Just that Langley needs you to be a part of the family, and so do I. And I'm trying to get my career off the ground while my parents are two hours away. I'm not running an Etsy shop out of the basement, David. I'm not baking while I wait for my next piano student to arrive. People rely on me. Human lives rely on me. I can't keep stretching myself thin every time you get another phone call from Jenio."

I looked sidelong to the crowds around us, considering a response that wouldn't dig me into a deeper hole with my wife. Jenio Solutions Consultancy, LLC was a private military company for which I worked, at least in name. It had a website, a corporate headquarters address, and a contact number that would be answered by a courteous, knowledgeable representative.

Jenio Solutions was also, of course, one of many front organizations covertly owned and operated by the CIA.

"Look," I said, "I'm sorry. But this is my new job. They say go, I have to go."

5

Incirlik Air Base, Turkey

Cancer took a pull of his cigarette, blowing another cloud of smoke toward the chain link privacy fence that blocked any view of his surroundings.

Above the fence's barbed wire were ordinary-looking pine trees, and beyond them he could hear the sounds of traffic and aircraft, indistinguishable from virtually any military base in America. There were no obvious visual indicators that he was in Turkey, and certainly none that the fence around him blocked off a small compound reserved for special operations forces passing through on their way to and from Syria.

Hell, he couldn't even remember much from the plane ride over: fifteen hours over the Atlantic had passed in the blink of an eye, courtesy of Ambien sleeping pills. With no opportunity for rest once they launched for the mission tonight, they'd had to get their sleep in advance.

Upon arriving at the air base, the old military axiom of "hurry up and wait" had proved true. An extensive chain of logistics was set into motion to get the team to and from their upcoming objective, and they faced hours with little to do but fuck off in the small area that had been temporarily allocated to them.

Taking a final drag, Cancer snubbed out his cigarette and tossed it in a trash can.

He pushed open the door to enter the planning bay and saw David at a desk with his planning materials spread across the surface—operational graphics, satellite imagery, infiltration and exfiltration plans.

David was looking at none of this. Instead he was ticking off numbers with the fingers of one hand, sounding frustrated as Cancer picked up his words mid-sentence.

"...the chair and ranking members of the Senate and House, and the lead Republican and Democrat in both the House Select Committee on Intelligence and the Senate Select Committee on Intelligence. That's it. No one's flying us to DC when they don't claim us in the first place."

Cancer followed David's gaze to Reilly, seated on a cot and holding a battered paperback.

Reilly shook his head. "That didn't stop Mitch Rapp, man."

David opened his mouth to reply, but Cancer cut him off.

"What in the fresh hell did I just walk in on?"

Leaning back in his chair and crossing his arms, David said, "Reilly wants to know why he can't meet the president."

"What?"

Reilly raised his paperback and waved it emphatically at Cancer.

"Don't you read thrillers? The government's secret super-assassin always reports directly to the president. Why not us?"

Cancer looked to David with a deadpan expression.

"He serious?"

"It's hard to say," David said, returning to his planning materials.

Reilly spoke in a defensive tone. "I *am* serious. After all we go through, I just want a handshake, man."

Cancer fixed him with a stony glare. "You wanna meet a president, join a campaign team. 'Cause he won't get any updates about us until something goes wrong. That happens, it means we're probably dead anyway."

Reilly shrugged, then opened his paperback to continue reading where he left off.

Cancer wasn't worried about him—he was a top-notch medic, and when the previous mission had gone sideways, Reilly reacted seamlessly to the shifting plans with little more than a word or two of guidance from his leadership. If there was one thing Cancer could credit to Reilly besides his medical and workout abilities, it was that he was in no danger of overthinking the tactical situation.

The same didn't hold true for the next man Cancer's gaze fell upon.

Ian, the team's little intelligence guru, was stretched out across a cot, any illusion of relaxation betrayed by his clenched jaw as he listened to headphones, his eyes pinched shut.

Cancer walked over to him and kicked the cot.

Ian's eyes burst open and he sat up, meeting Cancer's eyes in alarm as he removed his earbuds. "What's up?"

Nodding to his earbuds, Cancer asked, "What are you listening to?"

"'Piano Concerto Number Five in E-Flat Major.' Why?"

"Funny." Cancer grinned. "I took you for a gangster rap kinda guy."

"Really?"

"No. Shouldn't you be tinkering with some electronics?"

"Don't you dare project your technophobia on me, Cancer. I've already booted up, tested function, and shut it down on full power. It's packed, along with all my spare batteries. I'm good to go."

"Then why do you look nervous?"

Ian blinked, responding quietly, "Because I *am* nervous."

"You do share some DNA with your dad, don't you? Sure you weren't adopted?"

Ian bristled at the mention of his father, just as he did every time Cancer brought him up.

Grant "Mad Dog" Greenberg was a legendary Special Forces soldier whose combat exploits probably would have warranted his own statue at Fort Bragg, with the small complication that far too many of them were classified. Tales of his glory lived on in the spoken heritage of special operators across service branches and even the Agency, where he'd done contract work well into his sixties before retiring.

So when Cancer learned that his new team's tech whiz was none other than "Mad Dog" Greenberg's son, he'd been beside himself with disbelief and, ultimately, disappointment. Ian was technically proficient, but so far the only connection that Cancer could discern between the two men was a vague physical resemblance and a famous last name.

During the team's inaugural operation in the Philippines, Ian had to run his electronic gadgets from an offshore boat. And judging by the team's private accounts of Ian's abilities on their previous foray into Syria, that was probably the best thing for everyone involved. For all practical purposes, the mission ahead would be Ian's first real test not just as an intelligence operative, but a shooter—and Cancer was less than thrilled at the lack of confidence he saw in the man's face.

Finally, Cancer said, "Listen, Ian. You got nothing to worry about. Just make sure your little robot works."

"It's not a robot," Ian corrected him. "It's actually a pretty sophisticated IMSI-catcher called the Manta, which you'd know if you paid attention to my portion of the mission brief—"

"I don't care what it's called. Get it to make all the right beeps and boops to get us to the target, and we'll take care of the rest. Savvy?"

"Yeah," Ian said. "Sure."

Shaking his head, Cancer stalked off to find Worthy.

He heard Worthy before he saw him, a series of metallic scrapes and clangs echoing from behind the door to the hallway bathroom.

Pausing at the open door, Cancer saw Worthy standing before the mirror, wearing his tactical kit over gym shorts and a T-shirt.

Worthy raised his rifle to the mirror, pulling the trigger to elicit the hollow *click* of an empty weapon.

Before the echo faded, Worthy canted his rifle up and to the side, stripping the empty magazine and retrieving another one from his kit. By the time his empty mag finished its first bounce off the ground, Worthy had reloaded and resumed his aim on the mirror.

Lowering his rifle, he turned to face Cancer and said, in his Southern drawl, "What's up, Cancer—you need me?"

Cancer shook his head slightly. He never ceased to be amazed by Worthy's endless and obsessive weapons rehearsals.

A former competitive shooter at the national level, Worthy spent absurd lengths of time in front of a mirror, alternating between reload drills, dry fire drills, malfunction clearance drills, emergency transition from rifle to pistol...when your callsign was Racegun, apparently, the practice never ended. As a result, his hard-earned speed with a weapon was astonishing.

Cancer said, "Just making sure your trigger finger doesn't fall off before infil tonight."

"Absolutely," Worthy agreed. "Don't worry, I'm taking it easy. Bit of practice calms the nerves, you know?"

"No," Cancer replied, "I don't. That's what cigarettes are for."

Exiting the bathroom, Cancer stood in the hallway for a moment, watching David hunched over his planning materials, studying the pages for the hundredth time since they'd arrived.

Cancer had been surprised when David asked him to be second-in-command of the team. It wasn't a question of experience—Cancer had more of that than anyone else in their ranks, probably more than any two members combined.

He'd also fought alongside David twice, both times in the mercenary realm. The first was a multi-day operation in the jungles of South America's Triple Frontier, where David had first taken issue with Cancer's personal brand of warfighting. Which was, in a word, ruthless.

What else could it be? Combat was an unforgiving realm, and nothing was more important than removing as many enemies from the battlefield as possible, whenever and wherever you found them. If not, they would return the favor to you and your teammates at the first available opportunity.

David understood that much, but just barely. The kid had just enough skills to be good in a fight, but just enough morality to feel bad about the fallout. No matter, Cancer thought, some more experience would harden David into less of a touchy-feely team leader. In the meantime, it was up to Cancer to coach David whenever and however he could, and he intended to do just that.

"Hey, boss," Cancer called from the hallway. "Talk to you for a second?"

David looked up, then quickly rose and approached him.

"What's up?"

Cancer nodded toward a doorway at the end of the hall, and David followed him into the empty room.

Closing the door behind them, David asked, "How are the guys looking to you?"

"Fine," Cancer said. "I'm only concerned about one."

David gave an understanding nod. "Ian's out of his comfort zone, but he'll deliver on target. I've worked with him more than you have. And don't forget who his dad is."

"I'm not talking about Ian. I'm talking about you."

David recoiled, seeming uncertain if Cancer was being serious. "How so?"

"The guys told me about your little *Call of Duty* sprint to pull that little girl off the street last time we tried to slot BK."

"Yup."

"Ever think what would happen if you got shot in the face?"

David's eyes narrowed. "Ever think what would happen if *she* got shot in the face?"

Cancer shook his head. "We ain't Amnesty International, Suicide. You get smoked taking some dumb risk, and we gotta deal with it. We got one job: killing bad guys. Don't start thinking there's any good we can accomplish besides that. You make this morality sideshow too much of a hobby and people are going to get hurt. That girl may be safe, but how many people would die if Duchess couldn't find BK again?"

David was unconvinced. "What did you want me to do—let her get killed? We stand by and do nothing, then we're no better than they are."

He shrugged. "We ain't."

"I'm not talking about the civilians; I'm talking about the terrorists."

"So am I."

David's face turned to stone, his green eyes going flat. "Care to explain that?"

"Sure. You care to hear? Because my advice seems to be falling on deaf-fuckin'-ears lately, stopping somewhere short of your officer brain."

David huffed a breath, his expression softening.

"I picked you as my 2IC for a reason, Cancer. Tell me what's on your mind."

"Those terrorists are the same people as us—ruthless, violent, willing to do whatever it takes to accomplish their mission. They're on the other side of the ideological fence, sure. But don't think for one second that we're different from them. Because the biggest difference between us and the people we're hunting isn't our morality, it's our methods. Remember that."

6

Reilly followed his team into the closed hangar.

Along with his teammates, he carried his rucksack, weapon, and kit bag with parachute, helmet, oxygen tanks, and cold weather gear. The combined weight was considerable, though he'd be able to ditch most of it in their parachute cache after landing.

The hangar spread before him, revealing a single aircraft.

And man, what an aircraft it was.

The C-17 was a mighty plane, a bulbous gray giant with four engines and a tail rising fifty feet off the ground. At half a football field long, the massive bird could haul eighty-five tons of cargo just under the speed of sound.

The sight sent Reilly's heart racing. It was one thing to view such an aircraft sitting on a runway or even cruising overhead; it was another to see one that would soon catapult you across an international border just below the stratosphere, all while you waited for the order to jump.

The plane and its crew belonged to the Special Operations Division of the 437th Airlift Wing out of Charleston. While the same aircraft was used by a number of Air Force outfits, the Special Operations Division birds were heavily modified with a number of classified upgrades that allowed them to operate on dangerous missions involving nighttime flying, low-level and bad-weather operations, and anything sufficiently discreet to require top-secret clearances by all aircrew and maintenance personnel. They had a corresponding requirement for no-notice taskings from the Joint Chiefs of Staff, maintaining on-call aircraft at full alert at their home base.

David set his equipment on the concrete floor, and the rest of the team lined up their kit alongside his before following him toward the people lined up at the aircraft's tail.

The three-man flight crew consisted of two pilots and a loadmaster, each wearing flight suits devoid of insignia. None seemed to be strangers to meeting nondescript teams of shooters requiring transport into enemy territory. They knew David's team as OGA, a designation for Other Governmental Agency that usually signified CIA officers of one flavor or another.

But Reilly's gaze skipped past the two male pilots to the loadmaster, who was responsible for securing cargo and passengers before and during the flight. She was an olive-skinned brunette with curves Reilly could appreciate even amid her otherwise shapeless flight suit.

David and the pilots made a hasty introduction, then began going over the flight route, in-flight checkpoints, mission-abort criteria, airspeeds for cruising and personnel drop, and the location of the exit point based on prevailing wind direction at altitude. The plan had already been established, and the two leads—the pilot in command, and David as ground force commander—were simply confirming what they already knew in case a detail slipped through the cracks along the way.

When the loadmaster moved toward the rear of the aircraft, Reilly followed her.

"Hey," he said, "I'm Reilly."

She stopped and turned to him.

"Vanessa. So, you guys got a fun night lined up?"

"Just taking out the trash."

"Nice. Happy hunting."

"You guys are based out of Charleston, right?"

She nodded at the plane.

"That's what it says on the tail."

"Cool. I'm not far from there, living in North Carolina. Maybe we can meet up back in the States. You know, grab a beer or something."

"Sure, sounds great," she said. Reilly's face brightened until she continued, "Only I don't think my girlfriend would approve."

"Your—right. Got it. I'll just stick to flinging myself into freefall, then."

"Probably a good idea."

She continued walking, disappearing up the ramp and into the back of the plane as Reilly stood alone.

Worthy sauntered up to him.

"You couldn't tell she was a lesbian from a mile away? Or are you really that optimistic?"

Reilly gave a sad shrug. "Maybe a little of both."

"All right," David called out, "let's load up and get hooked up for our pre-breathe."

Hoisting their gear off the ground, Reilly and the team began shuttling their equipment up the ramp and into the cavernous aircraft interior.

7

Forty thousand feet over Turkey

The C-17's vibrating cabin was dimly lit in red, casting my team in an eerie crimson glow. At this point I could identify them by size alone; other than that, we were indistinguishable from one another in helmets and night vision devices flipped up on their mounts. The lower halves of our faces were concealed by oxygen masks, our air hoses plugged into a central console for an hour-long pre-breathing routine to eliminate nitrogen from our bloodstreams and reduce the risk of decompression sickness.

Our parachute harnesses were a complex array of webbing and buckles, rigged with rucksacks resting on our thighs and weapons strapped to our sides, barrel down. I checked the glowing altimeter on my left wrist, finding that we'd leveled off at forty thousand feet for our upcoming border crossing. I was already sweating under several layers of insulated clothing, which weren't optional at our current altitude.

The pilot transmitted in my ear, "*Five minutes to Sally*."

I keyed my radio and responded, "Ground Force Commander copies."

Then I held up one hand with the fingers outstretched, seeing the rest of my team was already doing the same to ensure everyone registered the time hack. "Sally" was the arbitrarily chosen brevity code for our border crossing, indicating that we were about to cross into Syrian airspace.

The female loadmaster walked past us, wearing a helmet with an oxygen mask and an emergency parachute but no combat gear. Lowering herself into a drop seat near the front of the cargo bay, she put on a seatbelt and tightened it.

This was the moment of truth—if Syrian radar "painted" our plane as we approached the border, the pilots would need to initiate the fastest turnaround of their flying career. And in the event that the Syrians launched a missile, our aircraft would drop flares and chaff while conducting a series of puke-worthy evasive maneuvers.

I tightened the seatbelt across my waist and looked at my teammates. From what little I could see of their eyes, they looked emotionless, utterly focused on the mission at hand.

The closer we got to the border, the less we talked. Our chatter naturally fell away to silence, preparation for updates surrounding our operation. Syrian air defenses catching us in the act. A change in the strength or direction of wind affecting where we'd have to jump. An intel update that our target had moved to a different location. A last-minute abort code from Duchess.

It was the last option I feared most. We'd already let BK slip through our fingers once, and were extremely lucky that he'd shown up again—luckier still that Duchess had allowed us to conduct one more operation against him. The most elite military assets had their hands full chasing top terrorist leadership, who were well-hidden and likely had several successful operations under their belt. People like BK were the up-and-comers, the young and intelligent next generation of terrorist visionaries.

And that's why my team existed.

It hadn't been my choice to draft our charter, of course. At the end of my mercenary career, I found myself at a lucky intersection with fate. Unbeknownst to me, a new presidential finding authorized this particular brand of covert action.

The president decided it was time to take the gloves off, to identify the rising generation of terrorist leadership—the future Osama bin Ladens—long before they rose to notoriety, and with it the access to an underground terrorist network that could hide them for years, if not a decade or more. Advances in the world of post-9/11 threat targeting had led to intelligence on rising terrorists outpacing the military's counterterrorism capacity to deal with them. Presenting a slight complication to this new reality was the standing executive order prohibiting assassinations, a document that had been signed by every president since forever, including the current one.

So the president had simply written a new executive order, one that bypassed the previous. In this new paradigm, dumb terrorist leaders got a free pass. It was the smart ones, those with immense leadership potential, who were selected for annihilation before they got the chance to massacre innocent civilians. Of course, this had to remain deniable, so the CIA—and Duchess in particular—found themselves ordered to expand their capacity from hunting only the top terrorist leadership to removing the rising stars flagged to become the next bin Laden.

This should have been a dream shot, but, of course, there was a catch.

Using a particularly sophisticated piece of malware, the Chinese government hacked the US database for top-secret security clearances, gaining exhaustive data on the names, faces, and careers of both Tier One military operators and members of the CIA's own Special Activities Center. The risk of capture for a qualified shooter now included US embarrassment and, more importantly, exposure for violating their own public stance against assassination.

But Duchess had also been tracking a transnational criminal syndicate that had recently been destroyed—and found that some of its mercenary force had survived, along with a clue that led her to me.

For her, it was a merger of necessity. My team represented people who'd officially left the military long ago but continued conducting global special operations as mercenaries. If we were captured behind enemy lines, not even China could prove the United States had sent us.

For me and my team, it was our one and only opportunity to continue doing what we did best.

The pilot transmitted, "*One minute to Sally.*"

I held up an index finger to my teammates and replied, "GFC copies."

Anticipating a sudden turnaround or evasive maneuvers, I was met with a wave of relief as we instead continued cruising forward in a thus-far anti-climactic flight.

Then the pilot spoke again. "*We are Sally at this time, situation Ice.*"

We'd crossed over the Syrian border, and the word "Ice" indicated what we all knew from our continued level flight: there was no radio chatter from Syrian air defense frequencies, no radar contact or incoming missiles. A mission abort prior to our jump was now extremely unlikely; no one wanted to risk repeating this little incursion if we didn't have to. Simply conducting a parachute jump in the first place was already a last resort for infiltration due to the sheer number of complications and variables involved. But we'd already burned one Agency ratline on our previous attempt to kill Bari Khan, and since he'd inexplicably remained in the same area, jumping was our only option.

My heart rate spiked when the pilot spoke again.

"*Preparing for descent.*"

I braced myself in my seat, seeing my teammates do the same a moment before the bottom fell out.

The plane dove in a roaring descent that caused my stomach to leap into my throat, accelerating until the pilots finally pulled up to level flight. Glancing at my altimeter, I saw we were at 24,000 feet, the altitude we'd maintain until bailing out of the aircraft.

Undoing my seatbelt, I tightened the straps of my rucksack for mobility rather than comfort, then turned on my oxygen bailout bottle before disconnecting from the console as the rest of my team did the same. Worthy was seated beside me, and he checked my oxygen pressure gauge, then examined my parachute pin and automatic activation device before tapping my helmet to indicate I was good to go.

I pushed myself to a standing position. The loadmaster followed suit, walking toward the closed ramp as I waddled after her under the bulky weight of my combat gear, looking considerably less graceful as I prepared for jumpmaster duties.

Stopping short of the ramp, the loadmaster placed her hand on a wall-mounted switch and communicated with the pilots on their internal aircraft frequency. I pulled my goggles over my eyes, then flipped down my night vision device and turned it on.

The cargo's dim red glow gave way to bright green. I cast a backward glance at my team, their torsos blazing with infrared chemlights that were visible under night vision. Turning to the loadmaster, I saw her give me a thumbs-up. I returned the gesture, and she activated the switch.

With a great shuddering rumble, the C-17's metal ramp began to lower.

A sliver of night sky became visible, widening into a gaping maw as an arctic blast of roaring wind spilled inside. The desert at ground level was relatively cold at night, but with a temperature drop of three and a half degrees Fahrenheit for every thousand feet of altitude, the sky outside the plane was freezing.

The ramp settled into its lowered position, exposing the Syrian landscape beyond.

I walked toward the edge, the howling wind growing in volume until I stood at the end of the ramp, surveying the world four and a half miles beneath us.

Glittering patches of villages were arrayed at irregular intervals, cut by swaths of vegetation delineating rivers and crops spread across the desert sands. At this height I could make out only the largest landmarks, but the pilots—guided by the aircraft's mission planning software—would be the ultimate authority on when we jumped.

A red light flashed on at the edge of the ramp, and a moment later, the pilot transmitted a wind speed advisory, followed by, "*Time on target, six minutes.*"

I relayed this to my team, who began buddy-checking each other's parachutes before Worthy gave me a thumbs-up, signaling the all-clear. I returned the gesture, then gave the command for them to stand up before watching my team struggle to their feet. They tightened the straps on their combat gear, donned their goggles, and activated their night vision devices. Ian was the last to complete this sequence, fumbling to tighten his rucksack straps until Reilly finally smacked his hand away and did it for him.

Ian was fully qualified to conduct freefall operations, of course, but there was a difference between completing tasks in training, no matter how realistic, and executing on an actual combat operation. Still, after the time we'd spent doing full-equipment rehearsals in a wind tunnel, it was a little early in the mission for Ian's nervousness to be on display.

"*Two minutes to TOT*," the pilot transmitted. I confirmed the call, seeing my team hold up two fingers to acknowledge.

I instructed my team to move to the rear, watching them shuffle toward me as the pilots throttled back power and lowered the flaps, causing the aircraft to lurch as it slowed for our exit. My team assembled a meter away from the hinge of the ramp and stopped, making last-minute adjustments to their equipment before freefall.

"*One minute*," the pilot called.

I caught a glimpse of Reilly waving goodbye to the loadmaster, ending his gesture with a solemn salute. She shook her head at him, then directed her focus to me.

Then the pilot transmitted, "*Fifteen seconds*."

I called out, "Stand by" and my team responded with a thumbs-up, moving forward onto the ramp. Turning to the open air, I stepped forward to within a foot of the steel edge hovering over oblivion and looked over the end of the ramp at the wrinkles of hills and canyons leading toward my team's last ambush point for BK. If he hadn't been suddenly escorted by two vehicles and a small army of fighters, we wouldn't be here.

But that was combat, I thought—random, unpredictable, chaotic—and in a way, it made more sense to me than my suburban existence in the States.

I felt a hand on my shoulder, sensed the men assembled in a tight pack behind me as the final seconds ticked away.

I was breathing faster now, as I was sure we all were—standing on a slab of metal 24,000 feet over foreign land, a surreal position made more so by the roar of the wind, the phantasmal green view through our night vision, the fact that we were assembled to conduct the US-sanctioned targeted killing of a terrorist in Syria.

I turned my night vision to the side, canting my head to observe the glowing red light with my naked eye. My heart felt like it was floating in my chest, the weight of my combat equipment seeming impossibly heavy in the last moment before the light blinked off and the green one beneath it illuminated.

The pilot called, "*Go, go, go.*"

I stepped off the ramp, flinging myself into the space beyond.

The chaos of exiting a high-performance aircraft took hold then: an overwhelming assault on the senses, the gale-force wind heated by scalding exhaust from the plane's four turbofan engines as my view was filled with the green shadows of the Syrian landscape.

The only control I could maintain for the time being was body position —arms outstretched, knees bent while arching my pelvis downward. The wind blew me vertical and head-down as the sound of the plane faded, replaced by the rumbling hum of my body splitting the air below.

It took a full ten seconds for me to reach terminal velocity, and after assuming a stable freefall position I dipped a shoulder to spin a 360 turn and search for my teammates.

They were dropping to reach me, falling like black spots out of the green sky through my night vision, the blazing glare of their chemlights marking their bodies. I couldn't make out who was who at present, save Reilly due to his size. But I counted all four, a good start, with one man higher than the rest, struggling to descend—had to be Ian, I thought.

Cancer reached me first, effortlessly dropping to hover a few meters off my right side. Reilly was next, falling like a stone as he overshot, dropping low before flattening his arch to rise level with Cancer and me. My hands and feet were already tingling with a frostbite-like sensation amid the frigid air that penetrated every layer of my cold weather gear.

I looked up, watching Worthy drift gradually toward us, making minor adjustments with his arms and legs to complete the semicircle formation as we faced one another. Terminal velocity didn't feel like falling; it was more like floating on a burbling pillow of air, all stability maintained through adjustments to a foundational body position.

Checking the luminescent dial of my altimeter, I saw we were descending through seventeen thousand feet. Ian was still flying high above us, working his way down with a hard arch. It took him another twenty seconds to fly into the remaining slot of our circle, by which time we were crossing thirteen thousand feet—the jump altitude for a normal civilian skydive.

Over my radio earpiece, I could hear my teammates breathing oxygen through their masks. Other than that, we kept silent; until we landed, the frequency was reserved for critical communications—a missing jumper, a malfunctioning oxygen system, a strap of combat equipment loosening and sending someone into a flat spin.

But our freefall formation remained intact and the scene almost tranquil despite the cold and howling wind. We held our positions facing one another, intending to stay close until it was time to deploy parachutes; at this altitude, winds were extreme, and any break in visual could cause us to drift far off course. I glimpsed the luminescent dial of the altimeter on my hand—we were at eight thousand feet and falling fast.

At four thousand feet, I brought my hands in front of my face and began waving them to the side. My teammates mirrored the gesture as we spun away from one another, turning away from our center point.

I locked my legs out and pulled my arms close to my sides, bending at the waist and cupping the air to begin tracking forward. In this way our circle formation turned into a starburst outward, each man gaining as much horizontal distance from one another as he could.

My hands were almost completely numb with cold as the audible altimeter began chiming in my helmet, and I broke out of my tracking position, resuming my previous arch to initiate my pull sequence.

Grabbing the ripcord pillow on my right side, I yanked it to full-arm extension and began a mental count. *One thousand, two thousand*—my body jerked upright, legs swinging forward as my main parachute deployed and filled with air.

Then I was suspended in a quiet sky, looking upward to see the squared corners of my rectangular canopy, fully inflated and flying cleanly forward. I quickly checked the airspace around me, prepared for an emergency turn to avoid collision with one of my teammates—but I was free and clear, and looked down to identify the flat patch of our landing area.

Activating the infrared strobe light on my harness, I grabbed my steering toggles and carved smooth ninety-degree turns to ensure my parachute was steerable. Raising my arms to resume full flight, I swung a right turn to locate my teammates as I transmitted, "Suicide, good canopy."

I made out my teammates' blinking infrared strobes, counting three dark parachutes as they reported in sequence.

"*Cancer, good canopy.*"

Ian was next. "*Angel, good canopy.*"

Then Reilly. "*Doc, good canopy.*"

Worthy was last, his transmission revealing why I'd sighted three parachutes instead of four.

"*Racegun, good canopy, but I had a thousand-foot streamer.*"

Looking down, I located his parachute far below as the result of a prolonged opening. He was already circling to enter the landing pattern.

I said, "Good copy, Racegun. Lead us in."

We flew into our slots to make a tight canopy formation, then shut off our blinking infrared strobes—while we didn't anticipate any observation out here period, much less by enemy scanning with night vision, there was no need to take any chances.

I ended up in the high position, watching Worthy enter the downwind leg of our landing pattern, passing a thousand feet over our landing area.

Then he turned ninety degrees to the base leg of his pattern, with the next man following in short order. By the time I initiated my own approach, Worthy had already turned to the final leg of his landing.

I watched him touch down lightly and pull his canopy to the ground as I reached 750 feet above ground level and carved a turn. A second man alighted a few meters away from Reilly, and a third was drifting toward the far edge of our landing area—Ian, no doubt.

Braking to maintain separation from the canopy to my front, I followed it through our final turn. Then I was facing into the wind, watching two men gathering their now-collapsed parachutes on the ground while a third did the same from a distance of fifty meters. Reaching down to grasp a fabric quick release handle, I yanked it from its housing and felt my rucksack fall free, tugging at my parachute harness a moment later as it dangled from an eight-foot lowering line.

The man in front of me touched down near the first two team members.

By then I was about two hundred feet off the ground, letting my canopy accelerate to full flight in order to build airspeed. At fifteen feet over the desert I pulled both toggles down to flare, hearing the whistle of wind against my face quiet as the sand rose up to meet me, and the thump of my rucksack making landfall resonating from the end of its lowering line.

Then my boots hit the ground, and I staggered to a standing position before grabbing a parachute riser to pull my canopy to the dirt.

"Suicide good," I transmitted. "Any injuries?"

I listened to my team check in, huffing breaths as they conducted the post-jump sequence: putting weapons into operation, stripping off the parachute harness, bagging canopies in preparation to cache them before we conducted our foot march to the objective.

"*Cancer good.*"

"*Angel good.*"

"*Doc good.*"

Worthy was last, his transmission confirming a successful infiltration.

"*Racegun good. Looks like we all made it here in one piece, boys. Let's go get him.*"

8

Angling his rifle upward, Worthy took his final measured steps to the rocky crest above him. Through his night vision, the sky was a dazzling green starscape flecked with innumerable points of light.

But his attention was focused on the ridge he approached at a crouch, and once he reached the top, Worthy took a knee to scan the landscape beyond.

The ground to his front fell away in a gentle slope, the buildings of the small village pooled among the landscape's curves and sliced by a single dirt road. He recognized the scene at once, and not just from his review of satellite imagery—this was the same village they'd fought in to kill Bari Khan, and the last time he'd seen that road, his team was speeding west to their exfiltration point.

Worthy scanned for immediate threats: observation posts, stray vehicles, figures strolling the periphery of the village.

But he saw no movement as a gentle dusty breeze crossed his sweaty face. He could hear a dog barking somewhere in the village, see a few exterior lights and illuminated windows among the buildings below him.

Slipping the shoulder strap of his ruck off one arm, Worthy rolled sideways to remove it and then assumed a prone position to continue watching for anything out of the ordinary. As point man, that was his responsibility as much as leading his team to their objective, and Worthy knew that the other four men would remain stationary behind him until he was satisfied.

After caching their parachute equipment near the landing zone, they'd made a swift four-kilometer foot movement across largely flat ground. It had been an easy hike; with the adrenaline from the jump, they probably could have covered twice that distance without breaking stride.

Scanning the outskirts of the village, Worthy located their target building: a squat one-story warehouse, the rear door closed and unlit. He knew from their mission planning that the opposite side held two rolling doors and a second pedestrian entrance—Duchess's sole intelligence asset in the area had done some daylight drives past the building, texting blurry cell phone snapshots of the building exterior to his Agency handler.

Satellite imagery and high-altitude drone passes had likewise revealed no notable enemy presence or fortifications outside the building. Bari Khan was lying low, having successfully evaded detection until an NSA algorithm had picked up his voice on intercepted cell communications from a new phone. Duchess had pinpointed his location using a range of intelligence assets at her disposal, placing him at this building beyond any reasonable doubt—at least, they hoped.

Speaking quietly, Worthy transmitted, "I've got eyes-on the target building. No movement in the village."

David replied, "*Stand by, I'm coming up to take a look.*"

Worthy keyed his radio twice, indicating that he'd received the transmission, and continued watching the village. Now that he'd established visual of the target area, he had to maintain it—the slightest distraction could cause him to miss some critical change in the situation, and that wasn't going to happen on his watch.

The rifle in his grasp was an HK416, the smaller, 5.56mm version of the weapon his team had carried on their previous incursion into Syria. The lighter bullets were a tradeoff in range and velocity, but the 416s fired much more quietly with a suppressor, allowed the team to carry more ammo—a key consideration given they'd had to jump in all their equipment—and allowed for faster shooting in the tight confines the team was about to enter in their hunt for Bari Khan.

He heard footfalls whispering up the rocky slope behind him, and then David crouched beside him, setting down his rucksack and slipping into the prone at whispering distance.

Worthy said nothing, allowing David a chance to take in the scene while the remaining three men maintained rear and flank security.

After thirty seconds of silence, David whispered, "Looks good."

"Yeah," Worthy agreed, trying to sound assured.

But David picked up on something in his tone. "What's wrong?"

"Nothing," he replied.

And while that was true, at least in the tactical sense, Worthy had his own reservations about this mission—namely, what was Bari Khan still doing here?

It didn't make any sense. After nearly being killed in the canyon, then being recovered from the village, returning to the area should have been the last thing he'd ever do. The fact that BK had done exactly that was deeply troubling to Worthy, who in his previous career had been privy to more mercenary assassinations than he cared to admit. When an attempt on someone's life failed and they fled the area, they *stayed* gone. But Bari Khan had done the opposite, and the fact that he wasn't an Arab at all, but a Chinese dissident who'd mysteriously appeared in Syria only for ISIS to roll out the red carpet, made this discrepancy all the more unsettling.

But no one on his team seemed terribly concerned about it besides, perhaps, Ian. The others were simply happy that their target had surfaced again, glad they'd have a chance to finish the job before Bari Khan achieved sufficient notoriety via a body count of innocent civilians.

Which, Worthy supposed, was noble enough—he just hoped his nagging gut suspicion was wrong.

David said, "Worthy, this isn't the time to hold back. Tell me what's on your mind."

"It's nothing," Worthy responded. "Just the fact that BK came back here after what happened, is all."

"It's weird, I agree. But keep in mind that by definition, terrorists aren't always rational actors."

Worthy considered a response, but before he could reply, David keyed his radio and transmitted to the team.

"Cancer, bring everyone up to my location. We're proceeding to our objective rally point."

9

CIA Headquarters
Special Activities Center, Operations Center F2

Duchess looked across the large room, surveying her kingdom with the full court present for the mission ahead.

The operations center was known in shorthand parlance as an OPCEN, the center of the universe for a raid-in-progress. It looked like a small movie theater more than anything else, with a few key exceptions.

Instead of a single screen, there were several—a large central monitor surrounded by smaller flatscreens, each broadcasting black-and-white surveillance footage from various aircraft and unmanned platforms. The largest screen was committed to broadcasting the main act, the feed from an Agency UAV, offset from the objective as it angled its camera toward a low crest adjacent to the target building. Descending from the crest were five tiny, shadowy figures that advanced with their rifles raised.

And instead of spectator seating, the ascending floor tiers around the screens were lined with desks and workstations, staffed by the myriad support personnel involved. At the front, paradoxically, were the least important personnel: the LNOs, or liaison officers, who existed to provide the CIA with a personal link to the many organizations capable of supporting the current effort.

Duchess's gaze flitted to them in sequence, their ranks representing ties to the Joint Special Operations Command, United States Special Operations Command, Joint Terrorism Task Force, and the Joint Personnel Recovery Agency, among others. Her LNOs had a difficult job, as nearly all of their partner organizations were denied information until the very second their assistance was required, at which time the liaison would leverage—and very possibly, at the same time burn—a long-held professional contact required to administer support.

Then she glanced to the higher tiers, both literally and metaphorically. These were the main staff shop representatives, each corresponding with their military equivalents. J1, joint personnel. They possessed the name, next-of-kin information, and pay status of everyone involved at the immediate and peripheral levels. If an Agency operator got shot in the face in the next six minutes, the S1 staff would have a car arriving at the parents' or wife's doorstep in a matter of hours, quietly explaining how their beloved had just perished in a training accident.

Then there was the J2, or joint intelligence. These fine representatives were wired into every Agency asset at all levels of intelligence whether HUMINT—human source, ELINT—electronic, SIGINT—signals, or COMMINT—communications. Their real-time analysis would be critical unless everything went according to plan, which it very rarely did.

Next up was J3, joint operations. Their personnel held a direct link not only to the operational assets required to execute the mission—the local driver serving as her team's primary exfiltration method came immediately to mind—but also to military and other governmental agency assets at every level of the chain of command, up to and including Duchess's direct representatives in the Office of the Secretary of Defense.

Beyond them was the J4 section, made up of supply personnel who could administer emergency airdrops for resupply, as well as the J6 staff, who maintained communications with the ground team and everyone they'd need to speak with in order to accomplish their mission. Which, at present, consisted primarily of Duchess herself.

Which was why, she knew, the concentric arrangement of desks was set up in increasing order of importance relative to their shouting distance from her. She presided like a judge at the highest point in the rear of the room, a throne from which she wielded the ultimate authority as far as this operation was concerned.

But since the outset of the Agency's targeted killing program, Duchess had to share her workstation with a second chair, one that held almost as much power as her own—and that seat was filled by Jo Ann's tall and bulky frame.

Jo Ann chose that moment to speak, her Northern accent ringing out with particularly choice words to commemorate the occasion.

"This never gets old, does it?" she said. "Watching our shooters terrorize the terrorists."

Duchess sucked her teeth, considering that Jo Ann had never actually been in the field. She replied, "'The best revenge is to be unlike him who performed the injury.'"

"Isn't it a little early in the day to be quoting Shakespeare?"

"Marcus Aurelius," Duchess corrected her, looking over to see Jo Ann appearing lost in thought watching the screens, as if she hadn't heard at all. She was methodically spinning her class ring around one finger, the garnet stone glinting as it turned toward the light.

Duchess sighed.

How a farmgirl from the Midwest had managed to choose the US Naval Academy was beyond her, but Jo Ann had done just that to begin a military intelligence career that had taken her to the staff offices of SEAL Team Six. Then she'd had a staff slot at the Joint Special Operations Command as the Intelligence Chief for Current Operations, overseeing operations from the Fort Bragg OPCEN that served as ground zero for every high-profile US military special operations raid in the world.

Her entire career progression defied logic—intelligence people were virtually second-class citizens in the Navy, with little influence over their career paths. They were considered lucky to get a single two-year tour with special operations. To make it to the Tier One level followed by a stint at JSOC implied some heavy-hitting personal connections that Jo Ann seemed outrageously incapable of establishing much less maintaining.

And as if that weren't enough, once her JSOC assignment was done, Jo

Ann had been handpicked—not by Duchess, of course—to serve as the head military liaison to the CIA for Project Longwing, the codename for the upstart targeted killing program that was entering its third mission execution without a single dead target to show for it.

Yet even as Duchess chafed at the presence of military oversight by Commander Jo Ann Brown, she had to admit the Navy officer had not just stood her ground on the matter of arguing against a drone strike, but also delivered the C-17 support for a HALO infiltration of her shooters. For the time being, that put her in Duchess's good graces.

The UAV representative called out, "Ma'am, we're about to lose coverage if I don't bring it closer."

Jo Ann was shaking her head before Duchess could get the words out.

"Don't you dare," she said. "Turn it around, but don't break the lateral boundary—we are not risking audible."

Duchess tapped her chin in momentary disbelief. The UAV community seemed to think their low-altitude drones were much quieter than they actually were, and the last thing she needed was for the faint buzzing noise to alert the quarry, causing him to flee their grasp a second time.

The UAV rep nodded, turning back to his workstation without a moment's hesitation. No one contradicted the OPCEN chief, who required instant compliance lest the mission devolve into chaos at the first complication.

But Duchess knew that her authority, while considerable, was relative rather than absolute.

That latter distinction belonged not to Duchess or Jo Ann but to one Thomas Gossweiler, the aging but very powerful senator chairing the Senate Select Committee on Intelligence. In addition to mandating the checks-and-balances arrangement of Jo Ann's presence, his current position allowed him a few abilities that served as a potential hindrance to her. Namely, he could invite himself to Agency ops provided they occurred while he was not in session, a technicality that she was currently circumventing by virtue of timing the assault with his weekly Senate Prayer Breakfast. Of secondary importance was his ability to impact her career or, worse yet, funding for special programs.

It wasn't that the senator was an insurmountable obstacle. The real problem, Duchess thought, was that Gossweiler wasn't *stupid*. Her ability to tap dance around the fringes of logic while pushing for a necessary tactical end was extremely limited with him, and for all the fervor with which he extolled his faith in Jesus and forgiveness, he was remarkably shortsighted with Agency leeway during the conduct of paramilitary operations.

Beside her, Jo Ann said, "I've been thinking about what you said. About why BK would return to the area, based on what you saw in Yemen."

Duchess canted her head to the side, curious about what conclusions her colleague would have reached in that regard.

"And?"

Jo Ann said, "He's tethered. There's something in that area he can't leave behind without forsaking his purpose. Some cargo, something he can't function without. Was that the case in Yemen?"

"That's right," Duchess said, mildly impressed. "It was a cargo that the terrorist wasn't willing to abandon."

"So, what was it?"

Duchess swallowed, feeling her face go slack.

"A bomb."

Then the J2 turned toward her, relaying information from a man in headphones beside him—a native Arabic speaker, kept on hand for just this eventuality.

"BK just activated his phone; looks like he's making a call."

Before she could reply, David spoke over the radio intercom.

"*Raptor Nine One, this is Suicide Actual. No movement on the objective, target phone location has been confirmed with ground scan. Request clearance for early execution.*"

Duchess replied first to the J2.

"Record full transcript for the duration." BK's call was about to get cut short, she thought as she lifted the hand mic and transmitted, "Suicide Actual, be advised target is using his phone at this time—he may have received early warning and be preparing to squirt. You are clear to execute."

David's tone was clinical. "*Suicide Actual copies all, executing time now.*"

Things happened quickly after that. The UAV feed shifted, flashing into adjusted focus settings as it captured the final glimpses of black specks—

David's team—splitting into two elements as they swept toward the target building.

The J2 was focused on the translator beside him, wearing headphones as he transcribed the content of BK's phone call to English.

Then the J2 turned to Duchess and shouted, "The team isn't compromised—BK says he's leaving in five minutes, requesting some pre-planned armed escort that's inbound. Call is connected to a mobile phone somewhere in Zaranj. They're discussing a scheduled transport coming to recover—"

Duchess snatched the hand mic from her desk and keyed the transmit button.

Her decision, of course, was no decision at all.

Gossweiler had threatened to shut down the program along with her career, yes—but the ground team had a perilous link to their exfiltration point in the form of one local driver preparing to speed to the target building upon David's order. If that link was severed by the arrival of an armed convoy, the five contractors would be trapped in Syria, desperately trying to evade capture until Duchess and Jo Ann could redirect military assets—and by the time that occurred, it would be too late to save them.

She spoke into the hand mic. "Abort. Abort. Abort. How copy?"

No response.

She transmitted again, "Abort. Abort. Abort. We have verifiable intel on enemy assets inbound to your location time now. Pull back until we can reassess the threat level, how copy?"

Silence. Total, abject, uncompromisable silence.

Then the UAV representative turned to face her.

"Ma'am, it's too late—the ground team is already making entry."

10

From his kneeling position, Worthy braced the buttstock of his suppressed HK416 against his shoulder as he heard the flat plastic *clack* of David triple-firing the initiation device behind him.

A deafening explosion to his front blew a hole clean through the outer wall—with BK remaining in place, they had to assume the doors would be boobytrapped—and Worthy rose to charge through a cloud of smoke into the now-gaping entryway.

He'd already flipped his night vision upward, prepared to utilize his rifle-mounted tac light once inside the building. There were many advantages to using "white light" in close quarters battle, the least of which was blinding your opponents before you shot them.

But as Worthy cleared the hole on his way into the target building, he saw at first glance that he wasn't going to need his tac light after all.

The interior was fully lit already, the windows taped over by sheets of black plastic. They'd been expecting a terrorist bed-down site, with their target asleep and defended by a personal security detail of two or three bodyguards.

Instead, they'd stumbled upon a massive logistical operation in progress.

Two covered trucks were parked facing the closed bay doors, and

Worthy saw in an instant that they were in the final stages of being loaded by what appeared to be a half-dozen Syrian men with assault rifles slung across their backs.

He charged for the nearest cover—a waist-high metal crate ten feet to his front—pivoting at the waist to open fire as he ran.

Worthy wasn't concerned at that moment with precision fire, instead ripping rounds from his barrel as fast as he could pull the trigger. They were fully committed, and if he didn't get some suppressing fire down ASAP, David and Ian were screwed as they entered behind him.

But Worthy had been first in the door for good reason—as a competitive shooter, his reflexes were without peer.

His first six rounds were directed at a cluster of men behind the nearest truck, and he registered two of them falling forward as he transitioned his aim right. Unleashing another half-dozen bullets at the men behind the second truck, he didn't have time to evaluate the results—by then he was slowing his forward sprint, crouching to take cover behind the metal crate as the first return fire began cracking around him.

Cancer flowed through the demolished rear wall to encounter absolute chaos unfolding inside the building.

The lights were on—problem number one—and a startled Syrian man was in the process of wielding an assault rifle in his direction—problem number two.

Cancer dealt with the second problem first, bringing his suppressed HK416 to bear on the man's chest and firing three times to drop him. Only then did he trip over something beneath him, regaining his footing to see a wounded fighter who'd been incapacitated by the explosive wall breach, or the rubble knocking him down, or both. Cancer ignored him, moving forward to bypass his first kill of the night to the sound of Reilly double-tapping the downed fighter in his wake.

But then the real shooting broke out—not the quiet, chuffing shots of his team's suppressed weapons, but wild automatic gunfire that exploded beyond the hall door to his front.

Racing down the short corridor, he heard a frantic transmission from David.

"*Cancer, can you isolate the trucks?*"

"Stand by," Cancer replied, kneeling at the open doorway and angling his rifle around the corner, feeling Reilly doing the same from a standing position behind him.

His first glance at the central warehouse bay revealed stacks of metal crates, scattered and open on a dusty concrete floor, partially blocking his view of two covered flatbed trucks facing away.

Men were piling into the backs of the vehicles, continuing to fire toward one side of the warehouse—the same wall through which Worthy, David, and Ian had entered.

At the moment, isolating the trucks was out of the question. He'd be dead in three seconds if he broke cover, and Cancer gladly obliged the ISIS fighters seeking martyrdom by responding in the only way he could at present: as a shooter.

Cancer took aim at one of the remaining fighters shooting his weapon overtop of the crate—what was it about terrorists, he wondered, that made them want to raise their guns over their head and fire without looking—and dropped him with a trio of rounds before directing his aim to the next standing figure.

As the low man, Cancer restricted himself to targets on the warehouse floor while Reilly engaged enemy fighters on the backs of the trucks.

Now the two team elements had the bad guys caught from perpendicular angles. Sure, they were grossly outnumbered by ISIS fighters, but establishing a crossfire was a good start. Cancer gunned down a man crouching behind one of the metal crates, then shifted to a fighter scrambling for the tailgate, lacing a burst into his spine and shoulder blades to drop him in place.

Cancer was scanning for his next target when he heard the bark of the truck ignitions turning over in the confined space, and before he could consider the implications, the rightmost truck throttled forward.

A shrieking scream of twisted metal erupted as the truck punched into the closed rolling door, ripping it from its tracks. The other truck followed suit, blasting through the second rolling door and out into the street.

Ian reloaded his rifle as the sound of the trucks receded, leaning out from behind the crate to take aim.

It was no use—the warehouse was empty or very nearly so, save the open crates and scattered bodies lying amid smears of blood.

David shouted, "Anyone hit?"

A chorus of negative responses.

The gunfight had lasted maybe thirty seconds, though to Ian it had seemed like half that. He'd certainly shot *at* enemy figures amid the din of battle, though whether he'd *hit* anyone was up for debate.

The gunfight itself was his team's area of expertise.

What happened in the minutes following that gunfight—or minute, singular, in this case—was Ian's.

David shouted, "One minute for SE!"

Ian scrambled to his feet, slinging his rifle and trading his grip for the small camera in his pocket. His task now was site exploitation, gathering as much intelligence as possible to feed back to the Agency. Ordinarily this meant prioritizing the collection of anything digital—cell phones, computers, hard drives—followed in short order by paper files and photographs.

But tonight, Ian's focus was almost solely directed at the metal crates scattered across the warehouse.

The air was rank with gunpowder and dust, vehicle exhaust and blood, as Ian took photos to document the number of crates. Each was olive drab in color, a sure indicator that they'd harbored military hardware. Ian flung one of the open crate tops shut, snapping a photograph of the yellow text atop it.

As the rest of his teammates checked bodies for phones, radios, and documents, Ian heard David transmitting to their exfil driver, a local Agency asset.

"Cobalt, this is Suicide Actual. Be advised two enemy trucks fleeing northbound. Do not *approach the objective. We're bumping to exfil point Bravo-Four, arrival in ten mikes."*

Cancer emptied a dead man's pockets as he called out, "Somebody tell me one of these bodies is BK."

Ian knew without checking that wasn't the case—the masterminds didn't stick around to fight. Everyone his team had gunned down were foot soldiers whose final moments were dedicated to covering the leader's withdrawal, and even if Bari Khan had miraculously caught a fatal bullet in the opening salvo, they would have done everything in their power to take his body with them.

Ian darted from open crate to open crate, stepping over the foam scraps of abandoned packing materials, until he found what he'd been hoping to spot.

One of the crates had some of its contents intact. It must have been the last one left to load before the team had made entry, and the enemy hadn't hesitated in abandoning it. Why should they? They already had the vast majority of their cargo aboard the trucks, which were now racing away from the warehouse to parts unknown.

But Ian recognized the contents at once, correlating the number of crates to his memory of an intelligence report with a growing sense of disbelief that his team had just stumbled upon something that the military community considered a statistical impossibility.

David yelled, "Thirty seconds!"

"I've got UXO," Ian shouted back, using the acronym for unexploded ordnance. "We need to blow it in place."

David said, "Leave it. We're in Syria, they've got more UXO than they know what to do with."

"Not like this," Ian said, snapping pictures of the crate's contents.

David appeared at his side, momentarily speechless. Then ran a palm across his forehead and said, "Well, shit."

Embedded in the remaining foam packaging were four identical rockets—three and a half feet in length, with body tubes ending in sinister-looking nose cones.

"PG-9?" David asked.

"Worse," Ian replied. "I'll explain later."

"You have what you need?"

"Yeah, serial numbers and batch codes. We can go."

"Exfil!" David yelled, readying a grenade to drop in the crate. "Get back to our gear—we're diverting to Bravo-Four."

11

Duchess focused on the central flatscreen projecting a grainy, low-angle shot of the target building from the unarmed UAV flying its orbit.

It was impossible to tell what was going on inside the building—they were reliant on David's communications for that—but the situation outside the structure complicated itself with the sudden appearance of two covered flatbed trucks turning onto the street.

The UAV controller said, "Two trucks leaving the objective, headed northbound. Do you want me to follow them, or keep eyes-on the target area for the ground team?"

Duchess answered without hesitation, "Stay with the trucks. J2, I want a geo-fix on the phone that Bari Khan called in Zaranj."

"Working it now," the J2 called back.

Duchess had promised herself she'd never be the person in an air-conditioned OPCEN pestering the ground force commander for updates. After all, a significant portion of the GFC's job was keeping the higher command appraised with timely updates on the tactical situation.

But it took David over a minute to check in, and when his voice came over the satellite communications relay, it was garbled amid intermittent static.

"*...Bravo-Four...no joy, eight EKIA, two flatbed trucks fled...heading north...airstrike...*"

Then the words faded to static altogether before ultimately cutting to silence.

But she'd heard enough.

Bravo-Four meant they were diverting to an alternate exfil point, no joy meant BK was alive, and his team had claimed eight enemy killed in action, which was notable for the same reason the two flatbed trucks were: namely, what in the hell were those transport vehicles and that many people doing at a supposed bed-down site?

Duchess's worst fears were coming true, her suspicion that the only plausible answer was a repeat of what she'd encountered long ago in Yemen.

Which would explain his use of the one word that should never have come over the radio frequency during a covert assassination.

Airstrike.

She keyed her hand mic. "Suicide, you're coming in broken. Say again."

"*Stand by...to high ground...when able...get an airstrike inbound...flatbeds headed north...*"

The only explanation was that David wasn't concerned with BK himself, but rather the cargo aboard the trucks. Without further information forthcoming until David reached the high ground to send a clear transmission, she needed more of the one thing she was losing by the second: time.

"What's our UAV station time?"

The operator called back, "Thirty-seven minutes before bingo fuel, but if those trucks keep going at max speed, we'll lose visual before that."

"Nearest airstrike capability?"

This time her joint terminal air controller answered. "Two F-15Es are on ready status one at Incirlik. If we scramble them now, they could be putting down munitions in just over two hours."

"JTAC, what's the fastest we can reacquire visual?"

A man responded, "Next wave of UAVs will be overhead in approximately one hour, forty-two minutes."

So no matter what happened, she was going to lose eyes-on the two flatbeds for just over an hour. And she had the creeping suspicion they'd just stumbled onto something much bigger.

Duchess checked her watch—Gossweiler would be stepping out of his Senate Prayer Breakfast in less than ten minutes, after which he'd be en route to the OPCEN at best, and able to shut her down completely at worst.

Now she faced the quandary of whether to trust her ground force commander and marshal additional assets that would likely expose a targeted killing operation that was supposed to be known only to a handful of Washington elites.

After a second of thought, she made her announcement.

"I'm calling in Agency authorization. Get those F-15s inbound now."

12

Ian struggled up the rocky slope, keeping Worthy in sight through his night vision as they moved in single file. They were racing against time, moving quickly toward the crest's high ground, where David could make effective radio contact with Duchess. From there, the team would swing south for three hundred meters to their alternate exfil point.

David fell in alongside Ian, whispering as they moved, "There must have been a dozen crates in there."

"Thirteen. And that's not the worst—"

David cut him off. "This is big. Those rockets were military grade. We've just stumbled upon hard evidence of state-sponsored terrorism. This has to be Iran."

"David, it's—"

"Or maybe," David continued, "Russia. Using the serial numbers, Duchess should be able to trace the shipment."

"David! Shut up. This *is* the result of state sponsorship—by us."

"What do you mean, 'by us?'"

Panting for breath as he moved, Ian replied, "Those were Bulgarian-made OG-9VM1 rockets. The CIA supplied them to the Syrian resistance. One of the shipments was lost in an ambush six months ago—thirteen crates totaling 650 rockets—and has been missing ever since. The Agency assumed that load had since been fired all over Syria, but we just found it intact. And since we only destroyed four, that means—"

"645 are still at large."

"646," Ian corrected him, "but that's not the point. This means BK was sent here to take possession of the rockets, and that wouldn't be the case unless he'd been handpicked to lead a major terrorist operation. With that payload, he could wipe a few city blocks off the map."

David continued huffing uphill for a moment before asking, "What do you think he's after?"

"One of our bases in Syria, maybe. Or a US Embassy somewhere. Could be anything. Duchess needs to hit those trucks ASAP."

As Worthy crested the high ground, Ian heard David transmitting beside him.

"Raptor Nine One, this is Suicide Actual, how copy?"

Duchess's response was faint over Ian's earpiece. "*You're coming in clear*," she said. "*Send it*."

"Those two flatbeds have the missing shipment of rockets intended for the Syrian resistance."

"OG-9VM1," Ian prompted him.

David said, "OG-9VM1. 645 are at large."

Ian cringed. "646, David."

"Correction," he continued, "646 rockets at large and presumed to be on the trucks, along with BK. Assess they will be used in a major attack. Need airstrike on those two flatbeds ASAP, how copy?"

"*It's in the works*," she replied. "*You're sure you found the entire load?*"

Ian whispered, "We're sure. They ship fifty to a crate and we found thirteen crates. You can double-check my math later."

David transmitted, "Positive. All crates accounted for. Will send serial numbers when able—"

An explosion in the village cut his transmission short.

The team fell into the prone, Ian the last to hit the ground. Orienting his weapon toward the noise, he caught a brief glimpse of a fireball ascending over the rooftops before fading to black, leaving only an ashy green smear of smoke visible in his night vision. There was a brief chatter of gunfire before he heard the revving of vehicle engines.

Ian asked, "What the hell was that?"

It was Cancer who replied, having assessed the situation at the first blast.

"*Hey, Suicide,*" he transmitted in an excited tone, as if he were pleasantly surprised if not enthusiastic about what had just occurred, "*I think that was our exfil vehicle.*"

13

Jo Ann watched the scene in the OPCEN unfold with a rapidity she'd witnessed all too many times.

Duchess thought her to be a dumb country bumpkin, she supposed, and Jo Ann didn't particularly care. All that mattered was that the job got done—the problem, up until this point, was that it hadn't.

And she knew as well as Duchess did that things were about to get a lot worse for everyone in the OPCEN, for the ground team, and for the future of Project Longwing.

The UAV rep called out, "Trucks are headed northbound toward Deshar, where the road diverges northwest and northeast. UAV will lose them before they get there—it's going offline in fifteen minutes."

Without prompting, the joint terminal air controller announced, "Our three-bird ISR stack will arrive twenty-four minutes ahead of the fighters, and I have recommended priorities for all three."

Duchess replied, "First platform on station goes to the center point of Deshar and flies concentric rings outward to search for the trucks first, and evidence of rocket transfer second. The next two proceed up the northeast and northwest routes to locate the trucks, and once they're found I want a full speed and distance analysis to determine if they had time to hand off cargo. Am I missing anything?"

"No, ma'am. I'm on it."

Jo Ann felt herself nodding at Duchess's order, grateful that she didn't have to intervene. It wasn't her role to bark orders, and interrupting Duchess was the last thing she wanted to do.

Instead, Jo Ann monitored the exchanges in the OPCEN with a clinical focus, trying to divine any vital information that had slipped through the cracks. Because while Duchess was ultimately in charge, Jo Ann was able to maintain an objectivity and perspective denied to anyone who had to answer the radio calls the instant they were received.

And her first opportunity to contribute came with the J2's next update.

"We've identified the location of BK's outgoing call," he said. "Geo-fix is on a structure on the east side of Zaranj, probable residence of a suspected ISIS logistician. It's a twelve-kilometer straight-line distance from the target building where BK scrapped his phone."

Jo Ann was already typing into the encrypted chat on her computer, linked directly to a counterpart at the JSOC OPCEN.

Duchess said, "I need to know what strike assets—"

"On it," Jo Ann replied, focusing on the response appearing on her screen. Looking up, she said, "There's a strike force at Forward Operating Base Presley: a platoon of Rangers and two CAG troops."

No one called them CAG anymore outside of the old breed who predated the myriad code name changes in the interim. But Duchess knew exactly who Jo Ann was referring to—an organization so elite that the military simply referred to them as "The Unit," and well-informed civilians called Delta Force: the Army's equivalent of SEAL Team Six, established three years prior to their Navy counterparts.

Aside from a few areas of specialization, there was virtually no difference between the two. Both were the apex predators of special operations, and either could accomplish their missions with a precision unknown to virtually any other military organization worldwide.

As Jo Ann saw the next line of text appear in her encrypted chat, she said, "They could be wheels-down in Zaranj in just over six hours."

Duchess winced at the ETA, and for good reason—far too much could happen in that period of time. "Put the Rangers on standby for a bomb damage assessment once we hit the trucks. I'll need a helicopter to recover our ground team, and I want the CAG troops on standby for no-notice launch in support of emerging intelligence as it is obtained. Questions?"

Jo Ann typed a swift response and said, "In the works."

Then the J2 said, "Intercepted radio chatter indicates an ISIS convoy was on its way to escort the flatbeds when they encountered a civilian truck on the road, and..."

"And what?"

"They destroyed it."

"What are the odds that it *wasn't* our team's exfil vehicle?"

"At zero one thirty Syrian time? Close to zero."

David transmitted, "*Raptor Nine One, be advised, we just saw a fireball in the village, and our exfil driver is no longer responding.*"

Duchess snatched up the mic.

"We're tracking. You'll have to initiate your escape and evasion plan until we can redirect recovery assets your way."

"*What's the status on that airstrike?*"

"It's inbound."

"*Are you going to have continuous eyes-on the trucks?*"

"There's going to be a gap in coverage."

"*Copy...stand by for Angel.*"

Duchess frowned. Angel was the callsign for the team's intelligence operative, Ian.

Jo Ann hadn't met him, but knew him by family reputation—his father was a special operations legend whose exploits for the military and the Agency had become canon among the community. Even the SEAL Team Six operators Jo Ann had worked with spoke "Mad Dog" Greenberg's name with awe.

Ian transmitted, "*By all means, hit the trucks—but don't be surprised when your bomb damage assessment doesn't find any rocket remains. BK's too smart to leave his cargo on those trucks for long, and we can't afford to lose them. They can fly nearly three miles, have a blast radius of ten meters, and there's over six hundred of them. You do the math. And if they've sat on those rockets for months, it means there's something big in the works. A catastrophic attack they've been setting up.*"

"No shit," Jo Ann muttered to herself.

Duchess was only slightly more diplomatic in her response. "Tell us something we don't know."

The next transmission came not from Ian, but David.

"So tell us how to help. We don't need to evade; we need to stay on the trail."

Duchess looked over to Jo Ann then, her eyes conveying what she likely had too much pride to speak—a search for confirmation, a second opinion on how she was about to respond.

Jo Ann, for her part, had been waiting for the chance.

This wasn't the first time she'd seen a mission's single purpose fragment into a constellation of unanticipated contingencies—though she had to admit, the wheels were coming off this particular operation with an intensity that rivaled anything she'd seen. They had two trucks on the move with Bari Khan presumably aboard, a dearth of air support, and a suspected logistician with potentially critical intelligence twelve kilometers from the objective, where the ground team was now stranded.

So when Duchess looked to her, Jo Ann was waiting with a thumbs-up gesture, nodding as she said, "We have nothing to lose by telling them."

Jo Ann's thinking in that moment wasn't that the ground team would have some miraculous ability to intervene. But in her years of working first with SEALs and then with the greater special operations community, she'd learned that a fully informed ground team could generate solutions that not even a full OPCEN staff would have the firsthand perspective to see.

Whether or not Duchess had been seeking confirmation for her decision, Jo Ann couldn't tell—but a moment later, she transmitted her reply.

"BK placed a call requesting an armed escort for the cargo. We think the call was made to a logistician who brokered the transport, and we've located the call's point of origin in Zaranj. But that's over twelve kilometers from your team, and you're not going to make it there before sunrise. We can have a special operations team there to snatch him in six hours."

"In six hours, this logistician is going to be gone. Keep tracking his phone and send us the grid."

"You're isolated without support," Duchess replied. "What can you possibly accomplish?"

A long silence followed, and the next transmission carried with it a tone of smug confidence that made Jo Ann crack a grin.

"*Duchess*," David said, "*you're lucky you have us.*"

14

I activated my rifle-mounted laser, the infrared floodlight illuminating the house interior in blazing emerald hues as I moved toward the stairs. This was no explosive breach, but a surreptitious entry: Reilly had pried open a door to let us in, and we spread throughout the small building as stealthily as we could manage.

The house was dead silent, and I wondered how anyone could sleep at the moment—we'd been in a gunfight not far from here about an hour earlier, and that was before our exfil truck turned into a fireball.

Yet I supposed if you lived in a war zone, there wasn't much choice. And when I thought about it, I'd had deployments where nighttime rocket attacks—even those that didn't miss my sleeping quarters by much—had been followed by going back to sleep in short order.

I ascended the stairs and paused at a doorway, feeling Ian squeeze my shoulder from behind. Pushing open the door, I slipped inside and saw two figures in the bed, a man and a woman.

I paused for a moment. There were ten different ways this could turn out, and nine of them were bad.

The woman's hair was a dark tangle over her pillow as she slept on her stomach. The man was on his side, facing away from me—and this was going to be really embarrassing, I thought, if he wasn't who I thought he was.

Circling to the opposite side of the bed, I found an AK-47 leaning barrel-up against the wall. I took the weapon in one hand and noiselessly passed it to Ian.

Then, kneeling beside the man, I examined his face.

His features were lean and angular, ending in a neatly trimmed beard that left no doubt—this was the father whose daughter I'd saved during our previous incursion to Syria.

I'd been in this home once before, glimpsing BK through the ground floor window shortly before handing the little girl back to the man I knelt before.

And here's where it got tricky, I thought. A surreptitious entry was no problem for my team; nor, in fact, was a gunfight. But there was no easy way to do what I was about to do.

Using a red penlight, I illuminated my face from below and shook the man awake.

"Shhh," I whispered, then summoned the most appropriate of my limited Arabic phrases. "*Hathahee lysat b'mushkula.*"

This is not a problem.

The man's face was calm as his eyelids fluttered open, and he seemed to register my presence with a serene acceptance. That was easier than I thought.

Then, as he awoke more fully, his eyes went wide and he screamed.

"Shhh!" I repeated, more urgently.

But he screamed even louder.

His cries were soon drowned out by his wife, who bolted upright and began shrieking loud enough to crack a windowpane.

Shit, I thought. This was going poorly.

I stood and turned on my tac light, pointing the beam downward to cast a soft glow and let them see us in full.

"It's okay," I said as reassuringly as I could manage, tapping my chest. "*Sadiq, sadiq.*" *Friend.* I held my hand toward him and said, "*Sadiqee,*" for *my friend.*

The woman was clutching a sheet to her chest, her figure partially covered by the man as he tried to shield her from harm.

They both looked terrified, the man in particular as he recognized me. He seemed to think this was some form of retribution, maybe us coming back to eliminate eyewitnesses to our previous operation.

I heard a girl scream from down the hall, followed by Reilly whispering in a failed bid to calm her. Looking to the woman, I extended an arm toward the door and said, "Please. *Raja*."

She hesitated, and I told Ian to look away.

Only then did she rise from the bed, sweeping out of the room as I transmitted, "Mom is inbound."

The man, sitting up to find that his AK-47 was gone from the bedside, gave me a smoldering glare.

"*Ana asif*," I said. *I'm sorry*. "*Wa laqin, intaj*—" *But I need*—Wait, I corrected myself, "*Noontaj musaeada*." *We need your help*. Had I said that right? I thought so, and waited for his reaction.

He shook his head slightly. "Your Arabic is...terrible."

"Look," I said, transitioning to English, "your family is safe. You remember me, right? I saved your daughter."

He shot back, "You started a battle. You almost got her killed."

"Well, yeah. But then I saved her."

"I assume you also started the battle earlier tonight."

I shrugged. "Yeah, maybe."

"What. Do you. Want."

I glanced at Ian, who looked even more uncomfortable than I felt.

Then I replied, "I need you to take us to Zaranj. You know this place?"

"Of course I know it. What do you want there?"

"There's a man I need to question. I'm not sure if he speaks English, and, well, you've heard my Arabic."

"I have heard your *attempt* at Arabic."

"So it's settled," Ian said cheerfully, "you drive us there, help us get some information, and we part ways. Oh, and maybe we could borrow some of your clothes because, you know, we're all pretty white."

I added, "We can pay you."

The man was unconvinced. "You cannot pay me enough. Zaranj is not for tourists. If they identify my vehicle, they will kill me." He rubbed his forehead, then stopped abruptly as he looked to me with renewed interest. "But if you can get my family to America...perhaps I can help."

I hesitated. I'd never discussed this prospect with Duchess, and while I was certain the CIA had the resources to relocate a family, I'd never explicitly received permission to offer them. Clemency to sympathetic locals hadn't exactly been a planning consideration prior to our freefall into Syria.

"Three people," I said. "You, your wife, and your daughter."

"Four. My mother as well."

Shit. Duchess was going to be pissed.

"I will request permission for four people." Seeing his gaze harden, I added, "And no matter the response, I will personally ensure you make it to America. I'll set it up myself if I have to."

I pulled the tactical glove off my right hand, extending a sweaty palm toward him.

He rose from the bed and shook my hand.

"Nizar."

"David."

Releasing the handshake, I said, "I'm sorry to be in a hurry, Nizar. But the sun will rise soon, and we need to leave immediately."

"Not yet." He shook his head. "First you need to meet my mechanic."

15

Duchess checked the wall clock, weighing the local time in Syria against US Eastern Standard Time as it applied to her at CIA headquarters and, more importantly, her Senate counterpart in DC.

The UAV rep turned in his seat, speaking the words that Duchess had been dreading.

"UAV is offline."

Duchess looked to the central flatscreen, catching her last glimpse of the two flatbed trucks and their armed escort of four technical vehicles traveling north as fast as they could manage on the potholed desert road. They vanished as the UAV banked right, the horizon on screen tilting out of sight until only the night sky was visible.

Now her OPCEN was timing the duration from losing visual with the UAV to re-establishing it with the inbound drones and fighter jets. Every second added to that count strained her ability to engage the trucks with an airstrike, added room for doubt as to whether the rockets would still be aboard by then.

Only a detailed bomb damage assessment would be able to say for sure, and even then, the number of rockets destroyed could well remain forever unknown.

Duchess announced, "Sutherland and Pharr, approach the bench. I'm ready for your brief."

The pair of men rose from their adjacent workstations and quickly ascended the platforms to her desk. They looked like a study in opposites.

Brian Sutherland was a youthful-looking, clean-shaven man in his forties. He laid a map before her, using a pen to point at a road junction at the village just north of the flatbeds' current location.

"This is where the road splits in Deshar. That gives us two likely routes, and we won't know which one the trucks will take—or if they'll split up—until our incoming birds arrive and establish positive identification."

Duchess nodded, waiting for the other shoe to drop. Sutherland was her JTAC, an acronym for Joint Terminal Attack Controller—an expert in the art and science of calling in close air support. He'd earned his bones at the ground level of special operations, first as an Air Force Combat Controller and later as an instructor evaluator at the schoolhouse. His active duty service consisted of calling in bombs and strafing runs while fighting alongside Green Berets and Navy SEALs, making him an ideal candidate for the Agency's JTAC requirements.

Now that he no longer served on the front lines but from an OPCEN at CIA Headquarters, he was tasked with the neurosurgery of close air support: directing fighters and bombers from thousands of miles away, relying on aerial surveillance and ground observer reporting to deliver precision ordnance at the ragged fringe of Agency authorities.

For this reason, his desk was located alongside that of the second man now standing at his side.

Sutherland continued, "But the truck's location, or locations plural, will determine how to proceed."

Duchess's shoulders fell. She knew where this conversation was heading.

"Let me guess: nearest location of allied forces."

"That's right, ma'am," Sutherland said. "If the trucks follow the northwest route, they'll be approaching a Special Forces ODA in Iskar. Once they break a five-mile barrier, we can justify close air support using Type 3 terminal attack control with blanket weapons release clearance in defense of US forces. That's our strongest legal justification, and it's pretty airtight."

"And the other possibility?"

He shifted the tip of his pen on the map. "One or both trucks take the northeast route instead. They don't pass within five miles of any allied forces, which removes our ability to justify close air support. We'd have to switch to AI instead."

"AI?"

The man beside him finally spoke.

"Air interdiction," he said flatly, and Duchess watched him closely for an explanation.

In contrast to Sutherland, Gregory Pharr was in his sixties. With his slicked-back silver hair and graying beard, he looked like the aging patriarch of a biker gang. Which, to an extent, he was—though it consisted of a group of his professional peers, most of whom looked considerably more bureaucratic than he did.

Pharr was an Agency lawyer, and he possessed decades of experience with the byzantine and often conflicting legal restrictions that governed covert action abroad. His role was to know every line of fine-print legalese that Duchess couldn't understand even if she had the time to read it all, seamlessly translating the authorities into clear, actionable guidelines. Pharr knew exactly what Duchess could legally approve, what she couldn't, and what fell into the nebulous gray area that could contribute either to mission success, the end of her career, or both, depending on which way the political winds were drifting.

She asked, "Why haven't I heard of air interdiction before?"

"Because it's a last resort, ma'am," Pharr replied quietly. "In the AI scenario, we'd be legally justifying the strike as destroying enemy military potential before it can be used against friendly forces. We'd be within our authorities, roughly speaking, but this scenario is subject to being dissected three dozen ways by every possible level of oversight. If the bomb damage assessment doesn't reveal any evidence of the rockets being onboard the trucks, and *especially* if this hits the news, the oversight committee, and Gossweiler in particular, are going to be looking for any possible way to distance themselves from your decision."

Duchess nodded, glancing to the wall clock and considering the timing of Gossweiler's next check-in. "Have both scripts ready to go. Barring any updates to the intelligence picture, I plan to authorize either scenario—or, if the trucks split up, both."

16

Ian's team arrived at the mechanic shop at quarter after four in the morning. The sky was still dark, though Ian grimly considered that they were losing that advantage by the minute as sunrise approached.

Once that happened, things were going to get complicated for five white men desperately trying to blend in. Granted, Nizar had provided much of his wardrobe to help with the effort—but to Ian, the results were predictably disheartening.

His team looked like a ragtag gang of homeless militia, the tan fatigues they'd arrived in now supplemented with checkered scarfs called keffiyehs, along with Nizar's unbuttoned overshirts and windbreakers worn atop tactical gear. The process would have been much easier if they could have simply donned full-body burkas, but aside from perhaps Ian's wiry frame, no one on the team was in any danger of passing for a woman.

As Nizar, David, and Ian approached the door, the remaining three men spread out into a loose defensive formation facing the dark street.

Nizar gave three hard raps on the door.

As they waited for the mechanic to answer, Ian considered the few advantages they had.

The locals in this part of the country wore clothes ranging from traditional Arab garb to Western casual. Most importantly, to hear Nizar tell it, was that the civilian populace tended not to let their gazes linger on anyone with a gun. There was such a wide spectrum of Syrian government forces, fractured ISIS militias, and resistance fighters roving throughout the country that you could more or less wear whatever you wanted without drawing attention—that is, right up until the moment you encountered armed fighters representing one side or another, at which point the situation became considerably more dire.

When Nizar knocked a second time without response, David whispered, "I thought you said this guy could deliver. If he's already bailed, I'm going to be pissed."

Ian knew that being pissed was the last of his team leader's concerns at present—if this mechanic had decided to turn on them in the minutes since Nizar called, the odds of him not ratting out the team for some ISIS bounty were slim to none, and they were stepping into an ambush.

But Nizar shook his head. "He hates ISIS more than anyone. But he is too smart. Be careful what you say around him. In any case, he will probably read your thoughts."

"What do you mean, read my—"

It was too late for David to finish the sentence.

The door creaked open, held by a single figure that Ian couldn't make out in the darkness beyond. David didn't hesitate, entering with Nizar as Ian hastened to follow with Cancer, Reilly, and Worthy collapsing their formation to slip inside. The smells of oil, gasoline, and rusting metal were thick in the stale air, and when the last man entered, the door swung shut behind them and locked.

Only then did their host flip on the light switch, illuminating a dank workshop packed with vehicles, motor parts, and toolboxes.

Ian got his first look at the man who'd let them inside.

The mechanic was short and squat, with a wide nose set over a bushy gray beard. His squinting eyes leisurely passed over the men, as if the 4:00 a.m. arrival of an American paramilitary team were a routine occurrence. Ian had worked his fair share of intelligence sources, and immediately assessed the abject lack of moral struggle in the mechanic's eyes, the self-assuredness he projected despite being immediately surrounded by armed men. It took Ian two seconds to arrive at the conclusion that he was dealing with a ruthless opportunist, and that could be a very dangerous thing.

David spoke at once.

"Which vehicles are we taking?"

The mechanic swung a weathered hand across the tight confines of the shop as he replied in heavily accented English, "These Toyotas are my most reliable."

He was pointing toward two Land Cruiser SUVs, one silver and the other white, appearing in decent condition given the country they resided in.

"Fully fueled?"

"I said I would fill them up, and I did. You may take as many gas cans as you wish from the back of my shop."

Cancer spoke to his men. "Get the gear loaded. Split Team One in the white truck, Split Team Two in the gray one."

As Worthy and Reilly began shuttling the team's rucksacks aboard, Cancer took a step toward the trucks.

The mechanic's hand shot out to stop Cancer, and then he stepped closer before inhaling deeply through his nose.

"You smell like cigarettes, my friend. American cigarettes. Camels?"

Cancer's brow furrowed in irritation. "Do I look like I'm trying to live forever? Marlboro Reds, Jack."

The mechanic smiled. "Perhaps some nicotine would help me wake up."

"Perhaps these rust heaps get us where we need to go, and I'll fucking think about it." Then he gently pushed the man aside, proceeding to help Reilly and Worthy load the trucks.

David intervened, extending his hand to the mechanic.

"I'm David."

The man shook it. "Elias."

"What kind of work did you do for Syrian intelligence?" Ian asked.

The question provoked a phlegmy noise from Elias, somewhere between a cough and a laugh, and he tapped his chest with a fist as if trying to clear some obstruction.

"I hunted the enemies of my country," he said, fixing Ian with his stare. "Just as I suspect you do."

Nizar quickly cut in, seeming to sense that this line of inquiry would produce less-than-favorable results.

"Elias, thank you for your help. You were the only one I could turn to."

Then Elias responded with a rapid-fire question in Arabic, and Ian interrupted before Nizar could reply.

"Gentleman," he said, "please communicate in English so we can understand as well."

Elias shot him an angry glare. "I said, 'what is in this for you.'" Then he looked back to Nizar and repeated, "And so, my friend, what *is* in it for you?"

Nizar shook his head. "It is not important. These men need our help."

Elias narrowed his gaze.

"Since I have never known you to care about money, Nizar, then I guess you have a trip to America all lined up for your family." Nodding, he turned to David and said, "This sounds nice. I will have one too, please."

"One what?"

"Trip to America. But I will make it easy on you. The arrangement will be for me alone. Do we have a deal?"

David said, "We can discuss this later. This is a matter of urgency—"

"You have no idea how urgent it is," Elias cut him off. "If you seek a man responsible for transport of a cargo that was very nearly captured already, who do you think will be the first to die when these men try to cover their tracks?" He gave a short, rasping laugh. "It has been some time since my work in Syrian intelligence, but my ignorant mechanic's guess is that the logistician responsible for facilitating the transport will be quite high on that list. We will very likely arrive to find him dead already."

17

Jo Ann's eyes darted across the screens at the front of the OPCEN, now filled with the camera feeds of UAVs streaking over northwestern Syria.

The first UAV to arrive had gone to Deshar where the road diverged, starting at the village's center and flying concentric circles outward with the first priority of locating the two flatbed trucks and, barring that, identifying any evidence of rocket transfer.

But that first surveillance platform had thus far observed only normal pattern-of-life activities within the village, transmitted in black-and-white images across the central flatscreen. The others were sweeping up the two main roads, searching for any trace of the flatbeds.

Then she heard the ground team leader transmit, "*Suicide element is en route to logistician using locally procured vehicles and guides. ETA just under two hours.*"

Seated beside Jo Ann, Duchess lifted the hand mic and transmitted back, "Raptor Nine One copies all. You are cleared to continue pursuit using maximum possible discretion."

"*Discretion is our middle name. Suicide out.*"

This comment made a faint grin appear on Jo Ann's face as Duchess set down her hand mic. "I'm glad you told them about the logistician."

"So am I," Duchess responded, her voice trembling with relief.

But there was nothing to be relieved about yet, Jo Ann thought. That ground team could get rolled up at any moment, and while they were non-attributable to the Agency—even accounting for China's data hack, which was no small achievement—they were still Americans, and to Jo Ann that made them the same as any active duty servicemember she'd sent into battle.

Before she could consider the thought any longer, Sutherland shouted, "We've got visual—looks like both trucks passed through Deshar and are on the northeast route. No US or Coalition forces ahead, so the strike would have to be authorized under air interdiction guidelines."

All eyes turned to the central screen as the image flashed from the orbiting view of Deshar to the feed from a new camera, this one sweeping up a road toward the distant shapes of two flatbed trucks. The four escorting pickups were nowhere in sight, and that bore dire consequences for their ability to authorize an airstrike—provided, of course, these were the same flatbeds in the first place.

"Fidelity?" Duchess asked.

"On it, will advise when able."

The analysts were capturing screenshots from the UAV feed, comparing them to previous images from the last surveillance platform before it went offline.

Within a minute, the lead analyst announced, "Side-by-side imagery of physical markings and thermal signature puts us at ninety percent fidelity that these are the same vehicles."

Sutherland turned in his seat to face Duchess. "Concur, ma'am. I've got more than enough for PID."

Beside him, Pharr shot a silent thumbs-up.

Jo Ann watched Duchess close her eyes and breathe an exalted sigh. PID—positive identification—was exactly what they needed. Duchess had just gotten her airstrike.

"What about the armed escort vehicles?"

"No sign of them," Sutherland replied. "Best guess is they waved off in or around Deshar, and are currently in hiding to minimize signature of the cargo trucks."

The only question now, Jo Ann thought, was whether the rockets were still aboard.

"How are we looking with the cargo?"

Sutherland gave a confident nod. "We've assessed the trucks' speed against the distance traveled—bottom line, if they stopped at any point since we lost visual, it wasn't for long. Less than ten minutes, tops. And with ISR continuing to observe normal pattern of life over the only likely transfer point at Deshar, I'd put our odds at seventy percent that the rockets are still aboard those flatbeds."

"I want PID handed off to the F-15s as soon as they've got eyes-on. Priority of fire is lead vehicle followed by trail, as close to simultaneous hits as they can manage. We've got continuous coverage lined up from here on out?"

"Yes, ma'am. I'll be able to rotate surveillance with Gray Eagles and maintain strike capability on site between Predator and Reaper flights."

"I want the flatbeds destroyed with a small enough munition to leave some evidence for the BDA. What do you recommend?"

"Based on loadout and given that both targets are moving, our best bet is the AGM-65 E2/L, which is the laser-guided Maverick missile variant with a three-hundred-pound warhead. They've got a total of four on the rails, which gives us two shots before they'd have to resort to larger munitions or a strafing run."

"Approved. Relay to the pilots and let me know if you get any kickback."

"Will do. Fighters will be on station in three mikes."

Jo Ann had already typed the launch order for the Rangers into her encrypted chat, but waited for Duchess's order before hitting send.

When Duchess didn't speak at once, Jo Ann prompted her, "Want the Rangers inbound for BDA? They've got just under a two-hour flight time on the MH-47."

Duchess, who looked like she'd just been awakened from a dream, quickly nodded.

"Confirm. Get them airborne."

Jo Ann hit send on her message, thinking that the amount of information to process at once was simply too much even for Duchess to manage—

with this many moving pieces amid a rapidly escalating situation, they were playing three-dimensional chess in Syria.

But the real players were the Rangers packed into an MH-47 helicopter, currently sitting on the tarmac at FOB Presley with its refueling probe hooked up to a fuel bladder while the engines idled, prepared for immediate launch.

Checking her screen, she said, "They're preparing to take off now."

Duchess nodded without speaking, waiting for the next update from Sutherland. It took less than a minute.

"F-15 flight lead has confirmed all, and assesses they should be able to achieve dual-impact within a three-second spread. They've got six miles of forward clearance before the next civilian population center, and there's zero traffic inbound."

"Gregory?"

The lawyer replied, "It's a clear shot for air interdiction, ma'am."

Sutherland added, "PID has been transferred to flight lead, we're offsetting our UAV from the bomb trajectory. Sixty seconds to weapons release; last call."

She responded, "Final clearance approved."

Whatever amount of time elapsed before the next spoken words in the OPCEN didn't seem like sixty seconds to Jo Ann. No matter how many times she'd watched a mission unfold on real-time footage, the magnitude of the ground events was rarely lost on her. She'd attended enough military funerals of the men she'd supported to forever purge herself of achieving total detachment, no matter how far from the fight she was.

"Weapons release," Sutherland called out, then repeated the statement a few seconds later.

Both air-to-ground missiles were streaking along a laser-guided trajectory, and the OPCEN went dead quiet aside from the chatter of the pilots emanating from a speaker box.

Jo Ann knew what would happen next.

All too often, footage of the seconds before a bomb or missile impact were filled with people racing away from the target on foot, having detected the noise of the aircraft or the projectile itself hurling through the air toward them—Jo Ann was never sure which. All she knew was that once the dark figures of humans on the ground scattered like insects, the explosion occurred on screen within three seconds or less.

Usually those fleeing figures were unsuccessful, vanishing in the blast despite their best efforts. Occasionally she could make out a human form half-crawling away from the destruction, making a last-ditch effort to survive before succumbing to their wounds. And in some cases, the fastest runners in a group managed to outpace the immediate blast, either vanishing offscreen or, in the event of high-value individuals, being tracked until a second bomb or missile could find its mark.

But the men aboard these trucks had no way of knowing what was about to occur; or maybe they did know, and were simply resigned to their fate. Either way, there would be no way to hear the fighters streaking in from fifteen thousand feet over the sound of truck engines, nor the descent of missiles until they were milliseconds from pummeling into the vehicle.

And even if those men knew they were about to die, what choice did they have? They were driving across the open desert, and there was no place to run where the unblinking eye of surveillance aircraft wouldn't find them. Would they even want to survive? Jo Ann wasn't sure; she only knew that these men were extremists who had, like many of the terrorists she'd targeted in the past, resigned themselves to the prospect of martyrdom in seeking some paradise beyond the confines of their physical existence. In the violent and poverty-ravaged lands where such fighters emerged, the prospect of heaven was a key ingredient in their justification for committing unspeakable atrocities against their fellow human beings.

Still, her thoughts were with the men aboard those trucks, considering what life events had transpired from their birth up until the moment of their death. Soon, it wouldn't matter; they'd be nothing more than ashes in the desert and forgotten numbers on an Agency casualty count.

And when it was all over, when the targets were nothing more than human remains smoldering in the dirt of some faraway nation, these same military and Agency professionals—herself included—would go to work finding more people to kill.

The first missile came streaking in from the bottom of the screen, a pinpoint of light that connected with the lead truck in a dazzling white flash. Then there was nothing but a vast cloud billowing outward, the trail vehicle braking in the final moment before it too vanished in a blossoming fog of sand and smoke.

Indistinguishable pieces of metal rocketed up and out of the explosions, pirouetting in spinning arcs until they crashed to the desert in a chaotic perimeter around the vehicle remains.

Jo Ann typed the grid of the impact site, sending it on her encrypted chat to vector in the Ranger platoon currently flying toward the strike zone.

Sutherland called, "Both targets destroyed, no survivors visible."

Duchess replied, "Keep the fighters orbiting for maximum station time. How's our stack looking?"

"No change to assets; we'll have manned and unmanned ISR rotating for the duration with continuous kinetic option."

"I want nonstop surveillance until ground forces arrive, with strike authority against anyone trying to recover materiel from the site." Then she asked Jo Ann, "How's our BDA looking?"

Jo Ann replied loudly enough for the rest of the OPCEN to hear.

"Rangers are airborne; flight time is one hour, forty-eight minutes."

Then Sutherland confirmed, "I've got comms with the Ranger JTAC and will be able to shift air assets as per ground force commander's guidance once they're boots-on-the-ground."

Duchess nodded her approval, her face as serene as a woman on her spa day.

But Jo Ann watched that placid expression vanish when a phone on her desk rang—this was the red phone, the one that could never go unanswered.

Duchess snatched the receiver. "Duchess here."

A long pause as her face became stern, and then finally, "Understand all."

She hung up the phone, giving Jo Ann an irritated glance before turning her attention to the OPCEN staff.

"I need everyone to prepare a formal brief of your actions and analysis up to this point," she announced, then cleared her throat. "Senator Gossweiler is on his way."

18

Sitting without his seatbelt in the lead Land Cruiser's rear passenger seat, Worthy practiced rolling to his left to reach for the pistol on his side. He repeated the maneuver several times without drawing the sidearm, his rifle resting barrel-down between his legs.

David was seated beside him, pretending not to notice what Worthy was rehearsing as the two-vehicle convoy threaded its way toward Zaranj, the sun rising over a rolling expanse of desert.

After Worthy's final rehearsal found his right palm married to the backstrap of his pistol in a fraction of a second, he relaxed and glanced at the buildings outside, never letting his vision stray far from the front passenger seat.

Based on his competitive shooting experience, Worthy was probably faster with a pistol than a rifle. But speed was only one factor in surviving the mission, and the rest—range, power, penetration—made his rifle not only the obvious choice, but the only one.

However, when shooting a fellow passenger in the tight confines of the vehicle, a pistol was the only option.

With five Americans and two native Syrians split between two Land Cruisers, David and Cancer had chosen the best load plan possible.

A team member drove each vehicle—Ian behind the wheel of Worthy's truck, and Cancer driving the trail vehicle—with a Syrian in the passenger seat who could identify anything out of the ordinary and stand at least a chance of talking or bribing their way through any checkpoints they encountered.

In the passenger-side backseat was another team member who could maintain physical security over the Syrian guide to his front, prepared to react in the event of sabotage.

And in the lead truck, that role fell upon Worthy.

They could never completely trust anyone outside their own ranks, much less the two civilians plucked more or less at random from Syria, a nation with some of the most complex tribal and militant factions on earth. So a team member had to occupy the "Godfather seat" behind their Syrian passenger, prepared to react if Elias suddenly grabbed the steering wheel and tried to crash their vehicle or any such similar nonsense. Worthy's first course of action was physical restraint, threading an arm around Elias's neck and muscling him away from the driver. His pistol was a last resort in more ways than one: if Worthy killed Elias, they'd lose half of their native guides and likely piss off the other half.

But Elias had proven to be a model passenger; in fact, he seemed more than enthusiastic about the mission ahead.

Elias asked, "So once we get the logistician back to my friend's workshop, what is it you would like to know?"

Ian replied from the driver's seat, "He facilitated the transport of an ISIS leader and his cargo from your town to an unknown destination earlier this morning. We need to find out the destination."

"And this ISIS leader is Syrian?"

"Not Syrian," Ian said. "He's a foreign fighter."

"Ah, the scourge of my nation. Where has he slithered in from—Iraq, Lebanon, Palestine?"

"China."

Elias considered this a moment. "Uyghur or Han Chinese?"

"Uyghur."

"Thousands of Uyghurs have traveled here. Most fight with the Turkistan Islamic Party. But their allegiance is to al Qaeda, not ISIS. And most return to China to fight for a homeland. Only a few hundred choose ISIS and remain in Syria, and these are probably the dumbest of them all."

Worthy smiled, wondering who in the hell this guy was. Nizar had been adamant that Elias held a background in Syrian intelligence, leaving his position to resume his childhood trade as a mechanic only when the national situation degraded to the point where he had no choice but to flee Damascus. And Worthy didn't doubt any of that. Elias seemed highly motivated to pursue anyone associated with ISIS, and seemed to view the Americans as a welcome if unexpected boon to his fortunes. But Worthy sensed the story was incomplete: Elias wasn't being completely open about something, and he hoped to God it wasn't some ulterior motive that would undermine the Agency's objective to locate the rockets.

Ian said, "Well this guy we're after is definitely leaving the country, and we need to stop that from happening."

"What has one man done to deserve such attention from America?"

Ian asked, "David?"

Rather than give permission, David replied to the question himself.

"He's moving a massive payload of rockets, and it's a safe bet he doesn't plan on leaving them unused."

"Ah," Elias said knowingly. "Yes, this is a problem indeed. But there must be someone else in charge. An ISIS Uyghur would be a foot soldier."

Ian said, "This one's calling the shots. Trust me."

"I believe your intelligence is mistaken."

"Are you familiar with what's going on in western China?"

Elias laughed. "The same thing that has always happened: China is crushing any dissent under the weight of her massive Communist heel."

"It's more like the Holocaust revisited," Ian said. "Between one and three million Uyghurs have been arrested, thrown aboard trains, and relocated to political re-education camps for no other crime than being born as Turkic Muslims. The abuse at these camps includes executions, forced labor, abortions, and sterilization. The children are being ripped away from their parents and sent to orphanages for indoctrination. It's demographic genocide."

"Please spare me the lesson. I dare say my country's president has done far worse."

"Well someone chose this specific Uyghur man for a reason, and it's not because he's dumb. Add in the fact that the Chinese government carted off his wife and daughter like cattle to slaughter, imagine how pissed you'd be, and then throw in enough rockets to wipe out downtown Damascus. Now I don't care if you believe my intelligence or not. We just need to find him, whatever it takes."

"It sounds like the Chinese should be afraid, not America."

"Everyone should be afraid," Ian said, "until we stop him and recover the rockets. If he can't get them back to China, he'll use them wherever he can."

"Well," Elias said, "this is unusual, but stranger things have happened in Syria. If you people can capture this logistician, I am confident I can obtain the information you require."

Worthy noted the eerie silence that followed the end of that particular sentence, but before he could consider the means by which a man like Elias would "obtain the information," the men in his truck caught their first glances of the town ahead.

Zaranj showed no obvious indications of the civil war. As the Land Cruisers made their way through the outskirts, Worthy saw the buildings intact, shops open for business as men, women, and children roamed the sidewalks freely, most of them in semi-Western clothes. There were no signs of government or militant oppression, and while Worthy's travels abroad had been more limited than anyone on his team, he imagined their current surroundings could have just as easily been in any number of underdeveloped Arab nations that hadn't descended into chaos and militia control.

As Ian threaded their way along the route, Elias spoke again.

"Once we get him, the interrogation may require some unique methods."

"No torture," David said flatly.

"I am telling you, Mr. David, it may not be needed. Those with financial motivations will quickly sing. But if he is hardline Islamic State, I will have to encourage him."

"Then use your head. Because you're not hooking up a car battery to some poor bastard's nipples on my watch."

Elias recoiled at the accusation.

"Car battery? What do you take me for, a Frenchman in Algiers?"

David shrugged. "If the shoe fits..."

"Perhaps I should simply dress the prisoner in an orange jumpsuit, then waterboard him for my country to prosecute me at some later point."

Worthy cringed. "Too soon, Elias. Pump the brakes."

This only seemed to enrage Elias further. "What is the problem? You lose a few thousand in 9/11—waterboarding is A-OK. No problem, my friend. Syria has lost *hundreds of thousands* since the start of the war, and Islamic State nearly took over the Middle East."

Then Elias clucked his tongue, going silent without immediate response from anyone in the vehicle.

David finally spoke in a flat tone. "You want to debate geopolitics? Get a side gig as a consultant on C-SPAN once you get back to the States. Until then, watch the road and figure out a way to get our detainee to talk that doesn't involve torture."

Elias turned to face forward in the passenger seat, sulking.

"Your friend could at least give me some cigarettes. I have not been able to find Marlboro Reds since Damascus."

Worthy said, "You should quit. Those things will kill you."

"If Syria has not killed me yet, perhaps I shall live forever."

This comment elicited a half-grin from Worthy, an expression that quickly faded as he considered the extent to which his team was operating on a wing and a prayer. Ian had been adamant that short of round-the-clock surveillance on the two flatbed trucks, Bari Khan would find a way to transfer the rockets undetected. Worthy wasn't so sure, but David's ultimate decision had been to remain in the fight however possible.

There was a certain logic to his judgment that Worthy couldn't argue. From what David had explained, their Agency handler was under incredible scrutiny, to say nothing of the pressure to deliver results. After the team's first outing in the Philippines had suddenly turned into a pilot rescue mission, and the second had seen Bari Khan escape despite a well-laid ambush, they were at risk of total dissolution if they didn't succeed. And while Worthy was no politician, he knew full well that America's foray into a covert targeted killing operation was no small leap. If his team couldn't prove some efficacy in the hours ahead, his country may well abandon the effort for years if not decades—and more than a few terrorist masterminds would likely rise to power as a result.

In the driver's seat, Ian consulted the tablet in his lap before glancing up at the road and then the adjacent buildings. "We're almost there. It's"—he gave a final glance to his right—"that one, blue door."

David transmitted to the trail vehicle, "Blue door at your two o'clock. Target building."

Cancer replied, "*Truck Two copies.*"

Worthy stared out his window, examining the building while keeping his back against the seat so David could see as well.

It was a tan, two-story structure wedged between a similarly unmarked building and an electronics store. Worthy could make out back alleys between and behind the structures, an urban maze that civilians were navigating with ease.

David transmitted, addressing Ian and the trail vehicle simultaneously.

"We're going to do a few passes around the block, case the alleyways before we take it."

Cancer confirmed, "*Easy day, boss. We're ready to drop when you are.*"

They passed the target house, taking in the details of the city block as Ian turned right to loop around it. Worthy felt his senses and instincts satisfied at the sight before him: unarmed men and women going about their lives, hustling over the sidewalk and across the street as the rhythm of daily life persisted despite the war around them.

But when Ian rounded the second corner, Elias spoke urgently.

"Mr. David, those men do not belong here."

Worthy scanned out his window, seeking anything out of place amid the bustling civilians. To him, the scene was indistinguishable from the previous city blocks they'd traveled, and he wondered if Elias was making some play to sabotage the mission ahead.

David must have felt the same. "Who are you talking about?"

"Blue jacket, white shirt, and the man in the shalwar kameez without a keffiyeh carrying a backpack. There may be more I cannot see."

"Who are they?"

"Islamic State sleeper cell, Syrian government proxies, who is to say? They will get our man before we can."

David said, "Ian, get us to the door." Then he keyed his radio and transmitted, "Truck Two, Elias sees suspicious military-aged males approaching the target house on foot. Likely trying to get the same guy we are. Advancing to breach now, primary plan in effect. Me, Worthy, and Elias will make entry. Reilly, you back us up and take control of our prisoner. I want both drivers staying behind the wheel and providing outside security, with Nizar on hand if there's any interference from the locals. Reilly will exfil the prisoner to his truck, and then we proceed to Elias's friend's workshop for debrief."

In the backseat of the rear truck, Reilly felt himself grinning as Cancer keyed his mic in response.

"Truck Two copies, let's hit him."

From behind the wheel, Cancer glanced at Reilly in the backseat and said, "If I gotta stay with the vehicle, you better crack some skulls for me, brother."

Reilly felt a smug sense of anticipation.

"It's been four days since my last workout. This is going to be fun."

"That's my boy." Cancer nodded, glancing over to see Nizar looking confused in the passenger seat. "What's the matter, you guys don't have roid rage here? No Syrian miscreants on the ol' gym juice?"

Nizar said nothing, clearly confused but having long since resigned himself to letting Cancer say whatever he wanted during the drive into Zaranj.

Reilly knew he was the ideal choice for manhandling a prisoner. If the slight frames of the Arab men he saw on the streets around him were any indication, he'd have no problem whatsoever in getting their detainee out of the building and into the truck. Armed with the knowledge that said detainee was a supporter if not an outright member of ISIS, an organization whose calling cards were mass murder and systematic rape, Reilly thought that he'd pursue his duties with exceptional vigor.

As Cancer wheeled their truck around a street corner and Reilly glimpsed the target building, he saw that Elias was already at the door, pounding on it with a fist. David and Worthy stood off to either side, weapons pointed down, waiting for the door to open.

Then it did, cracking a few inches as Elias took a step backward, and David shouldered his way violently through the doorway.

Cancer braked to a stop with the words, "Go get 'em, killer."

Reilly leapt out of the truck, rifle at the ready as he darted across a short strip of dirt before bursting through the doorway into the ground floor of the building.

He brought his rifle up toward three figures, none of them his teammates.

Then he lowered his barrel as quickly as he'd taken aim.

The trio of young teenage women were holding up their hands in submission, making no attempt to defend the man of the house. But these girls were too similar in age to be daughters, and Reilly realized that they were the man's wives—if you could call them that. More likely ISIS war brides provided in exchange for services rendered.

Oh, Reilly thought with a darkening sense of anger, he was going to manhandle this prisoner far more than necessary in the course of his duties.

From the far side of a doorway, he heard David shouting, "Doc, in here."

Reilly rushed forward, clearing the next doorway and entering an empty kitchen. The next door he encountered was open, and he jogged through it toward the sounds of men grunting in exertion.

But when he rounded the corner to see Elias standing triumphantly over David, who had his knee in the prostrate prisoner's back as Ian applied flex cuffs, Reilly stopped short.

David said, "Doc, come get this guy."

Elias waved a hand between Reilly and the prisoner, looking inconvenienced. "What is the problem? Pick him up."

But the prisoner that David was in the process of flex-cuffing was a bloated mess of a man, probably two hundred thirty pounds and very little of it muscle mass.

Gritting his teeth, Reilly stomped over and prepared to deadlift his prisoner.

That effort took more strain than he anticipated, even with David and Ian trying to help him. As Reilly hoisted the prisoner upright, the man spat into David's eyes.

David responded in kind, driving a fist across the prisoner's face and causing the fat man to go limp in Reilly's grasp.

He struggled to catch the logistician. "Suicide, you're not helping!"

"Sorry," David said, wiping his eyes clear. "Let's go."

The detainee was shouting in Arabic—presumably insults, judging by the tone—and did his best to resist the transport, locking his knees and trying to halt forward progress more than his considerable weight already was.

Reilly assisted his captive's motivation to comply by swinging him sideways, then flinging him into the wall.

The man's forehead cracked off the surface, driving his body backward into Reilly's grasp, and he exploited the gap in resistance by half-pushing, half-dragging the prisoner into the front room.

And that, he soon found, was where things got complicated.

The three teenage women who'd formerly cowed before Reilly's barrel had undergone some critical metamorphosis upon seeing their husband-slash-rapist being dragged out of the building.

They descended upon the prisoner with shouts and cries, assaulting him with their words and their fists as David and Ian struggled to keep them at bay.

But one particularly emboldened young woman broke free of David's arms, advanced before she could be grabbed again, and drove a kick to the prisoner's groin with a force that defied comprehension.

The big man went limp once again.

Reilly had to squat down to support the weight, wheeling the man away from his former captives and toward the door to the street.

And whatever Elias's intuition about suspicious men approaching the target building, Reilly saw in a glance that he'd been correct.

David and Worthy had their barrels raised, firing their first suppressed rounds at targets to their left. A collective scream erupted from the civilians around them as men and women darted for cover.

Then Reilly caught his first sight of an enemy combatant—a man running across the street toward him, drawing a pistol from beneath his shirt.

Reilly's only possible reaction was to throw his detainee to the ground, draw his rifle, and shoot the man that David and Worthy were too preoccupied to see. But by the time he did, Reilly knew, it would be too late.

Just as he prepared to drop his prisoner, he saw that he didn't have to.

Cancer's silver Land Cruiser roared down the street, mowing down the pistol-wielding man beneath the bumper before screeching to a halt. Then Cancer shifted to reverse, flooring the gas to back over the fallen enemy for good measure.

All of this occurred in Reilly's first six seconds outside the building, a surreal melee of violence that could have just as easily been dismissed as a bizarre dream. David and Worthy fired as fast as they could at the men closing in on the target house from all directions, and Reilly heard a single shouted order from his team leader.

"Get him off the street!"

Reilly turned to see a storefront door beside him and manhandled his prisoner sideways for three staggering steps.

Then, mustering all of his strength, Reilly swung the man to his right and hurled him into the door, which burst open as he landed on his stomach with a cry of pain. Reilly turned to provide suppressing fire, finding and then engaging a man crouched behind a parked car, his rifle angled over the hood. Firing two shots, Reilly saw the man drop out of sight before he swung his barrel to the right, blasting a half-dozen rounds at a building corner where he'd seen a flash of gunfire.

He continued shooting at another enemy sprinting into view, his peripheral vision registering three figures racing behind him to enter the store through the now-open doorway—first Worthy, then Elias, and finally David.

As David opened fire from the shop window, Reilly turned to plunge inside and saw the chaos within.

It was a small electronics store, the walls filled with cheap cell phones and wire attachments, and the owner behind the counter was red-faced, wild-eyed, and screaming at them in incomprehensible, rapid-fire Arabic.

"This way!" Elias shouted, waving Reilly into a back room.

Flinging his rifle behind him on its sling, Reilly squatted above his prisoner, still in the prone amid shattered glass, and deadlifted him upright. The prisoner was disoriented, but still able to resist—he dug in his heels, writhing his shoulders against Reilly's grasp.

"You dumb sonofabitch," Reilly grunted, swinging the man's massive body to his left. The prisoner's head smashed into the corner of a display case, buying Reilly a few moments to hoist his cargo through the doorway after Elias.

Beyond was a small storage room, with a single exit into an alley.

Devoid of options, Reilly hauled the logistician's mass through the next door, emerging into the alley and following Worthy and Elias toward a side street.

David was behind him, transmitting over the team frequency, though Reilly couldn't make out the voice in his earpiece over the shouts of civilians and enemy alike.

Instead he followed the men to his front, fully aware that he was the only team member capable of hauling the ISIS logistician's obese figure toward some unknown exfil, and trusting Worthy and David to manage the tactical situation with Elias's help. And while his trust in his teammates was absolute, it was Elias who represented the single point of failure for this operation.

Any lingering doubts faded when the combined element reached the side street ahead.

Cancer's Land Cruiser fishtailed to a stop before them, and Elias ripped open the back door as Reilly charged forward with his unrepentant cargo.

Reilly's next movement was performed with all the unceremonious grace with which he struggled through repetitions in the gym under enormous resistance: he took a final pair of staggering steps, squatted beneath the weight of his load, and, with as much force as he could muster, hurled the prisoner into the backseat.

The logistician's body sailed forward, achieving not any great distance but sufficient to cause his head to impact the far door so hard that Reilly feared he'd just broken the man's neck.

There was no time to confirm; Reilly leapt atop the backseat, feeling Cancer accelerate before he could close the door.

Glancing through the rear windshield, Reilly saw David, Worthy, and Elias leaping inside Ian's waiting truck, and together the two vehicles sped toward the workshop.

19

By the time Duchess received David's next transmission, his team's role in the mission was almost an afterthought.

"Raptor Nine One, Suicide element has recovered logistician. We weren't the only ones trying to snatch him. En route to an offsite location for tactical questioning, will advise when able."

"Copy all," Duchess transmitted back, acknowledging receipt of the message but offering no further guidance. At this point her only concern was the bomb damage assessment of the two destroyed flatbeds.

"ETA on the Rangers?" she asked.

Sutherland responded, "Wheels down in four mikes."

Duchess considered the phrasing on her next inquiry.

"ETA on the firing squad?"

This elicited a chuckle from the assembly.

"Senator Gossweiler's vehicle has passed the front gate," Pharr replied. "We've got fifteen to twenty minutes before he reaches the OPCEN floor."

Duchess nodded. "Sutherland, please advise the Ranger ground force commander that our PIR is time-sensitive. We request initial assessment as soon as they have eyes-on, followed by a detailed report once they've had time to sift through the wreckage."

Her priority information requirements were twofold: first and foremost, any evidence of rockets aboard the trucks at the time of their destruction. The Rangers making their way to the site to perform a bomb damage assessment didn't know that the rockets in question were provided by the Agency to the Syrian resistance, and they didn't have to—an untold number of indirect fire rounds were fired every day against warring factions in Syria, though none quite so accurate and deadly as the OG-9VM1.

For all of Duchess's continuous aerial oversight of the mangled wreckage of the two flatbed trucks, they'd been unable to positively identify any evidence at all. No visible rocket cylinders had been thrown clear of the blast, and Duchess desperately hoped that the Rangers would be able to find some scrap of a rocket body, some partial serial number that had survived the bombs and could thus provide an assurance that at least some of the cargo had been destroyed. If they could determine Bari Khan had been killed in the blast, even better.

That uncertainty was the reason for her second and final priority intelligence requirement: any identifying marks on the flatbeds themselves. Because in the event no rockets were found, Duchess would need concrete assurance that she'd bombed the right trucks in the first place.

At this point, however, there was nothing she could do about it either way.

Located almost seven thousand miles from the battleground in Syria, Duchess had made the best decision she could using the information she had available at the time. But the gap in aerial coverage of the trucks between the time they'd left the warehouse with the rockets aboard and the moment they'd been destroyed left a lingering doubt in her odds of success.

And now not just her career but the entire targeted killing program depended on this bomb damage assessment for survival.

The thought was fractured by Sutherland's next announcement.

"BDA element is one minute from wheels-down."

She turned her attention to the central screen, an orbiting high-angle view of the truck wreckage and the surrounding desert.

An MH-47 Chinook helicopter thundered into view, touching down at a two-hundred-meter offset from the blast site with its twin rotors forming shadowy discs over the ground.

Streams of darting figures raced off the helicopter ramp, spreading into a semicircle formation and kneeling until the bird had deposited the last man.

Then the Rangers were concealed within whitewashed clouds of sand as the aircraft lifted off again, gaining altitude and banking out of view at the edge of the screen.

By the time the sand cleared, the Rangers were already advancing on the vehicle wreckage, moving in tactical wedge formations as they divided into blocking positions on the road, perimeter security, and clearance elements.

Duchess watched the choreographed movements as she'd done countless times, supervising ground teams over a video screen as they executed their missions in more nations than she cared to count. Her focus was on the first men to reach the trucks, and she watched them raising their rifles in anticipation of possible survivors.

It was always easy to identify whether shots had been fired—the moment of enemy contact, before any radio call was sent, the tiny figures of men on the screen would immediately flex to fire and maneuver, overtaking the threat by any means possible.

But the Rangers continued their sweep unhindered, and she felt her pulse in her ears as she waited for Sutherland to relay the initial assessment.

He did so without turning in his seat, announcing, "The truck exterior components thrown free of the blast have bullet holes estimated to be from 5.56mm weapons."

That much was a boon to Duchess's spirits—in contrast to a majority of third-world Kalashnikovs chambered in 7.62mm, David's team carried 5.56mm rifles, so these were almost certainly the right trucks.

Then he said, "No rocket components whatsoever."

Duchess replied with composure, more for the benefit of her OPCEN staff than out of any sense of assurance. That particular resource existed in a very finite quantity, and it was dwindling away by the second.

She asked, "If you were a betting man, Sutherland, what would you put our odds at?"

He turned to face her.

"I *am* a betting man, and I wish I had better news for us. But given our use of the smallest possible bombs to achieve desired effects, the presence of truck exterior components with identifiable bullet holes, and the partially intact truck engine assemblies, the odds of 646 rockets vanishing without a trace are slim to none. At a minimum, they should have seen multiple rocket fins, warheads, or rocket motors by now. If there were rockets aboard, it wasn't all of them."

"Understood," she replied in a crisp voice. "Let's have them continue to comb the wreckage. I don't want them to exfil until they're absolutely certain."

Sutherland nodded and resumed communicating with the ground force, and the mood in the OPCEN was one of total control over the tactical situation.

Duchess, of course, knew better.

Sutherland was far too experienced to be mistaken about this. Duchess knew in that instant that she'd bombed the right trucks; but she also sensed, and painfully so, that they'd lost the cargo and Bari Khan along with it.

As for everything else—the operation at hand, the future of the program, her own career—all was uncertain. With her hopes of a positive BDA dashed, Duchess's every decision up to this point could—and would—be interpreted as questionable if not outright negligent by the one man who held the strings, and that man was on his way to the OPCEN at that second.

Gossweiler, of course, possessed the legal authority to insert himself on the OPCEN floor at will. If this mission occurred between Friday afternoon and Monday morning, when most of Congress was traveling home to meet their constituencies, she knew that Gossweiler would have been present from the moment of infiltration until his chief of staff ushered him away for his next scheduled commitment.

At present she was faced with the worst-case scenario: a failed mission resulting in Gossweiler clearing his schedule to personally supervise her efforts, thus making him even more irritable than usual.

She appraised her surroundings, considering the scene through Gossweiler's eyes.

The dress code in the OPCEN was business casual at best, unless the individual had some personal fashion sense. Pharr, for instance, wore a suit whether he had to or not—possibly just to offset his biker-gang appearance.

But for the most part, these people were selected on the basis of their brains, not their ability to dress well. Jo Ann's pantsuit looked like it was made of couch upholstery, more suited for substitute teaching in her Podunk hometown than a face-to-face with a senator in DC. With a short-sleeve collared shirt and tie, Sutherland could have fit in as middle management at a paper mill. And her UAV rep was in an honest-to-God polo shirt.

None of that changed the fact that Gossweiler would be striding onto the OPCEN floor as judge, jury, and executioner for the staff's combined actions over the past eight hours, and the hard facts were debatably just as questionable as their wardrobes. As with many key missions in Duchess's career, the outcome was usually more important than the means—if you bent every rule in the book and things turned out well, the administration was often more than enthusiastic to claim the victory.

But even if you stayed well within the lines of your designated authorities and things didn't go as hoped, the powers-that-be tended to find fault with everything you'd done, up to and including vague condemnations on seemingly obvious judgment calls. Politics was a dangerous game, and she was about to deal with a man who'd survived it longer than most.

And at the moment this thought crossed her mind, Gossweiler arrived.

She heard the door swing open behind her, held by a CIA staffer who announced, "Senator on the floor."

Duchess turned to see Senator Thomas Gossweiler enter alone, attired in a suit and tie, a seventy-two-year-old white man whose face was less creased than many of his peers who were ten years his junior. A shock of silver hair was combed back neatly over his ghostly blue eyes, and everything from his piercing glare to his erect posture projected an image of total authority that matched his tone as he spoke.

"Kimberly, what have you got?"

Duchess replied quickly, calmly, nodding to the screen at the front of the OPCEN.

"Our bomb damage assessment is ongoing. So far they've confirmed the presence of bullet holes consistent with weapons used by my ground team, which in addition to the analyst assessment indicates we hit the right vehicles beyond a shadow of a doubt. As for evidence of the rockets, they're still searching."

Gossweiler was unconvinced, watching the central screen with a skeptical expression. "Those trucks don't exactly look like they were vaporized, so if the Rangers haven't found any rockets yet, I don't believe they will. What else?"

Clearing her throat, Duchess said, "My team has detained the logistician who facilitated the transport and maintained direct communications with Bari Khan. They are conducting tactical questioning as we speak."

"And in my considerable experience with targeting terror organizations," Gossweiler coolly replied, "the logisticians are very rarely informed of the contents of their cargo. And they're *never* informed of what it's going to be used for, so I'm bracing myself for a dead end in that regard. What else?"

"During our gap in air coverage of the flatbeds, they passed through Deshar. We've maintained continuous surveillance for unusual activity, and I've got every Agency and military intelligence asset in the area monitoring for indicators of the cargo."

Gossweiler said, "As for the rockets themselves, how bad are we talking?"

Duchess called for Sutherland, who hastily rose and approached them, trailed by Pharr.

She said, "Brian, please brief the senator on the rocket specifics."

"Good morning, Senator. Brian Sutherland, Joint Terminal Attack Controller—"

"Cut the foreplay, son."

Sutherland said, "OG-9VM1, with fragmentary high explosive warheads. Maximum range 2.79 miles with a lethal blast radius of ten meters."

"Worst-case scenario?"

"Four rockets have been destroyed, leaving 646 at large. Simultaneous launch of that payload would achieve a kill box of 142 acres, and that's only accounting for the lethal blast radius. If he expands the strike to the lethal *fragmentation* radius of each rocket—fifty meters plus—he could cover a little over one square mile."

Gossweiler turned to Duchess. "So in the time it took me to have breakfast and make my way here, you lost your target, lost the rockets, and authorized a high-profile airstrike that resulted in exactly nothing."

Duchess suppressed the instinct to raise her voice.

"While you were at breakfast, Senator, we *found* the rockets. If they weren't going to be used for a major attack, they'd have been fired all over Syria by now."

"I appreciate that speculation, Kimberly, and can't say I disagree with you on that point. As for everything else surrounding this operation, I have to express my doubts, with the legalities being chief among them."

Pharr intervened, "Senator, I can assure you that every action taken has been to the strictest adherence to the mandated authorities of this program."

Gossweiler tilted his head, appraising Pharr as if he'd just noticed the presence of a particularly loathsome insect on his dinner plate.

"I don't remember asking you a damn thing, son. My committee lawyers will eat you alive and you know it."

Then he returned his gaze to Duchess. "As a humble and God-fearing man, I take no issue with making every possible effort to hunt down and kill every savage who would do harm to innocent civilians, whether those civilians hold American citizenship or not. But as Chairman of the US Senate Select Committee on Intelligence, I'm afraid I have other duties to attend to. And the biggest part of my job description is to provide, and I quote, 'vigilant legislative oversight' to programs such as these. On a personal level, I wouldn't have used my influence to get you this job if I didn't think you were the right person for it. But it's becoming apparent that I couldn't have been more wrong. And it's not just your abilities coming into question, it's the efficacy of this entire program."

"Sir, the program has merit," Duchess argued. "All responsibility for the failures to date rests with me alone and doesn't reflect in any way upon my OPCEN staff or the ground team I chose."

"The ground team you chose has burned through millions in my budget, and they've delivered exactly zero results in three missions, one of which is now off the rails in a way that defies my ability to comprehend it."

Jo Ann intervened, "Sir, there's an American pilot who escaped capture in the Philippines because of those men."

Gossweiler gave Jo Ann a bland smile, a contortion of his elderly features that fell a half-step shy of an outright sneer. "Couple problems with your logic there, Commander Brown. Yes, that pilot is alive. No, it was not what the ground team was sent in to accomplish. And I commend their actions on Jolo Island as much as the next guy, but their proximity to the shootdown was nothing more than a freak accident. The same applies for the team's identification of this rocket shipment. And if we keep hemorrhaging defense spending in the hopes that we land on lightning-strike odds of intervening in some peripheral incident, then our nation is in bad shape."

Before Jo Ann could reply, Gossweiler held up a hand. "I'd like to speak to Kimberly alone."

The trio scattered. Sutherland and Pharr returned to their workstations, trailed by Jo Ann, who followed them for lack of anywhere else to go.

Then Gossweiler spoke quietly, with far more patience than anything he'd said so far.

"Kimberly, I'm tired of the previous model of endless drone strikes and collateral damage. And I have a preference bordering on obsession for surgical direct action. I'm tired of the military operators writing tell-all books, so it only makes sense to move these activities back toward intel agencies that leak less. As such, I'm willing to let the leash stretch farther than I would for the usual programs I oversee on committee. But I'm not going to put an egg on the president's face over a team of former mercs doing wet work for the Agency, are we clear?"

"Yes, sir," Duchess replied, knowing that any other response would merely make the situation worse—if such a thing were even possible.

"So yes," he continued, "Project Longwing will continue—for the time being. But it's not going to be with the team that's struck out three times so far. And it's not," he added, his tone becoming grave, "going to be with you running it."

Duchess felt her stomach turning to stone, but she was unable to react outside of a hollow nod of acknowledgement.

Gossweiler looked for Jo Ann and called out, "Commander Brown."

As Jo Ann approached, Duchess braced herself for what was about to occur. There was a reason he'd insisted on military oversight in the first place, and that reason was about to play itself out.

Jo Ann arrived, and Gossweiler addressed them both.

"You're authorized to continue searching for the rockets using aerial platforms and intelligence assets. But as of this second, any further ground action belongs to the military, not the Agency. The ground team will take the captured logistician to the nearest exfil point, after which I want them out of Syria and on a plane to the States with zero delay. Then they're disbanded. You, Commander Brown, will stay on board. Kimberly, you've got exactly one week to prepare this program for transition to a successor that I nominate."

And then, before Duchess could think of any words that might change his mind, Senator Gossweiler turned and left the OPCEN.

20

Cancer rested his hand on the door handle, and I gave him a nod.

He swung it open and stepped aside, and I slipped into the room with my barrel raised, cutting right to find a largely open space as Cancer entered behind me and moved to the opposite corner.

My team was in the process of performing a "soft clear," not kicking down doors but nonetheless flowing from room to room at eighty percent speed, giving clearance to one another's sectors of fire as we moved.

Until we'd gotten eyes-on every space in the building, our security was a matter of assumption. That was the dilemma of our situation—too much paranoia, and we'd still be cowering in the desert outside our initial target, waiting for nightfall to bring a helicopter for exfiltration.

Too much audacity, however, and we'd wander into a trap.

But the building was unoccupied aside from us and the tall Syrian man who'd quite willingly let us in—a man Elias introduced as "a friend in Zaranj."

The man procured a chair from the corner and dragged it to the center of the room.

"*Munasib?*"

Elias gave a curt nod. "*Nem, nem. Shukraan jazilaan.*"

Reilly and Worthy entered a moment later, half-dragging the overweight ISIS logistician between them. Throwing him down into the seat, they began applying flex cuffs to bind his arms and legs to the chair.

When they'd finished, Cancer spoke without me saying a word.

"Doc, Racegun, make sure the trucks are ready for emergency exfil and go pull security. We need to make sure none of those bastards followed us back here. Make sure Nizar doesn't run off while you're at it, and send in Angel."

Reilly and Worthy swept out of the room.

Turning to Elias, I said, "Go ahead. Ask him where the cargo was headed."

"Sure," Elias replied, switching to Arabic and rattling off a question.

To my surprise, the man replied at once, his tone almost courteous. Perhaps, I thought, the reality of his situation was finally sinking in.

But Elias barked a laugh, glancing at me with a raised eyebrow. "He says he has engaged in sexual congress with my mother, sister, and daughter."

Ian entered the room then, walking to my side without a word.

"Try again," I said.

Elias did so in spectacular fashion, whipping a backhand across the logistician's face so hard I half-expected it to knock the man unconscious.

But instead, the logistician responded by summoning all the saliva he could muster and spitting it at Elias, who sidestepped the stream.

"So far, not too good." He asked another question in Arabic, with similar results.

Cancer raised an imploring arm and let it fall to his side. "Suicide, I'm telling you. Not everything we do requires a 'Cancer solution,' but this fat bag of fuck sure does."

Elias nodded. "He is correct. Someone like this man requires more...encouragement."

I shook my head. "We're not going to treat him like an animal."

"No," Elias agreed, "we will not. Because animals will not do what these people will do. You must treat them not like men, not like animals, but what they are." He looked to the man as I waited for some conclusion to his statement.

But when Elias met my gaze, he said only, "You want this cargo? It gets further from your grasp each minute we spend waiting here."

I walked to the corner of the room, waving for Ian and Cancer to follow.

"Shoot me straight, Ian."

He leaned in and whispered, "What do you want me to say, David? If the Agency grabbed this guy, they'd have a pro team of thirty-year interrogators breaking him down with days of sensory deprivation supervised by a full staff of doctors. And that's exactly what'll happen once we hand him off. Until then...well, we found the rockets about six hours ago, and until Duchess tells us otherwise, they're as good as gone."

Cancer was nodding in agreement, and I replied to Ian, "Go help the guys pull security."

"Whatever's about to happen, I've seen worse."

"I know." I left unspoken the real reason I wanted Ian gone—not because I was worried about him reporting me for any transgressions of our operational authorities, but because I didn't want him reliving this event in his dreams for the next few years. "Just the same, I want you to go. I'll get you if I need anything else."

Ian departed, slipping through the door as Cancer put a hand on my arm and whispered, "David, maybe this guy knows something, maybe he doesn't. But you're never gonna be able to live with yourself if we give him the VIP treatment and a bunch of civilians die as a result. So let's get it done, boss."

He released my arm and I looked to Elias. "Find out everything."

The old Syrian's eyes crinkled with satisfaction. "My way?"

"Yes. Your way."

He spoke Arabic to his friend, who nodded and moved off to another room.

As we waited for his return, Elias began circling the man in the chair with predatory anticipation, a series of footfalls I suspected he'd done many times before.

Cancer removed his fighting knife from its sheath and showed it to Elias, who shook his head and clucked in disapproval. Looking crestfallen, Cancer sheathed the blade and turned away.

Then Elias said to us, "I may need you both to hold him. He could be quite unwilling to remain still."

My stomach churned. Whatever was about to happen here, Cancer and

I were going to be not just witnesses but active participants. And when the torture ensued, it would occur because of my order. At best I was making a ruinous moral compromise for no reason at all; at worst, we'd elicit details of a terrorist attack that we were too late to stop.

In the middle of those two scenarios was a third option, one too unlikely to allow anyone but Cancer to witness the proceedings ahead. But it represented a small chance that the logistician knew actionable intel about a terrorist attack that we still had the opportunity to stop, and until we'd ruled that out, I was unwilling to let my personal sensibilities get in the way of continuing our mission any way we could.

I heard Elias's friend return and cringed at the thought of what his reappearance would bring. If Elias disapproved of Cancer's knife, and our guns had proven of no use to sway a hardline member of ISIS, then what exactly *would* work? Whatever the answer, Elias's friend was about to carry it into the room.

When he entered with a single item in his hand, I was momentarily confused, and then disgusted.

It was a clear plastic trash bag.

Elias accepted it with a brief exchange in Arabic, and his friend left the room. Then Elias let the bag fall open, looking to me with a single question.

"Shall we?"

Without warning, he threw the bag over the logistician's head, pulling the plastic tightly around his neck with one hand.

The man began thrashing immediately, and Cancer and I intervened to hold him still from the shoulders. "You better not kill him," I grunted.

Elias shook his head. "Look to the corners of his eyes. Still white. He is fine."

The suffocating logistician, however, was most decidedly not fine. The man's mouth was gasping like a fish, his eyes wild and panicked, as he began inhaling the plastic bag.

Then Elias said, "Only now do we start to have a problem. The corners of his eyes—you see the red dots?"

"Yeah. Blood vessels bursting?"

"Indeed. Only seconds remain to let him breathe."

"Then let him fuckin' breathe."

"Not yet," he replied, watching the man's legs, waiting for some signal I didn't understand, until the puddle of urine began spreading across the chair.

Elias whipped the bag off the logistician's head as the man took shrill gasps of air, heaving breaths as the crimson flush subsided from his face.

"Good boy." Elias patted the man's arm amid the stench of urine. "Have some air. Stay alive for me." Crouching next to the man, Elias waited for him to speak.

He didn't have to wait long—as soon as he'd processed enough oxygen to make a sound, he began speaking Arabic so fast that I doubted Elias's ability to comprehend the words.

But Elias was listening with his head cocked, nodding softly as he translated for me.

"There was to be a handoff of the cargo, which was to be routed to Sepaya. He says they told him no other details, but he overheard someone discuss some attack. It will occur five days from yesterday."

"What's the target?" I asked.

Elias didn't answer, instead throwing the bag over the man's head once more.

I grabbed Elias's shoulder. "If he dies, so do you."

But Elias shrugged off my hand.

"Too much air, and he will recover his wits. Then we have to start over, and it becomes impossible to tell when he is going to die. Trust me."

Cancer said, "Just let Elias do his thing. We already lost the rockets, man. Time to find out where they'll be used."

I had no way of knowing whether Elias was being truthful, or if he simply wanted to impart as much pain on a member of ISIS as he could. And in the end, I had little choice but to let him continue—if I didn't, those rockets would be sent into flight against some strategic target, and given what I knew about Bari Khan, my guess was that it would spell the death of thousands of civilians in some Chinese population center.

Elias removed the plastic bag, and the logistician once again took seizing gasps of air as his interrogator asked, "*Aistihdaf?*"

This time, some of the man's words sounded familiar.

"*Fee medina Sharlatsveel, fee wilaya Farjinia.*"

Elias said, "In the state of Virginia, a city named Charlottesville. You know this place?"

It took me a moment to respond—what I had just heard was impossible, and yet Elias was watching me lucidly, waiting for a response.

So too was Cancer, though his expression bore significantly more surprise. After all, he knew I lived in Charlottesville, and seemed equally as dumbstruck in that moment as I was.

But this didn't make any sense; Bari Khan's wrath should have been directed against his native government. The Chinese administration had killed his wife and daughter along with countless Uyghur civilians, and there was nothing of significance in Charlottesville—except, of course, my family.

"Yes." I nodded, feeling the color drain from my cheeks. "I know this place. Find out what else he knows."

The man was still speaking, though shaking his head as he did so.

Elias said, "He said this is all he knows about the target. That was the only comment he overheard."

"Hit him again."

"I believe he tells the truth."

"I didn't ask what you fucking believe. Hit him again."

Elias gave a leisurely shrug, throwing the bag back over the man's head and sealing the bottom with a fist against his neck.

"We must be careful," Elias explained. "He will not last as long each time we do this.

See there? The red dots are getting bigger."

Then he pulled off the bag, revealing the logistician's horrid expression. His eyes were wide but sightless, the whites blotched with blood, his round face a blighted vision of fear as he spoke in strained Arabic.

"What else?" I asked.

Elias shook his head. "This is all he knows. I believe he speaks the truth."

I turned to Cancer. "Let's get him gagged and ready to move."

It wasn't Cancer who responded but Elias, his voice alarmed. "Move where?"

"Sepaya. He's coming with us."

"No, this is impossible. My friend can release him once we are gone. Otherwise, he will slow us down."

I shook my head. "I'll see to it that he won't, and I have other friends who will want to speak with him. Let's go."

Elias nodded, relaxing as if resigned to my decision.

He brought a hand to his stomach as if scratching an itch, then dipped his palm beneath his shirt and drew a tiny automatic pistol.

I dove forward to tackle him, hearing the *pop* of a gunshot a moment before colliding with Elias and driving him to the ground.

Looking back, I saw I was too late—the logistician's head was marred by the round red mark of a bullet hole, a greasy slick of blood and brain matter sprayed from the exit wound along the floor.

Elias grunted under my weight as Cancer torqued his arm and recovered the pistol.

Reilly darted inside, taking in the scene.

Cancer said to him, "Get back out there and pull security. We've got it under control."

"What happened in here?"

"Elias just executed our prisoner."

But Reilly's eyes were taking in the truth of everything that transpired before that—the puddle of urine, the plastic bag abandoned on the floor.

Cancer repeated, "Get back out there and pull security. I ain't gonna tell you again."

Reilly left, leaving me to half-shout at Elias.

"What the hell was that?"

The side of his face was pressed against the floor as he replied, "You want to know why I did not ask you to bring my family to America? Because these savages raped my wife before butchering her and my sons. You want to shoot me? Help yourself. But if you want to find this cargo, you need my help. You will not get far with Nizar alone."

I pushed myself off Elias and stood.

He did the same, rising to brush the dust from his clothes in a dignified motion before Cancer threw his chest into the wall, frisking him for other weapons. When he'd completed his check from behind, Cancer swung Elias around and began sweeping the man's front from top to bottom.

I had my rifle poised, ready to gun Elias down for resisting.

But he made no move to stop Cancer's search; to the contrary, he held his arms out to make the process easier and watched me with a languid smile.

"Relax," Elias said nonchalantly. "My friend will take care of the body. It is no problem. And in any case, he was begging me to kill him."

For once, I didn't know what to say.

Whether or not the logistician knew any further information didn't matter now. Nor could I stay mad at Elias for long—he'd successfully procured the cargo's true destination, as well as the timing and location of the attack. I didn't doubt the information for one reason alone: the target was my hometown. That didn't make any sense to me, but the logistician could have listed any major city in the world—instead, he'd identified a location that I was one hundred percent sure he'd have no other way of knowing. Elias didn't know where I was from, and there were no elaborate circumstances by which this intel dump could have been staged as a diversion.

At the same time, I was angry at myself: as enthusiastic as Elias had been about going after ISIS, I should have thought something was wrong when he didn't ask us for a weapon.

But the revelation that Charlottesville was the target of a terrorist attack had shown me who I truly was at heart—all morality was stripped away in that moment, and if Elias hadn't risen to the task of torture as a means of procuring further information, then I gladly would have.

As I took in my last view of the dead logistician, blood and brain matter leaking from the hole in his skull as he sat in a pool of his own urine, the resting place of his final moment, I honestly didn't give a shit.

Of all the likely terrorist targets across the globe, what were the possible chances that a Uyghur separatist backed by seemingly extensive ISIS resources would choose Charlottesville, Virginia? The odds had to be in the millions, and it should have occurred to me then that the circumstances in which we'd found ourselves had transcended any possible coincidence.

Cancer took a step toward me and gave my shoulder a hard shake.

"Forget about it, boss. We'll get to the bottom of this. Nothing's happening to your family while I'm around, okay?"

Without waiting for a response, he spun toward Elias with the grace of a ballet dancer, producing his Marlboros and holding them out to him.

“Starting to like you, pal. Here—keep the pack. But surprise me one more time,” he growled, “and you’re going to think the logistician got off easy.”

21

Duchess resumed the vigil at her workstation after Gossweiler's departure. Her seat no longer felt like the throne of an Agency officer running a critical mission overseas; it now seemed like a prison cell rocked by the political winds that governed her every move.

But she wouldn't have to worry about that for long, she thought. Gossweiler was terminating her leadership of the program in one week anyway, and in the meantime she had to draw the current proceedings in Syria to a close before notifying David that his team was disbanded.

By the time she received her next transmission from him, it served as a welcome interruption to her thoughts.

"*Raptor Nine One, this is Suicide Actual.*"

She lifted the hand mic and replied, "Send it."

"*Logistician reported that the cargo was to be transferred to some other means of transport, then routed to a village called Sepaya. He wasn't directly informed of anything else, but overheard discussion of an attack set to occur, quote, 'five days from yesterday.' The target is in Charlottesville, Virginia. No further information at this time, how copy?*"

Duchess's first thought was that David was making some ill-timed joke. There seemed to be no other reason for a mention of his hometown, and certainly no motive for a terrorist attack there.

She transmitted, "Say again."

David responded with impatience, "*Cargo en route to Sepaya. Intended for use in attack four days from now in Charlottesville, Virginia.*"

"Copy all. Be advised, both flatbed trucks have been destroyed, BDA is ongoing but likely negative. Stand by for guidance."

Putting aside her skepticism, Duchess consulted her digital map, locating Sepaya and considering the time it would take David's team to get there. They wouldn't be able to beat the Delta operators out of FOB Presley—and those were the men she was concerned with at present.

If she tasked a helicopter to recover David's team and the logistician, it was one fewer for the raids she'd need to locate the rockets in Sepaya, and those raids would have to commence at the earliest opportunity.

She took a moment to consider how to kill two birds with one stone.

Gossweiler had said to send the team to the nearest exfil point—he didn't specify where, and Duchess had some leeway to dictate the tactical particulars according to her judgment.

Even then, what she was about to do was a sin she'd pay for in due time.

Keying her mic, she said, "Will send strike force to Sepaya to search for cargo. Proceed there for link-up and exfil."

"*Good copy*," David replied.

"And bring the logistician—we'll need to rendition him for further debrief."

"*Be advised, the logistician has escaped custody.*"

Duchess was unable to hide her displeasure at this statement—she saw Jo Ann's eyes dart to her, bearing the knowledge of what they both knew full well. No American element would let an asset like that get away, and whatever fate befell the man, his soul had since departed.

To David's credit, Duchess thought, he hastily added a bullshit explanation for the benefit of anyone who would have a problem with that outcome.

"*We were questioning him on a rooftop, and he took a two-story leap and ran off into the village. We can search for him, or we can move to Sepaya. Your choice.*"

She transmitted, "Understood. Proceed to Sepaya for exfil."

"*We're moving.*"

Duchess barely had time to set down her hand mic when Sutherland called out from his desk.

"Ranger GFC reports they've finished their search of the flatbed wreckage: zero evidence of rockets."

Duchess rose from her seat, assuming her command posture in front of the OPCEN as she issued her orders.

"Wonderful. The Rangers will redeploy to FOB Presley and refit as quick response force for Delta. Shift all available intelligence, surveillance, and reconnaissance platforms to Sepaya and get me a continuous stack of all available air support on a rotating basis."

Turning her attention to the J3, she continued, "I want target packets for known, likely, and suspected rocket transfer and storage sites in Sepaya in descending order of priority. Link in with JSOC and have the Delta shooters at FOB Presley ready to launch as soon as they've got a plan to action simultaneous raids. Follow-on targets are likely based on boots-on-the-ground intelligence acquired on the initial objectives.

"J2," she called next, "task the analyst staff with identifying any possible terrorist targets for an indirect fire attack in the vicinity of Charlottesville, Virginia, in four days. Then I want you working on refining our Sepaya objectives until the shooters are wheels-down."

Then she directed her gaze to the J4 staff responsible for supply and logistics considerations.

"J4, how could those rockets reach the US?"

A woman called back, "With a northbound trajectory from their last known location, and given the size of the cargo, most likely destination is one of three Turkish ports: Ambarli, Mersin, and Ismit."

"Lock down all border crossings however you can. Put the port staff on high alert, get some intelligence people in place at all three to screen incoming cargo using all classified means. Questions?"

There were none—her response came in the form of each section spinning to their workstation in turn, the clatter of keyboards and phones leaving their receiver, a collective hum of activity that signaled everything was in the works and order was being restored to the universe after Gossweiler's visit.

She dropped into her chair for a moment of respite, trying to process the bigger picture before setting to work on her next task.

Her reverie was broken by Jo Ann's deep northern accent.

"If there was going to be a terrorist attack," Jo Ann said firmly, "it'd be against an Independence Day celebration."

Duchess looked to the ceiling and took a breath. "Four days from now isn't the Fourth of July, it's the third."

"And that makes it even more unlikely. Someone's blowing smoke. There's nothing in Charlottesville. What makes you think that the intel on cargo headed to Sepaya is any more credible?"

Duchess looked at Jo Ann, appraising her with a newfound sense of annoyance. Maybe it was the sight of her atrocious wardrobe, or the wedding and class rings on either hand.

Or maybe, Duchess had to admit, because Gossweiler had just eviscerated her career and her Agency ground team in front of a military officer.

Duchess said, "You wanted me to tell them about the logistician. 'Nothing to lose by telling them,' I believe you said—now you're contesting the intelligence they've obtained as a result?"

"I'm contesting the validity of that intelligence based on the means they likely used to obtain it," Jo Ann said, leaning in so she could speak without being overheard. "And their detainee didn't escape. Your team executed him, and you know it."

Duchess locked eyes with Jo Ann, feeling the simmering burn of heat spreading throughout her chest. There were certain things you didn't speak aloud until you had some hard evidence, and accusations of war crimes were one of them.

Leaning in to match Jo Ann's posture, Duchess whispered back, "I *don't* know that, because I've been sitting here instead of in the field. But that wasn't always the case...which, unless I'm mistaken, is more than you can say for yourself."

There was a glint in Jo Ann's eyes then, a tick in her jaw muscle. The last thing any support person wanted to hear was a dismissal of their opinion because they'd never been on an actual operation, and Duchess had just hit the nerve she was aiming for.

Pressing the initiative, she said, "Charlottesville is too random to be coincidental. If someone wanted to send us on a wild goose chase, they'd have said New York or LA." Then, switching her .oice to the sternest possible tone, she concluded, "So do you want to keep pursuing Bari Khan and the rockets, or do you want to have a pissing contest with me? Because right now, there's only time for one."

22

Cancer adjusted his steering around another pothole in the road, trying to minimize the truck cabin's nausea-inducing jostle that had characterized their entire drive to Sepaya as he followed David's Land Cruiser.

In the passenger seat, Nizar seemed unfazed by the rough ride. He was gazing out the window at the rocky desert around them, a landscape that seemed desolate and alien to Cancer—but for Nizar, this was home.

Or at least, it would be until they made it out alive, and he could move his family to America. *If* they made it out alive, that was.

In the Godfather seat behind Nizar, Reilly looked considerably less comfortable.

He too was scanning the desert, one hand draped across his holstered pistol. But the team medic's expression—one of terse contemplation—was not due to the ride, but what he'd seen in the aftermath of the logistician's interrogation.

Of all the kids in the team, Cancer thought, Reilly was the most ill-equipped to deal with the sight: the plastic bag, the sight of a restrained prisoner who'd pissed himself before being shot in the head.

Cancer glanced at the medic in the rearview mirror and asked, "You okay back there?"

Reilly said nothing.

Returning his gaze to the road, Cancer dodged another pothole with a quick jerk of the steering wheel.

As the oldest member of the team, Cancer had been raised by the old-school generation of warfighters. Those men treated the job like they were coal miners: when it comes time for your shift, you get down in the mine and you do the work. When you come out, you don't turn your job into some philosophical dissertation. You don't go talk to doctors to find out what's wrong with you, you don't talk to shrinks about your feelings. You drink, you go to sleep, you get up the next day to do it over again. Simple.

But the younger generation of warfighters to which Reilly belonged was another breed entirely. With their tortured morality and ever-expanding social consciousness, they seemed to be more anguished about their jobs with each passing day. It was exhausting.

Still looking out the window, Reilly said, "We don't know if his intelligence was credible. And either way, he didn't deserve to be tortured. Or executed."

"I agree with you on the execution part. After directing his efforts to facilitating the mass rape and execution of everyone outside his organization, I'd feel better if he spent a few decades rotting at some black site. But hey, look at the bright side: we don't have to haul his fat ass around the country with us."

Cancer then looked to Nizar, sitting stoically in the passenger seat.

"For someone who lives here, you're awfully quiet over there, pal."

Nizar spoke calmly. "Elias lost his entire family to ISIS." Half-looking over his shoulder to Reilly, he continued, "If his pain was yours, you would do the same."

"Exactly," Cancer chimed in.

"But that does not make it right."

Cancer rolled his eyes, giving an exaggerated sigh. "Hey, is it too late to switch trucks? Because I'd rather be smoking with Elias. And I'm one hundred percent fuckin' *certain* that David doesn't have a problem with any of this."

In the rearview mirror, Cancer saw Reilly looking away, out the window. Nothing needed to be said about the rest—that David's wife and daughter were in Charlottesville. And while Cancer was unburdened by the moralities that seemed to plague others he worked with, David had a dark side, a capacity for self-destruction that flared at certain points in the fight. Cancer had seen it while fighting alongside him as a mercenary in Argentina, and during the team's first Agency operation in the Philippines.

Neither had anything to do with the man's family, which made Cancer inwardly eager to see what his team leader was capable of now.

Cancer's train of thought was interrupted by Reilly's voice.

"I've been thinking about why Bari Khan might hit Charlottesville."

Cancer replied, "So have I, and my only conclusion is that Charlottesville is too worthless for any self-respecting terrorist to hit."

"That's exactly my point," Reilly said. "That means there's got to be critical infrastructure in that area, and it's probably an electrical substation."

"You think he's trying to shut down power."

Reilly nodded. "My dad was a project manager for one of the largest power companies in the country. He had to deal with a blackout covering almost half of California because an electrical substation malfunctioned. And that was an accident. All BK would need to know is a little bit about the network structure. He picks the right substation, and he could cause a cascading failure that's nearly impossible to stop."

"What does that mean—cascading failure?"

"There's an initial failure when he takes out a substation. So the network rebalances the load, which causes a secondary failure. That starts a domino effect that continues until the entire network shuts down. And he wouldn't need all the rockets just to take down a substation; if I were him, I'd use some to hit the service centers, so the techs won't be able to fix what he's broken."

Then he continued, "Bottom line, I'm telling you for a fact he could take down the entire Atlantic grid if he hits the right spot. For all I know, there could be some really strategic substation in Charlottesville that would drop power across the US."

Cancer found himself nodding slightly. Reilly wasn't exactly going to split the atom anytime soon, but he had a good working theory if for no other reason than lack of options in that inbred backwater town that David called home.

Nizar said, "I do not think so."

"You don't think what?" Reilly asked.

"You say this terrorist is a mastermind," Nizar pointed out, "so there is no way he would allow his people to inform a mere logistician of his ultimate target."

Cancer said, "Well, speaking as the only person in this car who was present at the time he leaked that key piece of information, I'll tell you for a fact the logistician was telling the truth."

Nizar waved his hand, as if dismissing Cancer's words as irrelevant.

"I do not doubt what he told you," he continued. "What I am saying is he was deliberately misinformed. Whatever he told you is a diversion for the real attack. A large city, most likely."

Reilly sounded skeptical. "Then why wouldn't BK have given him a better alternative?"

"There is no telling. But no brilliant terrorist would risk giving that information to a man who could share it if captured."

Cancer intervened, "You forget all the bad guys trying to snatch him at the same time we were? If all he had was false information, they wouldn't have bothered."

"I disagree."

Before Cancer could respond, David's voice came over the radio.

"*Truck Two, be advised we have eyes-on armed men in the road ahead. Looks like a checkpoint.*"

Ian braked to a stop behind a civilian vehicle, scanning the single-file row of cars proceeding one at a time through the ISIS checkpoint.

David leaned forward between the seats.

"How many guys can you make out?"

"Looks like five or six total, but"—Ian angrily swatted at the pale cloud drifting in front of his face—"maybe I could see better if the cab wasn't filled with smoke."

Elias threw up his hands, offended. "America has the best tobacco in the world. How is that my fault?"

Ian didn't know who he was more pissed at: Elias for blissfully smoking cigarettes in the passenger seat, blowing smoke in his face and making his eyes sting, or David in the backseat for allowing it.

David seemed almost nonchalant toward Elias since the former intelligence agent executed their prisoner, and Ian found that was perhaps the most troubling thing out of this entire situation. Ian could understand David's gratitude—sort of—but no matter the alleged target of the terrorist attack, they couldn't have a foreign national imparting his own agenda on the mission at hand.

Every occupant of the lead truck was assessing the scene, evaluating their options as a single fighter leaned down to the driver's window of the lead vehicle, scanning and then questioning the occupants before waving the car past.

There were now five vehicles between them and the checkpoint, which in Ian's mind left precious little time before their cover would be blown.

The checkpoint wasn't a large affair. There was an ISIS pickup on either side of the road, and the one to the right had a fighter manning a vehicle-mounted medium machinegun.

In addition to the man checking each vehicle, Ian counted another four men spread in a loose semicircle formation, facing the row of vehicles waiting for their turn. The problem wasn't the men he could see—it was the unknown number that he couldn't, with his view blocked by the vehicles ahead. Pulling his checkered keffiyeh scarf over his lower face, Ian heard David ask, "Elias, can you talk our way out of this?"

"No," Ian responded, "Elias can't. I told you this would happen. As soon as BK learned the logistician was captured, he knew we'd be headed for Sepaya. This isn't some random checkpoint—it's a trap to find us."

"Then let's leverage that."

"How?"

"We can discuss that later. First, we've got to negotiate this checkpoint. Am I correct in assuming if we turn around, they'll open fire and pursue?"

Elias blew another cloud of smoke and said, "Yes, that is accurate."

Then David transmitted, "We've got one guy questioning the drivers, another four spread out between two pickups, and a machine gunner on the right-side truck. If they get a radio call out, I think it's fair to say we're fucked."

Cancer replied, "*Advise we let the other vehicles clear out. You can wait until that guard comes up to your window, then pop him in the face. Truck One dismounts and provides a base of fire, I'll bring Truck Two on-line with your left flank and transition to a dismounted maneuver element.*"

"Sounds good," David said. "Worthy will take the machine gunner, everyone else shoot from your flank to center line. Questions?"

"*Just one,*" Cancer replied. "*Is your driver shitting his pants right now?*"

David asked, "Ian, Cancer wants to know if you're shitting your pants right now."

The lead vehicle was waved past, leaving only four cars between them and the checkpoint. Ian said nothing, releasing the brake to follow the procession toward the enemy fighters.

Then David transmitted, "No, he seems pretty cool about the whole thing."

Elias offered, "I would love to help, but you took my gun."

"When I need a stationary target shot at point-blank range, I'll let you know."

"What do you mean, 'when?' That time is now." He waved an index finger toward the windshield. "These people are used to a terrorized populace. The man checking the vehicles is sticking his face right in the window."

The lead car was waved past, and Ian eased the Land Cruiser forward. Only four vehicles to go.

Finally, it was Worthy's turn to talk. "I'll take him from the backseat."

"The hell you will," Ian blurted. "You're not putting a rifle barrel across my face and pulling the trigger."

"No, I'm not. Because this situation has got 'pistol shot' written all over it."

Elias offered, "You give me the pistol, and I can take the shot."

"You're not taking the shot, I am. Ian, it'll behoove you to recline your seat just the slightest bit. Trying to be safe here."

"You can't be serious."

David said, "He sounds pretty serious."

Ian's voice assumed a tinge of panic. "Now *you* can't be serious, David."

But David was silent, allowing Worthy to continue. "And one more thing, Ian. I really can't stress this enough: keep your big-ass brain against the headrest, and don't move it until your face is covered in ISIS blood."

"What?!" Ian cried. "Why would you phrase it like that? David, there's got to be another way to do this."

Another car was waved through—three to go.

David said coolly, "Worthy's in the best position to take the shot. I'd listen to what he's telling you."

"And what am I supposed to do, just smile and nod at the guy until he gets his face blown off?"

"Pretty much," Worthy acknowledged. "But don't forget about reclining your seat. That part's fairly well critical to my whole process."

Ian felt for a handle at his side, then pulled it and leaned his seat back.

"Is this good?"

"That's just fine," Worthy said. "More than enough for me to take the shot."

Suddenly there were only two cars remaining, and Ian rolled the Land Cruiser forward with a growing sense of tunnel vision. At least this would occur quickly.

Only, it seemed, it wouldn't—the driver currently being questioned was driving a covered pickup, and the ISIS fighter made him dismount and walk to the back to uncover his cargo.

Initially relieved that action was imminent, this new wrinkle sent Ian's pulse racing as a hundred possible contingencies flooded into his mind.

David took advantage of the pause to chime in, "Hey, Ian, this is your time to shine. Say something really badass to the guy before Worthy puts a bullet through his head. Could boost your team rep. How about, 'Merry Christmas, motherfucker.'"

Elias offered, "'Islamic State is for dog-fuckers' would translate well. Perhaps you should try that."

"Wait, wait," Worthy said. "What about you grab your junk, then go, 'I got my license and registration right here.' And *then* I blow him away."

David sounded excited. "I like that. Let's go with Worthy's idea."

Then the covered pickup search was complete, and the truck rumbled off to allow the final civilian vehicle forward.

The man approached the car to their front, leaning down to stick his face in the open window.

Elias said, "Do not feel bad, Ian. This man is young. He probably has only five or six kids, all by rape of kidnapped young women."

Ian couldn't reply, instead pulling his keffiyeh higher atop the bridge of his nose.

The final car was a sedan, and Ian's assumption that the guard's questioning wouldn't take long was correct—before he knew it, there was nothing between him and the ISIS fighters but a few meters of dirt road.

Worthy spoke a calm, quiet reminder.

"Back of your skull against the headrest, Ian, and keep it there."

Ian complied, driving his head back into the cloth seat behind him with tense pressure. He regretted not reclining his seat any further, and now it was too late—the enemy fighter was pointing to Ian, then waving him forward.

Ian let his foot off the brake, trying for a gentle push on the accelerator but feeling the truck lurch forward uncomfortably before he braked to a stop again.

He was breathing quickly, feeling his pulse soar. He got nervous when pulled over for a traffic stop in the States; this current arrangement was so far outside his comfort zone that he wanted to curl into a ball on the floorboard.

The man approached, examining Ian with a frown, saying something in Arabic and motioning for him to pull down his scarf.

Then he froze as his eyes swept over Elias, and then the backseat, before widening.

Ian felt his breath hitch before blurting the only words that came to mind.

"America says hello."

The scalding blast of Worthy's pistol muzzle flared across Ian's face along with hot blood splatter, and he opened his eyes to see the ISIS man falling toward him, mouth agape, a bullet hole in his upper lip.

The body thumped against Ian's door, sliding out of view as David and Worthy leapt out of the truck.

Cancer floored the accelerator before the man's body hit the ground, whipping the second truck to the left of the lead vehicle as he assessed the situation.

Worthy and David were out of their truck and opening fire, and Cancer screeched to a halt beside their white Land Cruiser. Reilly was dismounted and shooting by the time Cancer's feet hit the sand. Now the far-left flank of this hasty battle formation, he immediately took aim on a man darting sideways, away from the battle.

He could have been maneuvering to a more advantageous firing position, though from the looks of it he was just trying to flee the scene and survive. But his intent made no difference to Cancer, who sent the man sprawling forward with three well-aimed shots before swinging his barrel toward the nearest ISIS truck.

An enemy fighter scrambled behind the bumper before he could open fire. Cancer instinctively dropped to a knee, rolling onto his firing side and spreading his heels flat against the ground. Laying his rifle sideways atop his support hand, he oriented his line of sight between the enemy truck's tires until he identified the partial figure of a crouching man.

Cancer fired two rounds, ejecting his brass into the ground and sending a stinging cloud of sand around his face. By the time he regained his sight picture, a wounded fighter was crashing to the dirt, and Cancer sent another three bullets sailing inches over the road. Blinking his vision clear from the sand, he saw the man splayed out, motionless, and scissored his legs beneath him as he fought his way back to a standing position.

By then the battle was in full swing, the chattering of unsuppressed enemy weapons barking from the right side of the objective. Seeing no further enemy at the pickup on the left, he took a bounding step toward the engine block, using it for cover as he assessed the locations of the surviving fighters.

Cancer saw first that the machinegun on the right-side pickup was unmanned and pointing upward on its pintle mount. Then he spotted David, Worthy, Ian, and Reilly trading lead with a few remaining fighters who'd entrenched themselves amid a rock formation on the far flank.

Without a clear line of sight, Cancer decided to maneuver to a more advantageous position—namely, the ISIS truck to his front. From there, he could make his way toward the downed machinegun and open up a new flank of the fight as he established a crossfire with the rest of his team.

He shouted a single word at Reilly—"Moving!"—and, not knowing or caring whether his teammate heard, took off at a sprint toward the enemy vehicle.

Granted, there was plenty of risk involved in this, starting with the possibility of surviving fighters engaging him from an unseen position. Cancer moved fast, prepared to slow to a shooting speed and engage any of the prostrate ISIS bodies before him.

But none moved. As he skidded to a halt behind the pickup's protective cover, he saw the man he'd shot between the tires was still alive, breathing shallowly in what appeared to be the final moments of his life.

Cancer hastened the process considerably, firing two suppressed rounds into the man's head. Then he executed a quick tactical reload, jamming a fresh magazine into his weapon and stuffing the partially expended one in his pocket.

He was just about to transmit to his team, to notify them that he'd be maneuvering to the next enemy truck with its unmanned machinegun before assisting in the fight against the remaining enemy, when the previously silent machinegun suddenly roared to life.

He tried to angle a line of sight toward the gunner, but the truck was positioned at a disadvantageous angle. And the gunner was being smart, Cancer noted—he was firing with his head and shoulders tucked low, concealed from Cancer's view and, due to his elevated position in the truck bed, likely from the view of his teammates scrambling for cover behind the team vehicles.

For all his eagerness to oblige enemy fighters willing to die for their cause, Cancer viewed the battlefield like a pro basketball player looked at the court, and this intrepid gunner was almost singlehandedly pinning down a team of five trained men.

Cancer transmitted, "Net call, hold fire on the machinegun—I got him."

"*Copy,*" David replied, adding sarcastically, "*take your time.*"

Cancer took off at a run, carving a semicircle to the left before angling his path toward the remaining ISIS pickup's open tailgate.

As he did so, the machinegun continued to rip long bursts of automatic fire, and Cancer didn't have to look right to know that his team's Land Cruisers were being turned into Swiss cheese.

Judging by the rate of fire, the gunner wasn't particularly concerned with getting blasted from the front. For all the advantages of suppressors, there was one considerable drawback: the bad guys often didn't realize they were being shot at. And while that was great for maintaining the element of surprise, it was a massive problem when you were trying to keep the enemy's collective head down.

Cancer was skidding to a halt behind the truck when the machinegun suddenly went silent, and he ducked beneath the tailgate in anticipation of the gunner spinning around to shoot him.

But the machinegun began firing again, the gunner probably long since deafened by the blasts. So far, so good, Cancer thought as he oriented his weapon and rose from a kneeling position to get his first clear glimpse of the gunner—or rather, of his legs.

Cancer took in the tantalizing sight of exposed hamstrings through his sights, and rather than waste precious moments in re-aligning for a kill shot, he stitched a short burst across the enemy fighter's rear thighs.

He had a momentary view of bloody holes opening through the fatigue pants, and the man was a machine gunner no more. Instead he fell to the truck bed like a puppet with the strings cut, screaming not in agony but anger.

The gunner's eyes found Cancer, transforming into a hateful glare as he began shouting in Arabic, his body sprawled atop a dead comrade who had initially manned the now-silent machinegun.

Cancer lowered his weapon, savoring this moment.

He had to hand it to the guy—his chosen side in the Syrian Civil War was probably the worst of many bad options, but for all the predatory cowardice with which ISIS operated, this man was fairly well a badass in Cancer's eyes.

Not that it would matter for much longer, he thought.

Because Cancer was going to end this fight on his own terms, before anyone else arrived on the scene to debate him on it. Reilly, being the delicate liberal snowflake that he was, would probably want to treat the wounded fighter with medical supplies they might need for their own team, then give the guy half his rations and a warm sponge bath.

Cancer, however, had a different plan in mind.

Reaching for the fighter's shirt with one hand, he dragged him backward out of the truck bed and flung him onto the dirt.

He writhed in agony, grabbing at Cancer's left leg in an attempt to drag him down. Cancer smiled at the man's sheer audacity, then responded by planting the tip of his weapon into his neck.

The suppressor was scalding hot, and it seared into the man's flesh with a sizzle as he cried out in pain. To his credit, he made a panicked reach for the gun—but Cancer's finger was on the trigger, letting the encounter proceed until its final ragged moment.

He fired once, and the weapon thumped sharply in his grasp as a 5.56mm round whipped through the man's jugular, sending a spray of dark arterial blood in a wide splatter.

Finally, the downed gunner was still.

"Clear!" Cancer shouted, then transmitted for anyone who hadn't heard, "Machine gunner is down."

Releasing his transmit switch, he heard David reply, "*Thank God—nice shooting, Cancer.*"

Then he realized that the sounds of battle had ended altogether—there was no more gunfire, whether incoming or outgoing, and he quickly mounted the back of the truck. Placing a boot atop the chest of a dead fighter below him, he assumed a firing position over the roof, searching for targets amid the rock formations and finding none.

David, Worthy, and Ian were scrambling toward the rocks, fanning out to locate any surviving fighters while Cancer and Reilly covered their movement. But no enemy reappeared, and Cancer heard the double *whuffs* of suppressed shots as the maneuver element dispatched any dead or wounded fighters they found.

Within thirty seconds, David transmitted, "*Objective is clear. We're heading back to the trucks.*"

I keyed my mic and transmitted, "Raptor Nine One, this is Suicide Actual."

Duchess replied, "*Send your traffic.*"

"We just engaged an enemy checkpoint, six EKIA. Conducting SE now." I sent a ten-digit grid location, then added, "Will update when able."

"*Copy all,*" she transmitted back, sounding inconvenienced by my radio contact. I understood why when she continued, "*Be advised, units are about to initiate raids in Sepaya. Expect to have cargo located within a few minutes. Be prepared for on-order helicopter exfil.*"

"Good news, we'll be ready. Suicide out."

Turning toward the sound of footsteps jogging to a halt beside me, I saw Cancer's sweaty face looking resplendently at peace in the wake of a gunfight.

"Hey, boss," he said, "the boys are almost done. What do you got?"

"Duchess is running military raids in Sepaya, expects to find the rockets in a few minutes. We need to be ready for helicopter exfil, and if none of the vehicles are functional, it's going to mean a foot movement away from the road."

"Hallelujah," he replied. "I'm ready to get out of this shithole."

"Amen."

Then Reilly jogged back to us, a quiver of foreign assault rifles slung over his shoulder.

"We're finished searching the bodies," he said, depositing his rifles on the ground. "Ian's got the intel."

Ian wasn't far behind him, carrying a burlap sack as he called out, "Found a half-dozen cell phones and some handwritten notes. Nizar can translate to be sure, but everything looks like personal effects. Doubt we'll get anything useful out of it."

Elias and Worthy arrived a moment later, returning from their vehicle assessment.

Worthy announced, "Both our team vehicles are shot to shit."

Elias nodded and sparked up a fresh Marlboro.

"They are beyond all hope," he said sadly. "You can smell every type of engine fluid from ten feet away."

"Even gasoline?"

"Oh yes." He took another drag, exhaling smoke as he added, "Especially this."

I raised an eyebrow. "Then maybe smoking isn't the best idea."

Elias looked at the cigarette in his hand with a renewed respect, as if the thought hadn't occurred to him until now.

"Well"—he shrugged—"this will be my last smoke until we are on our way again. The enemy vehicles are functional."

I looked to Worthy, who gave me a short nod of confirmation.

Then I turned to appraise the two ISIS pickups—they'd been dented and battered before our arrival, and courtesy of our brief engagement with the checkpoint personnel, were now pockmarked with bullet holes.

But they were otherwise intact, each draped with a black flag bearing words that translated to, "No God but Allah," and beneath them a white circle inscribed with, "Muhammad is the Messenger of God," all written in deliberately primitive-looking Arabic script though it had been originally designed on an ISIS computer in 2007.

What the hell, I thought, this made about as much sense as everything else on this mission so far. And after thirteen hours on the ground in Syria, if we were about to move toward a helicopter extraction, it was far better to drive than walk.

I announced, "Congratulations, we just became honorary members of ISIS."

Cancer, as ever, translated my impulsive statement into an actionable order. "Everyone but David and Elias, get to work transferring the fuel cans and equipment. We're on call for helicopter exfil, and I want us ready to move in three minutes tops."

They moved out to the team trucks, leaving me and Elias.

I asked him, "You ready?"

Elias nodded, leading the way to the ISIS truck with the machinegun mounted in the bed and a long-range radio antenna on the roof.

Elias sat in the driver's seat while I stood beside the open door, watching. He reached for the radio console and found the hand mic.

But instead of transmitting, he held his breath.

And then...nothing happened. He just sat there, holding his breath, until I rapped him on the shoulder.

"You going to transmit, or is this some Syrian meditation technique?"

Releasing his breath, Elias responded irritably, "I have listened to hundreds of radio transmissions from Islamic State. If there is a fight, they never speak calmly. Would you like me to do this thing, or do you want to find out how convincing your Arabic is to them?"

I took a step away from him without another word.

Elias exhaled, then postponed breathing until his face turned red.

Once it had, he brought the mic to his face and began shouting.

"*Laqad hasalna ealayhim!*"

A voice responded in Arabic, the intonation of a question rounding the end of the sentence.

"*Arbet kafaar wa wahid—aintazar.*"

He shouted a question in Arabic, releasing the transmit button mid-sentence, then resumed his radio conversation between gasping breaths. "*Khamset kafaar wa rajul suriun.*"

Then he looked at me and said, "Have someone fire an ISIS weapon the next time I speak."

Looking for the nearest team member, I found Reilly hoisting two fuel cans as he shuffled toward us.

"Doc," I called, "grab an AK and give some celebratory fire on my mark."

Reilly responded eagerly, setting down the fuel cans and retrieving one of his captured rifles before aiming it skyward.

When Elias began speaking again, I gave Reilly a thumbs-up.

He unleashed one long burst of automatic gunfire, then another. On the second volley, he added a shrill victory cry.

Elias lowered the hand mic and shouted, "Enough! I cannot hear their response."

"Sorry." Reilly lowered the rifle barrel. "I'm starting to see why they do that—felt pretty good, if I'm being honest."

Ignoring him, Elias was squinting in concentration as he listened carefully to the voice speaking in an authoritative tone.

Then he transmitted a final sentence before dropping the mic and looking to David.

"He said to load all the bodies and equipment for the purposes of propaganda. Then to proceed to their location and rejoin the force."

"In Sepaya?" David asked.

"No." Elias shook his head. "In a town called Ibrahimkhel."

23

Jo Ann watched the Sepaya raid commence with a sense of sheer awe.

She wasn't a stranger to viewing such proceedings—to the contrary, she couldn't have begun to estimate the number of live operations she'd seen unfolding, first during her staff time with SEAL Team Six and then JSOC Headquarters.

But the sheer audacity with which these men routinely operated was mind-bending.

They'd been wheels-up on their helicopters within literal minutes of the plan being finalized, lifting off to roar across the Syrian desert on their way to the objective.

And now, those aircraft were swarming into enemy-held positions in Sepaya.

On one screen, a Blackhawk helicopter hovered over a rooftop as the team of assaulters expertly slid down fast ropes. On another, a massive Chinook was touching down in a field, twin lines of men racing off the open ramp and heading to separate buildings. The third screen showed a helicopter waving off its planned landing zone when enemy gunfire erupted from a nearby tree line—the aircraft flew a wide orbit out of the area, displacing to an alternate landing zone and clearing the area for an inbound bombing run.

There was a strange order to the pandemonium, the threads of seamless military organization visible even amid the shifting maelstrom of multiple teams engaged in gunfights, clearing buildings, or moving toward secondary targets once they'd killed everyone at their primary objective.

Two Delta troops meant close to forty shooters, supported by a full contingent of enablers—medics, dog handlers, and radio operators—each at the pinnacle of training and experience.

When these hits occurred during the hours of darkness, as they usually did, their outdoor movement tended to be slower, more methodical, maximizing security under the benefit of the best night vision that money could buy. But this was a daylight raid, where any dickhead with a gun could see them plain as day from any window perch in the city.

That meant the operators were moving like greased lightning to force their way inside and between buildings. One second, the structures were standing as they had on any other day. The next, they were being penetrated from multiple angles simultaneously by teams of armed men moving with impossible speed. Somewhere in between those two moments in time were the door and window breaches, which an observer would miss if they so much as blinked.

Meanwhile, the entire OPCEN stood by to process intelligence that could lead to the rockets, with Duchess on split-second response to order all teams to consolidate to their location once found.

But their wait went unanswered.

One by one, the ground teams reported their objectives cleared, personnel accounted for, the number of enemy killed in action. A few men had sustained minor injuries, with a medical evacuation summoned for one who'd nearly been killed by an enemy hand grenade, but he had since been stabilized and was ready for transport.

And over and over, Jo Ann heard the same two words at the end of the radio reports.

No joy.

No rockets located, no intelligence gleaned that would lead to a follow-on objective. They'd conquered their respective targets and killed eighteen ISIS fighters, and that didn't include estimates of the fighter and attack pilots who'd executed air-to-ground strikes in the conduct of the mission.

Jo Ann and Duchess had brought every available shooter to Sepaya, to say nothing of the massive logistical chain connecting exfil assets, quick response forces, and aircraft rotation for refueling and rearmament, and it had amounted to precisely nothing.

Then the speaker box on Duchess's desk squawked with a new transmission.

"*Duchess, this is Suicide Actual.*"

This time, Duchess didn't pick up the hand mic as an afterthought. This time, the speed with which she replied indicated she'd realized the same two things Jo Ann had. First, the team leader referred to her by her personal callsign rather than that of the OPCEN, indicating that his transmission was of extreme importance.

And second, whatever he was about to say likely represented their last chance of finding the rockets.

"Duchess here. Send it."

"*Transmissions over captured enemy radio indicate cargo has been diverted to Ibrahimkhel, how copy?*"

The timing of this information couldn't have been much worse, arriving on the heels of maximum expenditure of all military assets in the area. If they'd found out even fifteen minutes prior, they could have redirected the strike force—now, it would take a major muscle movement from every supporting asset to refit and transport the shooters.

Duchess and Jo Ann immediately pulled up the village on their respective computers, and Duchess called out, "How long to relocate the strike force from Sepaya to Ibrahimkhel?"

Sutherland said, "Between the MEDEVAC and refuel times for transport assets, they could hit the ground in ninety minutes if we're lucky. I could get surveillance platforms on-line before that, but not by much."

"Get them moving, and shift all surveillance platforms to Ibrahimkhel," Duchess called back. "Everyone else get to work building target packets for suspected cargo transfer points. Same drill as Sepaya."

Jo Ann consulted the last reported location of David's team, unsure what she was supposed to feel about their current proximity to the city. On one hand, they could arrive in less than half the time it would take the strike force helicopters to land there—on the other, Gossweiler had expressly told her that all further action was to be military-only.

David spoke again. "*Duchess, I say again, cargo routed to Ibrahimkhel, how copy?*"

"I copy all," she replied. "The strike force will need an hour and a half to consolidate and move there before they can action targets."

The team leader's response was almost smug.

"*And fancy that, we're just under an hour away. Advise my team proceeds to Ibrahimkhel to reconnoiter for cargo location in advance of strike force arrival. We'll be continuing mission in two captured ISIS trucks, so please see to it that we don't get smoked in a Coalition airstrike.*"

He said the word "advise" as if he were speaking an order, and rather than be irritated, Duchess instead seized the opportunity to usurp Senator Gossweiler for the second time in five hours.

"Negative, my orders are to exfil you ASAP," she transmitted back, quickly adding, "However, since the strike force is rerouting to Ibrahimkhel, I assess that as the safest spot for exfil. Proceed there and..." She inserted some strategic pauses. "Stand by...for link-up...and exfil."

There was a long pause as the team leader interpreted the tone and spacing of Duchess's order. Jo Ann felt a wave of frustration at Duchess's insubordination, but she had to hand it to the woman: this wasn't her first time bending the rules.

Neither her tone nor the pauses between words would be discernable on the transcript of communications emerging in the aftermath of the mission, but both may as well have been a direct order for the team leader to proceed into Ibrahimkhel as recon element for the strike force, just as he'd recommended in the first place.

At least, Jo Ann thought, if the team leader was as perceptive as she suspected.

"*Copy all, we're en route and will be standing by for further guidance regarding link-up and exfil. Continuing to monitor enemy radio frequency, will advise if we hear any intel. Suicide out.*"

Duchess set down the hand mic, looking pleased that her unspoken order had been sufficiently received.

Jo Ann said, "Well, that was clever."

"Wasn't it?"

"Yeah, the only thing missing was one of you pretending to have radio issues. But this is a bad idea."

"The thought hadn't occurred to me."

"I'm serious."

Duchess tapped a fist against her opposite palm. "Gossweiler is already sending me to some outpost in the Arctic Circle to steam open envelopes until I retire. Let me worry about the fallout."

"Senator Gossweiler," Jo Ann replied angrily, "could shut down Project Longwing in its entirety as a result of this. This calls into question the Agency's ability to operate within very specific guidelines—it's not just about you anymore."

"It never *was* just about me. If Bari Khan makes it out of Syria with the cargo, it doesn't matter whether we protect Charlottesville or not."

"The analysts haven't found evidence in support of a terrorist attack in Charlottesville."

"Not *yet*," Duchess said, "and so what? Bari Khan could use them anywhere in the world, and depending on where he points those rockets, we could be looking at the highest casualty terrorist strike in history. And I'm not ending my command of this program until I've done everything in my power to stop that from happening."

24

Wei Zhao approached the bow of his yacht, stopping at the rail to let the salty breeze whip across his half-buttoned linen shirt.

He came out here often during his passages to think, to focus, to appraise the world behind mirrored sunglasses. From this leading edge of his yacht, he had a sense of acceleration, of limitless opportunity.

The horizon was an endless expanse of rolling blue ocean, the seascape both invigorating and humbling. On land he was a billionaire, a business magnate surrounded most of the time by an entourage of assistants and colleagues. But out here, he was a speck on the ocean, an infinitesimally small presence that Mother Nature could obliterate at any time. That was one of the reasons he liked going to sea and did it often—to remind himself of his mortality, to consider what really mattered in this world.

Another reason, of course, was to enjoy his yacht.

Named after Homer's six-headed sea monster, the *Scylla* was a 140-foot-long marvel of luxury yacht construction, one that had taken him three years and over twenty million dollars to build. It was a completely custom project, designed with the aid of a famed naval architect and built by the Italian firm Patrizio Limited.

He'd commissioned the yacht with an eye to the essentials required for easy access—namely, a helipad—as well as those required by cultural relevance, hence the square tables spread throughout the lounge for playing mahjong, the traditional Chinese tile game. There were also the "water toys," jet skis and scuba equipment, though they were largely reserved for his guests. Zhao had little interest in splashing around the water like a schoolboy on a family vacation. The same applied to the yacht's ten-guest capacity, only maximized when he was entertaining business prospects or loaning a charter to his most trusted colleagues.

Zhao's primary consideration was speed, and he'd spared no effort in that regard.

Powered by two Jedburgh diesel engines and a pair of Imar gas turbines, the *Scylla* produced 18,700 horsepower and topped out at sixty-seven knots, making it one of the fastest yachts in the world. He appreciated that speed—contrary to many of his island-hopping billionaire counterparts, Zhao preferred long voyages in total privacy, preferably to far-flung lands with diverse dining and culture.

And most often, he traveled with the company of what his Saudi counterparts in the business world referred to as their "pleasure wives."

These women were models and B-list actresses, usually with affinities for champagne and fine dining, diamonds and designer clothes. They weren't prostitutes—technically, at least. All were educated and dignified, carrying themselves with polished manners and quiet grace. They could all pass as a date or business colleague at any Michelin-starred restaurant in the world, if he'd decided to take them.

He never did, of course. Zhao preferred his temporary liaisons to occur on the seclusion of his yacht, generally finding his women through a network of fashion photographers who made personal referrals to the business elite and provided literal portfolios to aid in the selection.

Zhao had little interest in Asian women, preferring long-legged Nordic types, those tall blondes with an ice-queen style. He generally took four to six with him on his excursions, depending on availability and trip length. It wasn't that he needed the physical company—his sexual appetites were average at best, and unlike many of his colleagues, he didn't mistake any of the women's ego-boosting dialogue with him for any form of genuine enchantment.

The reason was much simpler: he merely appreciated the view.

An absurdly fast superyacht with 360-degree vistas of the sea or shore of his choice was a marvelous thing. But it was far more so when the deck was covered with nude or semi-nude women, usually draped in the jewelry he provided them unless they were sunbathing.

Growing up in a poor and conservative region of China, Zhao had an upbringing devoid of many things he now enjoyed—fine music, literature, even art.

It was that latter point he considered the women typically present during his excursions to be. Because he slept with them, yes. But most of all, he employed them for the sheer aesthetic beauty they added to his voyages. And when those voyages were over, those women received their gifts in a currency of their choice—the unit of measure was a "brick," or forty thousand dollars in wrapped bills. One brick per day aboard the boat, the payments—and non-disclosure agreements—taken care of by his crew.

He turned at the bow to look at his ship, the sleek white surfaces and bulbous black windows wiped to a mirror-shine by the constant efforts of the staff onboard the yacht. But he was alone on the deck; there were no women on this voyage, no businessmen. This time it was just Zhao and his crew, a rare solo excursion and a long one at that.

With the wind at his back, Zhao saw his yacht captain exit the cabin door.

The captain wore a pressed white shirt with traditional black shoulder boards, his eyes squinting in the sunshine until he covered them with aviator sunglasses. Locating Zhao, he strode across the bow until stopping at its apex.

Raising his voice over the wind and waves, he spoke in Mandarin.

"Sir, we are ten miles out. There are no vessels on radar, and with your permission I believe we can proceed as planned."

Zhao raised an eyebrow.

The captain smiled. "We have come a long way, haven't we?"

"We have," Zhao said. "And we will go much further yet, brother."

Then he turned to face the ocean before him, draping an arm around his captain's shoulders as the two men watched the rolling waves extending forward into the future, into oblivion.

25

Worthy adjusted his hands on the rifle between his legs, scanning out his backseat window for threats—enemy observation posts, spotters with radios or cell phones monitoring the vehicle traffic following the route to Ibrahimkhel.

And judging by the near-constant stream of conversation that had filled the ride so far, he seemed to be the only one paying attention to their surroundings.

Ian asked, not for the first time, "You sure this is a good idea, David?"

"Not really," he replied. "I mean, technically what she said was, 'stand by for link-up and exfil.' But what I heard was, 'reconnoiter for rocket location in advance of strike force arrival.'"

"And what if she didn't mean any of that?"

"She did, I assure you. And if anyone has a problem with our actions, I'll say we got lost and stumbled into Ibrahimkhel by accident. Let me worry about that. You just put your brain to use figuring out what BK could possibly want to hit in Charlottesville."

"You should know better than me—what's worth attacking there, the zoo?"

"No," David replied. "Charlottesville doesn't have a zoo. Have to drive to Richmond for that. But it's got John Paul Jones Arena for basketball and concerts; that has a capacity of fifteen grand. Scott Stadium, which can probably fit fifty or sixty thousand people. Could be the university, but we're too late in the year for a VIP commencement address. And all that seems too low-ball for that cargo he's got."

Ian said, "I just remembered—NGIC is in Charlottesville."

"What's NGIC?"

"National Ground Intelligence Center. It's an Army-run unit specializing in science and tech, with a focus on monitoring foreign ground forces. BK could make quite a statement by wiping out their headquarters."

Elias said, "I would like to propose another option: there is no attack on this date."

"What do you mean?"

"The logistician said he overheard this information, not that they told him. It could be the date and location of a transfer for the cargo. Does this town have an airport?"

"Yes," David said, "Charlottesville has direct flights to Atlanta, Philly, New York, Chicago..."

"DC?" Elias asked.

"Yeah, I think there's a line to Washington-Dulles."

"Perhaps you should consider this possibility."

David leaned forward and said, "Why haven't you thought of that, Ian?"

"Why are you picking on me?" Ian shot back. "Worthy hasn't said anything so far, and he may not be smarter than me but he's definitely smarter than you."

Elias asked, "And what about me?"

Ian shrugged. "Depends on whether your airport theory plays out, I suppose."

Worthy finally spoke. "With all you guys arguing over what BK's target is, one of us has got to pull some security. Besides, I'm not so sure Charlottesville isn't just a decoy anyway."

"Decoy for what?" David asked beside him.

"Oh, I don't know, maybe any major American city on the Eastern Seaboard. If I'm BK and I've got a rocket stockpile, I'm not wasting it on some dipshit town in the middle of Virginia. No offense, David."

"None taken."

Ian consulted his GPS while steering, and then he transmitted, "Should be about ten minutes out from Ibrahimkhel."

Cancer's response was almost immediate, crackling over Worthy's earpiece. "*If we end up having to sling lead again, you bastards better step up. Already been twice in this country that I've had to swoop in and single-handedly save the day.*"

David transmitted back, "Yeah, yeah, thanks for all your service and sacrifice. It's a miracle you've survived long enough to be a candidate for lung cancer."

"*No cancer with my genes. My dad made it to ninety-two, smoking two packs a day since he was fifteen. I go through less than a pack, tops, which means I'll probably live to a hundred twenty.*"

"That's good math," David conceded. "It's still disgusting."

"*At least I'm not Ian. Truck Two, out.*"

Behind the wheel, Ian asked, "What's that supposed to mean? I did good back there at the checkpoint. Didn't I?"

"It wasn't terrible," David said after a brief pause. "I mean, you could do worse than 'America says hello.'"

Worthy commented, "But you could do a whole lot better, too. Maybe some *Godfather* shit, like, 'America sends her regards.'"

"Oooh, I like that. Yeah, Ian, maybe use that one at the next checkpoint."

Ian shook his head. "Well if Worthy's one-liners are better, and his shooting is better—"

"And he's quite a bit more handsome," Worthy interjected.

"—then what the hell do you need me for?"

The truck occupants fell quiet then, conversation ceding to the rumble of engine and tires negotiating the path to Ibrahimkhel.

Then Ian loudly cleared his throat. "I said, then what do you need me for?"

"Hang on," David replied, "I'm thinking. Wait, that's it—we'll come to a point where actual thinking is required. You seem to do that better than any of us."

Worthy said, "Except Elias."

Elias gave a silent shrug as if this much were obvious, and David continued, "Well yeah, except him. He's pretty good at it too. And only when there's no pressure involved, like the risk of imminent death. In those circumstances—no Elias, and no pressure—you're absolutely indispensable, Ian."

Their driver fell silent again, probably deciding that he wasn't going to win any verbal battles. For all his intelligence, he was trampled underfoot when it came to the shit-talking abilities of everyone else on the team.

Worthy had no problem joining in the banter, and poking fun at Ian was always a good time. But he knew that, right now, the humor was largely a guise to conceal the reality of their circumstances.

The team's supplies were limited to what they had jumped into Syria, bearing dire implications where ammunition was concerned. Despite cross-loading the remaining ammo among the team, each man was down to a few magazines for their organic weapons. They'd mitigated that with a battlefield resupply of captured ISIS weapons and ammunition from the checkpoint, but resorting to local weapons represented a desperate last resort.

And the fact that none of them had been wounded or killed in the previous three engagements—exactly none of which had gone as planned—was less a credit to their skills than it was to the enemy's ineptitudes. Even wild, undisciplined, and untrained fighters got lucky, and they could miss ninety-nine percent of the shots they took and still succeed in killing one or more members of the American team that didn't have any men to spare.

Sure, the Delta guys who would be arriving to back them up faced the same risks. But they were fully equipped and had quick response forces standing by, to say nothing of access to emergency medical evacuation flights and pre-staged resupply waiting to be delivered if they got pinned down.

They also had the manpower and organization suited for the job they were asked to do; Worthy's team, by contrast, was like a scalpel being employed where an ax was required because no other tools were available.

Hell, he thought, at this point they probably owed their survival to Elias. His convincing radio transmission at the checkpoint was probably the only reason Bari Khan hadn't sent another wave of fighters to stop them, effectively severing any suspicion that the five Americans had survived and were far closer to the cargo than any of the special operations forces currently tied up with their move from Sepaya.

A transmission sounded over the truck's radio console, a voice speaking in Arabic followed by a short response. "Anything?" David asked.

Elias gave a dismissive wave of his hand.

"They are saying security is good. That is all. I will tell you when these savages say something useful to our purposes."

Worthy frowned. They'd overheard periodic transmissions throughout their drive, but thus far none had been useful to them—and he wondered if any would before Delta's arrival to the team's destination.

His contemplation ended the moment he caught a glimpse of the buildings ahead. At that second, he had no doubt that they were arriving at Ibrahimkhel.

I watched the surroundings pass by with a sense of disbelief.

The scope of destruction in Ibrahimkhel defied my ability to comprehend it. I'd seen war-ravaged lands before, of course, namely in Iraq and Afghanistan. Syria was a similarly ancient land—the capital of Damascus was the oldest continuously populated city in human history.

But Ibrahimkhel was a once-bustling city that had been transformed into a scene that was, to put it lightly, post-apocalyptic.

I was reminded of the World War II images of Hiroshima and Nagasaki, grainy black-and-white snapshots of half-standing buildings rising from an endless landscape of destruction.

But the sight before me wasn't the result of a marvel of technology being strategically employed to end a vast global war. These buildings, this city, the entire country had been beaten down by human hands operating relatively primitive weapons—artillery, mortars, rockets—with such incredible consistency that it looked like a vast reconstruction project had been abandoned midway through, leaving in its wake expanses of loose brick, exposed concrete siding, scrap material, and garbage strewn across the ground between buildings.

The truth, of course, was that those buildings had once been whole and functioning structures. I looked to a pile of twisted metal sheeting stacked nearly fifteen feet high, wondering where the hell it had come from. It was impossible to discern; trying to imagine how this city appeared before the civil war was like picturing a man's living appearance by looking at his skeleton.

And, I thought, that's what this region had devolved to—the skeletal remains of a once-functioning society. The strikes of countless bullets gave a blanket-acne appearance to every painted surface, once intact walls now as cratered as the surface of the moon.

To my left was an eight-story former apartment building with its entire front wall missing, revealing an X-ray view of dozens of abandoned rooms that looked like dark spider holes. How many families had it once housed? Where had they gone?

There was no way to tell, no hope of juxtaposing logic of any kind against the backdrop of what we were seeing. Virtually nothing was untouched by war—a building with an otherwise intact facade nonetheless bore a jagged hole big enough to drive a truck through, a black cyclops eye marking the path of some long-forgotten artillery round impacting at random. Rooflines had been chipped away by explosions, partially intact balconies were marked by bent and misshapen railings. Interior stairways were visible through missing walls, entire buildings charred and blackened by explosion and flame.

Yet the civilians I saw were carrying on with life, holding their heads high. I saw children playing atop piles of rubble, scampering up slabs of concrete that had once been walls. People were riding bicycles, wearing backpacks and carrying bags of food and supplies, seeming oblivious to the destruction around them. How they could exist with hope under these circumstances was almost beyond comprehension.

The few who looked at our trucks turned their gaze away just as quickly, trying to hide their dismay with varying degrees of success. They weren't looking to us as tacit allies in the plight against their oppressors; to them, we *were* the oppressors. There was a fair amount of vehicle traffic through the town, though every car and truck appeared to belong to civilians—so far we were the only idiots cruising down the streets in marked

ISIS vehicles, and I feared we'd take a rocket through the windshield from some resistance group waiting in ambush.

Ian asked, "Where do you want me to go?"

"Just follow the car to our front. Let's stay with the flow of traffic to get our bearings."

He did so, carving a left-hand turn after a battered white sedan.

As soon as we completed the turn, however, no more civilians could be seen—in fact, there was no traffic at all. We'd just entered enemy territory.

Elias spoke.

"We are lucky for these trucks. Look to our right."

I saw instantly what he was talking about. A trio of men were standing behind a partial wall on the second floor of a devastated building, and one of them was holding the unmistakable cone of a rocket-propelled grenade launcher.

But he didn't shoot at us or the car to our front, and I wondered what in the hell he was waiting for. Ian continued following the sedan, and for a moment I felt bad for the local driver—probably checking his rearview mirror to see the pair of ISIS vehicles trailing him through a second turn in the Syrian-nightmare equivalent of being tailed by a cop who you expected to pull you over at any second.

Sure enough, the car swung a hard right turn, disappearing into a short side street ending in an iron gate.

To my surprise, the gate was manned by a cluster of armed men. Two of them grabbed the gate's opposing doors, swinging them open for the vehicle to enter an open courtyard in the compound before we passed the side street and the scene vanished from view.

"Elias," I asked, "who were those guys?"

He gave an amused grunt. "Take your pick."

I knew exactly what he meant. At this point in the civil war, there were so many armed militia groups that it became difficult if not impossible to tell them apart—a rifle-toting man could be a member of the Syrian armed forces, pro- or anti-government militia, ISIS, Hezbollah—and we satisfied ourselves by assuming everyone with a weapon was hostile. But the fact that they hadn't reacted to the sight of our trucks indicated they were either ISIS or an ally, and there was no shortage of either in Ibrahimkhel.

Ian abruptly slammed a fist atop the steering wheel.

"Shit, David. That gate—that's where the rockets are. It's been staring me in the face this entire time, and I didn't even see it."

I was taken aback by his outburst. "Whatever's behind that gate could be one of a dozen enemy strongholds in this city."

"It's not about the gate," Ian insisted. "It's about the sedan that just pulled in. When we hit that ISIS checkpoint just over an hour ago, there were six cars lined up. The guard questioned every driver, but he only searched a single pickup truck."

"And that means...what?"

"It means that we didn't see six civilian vehicles—we saw *one*. The rest were transport vehicles redirecting to Ibrahimkhel to load the rockets. BK isn't transferring the cargo to flatbeds or marked ISIS trucks that we can bomb. He's going to divide the rockets among regular cars that can blend into the normal traffic pattern and be indistinguishable from the air."

Ian was a sharp guy, but I wasn't convinced—and the last thing we needed was to give Duchess false hope before we'd canvassed the entire city. She'd already launched a strike force into Sepaya upon receiving our previous transmission, and I didn't want to risk another expenditure of resources until we were certain.

"We have to be sure, Ian."

"I am sure. Think about it—in the time it took us to attack that checkpoint, clear the objective, and conduct our search, we didn't see a single additional vehicle pull up from either direction."

"No," Worthy said, "we didn't."

"That's because we weren't looking at the first vehicles in the transport fleet—we were looking at the last. And that's just out of the ones redirecting from Sepaya to Ibrahimkhel. There's no telling how many already traveled here from other towns."

I reached forward to tap Elias on the shoulder.

"What do you say, Mister Syrian Intelligence?"

Elias said, "I believe he may be correct."

Ian spoke quickly, continuing to follow the street. "I don't know how many cars BK is using, but the one that just entered has got to be one of the last. If we wait much longer, they're going to start coming back out. Even with air support, we couldn't follow them all."

"All right," I said, "this has got 'airstrike' written all over it. Let me see what Duchess has available."

But as I prepared to transmit to Duchess, my words were halted by an incoming transmission—not on my team's frequency, or even the command net, but from the truck's radio console.

It was another stream of Arabic, though this time Elias's reaction was notably different.

He looked back at me and spoke quickly. "The cars will leave in five minutes."

26

Duchess rubbed her temples, waiting for the next update.

The strike force was in the midst of redirecting to Ibrahimkhel, a nightmare of a logistical movement after they'd just expended vast amounts of fuel, therefore station time, for every aerial platform required to put troops on target with air support.

And in the meantime, she was on the brink of a knock-down, drag-out verbal brawl with Jo Ann, who'd proven herself to have all the narrow-mindedness of a woman who'd spent her entire career in an OPCEN much like this one. Devoid of any particular field experience to guide her perspective, Jo Ann existed in a self-induced cesspool of rules and consequences that eliminated free thought. The only way to forestall another verbal confrontation seemed to be to ignore Jo Ann altogether, and for now Duchess was trying to do just that.

She heard a flurry of activity from the J2 staff, saw three people converge around a computer as they spoke in hushed voices.

Duchess rolled her eyes and called out, "J2, something you'd like to share with the class?"

The J2 rose and faced her. "Ma'am, the analysts have reported back."

"About time. What took them so long?"

"The holdup wasn't them, ma'am. It was the White House."

Duchess paused, swallowing hard. "You have my undivided attention."

The J2 continued, "On July third, the president is going to visit Thomas Jefferson's plantation at Monticello with the president of India. It's been kept quiet so as not to disrupt a Pakistan defense contract that's being signed later today. Monticello is in Albemarle County, Virginia, and it's less than two miles from downtown Charlottesville."

Duchess felt the hairs rise on the back of her neck but surprised herself by calmly replying, "Thank you."

Then she spun her chair to face Jo Ann. "Convinced, Commander?"

Jo Ann looked pale. "I've never doubted the need to stop these rockets, or Bari Khan—but this is so much bigger, Duchess. An asinine level of sophistication. *We* barely found out about the POTUS visit, so how did they? There must be a leak in DC, and the NSA and Secret Service had better start looking for it."

"For once," Duchess replied, "you and I are in agreement."

"So what's the next step?"

Before Duchess could answer, David Rivers reported in over the satellite radio frequency.

"*Have time-sensitive intel requiring immediate airstrike. Assess we have found the location of the cargo—stand by for grid.*"

She typed the grid into her keyboard as he spoke it, pulling up the location for herself even as an analyst projected an overhead view on the central screen—it appeared to be an open compound between buildings, surrounded by multiple alleys and side streets leading into the city.

"Got it," she transmitted back. "Go ahead."

David continued, "*We assess that the cargo has been loaded onto an unknown number of civilian vehicles for further transport. Once those cars leave the compound, they're going to vanish into civilian traffic—and with the highway a half-kilometer from town, the odds of locating them after that point are around zero. We can't afford to wait for the strike force—you need to hit it from the air ASAP. Request the biggest munitions you've got dropped center mass of the compound. But we've got to move fast: intercepted enemy radio chatter indicates the vehicles will depart the compound en masse in five minutes.*"

Sutherland was already locking eyes with her, shaking his head as he flashed an open palm twice, then held up four fingers.

She transmitted back, "Closest air platforms are fourteen minutes out."

After a pause, David spoke again.

"*Well I guess it's up to my team.*"

"You don't have close to enough manpower to raid an objective of that size."

"*You're right about that,*" he replied. "*But we don't have to kill everyone; just disrupt their operation, prevent the cargo from leaving, and hold our own until the cavalry arrives. I won't know how to do that until I see the inside of the loading area, and by the time that happens you're not going to get much in the way of viable reporting. We're going to be fighting for our lives.*"

"You've got twenty-two minutes before the strike force lands, and that's if there are no mechanical issues with the birds."

"*Sure. Whatever. Doesn't change what I'm telling you, and we're ready to roll over here.*"

Duchess looked to Jo Ann, who cautioned her, "The senator said all further ground action is military-only."

"The military," Duchess shot back, "is too far out to make a difference. You have a problem with the way I do business, take it up with me after the rockets are back in our possession."

Then she transmitted back to David, "Want the strike force to cordon the area and fight their way to your location once they arrive?"

"*Hundred percent. This is going to be fast and loose—and as soon as we make our way inside, it's going to turn into the Alamo.*"

Well, she thought, this was it. Verbally authorizing David's team to conduct a raid was crossing the line into an outright rejection of Gossweiler's order to leave any further strikes to the military, and whatever the fallout, the stakes just got raised considerably.

"Godspeed, Suicide." Taking a final breath, she concluded, "You are cleared to execute your assault."

27

Cancer tightened his grip on the steering wheel, completing the turn onto the street where they'd seen the gated entrance to the compound.

They'd already rounded the large, angular city block, finding no less than four possible vehicle egress points aside from the entry gate. Each was blocked by an ISIS truck, limiting their options to the original gate.

Worthy rode shotgun in the otherwise empty lead truck. Reilly manned the machinegun in David's truck, with Nizar and Elias as passengers.

The hasty personnel swap was done for good reason. There was no telling how many enemy fighters were inside the compound; and while it was unlikely that all the transport drivers were armed, that was the only factor in the team's favor. With their dwindling ammo supply, it was a virtual certainty they'd need to resort to the enemy weapons they'd captured at the checkpoint. The problem with that, of course, was that they'd never be able to carry all those weapons inside without being noticed.

And the solution, David and Cancer had decided, was not to carry them at all.

Slowing the truck at the side street, Cancer whipped a quick ninety-degree turn to face the gate and its force of guard personnel.

They appraised the ISIS truck with routine disinterest, one man holding up a palm for Cancer to stop.

Cancer floored the gas instead, rocketing the truck forward. The guards reacted at once, their actions varying based on their proximity to the gate.

Those in his truck's direct path dove out of the way. The rest opened fire, blasting on full automatic as Reilly opened up with the machinegun atop the trail vehicle.

Cancer caught a fleeting glimpse of machinegun rounds wiping out the cluster of fighters to his left, then the muzzle flashes of men to his right. But his main focus was keeping his head low, maintaining just enough visibility to keep his truck pointed toward the center of the gate.

His bumper impacted with tremendous force, slowing the pickup to a near-halt in the span of one moment marked by a great metallic clang. But the gate blasted open, his tires regaining traction as the revving truck engine struggled to provide power.

Then he was inside the compound, catching his first glimpses of the scene beyond.

It was, he realized in a split second of muted horror, far worse than he'd imagined.

Worthy unbuckled his seatbelt the moment Cancer's pickup blasted through the closed gate, and he angled his rifle through the open passenger window to begin engaging targets.

As he did so, he took in the larger scene in the open compound, suppressing a sense of complete shock at the sight before him.

There had clearly been an orderly loading process prior to this; dozens of cars were parked in parallel rows, almost bumper-to-bumper. A few in the final row had their trunks open, still in the process of having rockets loaded by ISIS fighters.

But that process came to a screeching halt as Cancer's pickup barreled into the compound. To call the scene inside the compound total chaos would be an understatement.

The transport drivers may well have had no clue what they were hauling or why, but they were a hundred percent certain that they were about to get gunned down, and those standing outside their vehicle at the time of breach were leaping inside and firing the ignition. Half the cars seemed to be in motion already, the carefully lined procession disintegrating into disarray as they began wheeling toward multiple vehicle exits, some colliding with each other in the process.

Worthy observed all this in the two seconds it took him to take aim out his passenger window, and he opened fire on the closest two men he saw as Cancer shouted, "Fuckin' ISIS demolition derby!"

Worthy saw one of his targets drop dead and the other dart for cover, both lost in a blur as Cancer wheeled the pickup toward a corner of the compound.

As the truck lurched to a halt, Worthy threw his door open and jumped outside. They had to get away from the truck ASAP—it had just become the focal point of every enemy fighter inside the compound and currently served no purpose beyond carrying a cache of captured weapons in the bed. He already had one slung over his shoulder in anticipation of burning through his last remaining HK416 magazines in record time.

But as long as that weapon still had bullets, he'd put them to good use.

Worthy scrambled to a building corner a few meters beside the truck, transitioning his rifle to an opposite-hand grip to maximize his use of cover.

As he got his bearings, he began shooting at the men darting among the cars. There was no shortage of targets to choose from—instead, there were so many that he couldn't prioritize before one vanished into a car and two more appeared.

Worthy settled for lighting up the men as quickly as he could identify them, directing his suppressed fire with precise double taps before moving to the next without pausing to assess whether he'd hit his previous target or not. A few dropped in a spray of pink mist; others vanished from view without a visible impact. Right now, it didn't matter.

There was zero discrimination between targets—things were happening too quickly to be concerned whether the men in his sights appeared to be returning fire or not. They were all either currently armed or about to be, and anyone not dressed in his team's tactical kit received his precision fire with impunity.

As Worthy scanned and fired, he heard the enormous crescendo of Reilly's machinegun from the second truck, a wave of metallic sparks erupting across the vehicle roofs as men ducked between the cars.

Then a barrage of gunfire erupted to his front, the incoming bullets hissing and cracking through the air. He tucked himself against the wall, trying to identify the closest threat when a grenade explosion sent him flying to the ground.

Worthy's vision was a starscape of flashing color, his head ringing as he sensed the gunshots drawing nearer through the swirling fog of his mind.

Reilly's first words as his truck entered the compound were muttered with a sense of disbelief.

"Holy *shit*."

Cancer's truck was wheeling into a semicircle to his front right, and everything left of that point was a melee of moving cars and running bodies. Reilly pivoted his machinegun left and fired a long burst across the sea of vehicle roofs—there were too many for him to begin systematically shooting out engine blocks, and his first goal was to make the enemy forces too terrified to stick their heads out until his team had fully penetrated the compound and dismounted from trucks that had become rolling bullet magnets.

Reilly swept three long bursts of automatic fire over the formation of cars before glancing right, trying to locate Cancer and Worthy to establish the far limit of his sector of fire.

He registered a grenade explosion ahead, identifying his teammates a moment later and realizing that, if anything, he was already too late to stop what was about to occur.

A group of four men were advancing on the now-stationary lead pickup, three of them firing wildly as the fourth readied a second grenade to throw.

Reilly swung his machinegun to them, squeezing the trigger before his sights were fully aligned. Puffing explosions of sand erupted a few meters behind the group, and Reilly used the sight of his first bullet impacts to sweep the burst right into the mass of fighters.

They vanished in a cloud of sand and blood as he swept his aim left, lacing them with a second burst of fire before seeing the orange flash of the fallen grenade detonating among their ranks.

Then Ian braked his truck to a stop, the occupants bailing out of both sides as the crack of incoming bullets swept through the air around Reilly's head.

By then he was down to a short ammo belt for the machinegun, with somewhere shy of a hundred rounds remaining. Determined to provide his team as much covering fire as possible for their dismount into the compound, he swept the barrel back and forth over the cars streaming toward the vehicle exits, keeping the trigger depressed until the final bullet had cycled and the captured machinegun went silent for the last time.

Dropping behind the cab, he planted a hand on the side of the pickup bed. Then, using the opposite arm to steady the HK416 and enemy rifle slung across his back, Reilly leapt to the ground.

Ian did his best to keep pace with David, who was maneuvering forward in a zigzag pattern between covered firing positions as he engaged enemy fighters on the move.

Spraying bursts of fire wherever he saw movement, Ian leapfrogged forward behind David, knowing full well what was occurring inside the compound even before Cancer blasted through the gate. Bari Khan had intended to send all the transport vehicles out at once, flooding the streets and removing all possibility of US air assets tracking the now-dispersed rocket load.

But the team's raid had sped up that plan considerably, and cars were speeding toward the vehicle exits in a frantic race to escape.

For every car he could see, it seemed there was a dismounted fighter somewhere in the compound, shooting at the team and their pickups. While he couldn't hear his own team's return gunfire—they were operating their own suppressed weapons as long as the bullets lasted—he could tell that the enemy force here was in fearful disarray, taking casualties faster than they could sustain the fight.

Bodies lay in the open, and Ian saw a man limping toward cover. He aligned his barrel while on the move, almost in disbelief that he'd have a chance to shoot—normally his teammates would have gunned down every target before he could locate them, much less take aim.

But the fighter was still trying to hobble toward a car when Ian's sights landed on his torso, and he opened fire with a half-dozen imprecise shots that dropped the man in place.

"I got one," Ian announced to David, unsure why even as he did so—the statement sounded more like an announcement to himself than any critical piece of battlefield information—and at any rate, his team leader didn't seem to notice.

David had already emptied his final HK magazine and transitioned weapons to the AK-47 slung on his back before resuming fire as he took a knee behind a parked vehicle.

Slowing to a halt beside David, Ian looked sideways to see Cancer dragging Worthy's motionless body by the casualty handle on the back of his kit, then dropping him in the corner between buildings before returning to a firing position. Was Worthy dead? It was impossible to tell, though Cancer had notably failed to call for the team medic.

As David rose to a crouch to continue moving to the next piece of cover, Ian heard bursts of unsuppressed gunfire to his rear; he instinctively turned in place, knowing full well that he'd be too late.

But when he turned he saw not ISIS fighters but his team's two Syrian guides. Nizar was behind cover, carefully shooting his captured AK-47 at the enemy. But Elias was in a frenzy, standing in the open and spraying gunfire while shouting in Arabic. He halted abruptly as a bullet found his chest, then fell forward to the ground.

Ian shouted, "Elias is hit!"

"Leave him," David replied.

Then he was off again, shooting on the move as Ian followed. To David, Elias getting shot was a mere data point, and not a particularly important one at present. The two men plunged forward, Ian trying to discern exactly what David was moving toward, and why.

But by the time he could, he lapsed into utter shock at the sight.

Bari Khan should have been long gone, screaming away from the compound on the first moving car. After all, he was the highest value target on the objective, and his security detail's primary mission in life would have been to evacuate him at the first sign of trouble.

That knowledge made what he was now seeing impossible: a fleeting glimpse of Bari Khan himself, a Chinese man surrounded by Arab fighters, running not toward a car but into a doorway of the adjacent building. He wasn't even armed—though Ian saw he carried a satchel over his shoulder.

David shouted, "He's mine," and took off at a sprint faster than Ian could follow.

I closed with the building that Bari Khan and his security detail had just vanished into, slowing my final footfalls to give Ian a momentary chance to catch up.

Without waiting to see if he had or not—remaining in the open wasn't a viable survival strategy—I flowed inside, sweeping my AK-47 barrel across a short corridor with a single open door.

I ran toward the doorway, armed with the knowledge that if the procession at any point turned to set a hasty ambush, I was done for.

But what choice did I have? Bari Khan had slipped through our fingers once, the Delta soldiers were still twenty minutes away, and if I didn't kill him in the next thirty seconds, no one would. At that moment I didn't particularly care whether every rocket made it out of the compound. Illogical as the thought was, Bari Khan was my team's original target, and I was going to gun him down here even if the effort resulted in me getting wounded or killed.

There was one more important consideration, and it represented the only possible explanation for why he would still be in the compound instead of speeding away in a vehicle: he had evidence of his plan here, the ultimate target his rockets were intended for, and he valued the preservation of that plan far above his own life.

I cleared the doorway and saw at a glance that I was right.

The room had all the indicators of an impromptu command post—files of stacked paper, two computers, a satellite phone on a table—but my concern at present was with the men who'd disappeared inside and were now gone.

They'd exited through a window and onto the street, the last ISIS fighter vanishing through the window frame as I raised my AK-47 to engage.

But my vision registered movement on the floor to my front, an object of some kind coming to rest not two meters ahead of my boots.

Bari Khan's satchel.

I pivoted in place, turning to the doorway as Ian entered. Driving my legs hard, I tackled him at the waist, launching us both against the far wall of the corridor. Ian impacted with a grunt, and I spun him sideways to fling his body to the floor with savage ferocity.

Then I leapt atop him, freefalling with my arms outstretched. I was a split second from landing atop his prostrate form, my view entirely consumed by the sight of his tactical kit, when Bari Khan's satchel exploded.

The concussion of the blast sounded as a sonic boom of high explosives, a searing wave of heat flooding into the hallway as a tremendous shockwave sucked the air out of my lungs. I held tight over Ian's body, waiting for the heat on my back to recede before rolling off him.

"You okay?" I asked, faintly making out a groan from Ian amid the echo of the blast. Then I transmitted, "Doc, Elias is down in the courtyard."

"*Doc copies*," Reilly replied, indicating he'd search for and treat Elias as soon as the tactical situation allowed.

Pushing off Ian, I found my AK-47 hanging from its sling across my back and readied the weapon to re-enter the room that served as the focal point of our operation.

The former command post was a scorched wasteland of debris, the walls charred from the blast. Whatever the contents of those files, they were largely reduced to ash and paper fragments that covered the floor.

In the open compound behind me, I heard a few erratic pops of unsuppressed gunfire, but for the most part the battle seemed to be ending as quickly as it had begun.

I transmitted, "I've got eyes-on the enemy CP. Anyone need support?"

For the few seconds it took Cancer to respond, I desperately hoped the answer was no. Having found a treasure trove of enemy intelligence—mostly destroyed, but still—I didn't want to let it out of my sight.

Cancer replied over my earpiece, "*We're fine out here, gunfight's over. Worthy's fine, being a big ol' puss is all. What do you need from me?*"

I replied, "Ian will orient you to the CP; we need to strongpoint around it until the cavalry arrives."

"*Standing by, boss.*"

Then I turned to see Ian, his eyes wide and unblinking.

"Thanks for the save," he said.

"Don't think we're going to start taking warm showers together just yet. But if we find some viable intel in this mess, I'll consider it. Go find Cancer and bring him here so he can adjust our defenses—anything that matters to us will be in this room."

The final gunshots were still echoing as Reilly sprinted across the courtyard, scanning bodies until he located Elias. Unslinging his aid bag, Reilly dropped to his knees before the prostrate man.

Elias was lying on his stomach, shuddering faintly like a car running out of gas. Reilly said, "Hey, brother, you with me?" as he drew his knife, using it to slice the man's shirt down the middle and expose a backside free of obvious injury. Still, Reilly swept both palms down Elias's back, feeling for any deviation—some wounds closed almost completely, and other internal injuries were only detectable from abnormalities in the skin surface.

The second his initial sweep revealed nothing unusual, Reilly rolled Elias onto his back, seeing the bloody smear of a gunshot wound, his face an eerie purple hue.

Reilly tore Elias's shirt open, exposing a torrent of blood issuing forth from a bullet hole on the right side of his chest. But that part didn't matter—Elias's problem wasn't blood loss. Instead, the bullet's path had carved a one-way valve in his chest, allowing air into the pleural space and causing the lung to collapse. The resulting condition was known as a tension pneumothorax, and judging by the state of Elias's face, Reilly had a minute or less to stop it if he wasn't too late already.

He quickly unzipped his aid bag, telling Elias, "You're all good, pal, just a little flesh wound." Retrieving his supplies, he wiped the wound free of blood with a gauze pad and then applied a clear adhesive chest seal directly over the bullet hole. Then Reilly plucked a 14-gauge needle shrouded in a catheter from his aid bag and tossed aside the plastic cap.

Running his fingers across Elias's chest between his right nipple and the center of his collarbone, he stopped halfway and probed for a gap between bone—the space between the second and third rib along the mid-clavicular line.

"Bit of pressure," Reilly said, forcing the needle into Elias's chest.

It disappeared into his torso, and Reilly withdrew the needle to leave the catheter inside, the only sign of it a small circular valve emerging from the entry point. Sticking the needle into the dirt beside him, Reilly leaned down and listened for the hiss of air from the valve—there was none.

He grabbed a second needle and felt along Elias's right side, finding the midaxillary intercostal space that was lateral to the nipple. Forcing the needle inside, he performed his second thoracostomy in the span of fifteen seconds, pulling the needle back out and listening for air hissing out of the catheter valve.

But it too was silent, indicating that internal bleeding had flooded the space previously occupied by air. With no exit wound, there was a much greater danger of the bullet having struck a major blood vessel—and while two needle thoracostomies were enough for most stateside doctors to declare the patient dead, Reilly had one last-ditch effort to drain the internal bleeding that he now knew was preventing Elias's heart from beating.

He found the same spot on his casualty's opposite rib, holding an index finger in place as he aimed the tip of his knife.

"Sorry, buddy," he said, making a hasty incision, "going to be a badass scar."

Reilly dropped the knife and plunged his index finger through the cut to deepen the penetration, feeling Elias's hot flesh give way to a *pop* as his fingertip passed through all resistance.

Withdrawing his finger, Reilly watched the blood pour out of the wound, hoping it was enough to alleviate the pressure on Elias's heart. Looking to his torso, Reilly watched for the bilateral rise and fall of the chest.

There was no bilateral rise and fall, or unliteral, for that matter—Elias was dead, his vacant eyes staring up at the sky.

Reilly sat back on his heels, panting from the effort as he felt a hand alight atop his shoulder.

Looking up, he saw Worthy standing over him.

"Internal bleeding," Reilly said. "He's gone."

"He was gone two minutes ago." Worthy patted Reilly's shoulder. "You're a good medic, Reilly."

I leaned down to pick up the next object at my feet—the blackened remains of a satellite phone, half its receiver missing from the blast. It was beyond repair, but hopefully Duchess's digital forensics people could pull some data off of it nonetheless.

Slipping the phone remains into a cargo pocket, I knelt to continue sifting through the paper fragments that had partially survived the explosion. Most were covered in Arabic script, and I began assembling them in a loose stack beside a pair of incinerated laptops. The faster I could consolidate the remaining intelligence for a handoff with the special operators now inbound to link up with us, the faster they could speed it to the rear for analysis.

And at this point, every minute counted.

I had no idea what Bari Khan planned to obliterate with those rockets, but his plan was meticulous. The ashes around me contained paper shards of all sizes, most of them singed at the edges until only a few words remained. I collected them meticulously, watching where I set my feet, knowing that a single misstep could smudge some key detail about an imminent terror attack out of existence. Judging by what remained, a key detail or two might well be all that the intelligence analysts could decipher for our efforts to stop the attack.

And even while I sifted through the detritus of the enemy command post in the wake of a failed raid, I had to admit that Bari Khan had earned my full begrudging respect.

To remain on site after the first sign of US presence was impressive enough. But to expose himself to incredible risk in safeguarding his plan by destroying the evidence told me he was not just committed but courageous. Sure, his motives were misaligned with what most of society would consider acceptable, myself included. But as a terrorist operative, the man was a force to contend with.

Scanning for the next viable scrap, I found an oblong shred of blank paper a few inches in length. Carefully lifting it, I turned it over to see that the reverse side bore text that was not only neatly typed, but also in English.

My first glance at the words had a surreal, dreamlike quality. I blinked to clear my vision, certain that I'd been concussed by the blast and was currently looking at words that at any moment would morph into illegible Arabic.

But they remained clear and vivid, and any delusions faded to a tightening of my chest, a viselike grip on my heart as I struggled to breathe. Then the rage began to take hold, my pulse hammering with anger and a terrifying wave of fear.

Blinking again, I re-read the words printed on the partial scrap.

Laila and Langley Rivers, 427 Spring River Drive, Charlottesville.

28

Duchess mentally processed the current radio transmissions with a mounting sense of concern that everything was most definitely not going to be okay.

David's initial reports about the assault were virtually incoherent, and she seriously questioned whether he'd sustained some kind of head injury.

Now he was on a tirade, providing a stream-of-consciousness rant that Duchess visualized Gossweiler reading on the mission transcript even as she heard it.

"*They know my family,*" David continued. "*I want a protective detail on my wife and daughter yesterday, along with my entire team's next of kin.*"

At his first pause, she asked, "What's the status of the cargo?"

"*Fuck the cargo. Do you hear what I'm telling you? They have the info on my family, I just found the names in the CP.*"

Sighing, Duchess made her announcement to the OPCEN.

"Notify the FBI, we'll need low-vis protective details deployed at once. I'll wave them off if this turns out to be nothing."

Which, she thought, it almost certainly would.

Whether David had sustained a concussion or otherwise gone delirious in the course of the fight, she wasn't sure. But she knew one thing for certain: whatever David thought he knew, he was wrong. The only explanation for a link to his family was a personal vendetta, and there was zero chance one of those was playing out in Syria with the help of an ISIS-supported Chinese dissident pulling the strings. Duchess had initiated FBI support for one reason alone: so that she wouldn't have to lie on her next transmission.

"It's in the works. Now focus."

"*I am focused. You need to listen to what I'm saying. I'm looking at the scrap with my wife's and daughter's names on it.*"

"What scrap? What's the status of the cargo?"

"*Jesus, woman. All right, your precious 'cargo' is flooding out of the city in an estimated two dozen civilian cars and trucks. We stopped some of it still getting inventory, but I'd be surprised if more than ten percent is still here. You need to stop all traffic on the highway and start checking vehicles, especially any with bullet holes or body damage.*"

Duchess shook her head. He'd just described a significant portion of vehicles anywhere in Syria, and probably half of them originating from Ibrahimkhel. And with the logistical issues in deploying the strike force to that far-flung city in the first place, no magic wand would help them now.

No, she thought, any hope of stopping the rockets would have to occur at the border.

"I understand," she transmitted back. "The first element of the strike force is moving on foot to your position, will be on-site within ten minutes."

"*We're prepared for link-up.*"

"Now tell me about this intel you found."

"*The enemy command post was vaporized by an explosive charge, and we're sifting through scraps of paper at this point. I've got a sat phone and two laptops that are partially intact and need immediate analysis. Most of the writing we've found is in Arabic, but the information on my fucking family—that's in English.*"

Duchess lowered her mic, glancing sidelong at the woman beside her.

Jo Ann's face conveyed the unspoken accusation that Duchess had hand-picked this team leader—which was true—and that she'd chosen poorly.

That latter part may have been true as well, Duchess thought. She didn't have all the facts, but David's words cast a shadow on the inerasable transcript of a mission that had been called into question long before that point. Gossweiler was soon going to learn that Duchess had contradicted his direct order by authorizing an additional ground raid by her Agency team, and whether or not he would view the threat against the president as a worthy justification for that split-second judgment call remained to be seen.

Unable to bear Jo Ann's glare any longer, Duchess said, "Spit it out."

Jo Ann shrugged. "Your man is losing it."

"Yeah," Duchess agreed. "No shit."

Then she looked to the communications support rep and said, "S6, set up a direct line to my desk. I need to speak with the strike force commander."

29

Worthy approached Cancer as he spoke quietly to David, both men standing in the open compound amid the aftermath of the team's raid.

The fight was over, any surviving enemy having long since decided that discretion was the better part of valor.

Worthy would have liked to think that was due to the ferocity of his team alone, but their early warning network alerting them to helicopters approaching the outskirts of Ibrahimkhel was probably the determining factor. The strike force had already touched down and was proceeding on foot to the compound, and so far any remaining enemy in town hadn't taken so much as a pot shot at them.

Besides, Worthy thought, why would they bother? They'd already been successful, or mostly so. The vast majority of their cargo was already en route to whatever destination Bari Khan had dictated, and a handful of those rockets was sufficient to cause tremendous damage.

A few hundred of them spelled a catastrophe in the making, and that's exactly what was occurring now.

Nizar had been monitoring the radio in their captured ISIS truck, even sending a few hopeful transmissions in an attempt to procure some intel.

But the radio remained silent; the enemy knew their frequency had been compromised, and there was no way to tell how many were hidden throughout the city or otherwise proceeding alongside their cargo, currently dispersed across a fleet of civilian vehicles that had long since departed.

Leaving David's side, Cancer moved to one of their captured ISIS trucks and climbed aboard, stripping the black flag from its mast. He bundled the fabric and carried it away, probably for later hanging as a team room trophy. Though what they'd make of this chapter of their team history in the aftermath, Worthy wasn't sure. On one hand, they'd overcome incredible odds in making it this far, continually improvising to stay on the trail from the moment they'd discovered the rockets.

On the other, their best efforts had fallen far short of recovering them.

Now they'd been relegated to consolidating their defensive perimeter, assembling in open view for the imminent link-up with the special operations soldiers who'd be arriving at any second.

Reilly approached him and asked, "You still feeling all right? Any changes to vision?"

Worthy shook his head. "No, I'm fine. That grenade rang my bell pretty good is all. Spent most of the fight drooling on myself."

Cancer reappeared, speaking over his shoulder. "Learn to take a grenade blast like a man, Racegun."

Reilly looked irritated at this comment, but Worthy just nodded and said, "Yeah, I gotta work on that." He knew that Cancer had dragged him to safety, and the crusty sniper seemed compelled to rectify that momentary glimpse of his humanity by assuring everyone as quickly as possible that he was, indeed, still dead inside.

Then Reilly continued, "You start getting dizzy, seeing stars, feeling nauseous, and I want you to tell me right away."

"I will, but so far I'm good to go."

This was half-true, at least. He did feel nauseous, his stomach deeply unsettled as if he'd vomit at any moment. But his vision was clear, and upon testing the reflexes of his hands, he found that his motor control had returned in full. He could still fight, and that was all that mattered.

Besides, he was more concerned with his team leader.

David was as emotionally unstable as Worthy had ever seen him. One minute he seemed totally composed, conversing with the team as if it was business as usual, a normal day at the office. The next, he'd lapse into a stony silence, or begin pacing restlessly, or stop to stare at Elias's body.

Right now, he was doing the latter.

Worthy stepped beside David and said, "What do you make of your family's names in the CP?"

David spat into the dirt.

"It makes exactly as much sense as any of the rest of it. We've got a Uyghur-dissident-turned-Muslim-extremist who made his way to Syria, decides to attack the US instead of China, and then picks a nondescript college town in central Virginia for his effort. The record of my family is just one more ridiculous thing added to the shitshow."

He fell silent as a radio transmission came over their team frequency.

"*Suicide, this is Zombie Three Three. 27 Eagles prepared to make entry*."

David huffed a frustrated sigh and transmitted back, "Come on in. Try not to shoot the five gringos and a Syrian standing here like assholes."

Ending his transmission, he spoke to his team.

"All right, boys, get 'em up."

Cancer whispered, "God, this is so undignified."

The men raised their arms over their heads in unison, leaving their rifles slung and pointed downward. Granted, the guys waiting outside the compound were literal and figurative grandmasters of hostage rescue and thus highly unlikely to shoot anyone who didn't require it—but the team wasn't taking any chances.

The shooters utilized the gate entrance and vehicle pathways to make a simultaneous, and silent, entry.

The operators' movements were poetry, an expert choreography of synchronized motion as their formations dissolved into two-man elements that began clearing every facet of the compound perimeter as quickly as Worthy could process the sight.

A pair of operators approached the team, and Worthy could tell by the long radio antenna emerging from the second man's assault pack that the first was the commander.

His suspicion was confirmed when the lead operator stopped before them and announced, "Taylor, troop commander."

David stepped forward and spoke unenthusiastically. "David. Team lead. Have any trouble finding the place?"

Taylor smiled. "What do you got so far?"

David pulled a notepad and consulted it.

"Thirteen rockets found in the remaining cars. With four destroyed earlier, that leaves 635 at large."

Ian corrected him. "633."

"633," David echoed, then pointed to the door on the far building. "Command post is in there, just follow the smell of smoke. We consolidated all the intel we could, but there's not much left."

Worthy saw that Reilly had turned into a tactical lecher, shamelessly examining the operator's equipment.

And to be fair, that equipment was pretty badass—seeing Tier One guys in full kit was like seeing your first *Playboy* in fifth grade: an awe-invoking experience that you would never, ever forget.

Taylor was saying, "We'll get it all sped to the rear for analysis, and—"

He was interrupted by Reilly, who jabbed a bloodstained finger at a pouch on the man's gear.

"Are those the GPNVG-18s?"

"Hell yeah," Taylor said. "Why, what are you guys wearing foı night vision?"

Reilly cut his eyes to Cancer. "We gotta talk to Duchess about this bullshit."

The operator nodded. "Seriously. Agency can afford it."

David asked, "How'd you guys make out at Sepaya?"

"We gave better than we got. Didn't lose anyone, and that's something. How'd you all hold up?"

"Shit, man. You're looking at it."

The man's eyes swept across the team—every member filthy beyond recognition, eyes hollow after twenty-five hours awake, with over half that time spent in continual combat engagements. Then he looked across the objective, strewn with dead bodies between the remaining cars, and gave a nod of understanding.

Then he said, "My orders are to escort your team to a chopper for transport to FOB Presley for follow-on movement back to the States."

"Bullshit," David shot back. "We need to cross-load ammunition from your men and stay in the fight. I've got four shooters plus myself and a local guide who can accompany you to find this cargo before it's gone."

"Sorry, brother. We're full-up on shooters."

David's expression fell into a deadpan stare normally reserved for the moments before a fistfight. Cancer stepped forward and placed a hand on his shoulder.

"Suicide, it's over."

David spun and marched over to an operator closing on Elias's body to search it.

"Get away from him," David yelled. "He's one of ours."

The soldier stopped to let David approach the body. Worthy watched David kneel before Elias, seemingly in a moment of prayer.

But that wasn't David's style, Worthy knew, and he saw his team leader instead pat down the dead intelligence agent's pockets, reaching inside one and standing once he'd recovered the contents.

His prize was Elias's lighter and pack of Marlboros, and David put a cigarette between his lips before lighting it.

Ian took a step to Worthy's side, asking in disbelief, "He's *smoking*?"

"Yup."

"Shit," Ian remarked. "It's going to be a long flight home."

30

Duchess sat before the photographs of her family, stomach knotted with the burden of doing what she despised most: waiting. For her last two hours in the OPCEN, she wanted nothing more than a mug of tea.

Now that she was back in her office with a freshly brewed cup, she couldn't stand the thought of drinking it.

Instead she tried to savor the most respite she'd had since the mission began—the silence of her office, devoid of the radio chatter of ground troops and contractors and pilots, free of the constant updates on the status of UAVs and transport aircraft.

None of that mattered at present. She'd updated Gossweiler's office with the outcome of the failed raid along with the presidential threat and had heard nothing in response. Meanwhile, an alphabet soup of governmental agencies was combing through the roster of people with access to the president's schedule, looking for connections that could signify a traitor in the ranks.

Now it was a waiting game; everyone had been informed of the rockets, every sensor and agent had their ear to the ground, waiting for the slightest indication to emerge. Military assets had been stood up and forward deployed, aircraft fueled and ready to whisk them into a seizure operation at a moment's notice.

But so far, nothing had come over the net—not the slightest whisper of intercepted communications, not a single report from a field source, not a notable surveillance aircraft snapshot of a bullet-riddled vehicle traveling among the hundreds traversing the highways north toward the Turkish border.

When her phone finally rang, Duchess snatched the receiver immediately, prepared to run back to the OPCEN.

"Status?" she asked.

"No updates on the cargo, ma'am," a man replied without urgency. "But the team made it back to FOB Presley—I've got the team leader for you on the red line."

She felt her shoulders fall as she fixed her gaze on the picture of her son.

"Put him through."

"Stand by."

Duchess heard a click over the line, then a faint background static that preceded David Rivers's voice.

"We could have stayed in the fight."

Great introduction, she thought. Seven words into the conversation and he'd already pissed her off.

"That's not your call to make, and there *is* no fight. The last shots fired in anger were from your team, and even if that wasn't the case, it's time for you to come home."

"How appropriate," he quipped, "because my home is exactly what I'm concerned about."

She sighed. "The FBI protective details have been shadowing your team's next of kin for almost two hours. There have been zero suspicious indicators. Would you prefer we force them all into protective custody?"

"Yeah, that'd go over real well considering we're officially on a milk run in Jordan right now. You think it's easy to sustain a marriage while working for you? It's not. Not all of us have as much practice at lying as your organization does, though I dare say I'm catching up. What have you found out?"

Duchess gritted her teeth, thinking that if she were speaking to any normal subordinate, she'd fire them on the spot. But as much as she hated to admit it, she understood David's frustration. She'd seen the preliminary photographs of the intelligence he found, and her first reaction was that if her family's names had been on the paper, she wouldn't have responded much differently than he did.

And that's exactly what she sought to deal with now.

She said, "We have identified the target of the terrorist attack."

"Which is?"

Duchess felt a mirthless smile cross her lips. The presidential visit to Monticello with the Indian president still hadn't been officially announced, and David was the last person who needed to know about that particular item on the itinerary.

"You don't need to know."

"I'm the first person who needs to know. Do you have any idea what it took for us to follow the cargo? You think you can find a team who'd deliver what we did, go right ahead and hire them. Until then, don't keep me in the dark when it's my family on the line—especially when this leak could have come from your fucking office."

"You want to accuse me of something," she fired back, "then come right out and say it. But you've got a lot of nerve talking to me like that after I put my head on the chopping block for your team more times than I care to count since you identified the rockets. So you could start by showing me a modicum of respect, particularly after your little stunt with the logistician—jumped off a building and escaped my ass."

He remained silent, and Duchess took a breath to steady her anger before continuing, "What you *do* need to know is that the terrorist attack would generate a large number of casualties, and because of the target location, survivors would be taken to the University Hospital. We suspect your wife's and daughter's names originated from Laila's employee records. That doesn't mean they were targeted individually—it means the entire hospital was targeted for a second attack, designed to kill survivors from the first."

She paused then, allowing the information to sink in. The truth she couldn't say was that the casualty count probably didn't matter to Bari Khan—if the rocket strike didn't kill the US and Indian presidents outright, he intended to ensure his victory by detonating a bomb at the exact location both men would be taken to for extensive medical treatment.

And if he *did* kill them outright, the University Hospital would simply be the icing on the cake.

David replied, "So what's being done to stop this?"

"We're covering every possible port and border crossing. Coalition partners have been informed, and we've spun up multinational intelligence assets at the highest levels."

"The 'highest levels,' huh? Sounds like this is a pretty important target BK is going after."

"Any threat to our citizens represents an important target."

"What about Nizar? He was in as much danger as any of us, and—"

Duchess cut him off. "Not that you asked my *permission* before committing Agency assets to a relocation, but I will honor that agreement. Nizar and his family will be relocated to a state of his choosing."

After a pause, David said, "Thank you."

"There's a bigger team at play here. You guys dodge bullets, yes. But those of us supporting you have to negotiate a political minefield, myself included. And all that matters right now is finding the cargo."

"What about my men?"

Duchess leaned back in her chair, deciding how to frame her message.

"You'll fly home on the first bird back to the States. That wasn't my call, but I'd make the same choice if it was."

"We can refit and go back out—"

"After which," she cut him off again, "you will be on an extended hiatus in recognition of your outstanding service over the course of this mission."

"A hiatus," he repeated. "Sounds suspiciously like 'fired.'"

She felt her neck flush with heat. David *was* fired, of course, and within a week's time, so was she. But there was no reason to say that to a man in his current emotional state. She'd allow him the dignity of bringing his team stateside, let them turn in their equipment and return home before locking them out of their facility for good.

By then she'd be handing over control of Project Longwing to some Gossweiler-appointed successor, and the great game would be over—along with her career.

She said noncommittally, "Think of it more like R&R."

"I'll be sure to manage as much rest and relaxation as I can with the knowledge that there's a terrorist plot in my hometown."

"That terrorist plot," she said firmly, "is being dismantled as we speak. Now if you'll excuse me, I have to get back to work."

"By all means," David said.

She opened her mouth to reply, but heard the line go dead.

That kid is a real asshole, she thought as the feeling of nausea returned to her stomach.

Duchess hung up the receiver, then set her elbows atop the desk and watched the phone as she waited for it to ring again.

31

Forward Operating Base Presley, Syria

Ian paced the conference room, his mind racing in an attempt to piece this thing together while his team sat around a single foldout table covered in empty beverage cans and food trays.

Ever since their arrival by helicopter twenty minutes earlier, the Delta Force operators had been about as courteous as possible and provided all the food, protein shakes, and energy drinks the team cared to consume, along with access to their showers and latrine. They'd even assigned two escorts to take Nizar to the dining facility on base before leading the team to this conference room where they could have some privacy and taking David to their OPCEN so he could speak with Duchess.

While the team waited for David to return, they'd been debating any possible connection between Bari Khan and their team leader's wife and daughter.

But not even Ian could unravel that mystery, and the conversation had since devolved into speculation about the location of the terrorist attack.

From his position on a foldout chair against the far wall, Reilly said, "You know what? I forgot about this, but Clancy wrote about a terrorist attack in Charlottesville."

Cancer asked, "Who?"

"Tom Clancy. Let me think, must have been..." He snapped his fingers. "*The Teeth of the Tiger*. That's the book. A group of terrorists guns down a bunch of people at a mall in Charlottesville—not his finest novel, but when you start your career with *The Hunt for Red October*, you can pretty much do whatever you want."

"Let me guess," Cancer said dryly, "his hero gets to meet the president."

"Jack Ryan *becomes* the president, motherfucker. And his son—"

Ian said testily, "Can we get back on track? We've discussed the possibilities of an electrical substation, the logistician being misinformed, all the big venues in Charlottesville, and the chance that the town is a decoy for the real attack location."

Reilly added, "Don't forget the date and location being for cargo transfer, not an attack. Elias's idea, may he rest in peace."

"And the cargo transfer," Ian agreed. "But I'm not satisfied that any of those represent what we're after. I believe that someone handpicked Bari Khan for transport to Syria to take control of the rockets and lead an attack—and while we can't yet begin to answer who that 'someone' might be, we can infer from the seemingly impossible connection between an attack in Charlottesville and the link to David's family that none of this is a coincidence. All of it adds up to this thing being much bigger than we thought."

He went silent as the door swung open. David entered the room and slammed the door shut behind him.

"I just got off the phone with Duchess," he said. "She told me the Agency has identified the primary target but wouldn't tell me what it was. Claims that my family's names were off the employee roster of the University Hospital, which is a secondary target to kill survivors from the first. I don't buy it."

After a moment's pause, Worthy asked, "Did she say we're fired?"

"I'm not sure. Doesn't matter."

"Why not?"

"Because we're running our own op now. Whatever's going to happen in Charlottesville, you four fuckers are the only ones I trust to stop it. I say we get back, refit our equipment, and have Ian get to the bottom of this before anyone goes home. You guys in or out?"

Cancer replied without a beat of silence.

"In Ancient Greece, the politicians couldn't agree on anything including the color of shit. Their nation survived because when all their leaders were arguing in a tent, one guy put their warriors in a position where they had no chance of retreat. So they had to fight to the death, or face annihilation. That was Leonidas at the Battle of Thermopylae, it was Themistocles at the Battle of Salamis."

Reilly recoiled. "What are you, a military history major?"

Cancer gave a halfhearted shrug. "If I'm not at war, I'm reading about war—and I don't mean your bullshit novels. But my point stands: the Administration and the Agency are too concerned about political consequences. They can't make the hard decisions, but we can. We're the guys who have to do the killing. If we don't stop Bari Khan, he's going to set the world on fire." He looked to David. "So I'm in. We go rogue together or not at all."

Worthy nodded. "Well if you two are going down in flames, it's sure as hell not going to be alone. I'm in."

Reilly stood from his chair, snatching an empty soda can from the table and crushing it against his forehead. "I've gone along with too many of your dumb ideas to quit now." He spun and whipped the can at Ian, who gave a displeased grunt as the can's remains hit his chest.

"Lord knows you four are too dumb to figure it out—especially you, Reilly—so I suppose I'm in. And if it were my family's names we found on that objective, I know you'd do the same for me."

"Well," Cancer said, "maybe to save your dad, sure."

There was a murmur of agreement, and Reilly took his seat with the proclamation, "No one's fucking with 'Mad Dog' on our watch."

Worthy asked, "David, why don't you buy the hospital connection for your wife? You think Duchess is lying, or just mistaken?"

"Don't get me wrong," he replied, "I don't trust Duchess any further than I could throw her underwater. But even if she's trying to help, she's only looking at the current facts. My gut tells me that's not where the answer lies. I can't chalk any of this up to coincidence. Bari Khan could choose any major city in the world, he should be hitting China and not the US, and if he's going to the trouble of shipping rockets across the Atlantic, there's no shortage of targets on the Eastern Seaboard. Charlottesville is too obscure, too far inland to make sense. I'm thinking this has something to do with our previous career."

Cancer folded his arms. "It's possible. Keep in mind, Duchess found you in the first place because you were ratted out by an enemy survivor."

"That's true, but that guy has since died at a CIA black site. And to the best of our knowledge, he was the last survivor because we killed the rest. But to date I've pissed people off—"

"You mean killed people."

"Semantics," David said. "Let's say I've accrued enemies for good reason in, let's see, Somalia, a couple South American countries, Myanmar, and Russia. I know you've been to a lot more than that."

Cancer grinned. "I've been to a few. But Syria was notably absent from the list until recently, and I've never been to BK's backyard in China either. So I don't see the connection there. Maybe a better question is, who would want to kill us?"

"Jesus, man, throw a dart. How many criminal syndicates have we operated against? How many terrorist organizations?"

"Maybe we're looking in the wrong place," Reilly chimed in. "What if it's someone from the Outfit?"

David looked as if he hadn't considered that. There were certainly surviving members of their former mercenary unit, some who knew David's identity.

But in the end, he shook his head.

"I just can't see it. Those men were allies to the last, they were paid well for their services, and we went to what most would say were great lengths to assure their survival when no one else would. You have someone specific in mind?"

"No," Reilly said, "I don't."

Then Ian offered, "I don't trust Duchess any more than you do. Worst-case scenario, she could be holding our families as bargaining chips, in case things go sideways and one of us wants to wear a white hat to the press. The threat of putting our families at risk would shut us up pretty quick."

David ran a hand through his hair. "I'm not saying you're wrong, but that doesn't explain how BK could have that info already. None of us have exactly given Duchess any indication of turning informant for the media, have we?"

Cancer shook his head, then added, "No, but I think that theory explains it just fine. China's already hacked the top-secret clearance rosters. Maybe Duchess hasn't fucked us down yet, but her information got breached."

David nodded. "I've been thinking about the same thing. Deliberate or accidental, who knows, but Duchess got pretty upset when I brought up the possibility."

It was Reilly who asked the next question, one that immediately piqued Ian's interest.

"David, has Laila ever been to China?"

He thought for a moment.

"She did a mission trip when she was fourteen. I don't think that qualifies as making her a party to a terrorist conspiracy."

"Or does it? Just playing devil's advocate here, but she could have met Bari Khan then and been a plant this whole time. How else would he know her name?"

Worthy said, "Because Duchess is right about the hospital roster. Maybe it's that simple, boys. There's a target in Charlottesville, the hospital is a secondary, and the Agency is going to have it shut down by the time we get back."

"If that's the case," David replied, "we lose nothing by discussing other options."

"There's another possibility," Ian said quietly, but with such conviction in his voice that everyone else shut up to listen. "It's called the lone man theory."

"Which is?"

"We all know Charlottesville is too unimportant for a terrorist organization to care about. But sometimes all it takes is one person to make a whole lot of people suffer. My dad told me about one of his deployments to the Congo—there was a village that was the sight of some of the worst fighting he'd ever seen. They had no idea why—there was no strategic value in it, no high-value targets or key terrain. It wasn't even on his team's radar until the battle broke out—but when it did, there was a bloodbath. Two previously allied tribal factions converged there and began slaughtering each other and everyone else for six straight days."

"Well, what was the reason?"

"A woman, of course. Some tribal lieutenant defected and took the warlord's wife with him. He made it to the village before someone ratted him out, and both sides turned it into a battleground. The town was only important to one man, but that man wielded enough power to turn it into a firestorm. And when it was all over, four dozen people were dead, many of them innocent."

David nodded thoughtfully. "So you're saying Bari Khan has some personal interest in Charlottesville."

Ian shrugged. "Maybe it's him, maybe someone above him is pulling the strings. Possibly the guy who hired him for this job." Then he held up an index finger. "But it only takes one man."

His words trailed off to the sound of a cargo plane on approach, a rumble that shook the building as the plane touched down on the dirt airstrip outside and began slowing to a halt.

There was a double knock on the door before it swung open, revealing a bearded operator in sweat-laced fatigues.

"Sorry to interrupt, fellas," he said in a Texas drawl, "but your bird is here. Time for you boys to go home."

32

Cancer stepped out of the small toilet nook on the plane, zipping up his fly as he swept his eyes across the cabin.

His team was once again aboard an Air Force C-17, though this flight differed considerably from their high-altitude infiltration into Syria.

Gone were the oxygen masks and tactical kit; the cabin was fully pressurized and filled with huge metal containers held to the floor by ratchet straps. This was no first-class plane arrangement—they were aboard a routine flight, practical stowaways added to the passenger roster at Duchess's command.

The team was in civilian clothes, and spread across the cabin in varying degrees of comfort. Worthy had unrolled a sleeping pad atop one of the cargo containers and was currently asleep, while Reilly sat in a drop seat, resuming his progress in the same stupid paperback he'd been reading before infil.

Ian took the cake, having strung a hammock between two containers and resting in it as peacefully as if he were on the beach, though whether awake or sleeping, Cancer couldn't tell.

Cancer felt a dim sense of pride as he looked across the men. He liked to run a tight ship with the team, and wasn't the type to become overtly emotional. And in part he did this job for the sheer thrill of combat, sure.

But beneath it all, Cancer loved warriors. Even the ones trying to kill him were cut from the same cloth he was; and when that commonality extended to the men fighting alongside him, it bred a degree of loyalty so absolute that not even Cancer could shake it.

But at present his concerns fell to the last remaining member of his team: David, currently brooding in a seat at the back of the plane. Cancer grimaced at the sight—his young team leader was deep in some furious thought, looking as if he were about to burst into flames at any moment.

Cancer sauntered over to him and dropped into a seat, speaking without introduction.

"You figure out the target yet?"

David looked over as if he'd just noticed Cancer was there, then returned his gaze to the aircraft's shuddering floor.

"No. No idea. But once we get back, Ian's not going to sleep until he figures it out."

Cancer glanced over at the hammock, its occupant a motionless shape.

"Looks like he'll be pretty well rested by then." A sudden gust of turbulence rocked the plane, and Cancer steadied himself as he continued, "You do realize what you're asking the boys to do, right?"

"What do you mean?"

"Oh, I don't know. Going off the legal grid, subjecting ourselves to prosecution and incarceration at an Agency black site for the rest of our natural lives."

"I asked if they were in. Everyone volunteered."

"'Course they did, same as you would have for any of them. Doesn't change the stakes. The second we take Agency weapons out of our facility, there's going to be hell to pay if Duchess finds out. She'll crucify us, literally. Even if we just gain some intelligence and pass it along to her."

"Well, that's life in the fucking fast lane," David said. "Put yourself in my position, pretend it's your wife and kid on the line. Well," he corrected himself, "imagine you had a wife and kid, and then pretend they're on the line. There's something bigger at play here. We don't know what, and I'm not going to leave it to the Agency to figure it out. So we do," he repeated, emphasizing his next three words, "whatever it takes."

Cancer cracked the knuckles on his left hand, then the right, considering that there may be a mentorship opportunity in the middle of this train wreck that was the aftermath of their second operation in Syria.

"Slow down there, young Padawan. What happened to the guy who was so fuckin' touchy about letting Elias interrogate that logistician, so grievously concerned about our operational authorities in Syria?"

"That was before my family was involved."

"Oh." Cancer turned his palms skyward. "So *now* you're willing to do whatever it takes. Now that it's your family, and not someone else's."

David's brow furrowed. "Yes."

"No more born-again-Christian sentimentality?"

"Not this time."

Raising his voice over the wind that once again pitched the plane, Cancer said, "It's all or nothing, David. You want to survive in this business, you can't pick and choose your stance—"

David spun sideways and grabbed Cancer's shirtfront, pulling his face close.

"I don't need a lecture from you. My family's in danger, and we're goddamn well going to deal with it however we need to."

Cancer's eyes never wavered, and he felt his lips spreading into a wide grin.

"You may not like what I have to say. You may not agree. But you do have to *listen*. And don't get me wrong, I like the new you."

David let go of his shirt, glancing around the cabin to see if anyone from his team had just witnessed his loss of control. Cancer didn't care either way; they weren't colleagues on some corporate retreat. They were shooters, plain and simple, immersed in a business that was messy at best and fatal at worst.

Cancer continued, "Now you're seeing the situation for what it is. I told you before that the biggest difference between us and the terrorists is our methods. So take this pain you feel and use it as a lesson: what we do has consequences, and the cost of us failing to kill a target could be hundreds or thousands of civilian lives. They may not be your family, but they're someone's family. Remember that."

"We can discuss your philosophical leanings when my family is safe."

"We're discussing it now, because your family already *is* safe—you just don't realize why."

David looked at him sharply, his nostrils flaring. "Yeah? I must have missed the press release. Why are they safe?"

Cancer smiled again, a leering wolf's grin.

"Because you've got me."

33

Michaela Greene told her family to wait, and then sped up her pace on the bridge walkway. Stopping when she was abreast of the second flagpole in the road median beside her, she turned around and tapped her phone screen to film a video.

Then she called out above the noise—wind, traffic, rushing water, and a distant helicopter circling in the early morning sunlight.

"Okay, Greene family, go ahead."

Her husband lifted his hands from the shoulders of their son and daughter as he said, "Race you!"

Her son Dayton took the bait at once, darting forward and taking a single bounding leap that ended with both feet striking the sidewalk as he announced, "I win!" The ten-year-old was beaming as he threw up two peace signs for the benefit of Michaela's phone camera. She readjusted the angle to see that her daughter shared no such enthusiasm.

Raising her voice over the wind, Michaela announced, "Come on, Nora. You've got a whole year before you're allowed to act like a brooding teenager."

Nora uncrossed her arms, strolling forward for a few unapologetic paces before asking, "Happy?"

"Very," Michaela said. "All right, Dustin. Your turn."

Her husband raised his arms to the side, closing the distance to his wife with long strides before bringing his hands to Michaela's cheeks and giving her a loud kiss on the lips.

"You guys are so gross," Nora said.

He ignored her comment, announcing instead, "All right, Greene family, welcome to Canada! Let's take in the view."

Michaela slid an arm around his side, turning to see the majestic blue expanse of the Niagara River ending in the crashing white mists of the falls. The sheer power was incredible—even at this distance, the rumble of thousands of gallons striking the river with each passing second caused the bridge to vibrate with a steady hum, underscoring the sounds of vehicle traffic behind them. A few riverboats made their rounds toward the falls, and a sightseeing helicopter cruised above them, carving lazy circles in the sky.

"We better keep going," Dustin said to her. "Boat tour leaves in an hour."

"Not yet, I want a picture of us at the border."

She turned to locate a passing tourist—there wasn't much foot traffic this early in the morning, and while they'd succeeded in beating the crowds, the walkway leading back to New York was largely empty.

Looking the other direction, she found a man approaching from the Canadian side, his ballcap pulled low to shield his eyes from the sun's glare.

She pulled out her phone and waved it.

"Excuse me, sir? Would you mind taking our picture?"

He looked up, exposing an Asian face that quickly took on an expression of confusion at the sight of Michaela's proffered phone.

Then he spoke in what she assumed to be Mandarin, his hands gesticulating to his ear.

"Sorry," she said.

Then he broke into a smile and continued speaking in heavily accented English.

"I am joking, miss. I would be delighted to take your picture."

Michaela laughed as she handed him the phone, turning to stand with her family in a tight cluster at the rail. She preemptively nudged her daughter with an elbow. "Smile, Nora."

"This *is* my happy face," Nora replied, her jaw slack.

The man assumed a broad stance between the two flagpoles mounted on the road median behind him, aiming the phone at them before pausing to address Nora in a somber, reprimanding tone.

"Miss, this is a serious occasion—please stop smiling so much. It is quite distracting."

Then he raised the phone, tapping the screen before appraising the picture with a nod of approval.

"This will do." He handed the phone back to Michaela. "You have a beautiful family."

"Thank you," she replied, taking the phone as the man continued walking across the bridge without another word.

Dayton said cheerfully, "He was nice."

"He was weird," Nora muttered.

Checking the image on her phone, Michaela replied, "Well, it looks like he got a smile out of you."

Her husband gave a mocking gasp of surprise.

"A smile? From *Nora*? Maybe we should hire that guy to follow us around for the next week."

Looking down the sidewalk, Michaela saw the man's figure receding. He was strolling calmly, hands in his pockets, looking out toward the falls as he closed with the US Customs checkpoint.

34

Longwing Isolation Facility
Rockingham County, North Carolina

Ian entered the building before his team, flipping on the lights as they began shuttling in equipment bags from the truck outside, an Agency driver waiting at the wheel for their approval to depart.

They called this building their ISOFAC, or isolation facility. The term was a military one, but the exterior of these grounds was anything but: the main gate had an ambiguous sign reading *Operations Center, Public Works*, along with a phone number to call for access.

Beyond that, a half-mile-long road threaded through a section of woods, partitioned from the surrounding forest by a perimeter fence lined with cameras, sensors, and ominous government-produced NO TRESPASSING signs. While the fenced area included a few small ranges where they could fire suppressed weapons, most of their training was conducted in a network of military and Agency training sites up and down the East Coast. The vast majority of the fenced land surrounding their facility was simply a forested barrier to outside view.

And the interior of the ISOFAC wasn't much to look at—there were rooms for weapon and equipment cleaning and storage, a planning bay that had been cleared of materials before they'd departed for Syria, and individual workstations they used to prepare their respective segments of each mission brief.

As team leader, David handled the overall scheme of maneuver and actions on the objective, but each man planned in depth for their respective specialties: Worthy managed the route planning, Reilly covered medical contingencies and casualty care by phase of the mission, and as second-in-command, Cancer was in charge of the training and rehearsals, then overall logistical considerations from the moment they left the ISOFAC until they returned.

But every portion of mission planning occurred within the framework of Ian's specialty: intelligence.

As the men ferried their equipment from the truck, Cancer announced, "Reilly, get Ian's equipment put away and clean his weapon along with yours."

Reilly sounded appalled. "Seriously?"

"Listen, he may be deadweight in a gunfight—no offense, Ian."

"None taken," Ian said.

"But he's got the biggest brain on the team and when it comes to intel, he's our man. Ian, what else do you need?"

"Fresh pot of coffee."

"On it," Worthy said, moving to the coffeemaker.

Ian called after him, "And I don't want to see the bottom of my mug until I've found what I'm looking for."

Worthy halted in place and said in a measured tone, "Don't push your luck."

Ian barely heard him—he was already striding resolutely to his workstation, which was distinguishable at a glance from all the rest.

Four computer screens lined the desk, and everything was in order: his keyboard, mouse, and headphones exactly as he'd positioned them, ready for his bidding.

Which was a good thing, because Ian was in for a long night.

The team were phenomenal shooters, but when it came to good old-fashioned intelligence work, Cancer was right: Ian was their real asset.

And while finding the target was the most important priority at present, it was far from the last. Ian would have to divine every possible connection from a universe of data, trying to connect the dots between how a Chinese dissident had made his way to Syria and hooked up with an established terrorist network, to what his objective was in attacking the US instead of China, to how and why both the inconsequential town of Charlottesville and David's family factored into the larger puzzle.

Then there was the larger question playing at the back of his mind: who had put all of these pieces together in the first place?

Because Bari Khan didn't have the capacity to organize all this from either his native China or Syria, and ISIS was far too fractured to orchestrate such a sophisticated attack effort from the wrong side of the Atlantic. To Ian that meant someone else was pulling the strings, and he intended to find out who.

But at the moment, his first step was determining *what* in the hell Bari Khan intended to strike in Charlottesville. Right now, that mattered far more than *why* he was going to attack it—because once Ian had the target, he could reverse-engineer how Bari Khan planned to launch his strike. That in turn would lead him to possible avenues of getting the rockets into place, which opened up new threads he could follow outward in a spiderweb of possible intelligence leads.

And while the open-ended question of finding a terrorist target seemed overwhelming at first glance, Ian had more than enough to go off in beginning his search.

With Duchess's confirmation of the University Hospital as a secondary target, he could easily rule out a majority of public sites and key infrastructure based on the proximity to closer hospitals, thus narrowing his search down to a key operations box. Then it was a matter of identifying likely targets within that box, and mapping launch sites capable of fitting a launch assembly for six hundred-plus rockets. From there he would overlay the circumference of the rockets' 2.79-mile maximum range between launch sites and various targets, and look for the key overlaps between the two.

Of course, it all sounded easy when he thought of it in broad strokes. In reality, he was looking at hours of dedicated, highly caffeinated focus across multiple computer screens, all while wearing his Bluetooth noise-cancelling headphones with a classical music playlist spanning 168 songs.

All told, he expected to have a minimum of three targets ranked by probability no later than six hours after he started his work.

He settled in his chair, powering up his computer and seeing the quad-screen setup glow to life.

Pinching his eyelids shut, he took a final breath and released it slowly. Then he opened his eyes, seeing the login prompt on his main screen and thundering his fingers across the keys to enter his password. He reached for his headphones and was in the process of donning them when Reilly called out behind him, "I found it."

Ian spun in his chair. "You found what?"

"The target." Reilly was standing a few feet away, holding up the personal phone he'd just recovered from his locker, and showed the screen to Ian. "POTUS is visiting Monticello with the President of India. 2:00 p.m. on July third. It posted to CNN twenty minutes ago."

David said, "Let me see that," and snatched the phone. After a moment's pause, he looked up. "He's right."

Worthy entered the room holding the coffeepot, now filled with water in anticipation of brewing the first batch.

Holding the pot aloft, he raised an eyebrow to Ian.

"You still going to need that coffee?"

35

"Please have a seat," the young female intern said. "The senator will be with you shortly."

Duchess walked past the young woman—she was what DC insiders referred to as a "skintern," a leggy intern who pushed the limits of acceptable skirt length—and entered Senator Gossweiler's office.

She stopped inside the open door, scanning the office interior for a few seconds before taking a seat in a leather-bound chair facing the empty desk.

Rather than simply calling her with any updated guidance, Gossweiler had summoned her to his office at a time slot of his choosing. This would be her final reckoning, the last chance to justify her actions and find if the presidential assassination plot had granted her any leeway in ordering David's team into that final, last-ditch raid on the vehicle compound in Syria.

She suspected that Gossweiler wouldn't honor that judgment call in the slightest, and so Duchess had brought a single bargaining chip with her—a photograph hot off an Agency high-resolution printer, safely tucked into her pocket ahead of his return to the office.

And what an office it was.

Duchess's own personal workspace was arranged for utility—work, tea, and on occasion a nap break during extended shifts in the OPCEN. She didn't have anyone to impress; aside from her Agency colleagues and Gossweiler himself, no one was even allowed in the Special Activities Center, much less to the compartmentalized project corridor in which she ran the newly minted targeted killing program.

Gossweiler's office, by contrast, was arranged entirely to convey power.

She supposed this was a useful system in his line of work, where the closed-door negotiations with lobbyists and his fellow politicians were a fact of daily life.

The lone window was flanked by two flagpoles, one with the US flag and the other with the flag of Nevada. Framed photographs of Gossweiler with three presidents lined the walls, interspersed with various certificates from grateful constituent organizations. The shelves and tables were covered in files, polished wooden boxes, and displays of commemorative coins. There was also a large bronze statue of a cowboy riding a bronco, which she zeroed in on in the final moment before he entered the door behind her.

Duchess quickly stood.

"Senator."

He swept past her on the way to his desk. "I've got exactly five minutes, Kimberly, so let's make this fast." Dropping into his chair, he aimed a finger at her and said, "You violated my direct guidance to authorize another Longwing raid."

"I did so, Senator, only because the cargo was going to depart long before the military option arrived. And I'd just found out about the threat against the president, which raised my risk tolerance considerably."

Gossweiler leaned forward in his seat, folding his hands on the table as if in anticipation of a meal. "You're lucky on two fronts. One, your hunch paid off and some of the rockets were recovered. Two, you found out about the president's visit to Monticello before I did, and I'm not a man prone to being uninformed. But this program is in its infancy and it's already hanging by a thread. One more slip-up and I'm going to lose my funding, and then we're back to sending drones and racking up collateral damage. So your luck isn't enough to save you, not this time. In six days, I'll have picked a replacement and you're on your way out. I want a seamless handover—"

"Senator." Duchess produced the photograph from her pocket and slid it across the desk. "You may want to reconsider the timing."

He appraised the picture for a moment, then slid it back to her. "Is that supposed to be him?"

Duchess picked up the photograph, glancing down at the still shot from a black-and-white surveillance camera. In it was a man striding past, a baseball cap partially obscuring the features of his Chinese face.

"Our algorithms place it at ninety-six percent fidelity. It is him, Senator."

"When and where was it taken?"

"Just over two hours ago at the pedestrian crossing on the Niagara Falls International Rainbow Bridge. He entered the US using a doctored Canadian passport."

"Then why hasn't he been rolled up yet?"

She placed the photo back in her pocket. "Bari Khan is currently among a free population of one hundred million residents on the Eastern Seaboard. We've got every possible local, state, and federal agency searching for him, and the NSA has a priority tasking backed by every possible interpretation of the Patriot Act. But so far, he's been keeping a low profile."

Swallowing hard, she continued, "And my career considerations aside, the worst thing we could do is break leadership continuity among the staff who's tracked Bari Khan this far."

Gossweiler scowled, seeming to regard this as a form of intelligence-backed coercion—which, to an extent, it was.

"Have you disbanded your ground team?"

"They're stateside, and I've changed the codes on their facility so they can't get access."

"But you haven't told them."

"Not yet, Senator."

"Well, why the hell not?"

"Because I'm going to inform the team leader in person. I owe him that much."

"Do it fast. What else do you have for me?"

Duchess straightened in her seat. "Bottom line, we haven't found the cargo. Screenings at Syrian and Turkish ports have come up dry, as has extensive coastal and border surveillance. And the Secret Service is investigating possible leaks but has found no definitive leads yet. They're still in the process of administering polygraphs."

"Maybe the cargo was forced underground."

"Or maybe," she said, "it is on a boat crossing the Atlantic as we speak."

"You think the rockets were intended for maritime transport?"

"Bari Khan entered New York less than forty hours after the Longwing team reported seeing him in Syria. That is indicative of commercial air travel to any number of Canadian airports that have less security measures and scrutiny for flights returning from the Middle East—but there is almost no chance that he was able to smuggle such a large cargo in the same manner. We've been directing our primary focus to Syrian border crossings and major ports, and since both have come up empty, it's entirely possible that the rockets didn't move north to Turkey, but west to the unregulated coast. At the moment, my assessment is that the cargo is en route to the US via a trans-Atlantic crossing."

"Cut the shit, Kimberly. Are you trying to tell me you honestly assess a credible threat to the president?"

She tried to determine what to make of his flippant tone—he seemed like he was trying to disprove any possibility that there was a pending attack.

"I do, Senator. The exploitation of material recovered from Bari Khan's command post has resulted in no viable leads that would contradict a terrorist attack during the president's visit to Monticello. And if we don't have the rockets located in the next forty-eight hours, I believe that visit should be postponed."

"I dare say that altering the president's schedule is well beyond the abilities of a humble public servant such as myself."

"I wouldn't say that, Senator. Your humility has managed to put a Remington on the shelf."

He swiveled his office chair toward the bronze cowboy atop a bronco, then spun back to her.

"That's a reproduction, not an original. A gift from my wife after I was elected to the Senate. And for my first term, I slept on a cot in my office because I couldn't afford an apartment."

"Yet like every new member of Congress," Duchess countered, "you managed to become a millionaire within a few years. I would contend that like your political career, it's the outcome we need to concern ourselves with, not how difficult the path to get there."

Gossweiler looked momentarily furious, but before he could respond, there was a double knock at the door. His chief of staff appeared, announcing, "One minute, sir."

He nodded and the door closed again as Duchess waited for the inevitable reprimand.

But Gossweiler merely gave a frustrated sigh.

"I've spoken to a friend. The Administration views the Monticello visit as the leaders of the two largest democracies on earth coming together to agree on their countries' respective commitment to Jeffersonian democracy and human rights. The president has been informed of the threat, and he's refusing to change the location."

"He'd be playing into Bari Khan's hands unless we've located the cargo by then."

Gossweiler dropped a fist onto his desktop, knuckles down.

There was a sharp barking sound of bone on wood, and he snapped, "Then *locate* the cargo by then." He composed himself with a quick breath. "I'll approve you staying at the helm of Longwing until the rockets are stopped. Until then, that is your sole mission in life, are we clear?"

Duchess nodded. "There are thousands of possible ships. Given the timeline of the attack, we can narrow that down to a handful that are capable of crossing the Atlantic. Some of those ships originate from countries of questionable diplomatic relations."

He considered this statement. "Use Customs and Border searches at the ports whenever possible. Make it look random. If you have to, bring in the DEA to put a counter-narcotics spin on it."

"Understood, Senator. But there is one ship I'm particularly concerned with, and it will unleash a nightmare with the press if we raid it while cameras are rolling. I recommend a maritime raid, and I may need some overhead cover to accomplish that."

At that moment his chief of staff appeared in the doorway and said, "Sir, you're up."

Gossweiler rose from his seat, and Duchess hastily stood as he said, "Do what you have to. Keep it as discreet as possible, but get it done." Then he walked out of the office behind his chief of staff.

Duchess was escorted out by the young intern who'd seen her in. As they crossed through a lobby, Duchess glanced up at a television display to see Gossweiler live on CNN, striding onto the Senate floor.

36

I turned the corner into my driveway and saw Laila and Langley waving from the front porch.

Putting my truck in park and killing the engine, I leapt out in time to catch Langley as she barreled toward me. I hoisted her into the air and spun a circle to the sound of her delighted giggles, then pulled her into a tight hug and looked up to see Laila approach with a smile.

Laila and I kissed, and I started to carry Langley inside.

Then my wife said, "You want to get your bags?"

I turned as if looking at my truck. But my gaze fell to the street beyond, where I reassessed what I'd seen before pulling into my driveway: two nondescript SUVs parked with mutually supporting views of my house, Duchess's protective detail in action. Or what I could see of them, anyway. Probably FBI, and definitely not asleep at the shift.

"No," I replied to Laila, "they'll be fine. I'll get the bags later."

Then we turned to enter the house.

After that, everything was smooth sailing with Langley—she didn't seem to mind that I'd been gone, only that I was now home. She wanted to play, sit in my lap, and read books together. For the first hour of my return, I was like the center of her universe, and nothing made me feel more fulfilled.

But Laila was more distant, coming and going at irregular intervals. At one point I heard the sound of dishes clinking in the kitchen, and hesitantly entered to find her over the sink.

I said, "I thought we were going out to dinner?"

"We are. I'm just doing the dishes."

"I'll get them."

"No, go play with Langley. She's been waiting all day for you."

"You okay?" I asked.

"Yeah, of course."

"What's wrong?"

"Nothing."

"You're saying 'nothing,'" I acknowledged, "but what I'm hearing is, 'I'm bottling something inside and it's going to explode later.'"

"Well," she said playfully, "wait and see."

Then she kissed my cheek and moved off to continue the dishes.

I left the kitchen warily, feeling that armed confrontation with ISIS fighters was the safer play for me at present.

Returning to Langley's room, I found her busy making preparations at her play kitchen.

"Daddy," she announced, "what do you want for dinner?"

I considered the question. "Your world-famous pizza, obviously."

"Supreme?"

"Is there any other kind?"

She began sticking toy pepperoni and mushrooms to their Velcro attachment points.

I asked, "Have you been good for Mommy?"

"Yeah. We have fun."

"How has Mom been?"

"Good."

"Anything I should be doing to help her out?"

"Yeah," Langley said matter-of-factly, "make sure you let her sleep. She's been real tired after work."

I considered Langley's comment later that night, after we'd returned from dinner and put her to bed. After Laila and I made love, I expected her to pass out in my arms—instead, she began the inquisition.

"How is the contract?" she asked.

"Good. Great, everything's fine."

"Yeah? What happened to the contractor?"

"What contractor?"

"The one who had the disagreement with the Jordanian captain. The whole reason you had to go over there, David."

"Oh, yeah," I said quickly. "Sorry, all of our guys are contractors so I didn't know who you meant at first. Guy named Tom, good dude, and he was entirely in the right. But the contract takes priority, so we had to rotate him back home and replace him with a new hire, a young eager kid."

"Maybe you should start pissing off your host nation counterparts, too," she noted. "We'd certainly see more of you around here."

"Sure, all the way up until Jenio Solutions fires me."

"That's my point."

I looked over at her in the darkness of our bedroom. "What's that supposed to mean?"

"I'm about to finish residency. I've got student loans, sure, but so does everyone else I work with. And none of them are exactly living in squalor while they're paying them back. You don't need to be running all over the world anymore. You could find something local."

The idea repulsed me.

"Well as much as I'd love to work for your parents, they sold the metal-working business so that's out. Last I checked, UVA wasn't giving tenure to people with an undergrad degree, so that pretty much leaves me slinging ice cream at Chaps. Think I saw a 'now hiring' sign last time we went."

Laila wasn't amused. "I'm serious, David."

Frowning, I said, "I just don't know, Laila. I'm not cut out for most jobs, and I...I really like the gig I've got going now."

What I couldn't tell her, of course, was that I felt a paradoxical discomfort not about deploying to foreign lands—that part came naturally—but about coming home. Because strangely, suburban life tended to make me uneasy.

Things made sense to me in combat. The decisions were split-second and instinctive, and the bond between me and my teammates was absolute. It didn't matter that the enemy we fought believed in their cause as much as we believed in ours; we were simply two sides in the greatest game of all, the second oldest profession continuing a proud and gruesome lineage.

By contrast, it was the return to America that always confounded me.

The realities of peacetime existence were muddled; there was none of the adrenaline of combat, and none of the clarity. Talking heads were always screaming on the news. Everyone was seemingly in a competition to be the most offended or outraged by some political scandal or social issue, and the debates raged amid the billboards and commercials of a trillion-dollar advertising industry hawking designer clothes, fast food, and pharmaceuticals. People seemed to conflate the identity of themselves and others with their respective social media presence.

The refuge from this maelstrom was Laila's circle of friends, but they too stretched the bounds of my understanding. Social encounters seemed politely plasticine versions of reality, anything meaningful in my professional existence compartmentalized to my teammates, who were probably enduring equally awkward domestic existences elsewhere. Absent any relevant commonalities with the social circle of Charlottesville, Virginia, dinner party conversations were limited to banal and inoffensive topics that would be unbearable save the drink in my hand.

Then there was my family.

I loved Laila and Langley unconditionally. For Langley, this was enough; she needed the constant presence and playfulness, and that was my natural state with her. If I was brooding over something, she'd know immediately and cheer me up at once.

But Laila was vexing.

On the outside, everything was fine—we rarely argued, and seemed to get along well enough. But I sometimes got the feeling that we were each playing the role of spouse, and she was the only one holding up her end of the bargain. She'd describe her workday, venting as necessary, and I'd listen compassionately—then lie about my own job.

And it wasn't entirely because my security classification required it. I wasn't concerned about Laila accidentally divulging any secrets to a foreign agent.

The bigger issue was this: what was I supposed to tell her? That I was essentially a new breed of government contract killer? There was no gentleman's pistol-duel-at-sunrise aspect to what my team had been designed to do. There were threats to our country, and we were one small and extraordinarily violent cog in the machinery of national defense. We existed on the legal fringe of sanctioned paramilitary action, and when we were employed, it was to kill a designated terrorist efficiently, covertly, and ruthlessly.

What was Laila supposed to do with that information, even if I told her? Judge it against the backdrop of her upper-middle-class existence? Or do what I feared most, and leave me?

I didn't know, and had no intention of finding out. After all, my goal here was a happy marriage for myself and Laila, and a happy childhood for Langley. Neither of them needed to deal with my issues.

So I hid the obvious facts. Outside of combat, I wasn't even like a fish on land—I was like a fish catapulting through the sky. I'd spent so much of my adult life at war of one kind or another that the bucolic sanctum of peacetime felt like an alien realm. Everything was muted, strange to me, and I struggled to play my part as a normal member of society.

Finally I said to Laila, "You know what? Why don't we talk about this tomorrow."

It was no use—she was already asleep, breathing softly against my shoulder.

37

Chief Petty Officer Barry Steele steadied himself on the deck, watching the ocean view pitch beyond the bow of his twenty-eight-foot craft.

Squinting behind the shaded lenses of his shooting glasses, he felt the choppy Atlantic sea spray hitting his face as he tried to acquire visual of his target vessel. He could make out the distant orange specks of the circling helicopters, but the short waves obscured his view of the vessel to their front.

Then he heard the voice of an aerial gunner squawking over his radio mic.

"*Crew of the* Scyllis, *crew of the* Scyllis, *stop your vessel, stop your vessel. This is the US Coast Guard on channel one-six.*"

Turning to face the three Coast Guardsmen behind him, Steele shouted over the sound of the surf.

"There's the call."

The trio of men shot him a thumbs-up, each attired as he was in tactical gear with weapons slung. He looked forward, listening over the internal frequency as the gunner broadcasted, "*Vessel is compliant, cutting power. Two pax visible on deck, both unarmed.*"

Steele had personally led over a dozen boarding events in his nine years of service in HITRON. He'd since been promoted out of that job, reluctantly assuming more administrative and leadership positions as the next generations of Coast Guardsmen filled the ranks behind him.

But today was no ordinary interdiction.

His first sign that today would proceed like no other came at 5:00 a.m. that morning, when they'd received the tasking for a pre-planned interdiction of a vessel inbound for the World Ocean Superyacht Marina in Jacksonville. Their mission was to stop the craft, then board and search it for narcotics.

To Steele, there was just one small complication: that wasn't their job.

Well, that wasn't entirely true—as a unit, HITRON was born and bred to stop smuggling vessels inbound for the US coastline. To that end, they worked extensively with US and foreign agencies that provided intelligence on the shipping corridors and departure times, much of it obtained by agents embedded in South America.

However, that was where the similarities with today's mission ended.

Legally, HITRON could pursue a vessel only under very specific conditions: it had to be a "go fast" boat, or a high-speed open-hull craft in international waters, suspected of drug smuggling and without any visible indication of nationality. Nowhere in that job description, nor in Steele's years of experience, had a yacht ever been involved.

Especially not one flagged as a Chinese vessel.

Just the same, the mission was authorized straight from the top, the operations order having been signed by the commandant himself. Steele had never seen that happen, and it was far from the strangest thing about today's interdiction.

An older black lady had been ferried to his Coast Guard cutter by helicopter. She had DEA credentials, along with authority to monitor the boarding effort from the cutter's operations center. To Steele, that alone was a red flag—DEA agents never met a cutter at sea, mainly because they didn't have to. HITRON would deliver all captured drugs to DEA custody at the transfer point in Cecil Field, and there was absolutely nothing one of those agents could tell the Coast Guard about how to stop and board a boat at sea.

Then, of course, there was the whole matter of the SEAL platoon.

That was what bothered Steele the most. The Navy SEALs had forward deployed to the HITRON base, along with their contingent of Seahawk helicopters. They were currently airborne, orbiting just beyond the HITRON flight paths, ready to storm the yacht—but only if needed. In the event of enemy fire, Steele had orders to abort the boarding attempt and let the SEALs take the yacht by force.

Reasonable enough, he thought, except for the fact that HITRON was already armed to the teeth and fully capable of dealing with shooters. His gunners aboard the helicopters were armed with M240 machineguns for warning shots, Barrett M107 sniper rifles for disabling engine blocks, and modified M14 EBRs as a backup weapon. The tactical boarding team members, himself included, carried .40 caliber sidearms, M16 rifles, and shotguns with two separate loads—one with sabot slugs, the other with less-than-lethal bean bag rounds.

With all that armament, Steele thought the DEA should have either let HITRON do its job, or just punt the entire interdiction to the SEALs. He could only find one explanation for this half-measure of letting HITRON stop the yacht and board, while keeping the SEALs out of sight: unlike the other military service branches, the Coast Guard operated under the Department of Homeland Security. That gave them unique legal authorities in the waters off the US coast, and Steele suspected those authorities were being exploited by someone who desperately wanted to search the vessel he now approached.

He captured his first glimpses of it through the waves and watched in awe as the yacht drew nearer. The *Scyllis* was a big bastard, a 140-footer, and as beautiful as anything Steele had ever seen on the water. White surfaces and jet-black windows gleamed as the yacht bobbed in the waves, remaining in the watchful eye of the two MH-65C Dolphin helicopters that circled overhead, allowing their gunners to survey the deck for threats to the tactical boarding team.

Today, that boarding team was trailed by a second boat filled with Navy open-water divers. Their job was to search beneath the waterline, looking for a parasite, or torpedo-shaped storage container affixed to the hull. The alternative was a traditional torpedo setup, where the cargo pod was kept submerged by an internal ballast tank and towed by the overt surface ship. In the event the ship was stopped by authorities, the crew would simply detach the torpedo cable, abandoning the container to broadcast its location with a transmitter system until a new boat could recover it.

That particular contingency was covered by a third Dolphin helicopter, which was currently flying the ship's reverse azimuth along a two-mile zigzag pattern, searching for any sign of jettisoned cargo.

And as if the SEALs, the divers, and the search helicopter weren't enough, a *third* boat trailed behind them, this one loaded with a DEA search team complete with radar devices to check for hidden compartments aboard the vessel.

His boat began slowing behind the yacht, the operator steering the small craft toward a silver ladder leading onto the rear deck.

Steele was the first on the ladder, scrambling upward and setting foot on the deck to the near-immediate confrontation with a Chinese man in mirrored sunglasses and a white linen shirt.

"What is the problem?" the man nearly shouted at Steele as the rest of his tactical boarding team spread out across the deck, establishing immediate security.

Steele recognized the Chinese man at once—this was Wei Zhao, the yacht's owner.

"Sir, please have a seat and let us do our jobs."

"You have no business on my yacht."

"We have verified intelligence that there may be narcotics aboard this vessel, possibly being smuggled without your knowledge."

"Are you accusing my crew?"

"We are not accusing anyone, sir. This is a targeted search, and the sooner we conduct it, the sooner you can be on the way to your destination."

Though to be honest, Steele was just as suspicious of the search team as this Chinese billionaire seemed to be.

By now the divers were rolling backward off the side of their boat, entering the water to begin searching the hull as the search team from the third boat clambered up the ladder and onto the deck.

Maybe they were DEA and maybe not, but there was no doubt they knew *exactly* what they were looking for. They immediately split into two-man elements, combing the ship with a synchronization indicating they'd already analyzed the blueprints and identified the most likely hiding spots. He watched an agent use what looked like a stud finder on steroids to scan a wall while his partner watched a video display for any abnormalities.

Steele took a final look at the pair of sleek orange helicopters circling the ship, then entered the yacht's interior through an open doorway.

What he saw boggled the mind—every room of the yacht was like its own five-star hotel, filled with lavish furniture and fully stocked bars, gleaming marble floors and plush beds. For the staff on board, of course, this was a nightmare situation—luxury yacht crews were used to running around with a cloth, wiping down fingerprints on polished surfaces the moment the VIP had left a room.

Now, the DEA inspectors were sweeping across the ship, entering every nook and leaving no cabinet unchecked in their meticulous search for—well, whatever the hell it was they were looking for, Steele thought. Because it didn't look like a routine drug bust, and no billionaire in the world would risk his fortune by smuggling forbidden cargo in his personal yacht.

But just the same, Steele knew he'd been directed to interdict the *Scyllis* for a reason.

He looked forward to learning what that reason was, anticipating that he was about to have a role in some historic seizure for the Coast Guard.

But in the space of fifteen minutes, those hopes evaporated: the divers found a clean hull, the search bird swept two nautical miles on reverse azimuth without any sign of jettisoned cargo, and the DEA team announced they'd completed their search with zero results.

And just like that, the search was over.

He received the exfil order from one of the purported DEA agents, a further confirmation that his boarding team served little purpose beyond establishing a foothold on the boat.

"All right," Steele announced to his team, "get back to the ladder. We're out of here."

38

I quietly entered my house through the front door to the sounds of Laila cooking breakfast.

As I entered the kitchen with a hand behind my back, Laila turned to me.

"Hey, David, where were you this morning?"

"Oh, I don't know," I said, pulling the bouquet of flowers from behind my back with a flourish. "Just getting these."

Laila accepted the bouquet with a smile, then leaned forward to smell the blossoms."They're beautiful," she said. "To what do I owe the pleasure?"

"I thought you could take them up to Alexandria today."

"That *I* could take them?" Her smile faded. "What about *us*?"

I cleared my throat.

"Well, some work stuff came up. But it won't take long," I quickly added. "I'll be up there before the fireworks, I promise. Late on the third or early on the fourth. Just need to drive up separate, that's all."

"We were supposed to leave in an hour. As a family."

Why she decided to remind me of that, I had no idea. It wasn't as if I'd forgotten. Why did she always have to make telling lies about my work so damned difficult?

Since her parents had finally sold off the business and retired, they were spending their first July in Alexandria. At thei· invitation, we were supposed to drive up today, take Langley sightseeing for a few days in DC, and spend the Fourth watching the fireworks from the National Mall.

"I know," I said, "and I'm really sorry."

She set the bouquet on the counter.

"If you don't make it, David, you're going to break Langley's heart."

"I wouldn't miss it," I said, wondering how self-assured I sounded in that moment. Even as the words left my mouth, I considered the fact that I had no idea where I'd be by sunset on July Fourth—with the attack the day before, I could be in jail, or dead.

Then she turned to the stove, tending to her scrambled eggs as if I weren't there at all.

Laila was perplexing.

It wasn't that I didn't understand women—there was that too, of course, but it wasn't the primary issue. First and foremost was the fact that I'd spent years in the mercenary racket, and the women you met in the course of your duties weren't like Laila. At all. No, those women knew what they were getting with the damaged men they encountered, they understood the violence inherent in the job and the impermanence of any meaningful relationships. It wasn't a big deal to say you were leaving for "work," because they knew what that meant, and they didn't want to know.

By contrast, Laila and what I could only presume were a vast majority of regular wives were the direct opposite. They wanted to know everything, were accountants for every minute of collective family time, and had a long memory for any infractions to their expectations, however unrealistic. It was deeply unsettling.

"But look at the bright side," I offered. "You, Langley, and your mom have time for a girls' day before I make it up. And you won't have to worry about me drinking too much with your dad for another few days."

"A girls' day," Laila echoed, still facing the stove. "That's exactly what Langley needs. Great idea, David."

Things were getting difficult now. Laila had seen me coming out of the shower that morning, and her eyes went wide. My body bore the patchwork bruises, scrapes, and cuts of a long mission. I hastily explained that Jordan's

101st Special Battalion had their own obstacle course, and my cadre had to run it in full kit alongside the students. So, of course, I'd gone along with them.

I wondered how long this arrangement of lies could last. As long as the program continued running, I was going to be returning from a lot more "obstacle courses" with all the telltale signs.

But none of that mattered at present— today was July first, and in two days the US and Indian presidents would be arriving in Charlottesville.

"I'm doing the best I can," I said to Laila's backside, feeling like an idiot. "But I'm in charge of a team, and I can't just leave those guys hanging when work pops up."

She spun to face me. "Your team isn't your family, David. Me and Langley are."

"It'll get better," I said in a calm, clear voice. My eyes were level with hers, the composed and rational gaze of the dutiful husband doing what he must to support his family. The breadwinner, the hunter-gatherer sacrificing his personal interests for the sake of the whole.

It was all total bullshit, of course.

The truth was I wanted Laila and Langley as far from Charlottesville as they could fucking get. I didn't know exactly *what* would transpire on July third, but those six-hundred-plus rockets in BK's possession had some alarming statistics, starting with a maximum range of nearly three miles. Then there was the ten-meter blast radius, on top of a fifty-meter radius for lethal fragmentation. I'd be damned if I was going to risk an errant rocket smoking my family while they enjoyed the freedoms that the Western world had to offer.

There was another reason, too—a complication of my own design, though I hadn't thought that far ahead at the time.

In Syria, I'd demanded a protective detail shadow my family, and Duchess had delivered. Now, the agents rotating vehicles and surveillance points around my house represented not just an obstacle, but an obstacle who reported directly to the one woman who didn't need to know what was about to transpire. Or, put more properly, what was *already* transpiring.

I packed the car for Laila, then kissed her and Langley goodbye. After they pulled out of the driveway, I slipped inside the house and watched through the blinds as the surveillance vehicles drifted out of view, pursuing my family to their destination.

I let the blinds drop, then locked up my house and got in my truck. Backing out of the driveway, I turned onto the street and accelerated toward my destination.

39

Ian's computer chimed, and he looked over to the screen in time to catch the live footage of David's truck turning up the gravel driveway and proceeding toward the house.

Rising from his workstation, Ian moved to the front door and unlocked it before David had a chance to knock.

At first sight, his team leader looked frazzled, almost out of breath.

"Hey," David said, "what do you got?"

Ian nodded toward the back room. "Come on. I'll show you."

They walked through the ground floor of the rental house, David taking in the details for the first time. The rental property on the outskirts of town had been secured with a fake ID and paid for in cash. It also provided everything they needed: space to store their gear, bedrooms for team members rotating in and out, and most importantly, a place for Ian to set up his intelligence node.

That node occupied a corner bedroom that they entered now. And while it wasn't quite as posh as his work center in the ISOFAC, he'd done an admirable job of scraping together the furniture to support three computer screens with all the encrypted connectivity he'd need to do his work without Lady Liberty breathing down his neck.

"Have a seat," Ian said.

David dropped onto the bed as Ian slipped into his rolling chair, opening a satellite view of Charlottesville on a computer screen.

Before he could begin his brief, David asked, "Where is everyone?"

Ian tried to shield any annoyance from his voice as he replied, "They're doing exactly what you told them to."

After all, Ian wasn't confident that there was any purpose in canvassing Charlottesville by vehicle and on foot anyway. Bari Khan certainly hadn't done so in planning the attack—he would have been looking at maps and satellite imagery, just like Ian, and it was from that bird's-eye view that the attack plan would emerge.

In fact, Ian was relatively certain he'd already found it.

But David was an irrational, raging bull, so determined to uncover and stop the attack that there was little point in arguing with him. After all, it was his family whose names they'd found in Syria. If the roles were reversed for any other member, the team would be doing the same thing: taking every possible precaution, as much for their teammate's peace of mind as for any real tactical purpose.

Ian continued, "I've identified likely launch sites, and the guys are reconnoitering to confirm or rule them out. Worthy is on the north side of town, Cancer is toward the south, and Reilly—"

A radio handset came to life with Reilly's voice.

"*Angel, this is Doc.*"

"Speak of the devil," David said.

Ian picked up his mic. "Go ahead, Doc."

"*Confirm a high-risk site for the Water Street Parking Garage, four stories tall. He could conceal the cargo on the fourth floor and then transport it to the rooftop parking area for game time. Plenty of elevation to clear adjacent structures, and a two-mile straight-line shot to the target.*"

Ian made a mark on his clipboard checklist, then transmitted back, "Copy, proceed to your next priority at Tonsler Park."

"*I'll try to. It's just...these UVA girls, man. I don't know how I'm supposed to stay focused.*"

David snatched the mic from Ian. "You're going to stay focused because I'll pistol whip you if you don't. You can get laid on your own time—or don't, as seems to be your M.O."

Reilly was unfazed. "*I'm just saying, man...like, who invented yoga pants? Had to be a dude.* Had *to be*."

David tossed the mic on the desk, giving Ian an impatient nod.

"All right, so you've got a growing list of potential launch sites?"

Ian said, "Finding potential launch sites isn't a problem. The problem is finding spots that *couldn't* be used to launch the rockets, especially if he splits up the load. And we need to be extremely careful—you can't swing a dead cat in Charlottesville without hitting four plainclothes Secret Service agents from the advance element. Care to guess the odds of those guys having a sense of humor if they catch us rolling around with a truckful of assault rifles?"

"Then we don't get caught. You're the brain, so if you were Bari Khan, where would you set up to launch these rockets?"

Ian shook his head.

"I wouldn't."

"You wouldn't launch the rockets?"

"No," he said, looking up. "I wouldn't set up. BK has to suspect that we've figured out his target. Those rockets have a 2.79-mile max range—that's a long way, but not so far from Monticello that the Secret Service couldn't comb every inch of it long before Marine One touches down at Charlottesville Airport."

"That's smart. You think he's going to hit the president's helicopter when it lands?"

"I didn't say that. The air defense assets are going to be more concentrated around the airport than anywhere else, and BK knows that as well as I do. No, he's going to hit Monticello. It's the home of a founding father, a national landmark, and takes out the heads of state leading the world's two biggest democracies, one Christian and one Hindi, all in one shot. BK won't pass that up."

David frowned. "But you just said you wouldn't set up at all."

"That's right. To understand how he's going to do it, you have to understand that he's using rockets intended for an anti-tank recoilless rifle—that's basically a bazooka on a tripod. All he needs are the tubes to replicate that, an ignition system, and some trajectory math to put those rockets on target. Accuracy may be hit or miss, but when you've got over six hundred pointed at the same spot, you're going to kill what you're aiming at."

"And you think there's no way the Secret Service would miss that many rocket tubes."

"Right," Ian agreed. "No way he's going to risk concentrating those rockets and a launch assembly in a fixed location that could be observed from the air."

"Well, on with it, then. What's the answer?"

"He's going to shoot them from a truck."

"Ah." David nodded. "Modify the trailer for an eighteen-wheeler with the launch tubes facing out and a removable sidewall?"

"Yeah, something like that." Ian moved his finger to the computer screen and traced the line of a road. "You've got Interstate 64 running east to west here. The Secret Service isn't going to shut it down for the entire duration of the visit, and they're certainly not going to be able to screen every car that passes through. Based on road curvature, that gives BK a 7.27-mile stretch to fire the rockets from and still hit Monticello. If he's firing from the center of that stretch, they'll only need to fly half a mile or so—that's less than twenty percent of their max range, and based on how precise his planning was, I'd guess he'll have no issue putting three-quarters of his payload on target. Maybe more."

David visibly relaxed. "Ian, you're a genius. How do we stop it?"

"If I'm right about this," he replied, "we don't. It's going to take the Secret Service."

40

Through his binoculars, Gary Conrad scanned the water for any sign of the buoy.

He'd powered down the boat almost completely, proceeding with minimum forward throttle as he searched the Atlantic surface for anything out of place.

Beyond the cabin window, he saw his men scattered across the deck below, already exhausted from the day's work aboard the *Amelia* and still with a long way to go before they could shack up for the night. Some twelve years ago, Gary had been one of those poor bastards down on the deck, sweating and hauling up all the dead and dying contents of his nets. It was filthy, tiring work, the smell of fish permeating everything from your clothes down to your very skin.

After eight years of working his Irish ass off, though, Gary had become a first mate, and within another two years he'd saved enough to buy his own boat, naming her after his wife at the time.

Now he was captain, responsible for everything from outfitting the ship and hiring the crew to plotting the course and selling the catch. Having started from nothing, he provided a good life for his family, with young fishermen competing for his attention in the hopes they could join his crew.

But he still couldn't see the damn buoy.

Occasionally they were visible as plain orange and white buoys bobbing in the waves. But the really good ones were concealed as something else entirely—a piece of trash, a small rescue float that appeared to have fallen off a passing ship.

And when he finally located it, he realized this one was the best he'd seen yet.

It was a simple piece of driftwood, measuring perhaps three feet in length. There was no outward indication that it contained a location transmitter system, which had been broadcasting to the *Amelia* on a designated frequency.

He maneuvered the boat so its side roller and power winch were positioned over the buoy, watching his men scramble across the deck in their orange bib pants, preparing to hook the line and begin the retrieval process.

Normally the cargo was recovered at the beginning of a fishing trip—usually around the first quarter of the moon cycle, when the tuna and swordfish were out. They'd throw the recovered items far forward in the hold, and pack it with ice and then fish—no Coast Guard inspection ever unpacked twenty tons of ice to look at everything.

Once the ship returned to shore, it was easy enough to get the cargo where it needed to go. The fish house trucks were fully refrigerated, chock full of fish and ice, and went all over the country. The best sushi-grade tuna came from the East Coast, after all, and the trucks made their way to every state in the continental US.

The late notification of this load presented a pain in the ass to his crew—they'd already unpacked tons of ice and fish to clear room far forward in the hold, where the inspectors never searched—and once the cargo was safely stashed away, they'd have to repack it all.

But his crew's objections had faded to nothing when he told them what they'd be getting paid for this load.

They'd not only be well compensated for the inconvenience, but virtually problem-free for the rest of their lives. This haul alone was the mortgage, the new car, the kid's college fund, the alimony, and plenty to spare.

It wasn't until he caught his first glimpse of the cargo that Gary became uneasy.

He'd been expecting to see the usual haul—marine bags filled with shrink-wrapped packages. All the coke you cared to snort, he imagined, though he never looked inside. The people responsible for these transfers liked to install anti-tamper measures, and if one of those was found broken, it was his ass on the line to explain it. At worst he'd be killed and at best denied any further gravy, which was just as bad.

Having seen his father wither away to nothing after a forty-year fishing career that accomplished little more than advancing his family a half-rung above the poverty line, Gary had no intention of following in those footsteps. When he'd earned enough experience to join the word-of-mouth referral network to get "extra work," Gary leapt at the chance.

But the huge objects being pulled out of the water weren't marine bags—they were blue marlin.

The cargo must have been packed in the belly, against the fish's spine. He'd seen that kind of thing before with swordfish, but never marlin, and certainly not for a load of this size. How long had those people been catching and refrigerating marlin?

Then there was the obvious problem of sharks destroying the load.

Whoever had made the drop circumvented this the same way he'd seen with swordfish—by sealing the animals in huge plastic bags, trapping the smell of dead fish as they floated beneath the buoy, weighted by the contents of whatever illicit cargo they harbored.

But they'd taken an additional precaution as well, one Gary had never seen.

He watched his men pull a large yellow cylinder out of the water and examine the black wires extending from it.

"*Hey, Cap,*" one of his men called over the radio, as another held the object up toward Gary, "*what's this?*"

He transmitted back, "Lithium net. Puts out an electric field that keeps the sharks away."

"*Got it. There's four of them daisy-chained around the load.*"

He'd seen those devices used by dive boats but never employed to safeguard a load. It was a smart enough idea, he supposed. These people had to have deep pockets anyway—that much was evident by the fish.

Gary wasn't sure why the sight of marlin bothered him. He supposed it was their size—a full-grown swordfish was a sight to behold, but nothing compared to an adult female marlin. Their cobalt blue sides were visible even through the opaque plastic sheeting around them, with more than a few thousand-pounders in the lot. These were trophy-sized fish with the storage capacity to match, and given the number of them being hauled up, Gary estimated he was about to be sitting on tens of millions' worth of cocaine. Maybe even a hundred million or more.

Jesus, he thought, he'd smuggled drugs before but never anything of this magnitude. As soon as he made it to shore, his employers would be watching his every move from afar, making sure the marlin were loaded on the right truck. He hesitated to think what would become of him if there were any complications in the transfer.

Gary was startled by a man entering the cabin behind him—Jack Bowen, his first mate.

"Cap, I think we got a problem."

"Oh?"

Jack nodded. "It's the new kid you hired—Robbie. He's getting spooked by the size of the load, says this wasn't what he signed up for."

"You think he's a snitch?"

Jack shrugged. "If you have to ask, then he's a snitch."

"Goddammit." Gary sighed. Robbie had seemed like a sharp kid, likeable from the first and a good personality match for the crew.

But sometimes you didn't see a man's real character until you saw him at sea.

"All right," he said after a moment's hesitation. "We gotta do it, I suppose."

"Man overboard?"

Gary nodded. "We'll call it in at sunrise tomorrow. He went out for watch eight hours ago while we were asleep, and we called the Coast Guard as soon as he was unaccounted for."

"What about the investigation? They'll have to come out on the ship."

"If they're filling out reports for a man overboard, they're not looking at our fish." He glanced over at Jack. "You need me to take care of it?"

"No, Cap, I'll do it."

"Good man. This kind of thing can be hard on a crew, so make sure everyone knows: Robbie's share gets divided equally."

"Sure thing." Jack turned to leave, and Gary called out to stop him.

"You still got those four shark deterrent cylinders?"

"We do, Cap. We were going to throw them back in once the load is recovered."

"Throw in Robbie instead. Toss some chum over the side to make sure there's nothing left. I want it done before we leave—no sense in risking his remains near the search area. We'll get rid of the shark cylinders later."

41

I walked down the sidewalk amid light morning foot traffic, mentally reviewing the day ahead. I'd detected some unspoken pushback from Ian—he seemed to be patronizing my attempt to influence the events of tomorrow's presidential visit, as if there were nothing we could do—but in all honesty, my theory was pretty simple. If local and national assets were able to successfully deal with the threat, then what was the harm in having my team mobilized to respond? None whatsoever. Just a little extra-legal planning for a rainy day that never arrived.

But if the threat went unchecked, if Ian was able to find some detail that everyone else missed—well, then the value of having our team ready to go was immeasurable.

I needed to get the lay of the land myself, to see Charlottesville and the surrounding area not through the lens of a happy hometown but as a tactical objective. I didn't doubt Ian's theory of a mobile rocket attack from I-64—but in the meantime, I wanted to put eyes on the main possible launch sites identified by my team. If we did have to raid one of those locations, there may be only minutes to come up with a hasty plan. I needed to see every possible location for myself.

And before that happened, I desperately needed one thing: coffee.

I pulled open the door to the coffeeshop, then entered the back of the line and checked my watch. I only had four minutes before Worthy was supposed to pick me up, serving as driver so I could take notes on the best assault options for each location.

Reaching the counter, I was in the process of ordering a large black coffee when I heard a woman speak behind me.

"Buy you a drink?"

My stomach lurched into my throat before I'd consciously registered why. The voice was polite, a little too firm, and far too familiar.

Turning around, I saw Duchess.

I flashed her a smile. "Why Duchess, I didn't know you were in town. What a delightful surprise."

She ordered tea for herself, paying the bill as I shot Worthy a text with the word *ABORT*. Then I glanced over my shoulder to try and spot him without alerting Duchess. She was far too cunning to buy into the notion of a social call, and there would be severe consequences if she learned what we were up to.

But I didn't see him among the passersby outside, and so I quickly followed Duchess to a table with two seats. Only one chair faced the glass storefront, and I desperately needed it—if Worthy came strolling up to the door, as he would at any second, I was in a world of hurt.

Duchess made the first move for the chair facing the door.

I tried to cut her off.

"That's my seat."

She turned and said, "Really, David? Are you trying to play the rule that the PTSD-ridden veteran always gets the seat with a view of the door?"

"I wrote that rule, and yes. Or you could talk to the back of my head as I sit there and stare at it from the wrong side of the table. Your choice."

She conceded after a brief pause, moving to the opposite side of the table and not a moment too soon.

As soon as she turned to face me, I saw Worthy appear through the storefront glass. I shot him a momentary head jerk—*get out of here*—and then pulled my chair back as Duchess turned to look through the window.

To his credit, Worthy's gunfighter reaction speed must have applied to ducking out of sight as well—he was gone, the flow of pedestrians proceeding without interruption.

"You were saying?" I asked, taking a seat.

Duchess did the same, eyeing me with thinly veiled suspicion.

She said, "The security detail told me you didn't accompany your family to Alexandria."

"So?"

"So as concerned as you are for their safety, I'm curious why that would be."

"Look, Duchess. I'm glad you're confident in your theory about the hospital being a secondary target. But I've got enough skeletons in my closet to fill that hospital to capacity, and until I'm certain there's no personal vendetta against me, I want to be as far from my family as humanly possible."

"That's not true."

"It's not?"

"If you wanted to be farther from them, you could head west. You didn't. You chose to stay right here in Charlottesville. Why?"

I took a sip of scalding coffee. "The weather this time of year suits me. Now, to what do I owe the honor of your presence? I trust that the terrorist attack you identified was the president's upcoming visit to Monticello."

"It's not your concern."

"Really, Duchess? You're trying to tell me that I don't deserve any updates after all the shit my team went through in Syria?"

"No," Duchess said flatly. "For that, you deserve a debt of gratitude."

I relaxed. "Well, thank you."

"That's why I take no pleasure in delivering this news, David."

"What news? Did BK make it into the country?"

"The news that your team is officially disbanded."

I felt a lump forming in my throat then, a stomach-churning sense of betrayal that robbed me of the ability to speak for five long seconds.

Finally I managed, "You're honestly telling me you think we're unfit to continue operating?"

"I think you're perfectly capable," she said, "but it wasn't my decision."

"Then whose was it?"

She closed her eyes for a moment before opening them and replying, "Someone who outranks us both by several orders of merit."

"You have to fight this, Duchess. You have to get us reinstated."

"I can't," she said, "because I've been given my notice as well. The only reason I'm still heading the project is because no one wants to disrupt continuity of staff leadership until the cargo is located. After that, you can bet the bank I'll be reassigned to the mailroom and forced into retirement. Not exactly what I've been working for all these years."

"For what, finding the cargo in the first place and then doing everything in your power to stop it?"

"We were both forced by circumstance to color outside the lines to do what we had to do. There are political consequences for that, whether deserved or not."

"How long have you known about my team being disbanded?"

"Since you snatched the logistician. What happened to him, anyway?"

"You wouldn't believe me if I told you."

"Try me," she said firmly.

I rubbed a hand across the back of my neck. "Unbeknownst to me at the time, one of our local guides had his family killed by ISIS. He had a hidden pistol and blew away the logistician when he found out we were trying to take him alive. Okay?"

"Okay," Duchess said. "I believe you, David."

"Did you recover any other intel from the command post, or locate the cargo yet? Or find a lead on Bari Khan?"

She said nothing, and I gave her a knowing nod.

"Well there's my answer," I said, understanding from her tense silence that they hadn't made much if any progress. "And since we're both coming clean, shoot me straight: the target you're anticipating is Monticello during the president's visit tomorrow. Right or wrong?"

"You didn't need to know that when you were under Agency employment. What makes you think that's changed now that you're not?"

"Because my wife and daughter were mentioned by name, that's why. If that weren't the case, I'd be drinking bourbon with this coffee. But I can't exactly relax when I still don't know how their names ended up in Syria."

"Speaking off the record," she began, taking a moment to examine her cup, "the last update I provided you on this situation remains the current assessment. Furthermore, I feel compelled to remind you that your team had no authorities to operate in the US, even in the capacity of collecting passive intelligence. Now that you're disbanded, that holds doubly true."

"I know that."

"And the consequences for any infraction will result in imprisonment. I'm not talking about a minimum-security camp, David. Due to the nature of your former employment, you and your men would proceed directly to Supermax or a black site following a closed trial."

Waving a hand around the room, I asked, "Do you see my team anywhere? Am I running around with a knife between my teeth, looking for BK? Does anything in our past indicate that I'd be eager to leave my family behind? I was getting a cup of coffee. Besides," I added, "if there's anything I could possibly contribute to all the federal agencies working to stop this plan, I'm all ears."

Duchess's face abruptly went slack, her eyes wide and fixed on mine. I'd seen her pull this move before, and it never got more comfortable to watch.

I took another sip of coffee and set my cup between us. "Look, can you stop doing your human lie detector scan-for-signs-of-deception thing? It's creepy. Your face looks creepy. Just talk to me like a human being."

She relaxed a bit then, and I continued, "Why doesn't the president just cancel the visit? Just cancel the stupid visit."

"Well unfortunately I wasn't consulted, and someone significantly higher in the food chain hasn't had any better luck despite his best efforts. But honestly, it may be a good thing this visit is still on."

"Yeah? How's that?"

"If they cancel the president's trip, BK could turn those rockets on any densely populated civilian area in the country. None of them except DC and Charlottesville have the advantage of Secret Service oversight. Where the president goes, his security follows...so an attempted attack here is the best chance of stopping BK and his rockets."

"That's one kind of logic, I suppose." Then I assumed a thoughtful expression. "You know, I was thinking about how BK would pull this off."

"Oh? And what did you conclude?"

I shrugged nonchalantly, eager to claim Ian's theory as my own. He wouldn't mind, I thought, and precious rare were the opportunities to outfox Duchess. "I'm no intel guy or anything. But it seems to me that the smart play would be to set up a mobile launch system in the back of a semi-trailer. Drive to a pre-planned spot on I-64, drop the side of the trailer, and launch it all in one volley."

"That's a good theory."

"What can I say, every once in a while even a knuckle-dragger comes up with something smart."

"Well, in this case the 'something smart' occurred to the Secret Service long ago. Precautions are being taken."

"Precautions as in special sensors, air defense capability, or an interstate shut-down?"

"Precautions," she said, "as in, you don't need to know."

Her comment should have upset me, but it didn't—instead, I was met with a long-overdue realization.

For some reason, it took until that exact moment in the conversation for me to register the obvious: my team had our Agency-issued weapons and equipment on hand, and the second Duchess discovered they were missing from the ISOFAC, we may as well drive ourselves to the nearest police station and wait for the proverbial black helicopters to come and take us away.

"Are you okay?" she asked.

"Yeah," I said, "I guess this whole being fired thing is just starting to sink in."

Her expression fell from stern to sympathetic, and I added, "Wife will be happy about it, at least." Waiting a beat for good measure, I continued, "I suppose I'll just head down to collect my team's personal effects from the ISOFAC."

"The codes were changed the second your team left," she swiftly replied. "I'll have the cleanout team inventory all personal effects and forward them to your men."

A balloon of panic rose from my stomach.

But I nodded amicably, knowing full well that to do otherwise would be to cause that cleanout team to arrive sooner rather than later. Duchess had her hands full at present; she'd outright admitted that she was only in command of Project Longwing because the rockets hadn't yet been located, and I expected her administrative duties—with transitioning the ISOFAC to its next occupants chief among them—would proceed immediately after July third came and went, with or without a terrorist attack to show for it.

Now we were fugitives whether the Agency realized it or not, and I'd placed my team yet again in danger, albeit of a very different sort.

So I merely thanked her, adding for good measure, "I appreciate you coming down to tell me in person, Duchess. That means a lot."

She smiled at that—or was it a sneer?

"You don't have to thank me, David." Her face went slack again as she continued with an edge in her tone, "It was the least I could do."

42

Ross Sidor accelerated his Subaru WRX up the fast lane of I-95, scanning for speed traps in the trees to his left.

Looking forward, he saw a minivan abruptly change lanes in front of him, and slammed on his brakes to avoid hitting it.

From the passenger seat, Stephanie said, "Jesus, babe, watch out."

Ross said nothing, directing his energies instead to trying not to explode into a screaming fit of profanity at the minivan driver who trundled along, completely oblivious to the outside world.

That driver had suddenly changed lanes in an attempt to overtake a semi; but upon blocking the fast lane to all progress by sentient drivers with an eye for punctuality, he or she had since forgotten to accelerate.

Now both lanes were blocked; and Ross was in ever-increasing danger of failing to deliver Stephanie to her wedding rehearsal on time.

Of course, it was technically his rehearsal, too. But the entire wedding process, he'd learned, really had nothing to do with the groom. Aside from offering a few trite opinions on the decorations, attire, and reception menu options, his role was largely relegated to showing up.

And, of course, getting them both to the church in time for the rehearsal.

That minor detail was currently his chief concern. Having been unable to knock off work completely, he'd been relegated to packing the car in advance, then squeezing out as soon as he could to set out northward to Stephanie's hometown.

Now he was barreling up I-95, fighting his way through traffic to reach Northside Church in time for their latest possible rehearsal slot at five.

With the obstinate minivan driver refusing to apply a few pounds of pressure to the gas pedal, Ross whipped into the slow lane and tailgated the truck instead. He hoped the semi driver would take mercy on him, accelerate by just a few miles an hour to create a gap big enough for him to exploit, but the big truck ambled along on cruise control that, by Ross's estimation, appeared to be set exactly at the speed limit.

He tailed the minivan again, then the semi, mentally pleading with either or both of them to hurry the hell up and let him pass.

Finally the minivan edged forward, Ross trailing a half car length off the rear bumper and finally creeping up the side of the semi-trailer to see the logo of Blackwood Seafood Company. Looking over to shoot an angry glance at the trucker, he saw a rotund Chinese man with a beard. The driver didn't look back, keeping his emotionless eyes forward.

"No wonder he was so slow," Ross said. "He's DWA—Driving While Asian."

"Ross, stop it."

"What? I'm not saying they're terrible people. Just terrible drivers."

The minivan finally—*finally*—engaged its turn signal, and then began a ten-second lane change back onto the right side of the road where it belonged.

Ross floored the gas, roaring past the pair of sloths and letting out a whoop of victory as he flew by a large sign with a red heart that read, *WELCOME TO VIRGINIA.*

43

The crowd around Worthy began cheering at the first sound of the aircraft approaching the Charlottesville airport. He caught a glimpse of them seconds later, flying low over the horizon on their final approach.

The helicopters were unmistakable: a pair of Sikorsky VH-3D Sea Kings, their bodies olive drab and bearing the Seal of the President of the United States beneath gleaming white upper surfaces marked by the American flag. Whichever one held the president—and Worthy had no idea—flew under the callsign of Marine One.

The two helicopters thundered over the tarmac as three trailing aircraft swept into view. These were MV-22 Ospreys, whose tilt rotor assemblies gave them the appearance of an insect-like mashup between a cargo aircraft and helicopter. The Ospreys carried White House staff and an additional contingent of Secret Service agents, descending to land in sequence only after the two Sea King helicopters had touched down and begun taxiing behind the main terminal building, out of Worthy's view.

He pulled out a phone and texted the designated brevity code, *see you soon*. Even though Ian had performed some cyber-wizardry to prevent Duchess from tracking their personal phones, today they relied on a network of prepaid cellular devices complete with brevity codes for fear of some classified Secret Service capability intercepting their communications and finding them suspicious.

Yesterday, David had informed the team of his meeting with Duchess. To his credit, he said that once the Agency realized their weapons and equipment were missing, David would assume all responsibility, claiming he lied to his team and said he was under orders from Duchess herself—as if she'd believe that. Still, it was a noble effort on his part to manage a situation that had spiraled out of control. Whatever the fallout, the ISOFAC was cleaned out and they were a day if not mere hours away from being caught in the act of usurping not just their previous authorities but the legal sanctions governing all US citizens.

But until they were busted for sure, David's plan was to have the team strung out along the president's route, so that even if a response wasn't required, they could at the very least be informed in real-time.

At his overwatch position outside the Charlottesville Albemarle Airport, standing amid throngs of civilians lined up for the spectacle currently unfolding, Worthy was the first of his team with eyes on the presidential motorcade.

And when he caught his first glimpses of it, he felt a keen sense of humility.

Before his assignment to the team, Worthy had been a bodyguard to unarguably the most feared and respected leader of any criminal syndicate. He'd been selected for his competitive shooting abilities, having none of the public relations considerations of the suited Secret Service agents that the public observed on a regular basis. Instead he'd openly worn a highly modified competition pistol with a barrel extension, reflex sight, and extended magazine that would allow him to react to any close-range threat with lethal precision.

But even he was merely the central cog in many concentric rings of security around his primary—and even that sum collective protection paled before what he saw now.

The first vehicles to pass him were a mix of Virginia State Police and Charlottesville PD cruisers, a melee of patrol cars, SUVs, and motorcycles that ripped past with their lights blazing. Some would remain ahead of the convoy while others were designated to block intersections, and it wasn't until a dozen vehicles had passed that he caught his glimpse of the real convoy.

The first jet black Suburban to pass him was known as the Route Car, the vehicular equivalent of a point man for the president's convoy. It was trailed by an identical SUV called the Pilot Car, flanked on all sides by state police motorcycles.

Then came the Sweepers, a half-dozen police cars serving as a protective buffer before the lead car, a Secret Service Suburban that preceded the presidential limo. Or, to put it more properly, one of *three* presidential limos.

They were indistinguishable from one another down to the license plates, a trio of hulking black limousines whose front headlights were crested with the American flag on one side and the presidential flag on the other. While they looked big enough to transport a large group of people, Worthy knew that the rear seating was virtually shoulder-to-shoulder beneath the extensive armor and internal oxygen supply that would protect the occupants from any conceivable attack.

Though who those occupants were was a mystery to anyone outside the convoy.

While the limo carrying the president was designated Stagecoach, the other two were merely Spares, implemented to conceal the president's location as they swapped positions in a fluid choreography. In the event of a ground attack, the two Spares would serve as blocking forces or outright battering rams to pummel the Stagecoach away from the threat.

The limos were trailed by two more Suburbans, their purposes distinguishable to Worthy at a glance.

First was the Halfback, carrying a heavily armed contingent of Secret Service agents with body armor and assault rifles. The tailgate was open, revealing a rear-facing third row with shooters facing out.

The second was called Watchtower, its roof and rear bumper bristling with antennas. This was the electronic countermeasures vehicle, capable of jamming electronic explosive devices. If Bari Khan tried to employ the rockets against the convoy, the Watchtower truck would detect the incoming projectiles and deploy flares and chaff upward in an attempt to cause early detonation.

Then came the Support Vehicle with the president's key staff, and the Control Vehicle carrying the top military aide with his "football," a forty-five-pound briefcase whose contents allowed the president to authorize retaliatory options ranging from a single cruise missile to a full nuclear strike.

Behind the Support Vehicle was the CAT, a counter assault team whose shooters filled two Suburbans. The men inside were the closest approximation to Worthy's team, outfitted in body armor and with enough weaponry to maneuver on heavily armed enemy forces if required. They were trailed by the Intelligence Division Vehicle, where people like Ian were hurriedly compiling real-time reports from local and national intelligence assets to determine if any changes to the convoy's route were required, or if an immediate evacuation was in order.

And the show wasn't over yet: a giant quad-cab pickup with a covered trailer served as the Hazard Materials Mitigation Unit, capable of detecting and responding to chemical, nuclear, and biological attack.

The final elements of the convoy included vans transporting the White House Press Corps and reporters from national news outlets, and a mobile command and control vehicle known as Roadrunner that kept the communications relays to the White House running securely. Behind it was the president's personal ambulance, and finally a bevy of marked and unmarked police vehicles serving as the Rear Guard.

Impressive as the convoy was, Worthy knew it was merely one of more than a dozen that forward deployed ahead of the president, who, during campaign season, could require them in two or three cities in a single day.

The convoy threaded its way along Towncenter Drive toward US-29 South, its immediate defenses just one of many elements put into place ahead of the president's travel. Worthy could still see sniper and spotter teams atop the terminal building, their rifles out of sight as they scanned the crowd with binoculars. And it didn't take a tactical genius to spot the plainclothes officers and agents in the crowd around him, to say nothing of those circulating around Charlottesville during the team's reconnaissance efforts over the past few days. He didn't know the full extent of protective assets staged along the convoy route and around Monticello itself, though he could reasonably suspect the number of men and women involved numbered in the hundreds.

Worthy just hoped that today, it would be enough to protect the President of the United States.

44

Reilly's position in the outdoor seating area of C'ville Burger & Brew afforded him a complete, if somewhat noisy, view of US-29 as it merged with US-250 and circled around the west side of Charlottesville.

He'd spread out his meal as long as he could to occupy the table, starting with a twin round of appetizers before putting in the order for a medium-rare burger with all the toppings that the restaurant had to offer—bacon, fried egg, and jalapenos for starters. For Reilly, this wasn't exactly a hardship duty. His physical size required a lot of calories to maintain, and he had a ravenous appetite. There was little that even an American menu could throw at him that wouldn't be quickly suppressed by the energy expenditure of his workouts, and that held doubly true as he faced the imminent prospect of lifelong incarceration with food that would be far worse than what he could buy in Charlottesville. Matter of fact, he hoped to have time for a quick dessert before relocating to his next position to survey the presidential convoy's return to the airport—that was, if the convoy made it that far.

The traffic noise beside him abated considerably in one fell swoop, the stream of vehicles in the southbound lanes trailing off to nothing as temporary roadblocks took effect. This was followed by the excited chatter of his fellow diners as the motorcade appeared, its arrival heralded by a fleet of police vehicles with their red and blue light bars flashing.

Reilly texted his brevity code to the team—*on my way*—and then waited for something further to report.

But the long row of sleek black vehicles surrounding a trio of presidential limousines continued past him unhindered. There was no drama, no thunderclap of rockets from the sky, nothing but the sun and sky and civilians around him enjoying their lunch.

Reilly looked up as his waitress reappeared, setting his burger down in front of him.

"Thanks," he said. "Name's Reilly, by the way."

She smiled politely, muttered some blithe response, and walked away.

Shrugging indifferently, Reilly turned his attention to his plate.

Then he lifted his burger in both hands, gave a sigh of delirious pleasure, and took the first bite.

45

Jo Ann sat beside Duchess in the OPCEN, watching the president's address at Monticello as it unfolded live on CNN.

The OPCEN was down to a skeleton crew. With no mission in progress, their role was to monitor the situation in Charlottesville and serve as an additional conduit to the Intelligence Division Vehicle in the presidential motorcade, supplying any real-time data regarding Bari Khan's plans as that information became available through a network of overseas sources.

Which, of course, hadn't occurred.

There had been no further intelligence on the location of the rockets or Bari Khan's whereabouts. Duchess had expended virtually all her remaining credibility on raiding a Chinese billionaire's yacht, which at the time represented the highest possibility of affiliation with the Uyghur separatist who'd taken control of the rockets in Syria.

And this lack of progress seemed to be reflected in Duchess's posture; she was currently seated beside Jo Ann with arms folded, watching the screen as if it were a funeral procession.

What she had to sulk about, Jo Ann wasn't sure—Duchess had somehow pulled her career out of the ashes, having been granted an extension from Gossweiler under the condition that she find the rockets at all costs. And rather than relish that fact, Duchess appeared upset that the Charlottesville visit had proceeded against her best advice.

Jo Ann asked, "Are you pissed because the president didn't cancel this visit?"

"One hundred percent. You?"

"Not really," Jo Ann admitted. She knew this wasn't what Duchess wanted to hear, but it was the truth. "There is no indication that the rockets have made it stateside. For all we know, Bari Khan could be hunkered in a safehouse, waiting for the arrival of his cargo."

Duchess countered, "But those rockets are a lethal threat. One that exceeds even the Secret Service's capabilities to stop them. There's not an air defense network in America outside of DC that could shoot them all out of the sky at once. And just one of those rockets could take out a tank. That's what they were designed to do, and that's why we supplied them to the Syrian resistance fighters. Can you imagine the effects of *hundreds* of them impacting within our shores?"

"But it's still a hypothetical. If we had some concrete intelligence that the attack was proceeding on time after everything that happened in Syria, I could see altering the presidential schedule."

As if in vindication of her statement, the president concluded his address, pausing beside the Indian president for a final photo op before both men stepped out of the room in Monticello to the flickering lights of journalist cameras. He was now leaving, without the slightest whiff of a terrorist attack against him. For a moment Jo Ann felt proud of herself; no matter the dark realities of her job, she refused to lapse into the void of cynicism and despair that seemed to overcome Duchess and, to an extent, many of the old hands on the Agency team. Some of them showed up to work with the grim determination of factory workers, seeming not to relish their job but resent it.

Duchess said, "Looks like you were right, anyway. No terrorist attack, not even an attempt. Congratulations, Jo Ann. Who knows, maybe we're one step away from being shut down no matter what happens."

"Would that be so bad?"

Her counterpart seemed thrown off guard by that comment.

"You sound like you're questioning the efficacy of this program," she replied incredulously.

"By this point in time, aren't you?"

"It doesn't matter what I think," Duchess replied. "You'll probably be around long after Gossweiler throws me to the wolves. What are your thoughts?"

Jo Ann swallowed, considering her words. "I think this program is indicative of the fundamental miscalculation in how we as a nation use our military. We don't send enough troops when they're needed, and then we send too many once the situation has already spiraled out of control."

"Case in point?"

Jo Ann looked like she'd been slapped.

"How about bin Laden?" she replied. "We had *so* many chances to put a bullet in his head immediately after 9/11. He spent a month in a Kandahar safe house, then another month in Kabul before making any attempt to flee the country. Another two months near the border being hunted by a literal handful of Delta operators and CIA officers, the leader of which requested a few *hundred* Rangers—who were located a few hours away in Bagram, mind you—to block off the mountain passes in Tora Bora."

Duchess smiled. "Gary. Hell of a good officer."

"And he was refused because the Bush Administration believed that the Pakistanis would turn over bin Laden if he made it across the border. So bin Laden walks into Pakistan uncontested, where he had safe haven for the next decade while we deployed close to a *million* troops to the desert for an endless counterinsurgency."

"And you're concerned that we're seeing the new Tora Bora?"

"I'm concerned that Longwing is an extension of the mentality that fetishizes the surgical application of force when more assets would accomplish twice as much in half the time. Look at what happened with Bari Khan—he escaped because we're using a five-man team with minimal local assistance. It's not enough."

"Jo Ann, I have to say I disagree with you completely."

"Not for the first time," she replied, throwing her hands up. "But I haven't stated anything that isn't a known fact."

"I'm not questioning your facts, I'm questioning your logic. The time to put a 'bullet in his head,' as you so eloquently put it, wasn't after 9/11. It came and went long before then."

"If we're speaking with the benefit of hindsight, sure."

"How much hindsight do you need? We could have snatched him in the '98 Tarnak Farms raid, which we rehearsed for months before the Agency leadership lost their nerve to seek presidential approval. Three months later, bin Laden bombed our embassies in Kenya and Tanzania and killed a couple hundred people."

"There was a cruise missile strike after that," Jo Ann pointed out.

Duchess nodded. "A strike that missed him by a few hours, which brings us to spring of '99, when bin Laden was at Sheikh Ali hunting camp in Afghanistan. That strike was scrapped due to diplomatic considerations about the presence of Emirati nationals—who, mind you, were his personal friends if not financiers. Three months later, he was stationary in Kandahar for five days and no one was willing to launch cruise missiles despite arguably the best intelligence to date. So he bombs the USS *Cole* in 2000 and kills another seventeen people. CENTCOM then presented *thirteen* options for phased bombing campaigns against bin Laden and his organization, all of which went unused.

"All the while, the Administration waffled back and forth over whether it was permissible to kill him if a capture wasn't possible, there were miscommunications between the Administration and the Agency, later redactions of clear kill authority in the memorandum wording, and opportunities slipping through our nation's fingers like so many grains of sand."

Jo Ann replied, "You seem to be advocating a blanket approval policy regardless of the fidelity in intelligence. I can list a few regimes that have done the same, and none of them represent what I think America should become."

"You're missing my point, and I'm not finished."

Jo Ann fought the impulse to roll her eyes. "I thought you were about to run out of breath. There's more?"

"There is. I haven't mentioned the December '98 rocket strike refused by Clinton on the grounds of a prospective three *hundred* civilian casualties —a decision he later praised himself for in a speech less than twenty-four hours before the 9/11 attacks commenced and killed nearly three *thousand*

Americans. And let's not forget the CIA officers operating in Sudan in '92, who watched bin Laden every day and had a plan to assassinate him that made it all the way to the director before being shut down."

Spinning her chair to face Jo Ann, Duchess continued, "It doesn't matter who pulls the trigger, so long as it gets pulled. There's no shortage of people willing to go into harm's way, regardless of what uniform they wear —or don't wear, as the case may be. The real lynchpin is political approval; we've got that for the time being, and for once it's in alignment with our nation's capabilities. But this represents a precious and fleeting opportunity. Longwing is still a burning coal; far from the fire it needs to be. Those five men you consider insignificant represent the future of stopping not catastrophic attacks, but the junior terrorists before they become masterminds capable of planning them. And it's up to us to prove the efficacy of this concept by writing a playbook that *works*. You thought that I only cared about my career when I authorized the final raid in Syria. But this program is my real concern, regardless of whether it's me running it or not."

Jo Ann replied in a challenging tone, "How noble of you."

"It doesn't matter if it's noble, only if it's necessary. In a way it's not even about the attacks we can prevent—those are just the beginning."

"The beginning of what?"

Duchess closed her eyes and drew a breath.

"Three thousand died on 9/11. But since then, there have been over seven thousand US military deaths in Afghanistan and Iraq alone. Civilian casualties abroad are in the six-figure range by the most optimistic estimates. Some say that number is a million or more."

"I'm aware of the statistics."

"Then be aware that what this program is designed to stop isn't just terrorists; it's the war, or *wars*, that would very likely follow an attack of that magnitude."

She leaned back in her seat. "And don't ever underestimate our enemies. There is no limit to what a smart, determined terrorist can accomplish. Make no mistake, Jo Ann: until those rockets—and Bari Khan himself—are found, we are living each moment on the razor's edge."

46

Cancer threaded his way through the crowd at the airport, having followed the convoy back to its point of origin.

And he was severely pissed.

There was some silver lining to the situation—the leader of the free world had survived what the team had suspected was an imminent rocket attack, after all—but that was about the only happy consequence at present. Sure, he supposed there was technically a chance that BK would hit the president now that he'd returned to the airport, but Cancer knew in his gut that wouldn't be the case. If Bari Khan had the ability to point 633 rockets at the tarmac, he damn sure wasn't going to give the Secret Service an extra few hours to locate them by waiting until his target was on his way back out of the state. He would've let the president land, stroll from the helicopter toward his armored limo, and let 'em rip.

And beyond that, there was nothing for Cancer to react to, shoot, be of good use in furthering as he slipped back into the banal Western existence that was completely devoid of adrenaline or conflict of any kind. Even that existence, he thought, was soon going to be reduced to the confines of a prison cell after Duchess realized what they'd done.

After all the preparations, the speculation as to what Bari Khan would do or how, the team was back to square one: fully aware that their terrorist was in the wind along with the rockets, and nothing to do about it.

Finding a vantage point overlooking the tarmac, he plucked his trusty pack of Marlboros from his pocket with a mournful shake of his head, withdrawing a fresh cancer stick and expertly lighting it with the first spark of his lighter.

Then he watched the president depart his limo and stride across the tarmac with a Secret Service agent moving one pace to his front right. They approached Marine One's waiting stairs, the helicopter's twin engines spooled up for the flight ahead. The president crossed in front of a Secret Service agent standing with his hands folded, facing the motorcade. Then his escorting agent peeled off, and the president approached the helicopter alone, the lowered front stairs flanked by a pair of saluting Marines in full dress uniform. Returning the salute without breaking stride, the president mounted the stairs, and disappeared inside the helicopter.

A somber procession of seven men trailed him, four carrying large briefcases as they moved up the aircraft's rear set of stairs. Only then did the president's original escorting agent trot up the front steps, followed by one of the Marines who pulled up the steps behind him as the other fired off a crisp salute to the aircraft, turned an about-face, and marched away.

Cancer knew what was occurring outside of the camera's purview: the remainder of the president's top staff, along with a considerable Secret Service escort, had already boarded the trailing helicopter and trio of Osprey aircraft, unaccompanied by the ceremonial Marines who greeted the president upon his arrival.

By then Marine One was already taxiing down the tarmac, trailed by the four aircraft.

Cancer took another drag of his cigarette and muttered to himself, "Well, shit."

47

I stepped through my front door, slamming it shut and locking it behind me. Entering a code onto the keypad, I silenced the repetitive beeping of my security system and whirled toward the stairs.

Ascending them two at a time, I felt the anger surging inside me, a white-hot coal of rage. I'd given every possible warning about the attack to Duchess, and waited for Bari Khan to make his next move only for nothing to happen at all. I'd assembled my team in Charlottesville with their Agency equipment, and in doing so inadvertently committed them to life in prison. And in the process of burning my team to the ground, I had absolutely nothing to show for it—it would be one thing if thousands of civilians were saved in the process; to be incarcerated until the end of time over a series of miscalculations seemed a far crueler fate.

At the same time, I couldn't reconcile the bare facts with my present reality. Any individual data point was bizarre unto itself; the combination of them was so fucking weird that there had to be something I wasn't considering—there simply *had* to be.

Reaching the second floor of my home, I strode down the hall and stopped at a door. After resting my palm on the handle for a second of hesitation, I threw it open.

It was Laila's home office.

I surveyed the interior for a moment, her desk and houseplants in the same tidy configuration they always were. Circling the room, I used my phone to photograph it from all angles, then opened the desk drawers in sequence and took pictures of the contents. Before she returned from Alexandria, I'd have to restore everything to its original position.

Because right now, I was about to tear this fucking room apart.

It was possible, of course, that the rockets were still in Syria or otherwise tied up in whatever logistical means Bari Khan had set in place.

But that explanation didn't sit well with me; it was too convenient, too hopeful, and in my experience with criminal and terrorist organizations over the years, the real answers were anything but.

I had to look at this from a new angle, one that would have previously seemed inconceivable. Central to that were two questions I hadn't previously asked myself.

What if the intel we'd uncovered in Syria had nothing to do with my team's past in the mercenary realm?

Shortly behind that, but equally valid, was the second hypothetical.

What if our intel on the attack had *nothing to do* with the president's visit to Charlottesville?

Both lines of inquiry were ludicrous, but since the president had come and gone without the slightest blip, I had little choice.

And when I pursued that line of inquiry deeper, the plain fact was that the scrap of paper had mentioned Laila and Langley, not myself. Since my daughter was unlikely to have many enemies of substance at her age, this led me to consider what I knew, or thought I knew, about my wife.

Her brother, Steve, was my roommate at West Point. I met her on a weekend trip to his mom's home in a Philadelphia suburb, when she was visiting from Ohio State. We'd been college sweethearts until she broke up with me prior to my graduation and medical discharge from the military. I knew that her biological father had committed suicide, and her mother later remarried and moved to Charlottesville to take up residence with her new husband. There was nothing suspicious about any of that, nor of her stepfather, who had until recently run a very successful local metalworking business before selling it and retiring to Alexandria.

Laila's mother was a nice woman, if slightly judgmental of me—in that she was fully justified, though neither she nor my wife knew the full extent of why—and her stepdad and I got along as well as could be expected. I couldn't envision any scenario in which either had some ties to organized terror or even international finance that held some nefarious link they were unaware of.

As for Laila, what was there to be suspicious of? She was a loving and kindhearted person, passionate about her budding career as a pediatric doctor though frazzled as of late from her residency. And, if I was being honest with myself, from the lack of parental support from my end. If she'd married a nine-to-five banker or one of her fellow doctors, I suspected she'd have no problems at all.

And maybe that was the key, I thought. I'd never suspected her of infidelity, though if she was having an affair with someone, there was little chance I'd be aware of it. Laila's residency involved long hours in close proximity with her fellow doctors, and while I'd met some of them at dinner events and cocktail parties, none had raised my hackles of suspicion in the slightest. For all my shortcomings as a husband and father, I trusted that I'd detect a fellow participant in the covert world of espionage or military action, justified or otherwise.

Unless, of course, I'd never met him in the first place.

Once my phone held the reference photos for Laila's arrangement of her personal and professional items, I began my search.

Much of it could be dismissed at a glance—medical journals and reference works, piles of med school textbooks and academic case files with the patient names redacted. It was possible she'd hidden something within those pages, and I'd flip through them one by one if I couldn't find answers elsewhere.

My thoughts were jarred by the sight of a leather-bound notebook in the top sliding drawer, an object familiar to me though I'd never once touched it.

This was her journal, and there were dozens like it stashed away upon completion.

Considering the implications of what I was about to do, I lifted it and flipped open to the last written page.

My eyes settled on a handwritten line selected at random. *Is it another woman? After a year of marriage, I already feel like we're growing apart...*

I slammed the journal shut, setting it down as hot tears hit my eyes. She deserved her privacy more than I deserved mine, and at the moment I couldn't bear the thought of seeing my domestic inadequacies through her eyes. If I couldn't find anything else, I'd go through that journal line by line in search of a clue, maybe something that Laila herself didn't recognize. I'd read it alongside Ian if I had to. A terrorist attack was in the works whether I liked it or not, and if it took getting my feelings hurt to stop it—or breaking my heart, as the case may be—then that's exactly what I was going to do.

But for now, there were other places to search, and I began poring through her remaining desk drawers.

Then I found another mess of paperwork, neatly filed in large manila envelopes and labeled by date. Most of the stacks of paper within seemed to be too pristine for her to have handled much, photocopied packets of some kind. I was quickly able to discern why: these were the documents of her parents' sale of their metalworking business, a process that Laila had been peripherally involved in by way of helping them make the transition to Alexandria.

This should have been a dead end, but something caused the hair on my forearms to rise before I realized what it was. Something both strange and familiar at the same time, though I spent no small amount of time flipping through the packets to figure it out. Eventually I realized it was the typeface itself.

And reaching the page that changed everything I thought I knew, my eyes settled on a line that made my breath hitch.

Beneath the legal documentation of her parents' new residence in Alexandria was a second line. It read, *Next of kin: David, Laila, and Langley Rivers, 427 Spring River Drive, Charlottesville, VA 22901.*

At that moment, I didn't need to consult the photograph I had of that scrap of paper I'd found in Syria. That image was emblazoned in my memory, as startling and vivid as if I were looking at it that second; and I knew beyond a shadow of a doubt that this particular sheet of the public domain was the same piece of paper.

And that's when I realized the truth, however improbable.

The Syrian connection with my family had nothing to do with me. Instead, it had to do with Laila's parents, and their sale of the metalworking business in Charlottesville.

Finding the phone in my pocket, I dialed Ian and breathed quickly, my heartbeat racing as I waited for the goddamned call to connect.

48

Ian spun his chair away from the computer, the phone pressed to his ear.

"Just slow down," he said. "You're sure it's the same piece of paper?"

David was frantic. "Do I sound like I'm in doubt? It's the exact same page, and if you need me to come down there and do your job for you, then I will—"

"All right, all right," Ian said, "take it easy. Let's think this through."

"Thinking is your job. I have no idea what to make of this, so start using that thirty-pound brain of yours."

"It could...no, wait...unless..."

Then he stopped abruptly, looking up.

"It's probably a strongarm ploy."

"A what?"

Ian spun his chair to face the computer, speaking quickly.

"Think about it: if these people wanted to acquire that business for something shady, then they could feasibly need the next-of-kin information so that if they needed to intimidate some people, that's who they'd strongarm. Don't you get it? It wasn't a threat against your family. You were just backups in case something went wrong with the sale. Or the aftermath. If they needed to hold leverage over the original owners of that metalworking facility, then they had three hostages in Charlottesville. Either way, it's not about you or us. It's about that business."

"What's the connection?"

Ian thought for a moment.

"It could be two possibilities. The first is storage for the cargo. Why risk renting a storage unit and subjecting yourself to surveillance footage when you can buy a factory in advance and use it as you please?"

"That's smart," David said.

"No, it's not. Far too high-profile, and too much effort for such a simple purpose. That brings me to the second possibility that a metalworking factory would serve: production of the launch assembly. Now you could launch those rockets from properly-sized PVC tubes if you had to. But given what you just found, there's a possibility that the metalworking factory was acquired for the express purpose of building an assembly capable of launching the entire load at once, and doing so with extreme precision for the kind of meticulous attack we've been looking for."

"So you think everything's at the factory now—the missiles and the launch assembly?"

"I didn't say that. Bari Khan is no idiot, he wouldn't pair the launch assembly with the rockets until the last moment. And how much did the factory sell for?"

"$5.2 million."

"Jesus, I got in the wrong line of work," he said. "But think about that: there's no way BK has the means—or the connections—to facilitate that sale himself. Someone handpicked him because he was smart and motivated, but the guy comes from a poor village in western China that had almost its entire population imprisoned or killed by the government. That means we're looking for a financier. Find me the buyer data. Names, addresses, all of it."

Ian put the phone on speaker and set it on the desk, then set to work opening browser windows on the computer and inputting information as fast as David could relay it to him.

"POC is Sam Burgess, making the buy on behalf of Steno, LLC in Richmond."

"Address of record?"

Within minutes, Ian had fourteen browser windows open, tracing the chain of business links as high as he could.

And when he found what he was looking for, it was with a sense of exhilaration that he couldn't keep out of his voice.

"Steno, LLC is one of seven under a corporate umbrella owned by a multinational conglomerate called Palvita International. That conglomerate is headed by a businessman named Wei Zhao. Now there's plenty written about this guy; he's one of the hundred richest men in China."

"So you think Zhao has some Uyghur connection," David replied, "and is bankrolling the attack through one of his business entities?"

Ian didn't answer immediately—he was too preoccupied with the connection he'd just found, a potentially groundbreaking development added to the mix of already perplexing factors surrounding this case. Zhao couldn't be the mastermind behind this; wealthy businessmen didn't involve themselves in the tactical specifics of terrorist operations. At most they were financiers behind the scenes, a craft that had been perfected by rich Saudis over the years as they funneled vast sums of cash to Islamic terror organizations via a series of cutouts and laundered transfers.

Zhao could have paid into the attack, but he hadn't constructed it.

David asked, "You still there?"

"Yeah," Ian responded, "and it's too soon to say for sure, but Zhao as financier makes sense to me at present. And in lieu of everything else about this that has defied logic, it's a pretty good start."

"All right, this has gone far enough. I'll notify Duchess."

"Slow down," Ian cautioned, taking the phone off speaker and bringing it to his ear before continuing. "We do that, and she knows we've been pulling strings even before she finds that we cleaned out the ISOFAC. This is a working theory, but it doesn't mean I'm right—and if I'm not, or there's something I'm not considering, then calling Duchess now will accomplish nothing but putting ourselves in prison on an educated hunch."

"I'll have Worthy put eyes-on the factory. If there's any sign of the launch assembly being transported, we signal the alarm."

"Agreed. And the next step is to confirm or deny that the facility was used to manufacture a launch assembly. If it wasn't, no harm, no foul. We keep looking. But if it was, we need to find out two things: if it's still at the factory, and if not, where it's headed."

"How do we do that?"

"Only one way," Ian said. "I need to get inside that factory."

49

Cancer was the last man to arrive at the team house.

He followed the sound of murmuring voices toward the back, where he found David and Reilly standing behind Ian's workstation. Their intelligence specialist was responding to the other two men's requests to zoom in on the overhead imagery of a large building.

No one looked up at Cancer as he entered, and he announced, "Hey, shitheads. You start planning this thing without me?"

Ian spun his chair to face him. "Yes."

"Good, 'cause I'm tired of doing all the work around here. Reilly, why do you look so bloated?"

The huge medic shrugged helplessly. "I had a second lunch." Then, a moment later and in response to the team's collective blank stare, "What? I had two surveillance positions. Both were restaurants."

Cancer asked, "Suicide, what do we got?"

David said, "We're waiting for Worthy to get eyes-on. But I've got a plan based on imagery."

"'Based on imagery.' Does that mean you've never been inside this factory?"

"No."

"Not once?"

"I said no," David replied testily. "I've been a little busy traipsing around the world with you dickheads."

Reilly added, "We'll have to do a surreptitious entry after nightfall."

Cancer smiled at him. "Ain't no 'surreptitious entry' about it, boys. This is a B&E, pure and simple. Starting to feel like a teenager again. Let's see the game cam."

Ian maximized a satellite photo on his computer screen showing an overhead view of the facility, most of which was the huge square rooftop. The remainder was an L-shaped addendum to the workshop, which Ian traced with a finger. "Offices are in this portion, and that's where I'll need access. The rest is primarily a workshop for metal fabrication."

Cancer nodded, quickly scanning the graphic markups indicating windows and doorways in the form of red arrows with breakout boxes listing the dimensions from construction blueprints—Ian must have already hacked the city land records.

"What's the size?"

Ian replied, "32,000 square feet."

Cancer gave a low whistle, then cut his eyes to David.

"What's the plan?"

"I was thinking Ian bypasses alarm power," David said, pointing to the building on the screen, "and then we all enter through the northeast corner of the office portion, start our clearance there and let Ian do his hard drive cloning while the rest of us clear the building to search for the launch assembly."

Cancer squinted hard, looking physically pained by the words.

"What's the matter?" David asked.

"Boss, with a building this size, that's asking for trouble. Anyone in the workshop could hear us enter, if not be tipped off by a silent alarm, and make a call or be on the run to the main road before we had any idea. Now I've been in my share of factories, and the workshop is usually a wide-open space that can be largely cleared by visual. So I say we make entry through two sides of the building simultaneously—Ian and Reilly through the south end, me and you through the northeast."

"You and Reilly," David corrected him. "I'll stay with Ian."

Cancer looked to David, then to Reilly, then back to David.

"What's the matter, you don't trust me unless our resident Boy Scout is at my side?"

"Those are your words, not mine. I didn't say that."

"Then what are you saying?"

David gave an exaggerated cough, then cleared his throat. "I'm not saying anything, other than I didn't say that."

Cancer glared at Ian, who was doing his best to suppress a laugh.

"Fuck is so funny over there?"

Ian shook his head, saying nothing.

"Fine," Cancer said, "David and Ian break into the short side of the L-shaped building on the south end, start clearing offices and ripping hard drives, while me and our Geneva Conventions expert enter through the northeast corner, then clear the workshop. If we find the rockets, everyone pulls out and we tip off the cops. Attack stopped. If it's empty, we consolidate for local security and Ian can take his time. Anyone gets interrupted, we bail out the backside because the first cops will come to the front of the building. What do you think, Suicide?"

David was motionless, his gaze focused on the screen as Cancer waited for a response.

Finally, he began to nod slightly.

"Yeah, that's a better plan. We can't risk getting rolled up on this. Let's go with Cancer's idea."

"So it's settled," Cancer said. "But we got a problem."

Before he could elaborate, Ian's phone rang.

He announced, "It's Worthy."

Answering the call on speaker, he said, "Racegun, the guys are here and we're looking at the overhead imagery. Where are you at?"

Worthy's Southern-accented voice was calm as he replied, "Adjacent parking lot off the north corner. Got a clear line of sight through the trees to the service road and around the side to the loading dock."

Ian scrolled across the satellite view on his screen. "Looks like a good spot. What do you see?"

"No movement during my drive-by or since I've been in position, but there's a few company trucks parked at the back of the lot. Don't see any privately owned vehicles, so it could be empty. If there were any major muscle movement I'd be able to see it, but it looks like the factory has shut down for the holiday."

David said, "Stay there and call us the second that changes. You see any trucks departing with possible launch assembly components, I want you to follow them. We'll scramble from here to back you up, and I'll notify Duchess."

"She's gonna be pissed," he replied.

"Yeah," David agreed, "but it's better than the alternative. Hopefully it doesn't come to that. We'll be standing by."

"You got it, boss."

After Ian ended the call, Cancer said, "Now about this problem."

"What problem?" Ian asked.

"What are we supposed to raid the factory with, our dicks? We gotta procure some firearms."

David said, "Firearms are the one thing we have."

"No, they ain't. We fire one shot in there, and the police find a piece of brass that Duchess can trace to our Agency-issued weapons, how do you think that's going to work out for us? Hell, I wouldn't put it past her to check the ballistics on any team-caliber kills in the Charlottesville area. She's already going to find the ISOFAC cleaned out any day now. No need to speed up that process."

After a moment of silence, Reilly said, "I could do a round trip to my house, raid the gun collection. If I leave now, I could make it back by"—he consulted his watch—"midnight, maybe one o'clock. We could probably be in the door by two."

"Get moving," Cancer said. "We'll get to work refining our plan for the B&E."

50

Worthy sat in his car, alone in the darkness, stretching his legs so they wouldn't fall asleep.

He'd been there for close to eight hours, peeing in bottles and trying to stay awake as his vision blurred and he yawned repeatedly. Giving his face a slap to restore some alertness, he refocused his gaze on the factory through the trees beyond his windshield.

He'd initially been apprehensive about someone knocking on his window, asking what in the hell he was doing there. Or worse yet, a patrol officer being called in by a neighboring business that had reported a suspicious vehicle with a single occupant remaining behind the wheel for hours on end.

He'd dreamed up a few cover stories tailored to whoever discovered him there—he'd certainly had time to do so, all the way up to verbally rehearsing them to himself—but after the sun set without the slightest whisper of movement around him, it became apparent that the industrial park was a ghost town.

And why wouldn't it be? Tomorrow was the Fourth of July—actually, today was, since his watch had crossed the stroke of midnight just over two hours earlier—and any business not owned by a complete and total

Communist would have closed early to allow their employees a head start on travel plans for the holiday weekend.

So Worthy had sat, and sat, and sat some more, watching the metal-working factory with no more action than the security lights ticking on automatically before sunset. This kind of assignment would have been fine for someone like Cancer, a trained sniper used to observing the world through a scope for hours on end.

But Worthy wasn't a sniper—his specialty was running and gunning with blazing speed, reflexes honed for split-second response. The wait would have been bearable given the knowledge that he'd soon be slipping inside the building, joining his team for the intelligence collection ahead.

That wasn't, however, going to be the case.

David had sounded almost apologetic when he'd handed Worthy his marching orders: sorry, but we'll need you to stay on lookout duty. It wasn't even a matter of monitoring the police scanner, which they'd be able to do as well as he could. The simple fact was, they suspected this facility of being owned by some very bad people, and those people wouldn't necessarily call the cops if they became aware of unwelcome visitors.

Worthy doubted the building even had an active, normal security system. That would put the police on automatic response in the event of a break-in, complete with carte blanche to make entry if they found a door or window ajar.

No, Worthy suspected the reality was much worse.

They probably had a silent alarm of some kind, complete with their own personal response force designated to appear on command, intent on ensuring that anyone who penetrated their lion's den didn't live to tell about what they'd found inside. That would hold doubly true if the rockets were present, a possibility that Worthy discounted based on the simple fact that he hadn't seen any sign of personnel since arriving.

Ian was aware of that too, which explained why he'd spent several hours making provisions to set up a cable relay in a nearby electrical junction box, ensuring that any security systems reliant on building outlets would detect a steady stream of electricity and not switch to their internal power supply. This would, in theory, prevent the alarm from being raised even if the entry team tripped a sensor—as far as the electronics were concerned, all circuits would appear complete and unbroken, and the team could take their time sifting for intelligence within the main offices.

It was far from a failsafe, however. There could be any number of security measures running off an internal power supply in the first place, necessitating the entry team to carry cellular and wireless jammers on their kit. But they'd have no way of knowing whether that effort was successful or not until one of two things occurred: they slipped out of the building upon mission completion, or the effort was cut short by some outside response, law enforcement or otherwise.

So Worthy's duties as team lookout were far from over.

He just hoped that the team's entry into the building was as uneventful as his surveillance had been. Otherwise, things were going to get very interesting, very quickly.

David's voice came over his earpiece then.

"*Angel is relay-complete,*" David said. "*Team One is moving to make entry.*"

Reilly rose from his crouch at the string of trees lining the factory and darted across the open ground toward the building.

The single-story row of offices was phosphorescent green in his night vision, backed by the two-floor warehouse attachment behind it. Cancer shadowed his movement by a few paces, his voice in Reilly's earpiece broadcasting their intent.

"*Team Two copies, we're on the move.*"

Reilly approached the side of the building, slowing as he reached the window designated as their point of entry. He prepared to breach the building's exterior, completely dependent on Cancer to provide cover. As much as he hated to concede that Cancer's plan was a good one, there was good reason for splitting the entry team into two-man elements.

While only Ian had the equipment and training to pilfer digital evidence from any computers they found, Reilly and Cancer provided another intangible benefit: security.

Granted, Worthy hadn't seen any activity or even lit windows, but that didn't mean the building was empty.

With David providing immediate security for Ian, Cancer and Reilly could begin sweeping the building for any human presence. And while David had been adamant that any personnel found inside should be restrained uninjured—if they were affiliated with terrorists, they'd need to be interrogated, and if not, there was no need to harm helpless civilians—Reilly was concerned about his partner's degree of restraint. Or lack thereof.

The bottom line was that Cancer liked killing people, plain and simple. If Reilly was the team's moral compass, then Cancer was like an iron ore deposit that would swing the needle askew at the first possible opportunity. Reilly saw the team's mission as a force for good, and he'd clashed with Cancer on this issue at every conceivable juncture. In that regard, David had been right to pair him with the team's second-in-command.

None of that mattered tonight, of course, until they made it into the building.

With the security systems disabled—hopefully, at least—by Ian's bypass on the junction box, Reilly had no choice but to trust the cellular and wireless jammer in his assault pack as he employed his Halligan bar on the window.

More commonly known as the hoolie tool, the iron bar had a giant forked chisel on one end and a wedge with a perpendicular pick on the other. Most law enforcement and firefighter applications, even military, employed the "break and rake" technique of smashing a window, then scraping the broken glass from the frame for follow-on personnel to enter.

But nothing so overt would suit their purposes tonight, and instead Reilly wedged the chiseled end into the frame, prying the sliding window upward with a sharp crack of the surrounding molding.

Cancer whispered, "Can you get any louder, asshole?"

Ignoring him, Reilly used a gloved hand to push the window up and out of the way, dropping to all fours for Cancer to step on his back—which he did a little more harshly than necessary—to enter through the window frame.

Grunting under the footfall, Reilly felt Cancer's weight vanish.

Rising quickly, he adjusted the hoolie bar on its sling and placed both hands on the open frame, then leapt through the window and into the building.

Ian stepped inside the building, pulling the window shut behind him as directed before turning to scan through his night vision.

David was a black shadow in the hallway, sweeping his weapon across a green swath of the building interior as he cleared for immediate threats. Wasting no time, Ian tested the handle of the office door to his right, found it unlocked, and quickly cleared it.

The process was clumsy, and not just because Ian lacked his teammates' tactical experience—there was also the matter of his weapon, a Colt 1911 handgun from Reilly's personal collection. The family heirloom was passed down from his grandfather, and he'd entrusted it to the team's intelligence operative not as a sign of respect but rather because Ian was the least likely to fire a shot. The .45 caliber pistol felt alien in his hands, and he desperately wanted to use the Agency-issued rifle slung on his back as a last resort.

It didn't matter anyway, he thought. The office was empty, a pair of computer workstations facing the wall and window.

Ian holstered his pistol and moved toward the computers, finding the small, box-like device secured in his cargo pocket and plugging it into a USB port.

A flashing red light blinked at a corner of the device, indicating that it was in the process of copying the hard drive. At that moment, Ian wasn't concerned whether the launch assembly was present in the facility. If so, Reilly and Cancer would uncover it in minutes, and the team would exfil and overwatch the building until police responded to their anonymous tip. And if any terrorists showed to secure their cargo before then, well, Ian's team would get a chance to put Reilly's weapons to good use.

Barring that possibility—and Ian guessed from the building's lack of guard personnel that the odds were slim indeed—anything of value from tonight's raid would come from the hard drives.

When the light on his device turned from blinking red to steady green, he pulled the USB cord and hastily moved to the second computer.

Reilly followed Cancer into the warehouse portion of the facility, seeing a two-story-high ceiling packed to capacity with giant machines, welding equipment, and parked forklifts.

As Cancer flowed left, Reilly proceeded toward a row of tall shelving in the opposite direction and tucked his body behind a stack of empty pallets. He saw a large sign on the wall proclaiming the original name of the business, DOMINION METALFAB, and briefly wondered if there was cause for suspicion in the new owners not immediately changing all branding to their own title.

No time to consider it, though—he was on a hunt first for any enemy in the facility, followed by any trace of the rockets—and he continued moving forward down the long axis of the warehouse, sweeping his barrel left and right to search for threats.

Then he heard a noise to his front.

It was immediately more terrifying than footsteps or even a gunshot, both of which might have at least come from his teammates.

But what he heard was someone calling out, "Jessie?"

He spun to the side and angled his rifle up, but it was too late—he was in the glare of a flashlight held by a man stepping out from behind a machine in the workshop, and Reilly's night vision flared to a blinding shade of white-green.

Squinting through the glare, Reilly desperately tried to determine if the man held a weapon in his opposite hand.

He was unable to tell before another figure appeared, this one a shadow closing with the first man and driving his fist into his exposed side—it was Cancer, and Reilly didn't need to register the choking gasp to know that his teammate had just plunged a blade into the man's kidney.

The effect was devastating. A stab to the kidney caused such crippling pain that the victim was rendered incapable of crying out, and the man fell to his knees as the flashlight clattered and rolled sideways.

Reilly's night vision focused on the view of Cancer finishing the job, thrusting his blade into the side of the man's neck and ripping it out the front before flinging the body downward. There was a wet, suctioning noise as the man gasped his last dying breaths without so much as a scream, and Reilly raced forward amid an exploding sense of dread and horror.

Even as he moved toward the casualty, he knew he'd be too late. There was no treatment Reilly could administer that would delay this man's death, even if he'd had a full complement of medical supplies on hand.

"Jesus," he whispered as he stopped before the body. "What have you done?"

Cancer said, "Relax. Not a lot of security guards packing MAC-10s."

Reilly glanced down to see the submachinegun lying on a sling at the man's side.

When Reilly didn't respond, Cancer said, "You're welcome." Then he patted down the man's pockets, removing a cell phone and sliding it into a drop pouch as he transmitted, "Tango down, one EKIA in the warehouse."

Ian heard David's whispered response over his earpiece.

"*Copy tango down. Any sign of the rockets or launch assembly?*"

"*Negative*," Cancer replied. "*Continuing clearance*."

Pulling the USB cord from the second computer, Ian secured the cloning device in his pocket and moved out of the office with his senses aflame—Cancer had just transmitted a confirmed enemy kill in the warehouse, though David didn't seem to mind at all.

Instead, at the sight of Ian he advanced further, entering an office as Ian pulled security down the corridor, waiting for David to reappear with the signal that everything was okay.

He did so a moment later, taking up a security position with his shoulder flush against a doorway to the left, his rifle aimed down the hall as his body remained behind cover.

Ian rushed inside to assess the contents of the office. There was only a single workstation here, and he moved to clone the hard drive as he considered the implications of a team kill on domestic soil.

At present, the magnitude of that particular event seemed lost to everyone but him.

Duchess would find out about this—how could she not? Surely she was casting an analytical eye to the goings-on in Charlottesville, particularly after she'd seen fit to personally follow and confront David in his hometown. And when that happened, she'd have them all carted off to a black site in the time it took them to realize what was happening.

The light on his device flared to a steady green, and he detached the USB cord.

With the third hard drive copied, Ian moved back to the door. He squeezed David's shoulder, and his team leader moved forward once again, cutting into the next office as Ian covered down the hallway and waited for him to re-emerge.

Once again, David did, though this time under less voluntary circumstances.

He was flung against the far wall against the weight of a silverback of a man who pummeled him in a half-tackle. A single unsuppressed gunshot sounded from David's barrel, the flash of light momentarily illuminating the hallway before everything went dark again. As Ian oriented himself through his night vision, he heard Cancer transmit over the net—"*Status?*" —before focusing on the dark mass of two bodies on the floor, the distinction between where the giant's body ended and David's began impossible to tell at this distance.

Ian reacted instinctively, a hundred shooting range lessons imparted from his teammates congealing into a single reflexive action that he performed with astonishing quickness.

Launching forward a step, he fell to his knees and slid forward, angling his handgun upward for a shot that would send the bullet through the attacker's head and into the ceiling without injuring his team leader in the slightest.

The maneuver played out with impossible perfection, the 1911's sights aligning with his opponent's blocklike head in the time it took him to flick off the thumb safety.

But before he could squeeze the trigger, the giant's fist sailed out of the darkness, cracking against the side of Ian's head and flipping his night vision device sideways.

He fell backward, involuntarily firing a second round into the wall, the ricochet sending the bullet careening down the hallway as Ian's head exploded into ringing flashes of color.

Cancer moved at a sprint with Reilly at his rear, both racing to back up their teammates by the time the second shot fired. Worthy transmitted, "*Do you need support?*"

"Standby," Cancer replied, slowing as he approached the doorway leading into the office hallway.

The doorway was open, lacking even a closable panel, and Cancer stopped in front of it before stepping sideways to clear the space beyond.

Once he'd come parallel with the opposite wall, he dropped his barrel as Reilly cut past him into the hallway, and Cancer moved forward to clear in the opposite direction.

Seeing an empty corridor, he spun in place to view the scene before him: Ian on the ground, David being choked to death by a monstrous figure, and Reilly standing motionless, momentarily stunned.

"What are you waiting for?" Cancer asked. "Hit him."

It was easy for Cancer to say, and he knew it.

Reilly was the biggest guy on the team by a long shot, and he looked like a child beside this hulking monster trying to choke the life out of their team leader. The man was an absolute beast, and he was too close to David for anyone to risk firing a shot.

Undaunted, Reilly flung his massive body atop the figure, trying to choke the man before being flung sideways, his hoolie tool flying off his side upon impact and clattering against the floor.

Shaking his head, Cancer slung his weapon and drew his fighting knife for the second time in the space of three minutes. He knelt beside the mass of human bodies before him, driving his blade into the stomach of the barbarian currently manhandling his teammates with savage ferocity.

The giant was unfazed by the effort, knocking Cancer backward as he spun sideways with Reilly atop his back.

No matter, he thought. The knife was still firmly within his grasp.

What most people didn't know about knife kills, save the police who investigated the aftermath, was that the blade frequently lodged on bone, causing the attacker's hand to slide onto the exposed blade and leave a smattering of DNA residue in the form of blood.

It was for this reason that Cancer used a fighting knife with a hilt, ensuring that his stabs left him uncut. He delivered another two blows to the man's belly, knowing that they would cause an astonishing amount of pain while leaving the man to die a slow, agonizing death with plenty of time left over for tactical questioning.

But the immense man was fighting his way to a standing position, struggling mightily against the best efforts of three men trying to stop him—Ian was still semi-motionless on the floor, struggling to regain his senses.

Cancer was pushing himself to his feet in preparation for the next attack when a sixth figure appeared.

A moment's analysis proved it to be Worthy, summoned either by the audible gunshots or the sporadic radio transmissions that had continued without resolution—and Cancer saw him pick up Reilly's hoolie tool from its resting place on the ground.

Bracing his feet for the effort, Worthy raised the chiseled end over his head and brought it down with a sickening thump atop the man's head.

The giant figure jolted violently and then dropped to the floor like a stone, David and Reilly collapsing atop him in a pile of human bodies.

Sheathing his bloodied knife, Cancer knelt, feeling for a pulse through his gloved fingertips and then looking up at the murderer before him.

"Why'd you have to kill him? Can't get information from a dead body."

Worthy was panting for breath, holding his hoolie tool like a fireman with an ax.

"I couldn't...he was...aw, shit."

David rose from the ground, giving Worthy a pat on his shoulder.

"It's all right, buddy. You don't know your own strength. Thanks for the save."

Before anyone could respond, they heard the shrill wail of police sirens, as loud and piercing as if they were inside the building.

David called out, "You guys are on your own. Get that intel back to the team house, find out where BK is headed."

And then David was gone—sprinting toward the warehouse in what seemed to be a determined attempt for suicide by cop.

Without alternatives to intervene, the team scattered out of the building and raced toward their vehicles.

I burst into the warehouse facility, momentarily overwhelmed by the sight before me—shelving and equipment, machines and forklifts as far as the eye could see—before focusing my night vision on a dark panel of doorway to the front of the building.

This was stupid, I realized even as I completed the action.

But as with every time that thought had occurred to me, I proceeded nonetheless, charging through the door's push bar into the outdoors.

With team vehicles parked to the north, east, and south, there was only one direction I could move to direct police attention away from my team as they escaped the facility—west, directly out the front door.

I did so at a run, emerging outside to the swirling red and blue lights of multiple police cruisers and the sounds of men shouting, "*Police! Stay where you are!*"

Both statements seemed redundant given the circumstances, and I cut left to break into a dead sprint along the front of the building toward the far tree line.

This was pitting my speed against police marksmanship, pure and simple—the odds of me falling in a hail of gunfire were too high for this to make any rational sense whatsoever.

But the cops didn't shoot, instead relocating to give chase as evidenced by the sound of car doors slamming and engines revving from the main parking lot.

Then came running footfalls and shouted commands behind me as an unknown number of officers pursued me on foot. It was hard to tell which side held an advantage in physical fitness, and we both certainly had adrenaline on our side.

However, I had one thing going for me over the members of law enforcement currently chasing after a shadowy figure in the night. They were, as a rule, consummate professionals dedicated to public safety and their own duty.

I, by contrast, was a reckless amateur, and reckless amateurs got lucky.

My thought process was questionable, but in my mind there seemed no other way. If I hadn't distracted the police, they would have quickly surrounded the building and captured one or more of my teammates.

And while I didn't doubt my colleagues' ability to serve time in jail—they'd been to arguably worse destinations around the world, with Syria a prime candidate among them—there was a larger consideration at play.

In providing security for Ian, I definitively knew that I had no discernable intelligence that would stop Bari Khan's attempt at, well, whatever it was he was attempting. Now that Monticello had been ruled out, the sky was the limit for a well-equipped terrorist like him.

But I couldn't say the same for any of my teammates. Not Ian, who carried an assault pack full of data from cloned hard drives, nor Reilly and Cancer, who had seen the bowels of the warehouse and could have a clue that possessed the missing link we sought.

If any of them were rolled up by the cops, then Bari Khan could very feasibly succeed in slaughtering hundreds of our countrymen in the time it took for the captured member to explain their situation, probably without much assistance from Duchess, who had her own legal and political justifications to consider.

I ran west, armed with a basic orientation of my surroundings from analysis of overhead imagery. In the industrial park, I was a sitting duck: the paved expanses and large parking lots lent themselves to easy police vehicle access, to say nothing of the fact that I had four team members who needed to slip out of there as discreetly as possible.

My shadow was cast as a long and distorted phantom before me, the police flashlights lighting my back as I took surging breaths like a sprinter on the hundred-yard dash. Which, for the moment, I was—a short stretch of woods was visible to my front, and I desperately needed to reach it. For one, it would provide concealment to block cops' view, allowing me to disappear if only for a short time.

And second, I desperately needed a reprieve from the all-out sprint that was setting my muscles and lungs aflame.

Plunging into the trees, I transitioned from a straight-line sprint to an erratic, zigzagging course to dodge the trees. Grateful for the necessary reduction in speed, I relied on the swirling glow of police flashlights casting nightmarish shadows through the branches as I moved. I emerged into an open stretch, landing a single step on a paved walking trail before launching through the trees beyond, pumping my legs up a steep incline that made my hamstrings and calves cramp with effort.

Then I was over the top and descending, scrambling down the wooded embankment. I lost my footing, tumbling sideways through brambles and leaf litter before rolling into the open. Struggling to my feet, I found myself on a short expanse of grass between houses.

I'd made it to the neighborhood beside the industrial park, a critical step in my escape. Next I'd have to cross the subdivision, a process that began with launching into a run onto the paved cul-de-sac before me. Racing down the street with a row of houses on either side, I entered a surreal suburban reality, risking the exposure of streetlights for the sake of gaining distance from my pursuers. My lungs were screaming for air, legs on the tremulous brink of giving out as I exploited every milligram of adrenaline in my system.

Closing with the main road, I caught a glimpse of a street sign—Running Fox Lane—and thought, how appropriate to my current situation. The only thing my hunters were missing at present were the dogs to follow my scent, and those were surely on the way. And while I could temporarily outpace the officers currently swarming into the neighborhood, my running abilities wouldn't count for much the second a seventy-pound German Shepherd was let off the leash.

I dashed across the street, seeing the red flickers of a patrol car screaming toward me from the left. They'd moved to surround me with astonishing speed, reacting to my direction of movement and trying to cut me off at every possible junction.

Now that I'd been spotted, their search radius was immediately narrowed to a single point in the neighborhood, and as I reached the far side of the street, I cut left between houses, feet pounding across a manicured lawn as the patrol car followed my progress.

I cut right, tucking myself behind the backside of a house as a blazing white spotlight illuminated the space I'd just departed.

Then I continued moving west, toward the final yard separating me from a large span of woods bordering I-64 to the south. At present I was merely an armed suspect in a B&E—but once the first officers searched the metalworking factory, that would immediately escalate to murder and my odds of getting shot would rise by a factor of ten.

As I made it to the woods and began racing uphill, I took a fleeting glance behind me—the night sky above the housetops was lit by the ethereal blue and red glow of flashing police lights, the barking of every dog in the neighborhood punctuated by the slamming of car doors and shouts of officers.

This entire raid had turned into a disaster in record time, and for a moment I wondered if my team had made it out of the industrial park undetected.

No time to consider it now. I turned and continued moving uphill, staying on a westerly course. When the K9 units arrived, they'd hopefully suspect I was proceeding to the next neighborhood, or north toward I-64. After a hundred meters I cut left instead, then turned south to follow the woods that presented multiple link-up points on the roads adjoining either side.

I pushed onward, struggling to cover ground and fighting the overwhelming impulse to stop and rest. Everything hit me at once then—the failed attempts to kill Bari Khan, the moment we'd lost the rockets in Syria, the state of my relationship with Laila and Langley.

I didn't know where this would end, or what the ultimate outcome of my actions would be—not as it related to my imprisonment or death, and definitely not as it pertained to the family I'd set out to protect.

The only certainty in that moment was that I needed to run, and so I did. I was a desperate fugitive, and the only recourse was to continue fleeing deeper into the woods, changing direction on a course that would lead miles into the night before I could call upon my team for help. Above it all was a sense of total exhaustion—mental, physical, and emotional—that I fought to suppress.

And as I moved, the branches and thorn bushes whipping across my body in the black surroundings, I felt the sting of hot tears against my eyes.

51

Duchess was awakened by a phone ringing on her nightstand.

Her eyes opened in the darkness. She knew from the ringtone that this was business—when your duties required you to be on call, the Agency paid to outfit your home with a secure line—and she rolled sideways to reach for the receiver by feel in a motion she'd executed many times before.

Sitting up and bringing the receiver to her ear, she said, "Duchess here."

A man replied, "Ma'am, we've had an update in PIR 08."

She felt a slight tremor in her hand as she turned on the bedside lamp, illuminating her solitary bedroom.

A limited number of "wake-up criteria" would result in her receiving a call like this, and Priority Intelligence Requirement number eight was the last one she wanted to receive a notification about.

She'd crafted the wording to be sufficiently vague—*Any law enforcement reports with possible links to terrorist-related violence or intelligence gathering in Charlottesville or Albemarle County, Virginia, USA*. That line of PIR wouldn't look out of place amid the others pertaining to Bari Khan, all of them worthy of a call at 3:16 in the morning.

But Duchess's unstated reason for instituting it had nothing to do with Bari Khan, and everything to do with David's team.

And as the man continued speaking, she realized her fears were coming true.

"Charlottesville PD responded to a report of gunshots at a metal-working facility. They found two unidentified victims, one with a stab wound and a slit throat. The other had multiple stab wounds, a bullet in his abdomen, and a cracked skull from blunt force trauma of some kind."

"Did they arrest anyone?"

"One suspect fled the scene and is currently at large. Bloody boot prints leading out of the building indicate two to three additional suspects that escaped. No one is in custody at this time."

"Name of the facility?"

"Patten Metalworks. Formerly Dominion MetalFab."

Duchess's heart sank. As part of the security clearance process, CIA officers and contractors had their friends and family screened with an eye to indiscretions lending themselves to blackmail, and business holdings that could be used to launder illicit earnings. Both represented a risk for manipulation by foreign intelligence services trying to flip an Agency employee, and Duchess had screened the backgrounds of David's team with a particularly wary eye.

She knew that David's next of kin had recently sold Dominion MetalFab.

"Find out everything you can about the facility. Sales records, buyer background, all of it. I'm coming in."

"There's something else, ma'am."

Duchess's heart fell. After the bomb this man had just dropped, what else could there possibly be?

"What is it?"

"The cleanout team arrived at the Longwing ISOFAC twenty minutes ago. They reported some missing equipment."

"Such as?"

"I've got the itemized list with serial numbers, but for starters, weapons, lasers, suppressors, night vision devices—"

"Got it," she said. "I'll be there in forty minutes."

She hung up and wiped the sleep from her eyes, rising quickly to get dressed.

Gossweiler wasn't going to miss the Charlottesville killings on the morning news, and she couldn't risk him finding out about missing Agency equipment from any source besides herself. There was precious little time remaining before he was awake. If she hadn't taken action by the time that happened, he'd suspect her allowance of, if not outright complicity in, her former targeted killing team taking unsanctioned paramilitary action in the homeland.

So Duchess hurried to her car, beginning the drive to Agency headquarters and considering how to best handle the delicate matter of arresting David and his team.

52

Worthy cruised down the road, his thumb tapping the steering wheel in time with the country song playing on the radio.

The sun was rising, casting its light over the richly forested countryside on either side of the road.

Glancing at his GPS, he knew he was getting close—and rounding a curve a moment later, he saw the load signal in the form of a pair of crossed branches ahead, both lying at the edge of the forest as if they'd fallen haphazardly.

Checking his rearview, Worthy activated his four-way flashers and pulled off to the side of the road. He was prepared to make a go-around in the event of other traffic on the road, but for the moment the coast was clear.

Worthy barely had time to press the unlock button before David lunged out of the trees and wrenched open the back passenger door.

"Go," he said, as if Worthy would have preferred to loiter around the pickup site until a patrol car cruised past.

Killing his flashers and accelerating back to cruising speed, Worthy texted Ian with news of his successful recovery of their team leader, and then briefly turned to look at the passenger behind him.

Then he returned his eyes to the road, giving a grim shake of his head.

David, to put it lightly, looked like shit. His eyes bore dark circles, face and clothes covered in dirt, looking more homeless drifter than shooter.

"Everyone make it out last night?" he asked.

"Yeah," Worthy replied. "You were the only—"

"What the hell are you listening to?"

Pausing, Worthy said, "That's Merle Haggard right there. Want me to turn it off?"

"No," David said. "Depressing country music is the perfect way to tie up that train wreck of an operation."

Worthy read between the lines of David's statement and turned off the car stereo. They rode on in silence for a few moments before Worthy spoke again.

"Looks like you had a rough night."

"I needed to crush some cardio anyway. How are the guys?"

Worthy sighed. "We spent the night bleaching the blood off our kits, and burning the boots that weren't going to be clean anytime soon. You and Ian fired the only shots, so Reilly's down two weapons once we get rid of yours. The one Ian used is already at the bottom of the Rivanna River, along with Cancer's knife."

David shook his head. "Cancer loved that knife."

"Thought that inhuman bastard was going to cry. But I'm sure he's got plenty more."

"If Ian or the cops had found anything useful, I'm guessing you would have led with that fact."

"Yeah, boss, I would've. Police didn't find any rockets. The hard drives haven't revealed anything suspicious—matter of fact, there's no digital record of any production at all under the new company, but that could just be because they hadn't started operations yet."

"Well, shit. Cancer and Reilly didn't see anything in the workshop?"

"I wouldn't go that far. No sign of the launch assembly, or any tubes consistent with rocket size as best as they could tell. But Cancer pulled a phone off the guy he killed."

"And?"

"That's where it gets interesting. No contacts, no calls made, so he must have memorized a number and erased the record each time he used it.

These guys ran a tight ship. Ian's working on restoring the phone data, but apparently that can take some time."

"I don't suppose Duchess overlooked our little party last night."

"Good guess. She's been calling nonstop."

"And?"

Worthy looked at David as if he were crazy. "'And' nothing. None of us are answering that call, but I'm guessing she's either seen the local news, or found the ISOFAC cleaned out, or both. But explaining that is your job, boss. Happy Fourth of July, David."

"Yeah." His team leader nodded, still facing the window. "Happy Fourth."

53

Ian looked up from his computer as Worthy and David entered.

David looked like he'd been chewed and spit out from the wrong end of an industrial-sized blender. His green eyes ticked across the team before settling on Ian.

Worthy smiled, placing his hands on David's shoulders and giving him a light shake.

"Our fearless leader was rode hard and put away wet last night, but he made it back none the worse for wear."

Cancer stood from his seat and said, "Welcome back, boss."

David ignored him, and even Reilly, for that matter. Instead he kept a dull, almost threatening stare on Ian.

"What have you found?"

Ian detested the sight of David when he got this way. When pushed to the wall, he assumed a recklessness that had no place in tactical operations —even the way he phrased his inquiry was telling. Not *have you* found anything, but a demand: *what have you* found. As if there had better be something, or else.

Fortunately, in the time it had taken Worthy to pick up their last remaining fugitive teammate, Ian had his one and only break so far.

He said, "I've finished exploiting deleted information from the captured phone. Whoever this guy was, he was dialing a single number, checking in every hour and deleting the call record afterward. To me, that's indicative of a stay-behind element, issued phones for the purpose and left in place as early warning in case anyone picked up the trail. Those two guys were probably just hired guns, with no idea who they were working for."

"Well that's good," Cancer said, "because Worthy clubbed the last one to death before we could ask him anything."

Worthy frowned. "I've apologized for that multiple times."

"Ian," David cut them off, "what did you find out about the number he was calling?"

"Captured phone is a Missouri area code while the number it was used to dial was an Arizona code; all that means is they established a solid burner network in advance. The key info, however, came from the cell tower records that the calls pinged off of—captured phone was hitting here in Charlottesville every time. But the number it was dialing went through a tower in Fredericksburg."

"Could it be a false ping, a call relay like we use?"

"Could be," Ian admitted. "But if you had the technical sophistication to do that, why not use a more distant location?"

"Because a close one is more convincing, that's why."

"I can't say for sure, but I don't think so. Fredericksburg is pretty strategic."

David grunted his disapproval. "Fredericksburg is an even smaller pimple on the ass of Virginia than Charlottesville is. I don't think we're going to find anything significant for BK to destroy there."

Ian said, "I told you before that Bari Khan wouldn't pair the launch assembly with the rockets until he was ready to attack. We don't know where the rockets made landfall in America, but it's a safe bet that the launch assembly was fabricated here in Charlottesville. That makes Fredericksburg an almost ideal location to pair the two because it's located along I-95, and that goes past every major city he could possibly want to attack. If Bari Khan is launching a weaponized semi rig, as I suspect he is, he could drive north to DC, Baltimore, Philly, or New York. If you want to clear out a few city blocks, New York is a hell of a place to do it. Especially if he's attacking the Freedom Tower."

"Boss," Cancer offered, "for the record, I agree with Ian. In lieu of any other meaningful information, and owing to our popularity with the Charlottesville PD at present, I say we get the hell out of town. Take our kit and stage in Fredericksburg until Ian finds another thread for us to follow."

Ian blinked. "What if I don't? I can scan the available data, but if I don't find anything, I don't find anything."

Cancer shrugged. "I haven't thought that far ahead."

"Neither have I," David said. "But that's the best idea I've heard so far."

Then he placed a hand on Ian's shoulder, gripping it a little too firmly for comfort.

"And you're a smart guy," he said, a hint of malice in his voice. "I'm sure you'll figure it out. Just ask yourself what your dad would do."

As Ian sat there, dumbstruck, the phone beside him began to ring.

He checked the display, then looked at David.

"It's Duchess."

54

Duchess's office phone rang, and she set down her mug of tea to pluck it from the receiver.

"Duchess here."

A male answered, "I've got David Rivers on the secure relay."

She felt her stomach grow warm—when her first call to David went unanswered, she instinctively assumed he was the suspect-at-large who had fled the metalworking facility. By the time her next half-dozen calls were met with the same fate, she was certain of it.

"Put him through," Duchess said, "and push his location tracking to my computer."

"Yes, ma'am. Stand by."

Duchess saw the invitation window appear on her computer screen and clicked it to see a world map that centered on North America before zooming in on the call origin.

Hearing a click over the phone line, she said, "You've been a difficult man to reach."

David Rivers answered, sounding nonchalant.

"Sorry, slept in this morning. What's up?"

"Where are you?" she asked.

"At home."

"No, you're not. And with your wife out of town, I'd like to think you're either having an affair or you woke up drunk in a gutter somewhere. Knowing you, I'd suspect the latter."

She continued watching her computer screen, frowning as the call location was confirmed.

"Hang on." He paused, then said, "You're right. Thought it was my house, but this is actually a gutter. But you work for the Christians In Action—shouldn't you be able to trace this?"

Duchess felt her jaw settle.

"I have, and it's pinging you in eastern Los Angeles. Since you don't have the sophistication to reroute a call like that, I'll take that as hard evidence that Ian is assisting you."

"Now now, Duchess. Who says I can't be devastatingly handsome *and* technically proficient?"

She felt a hot pit of anger welling up in her stomach and rising into her chest.

"I've heard some disturbing news about two killings in Charlottesville."

"I heard about that, too. Murders at a metalworking factory, I think it was. Strange times we live in."

"Two murders," Duchess said, "at the business formerly belonging to your wife's parents. We're well outside the bounds of coincidence."

"Was it the same business? Good thing my father-in-law wasn't present. But just because I live in Charlottesville doesn't mean I control everything that happens in it. Who knows what criminal miscreants pulled off that stunt."

"So you're denying it was your team?"

"Categorically."

"I'm glad to hear that. I'm going to need you all to report to the flagpole so you can tell me that while hooked up to a polygraph."

"Sure, let's pencil something in after the holiday."

"I'll rephrase. The cleanout team arrived to find your ISOFAC devoid of Agency-issued equipment that is currently at large in blatant violation of a mile-long list of legal statutes. You and your men have exactly thirty minutes to turn yourself over to the authorities, who will detain you until Agency reps arrive to transport you."

"Or else...what?"

"After hearing your denial, it's quite clear you have a vivid imagination. So you tell me."

There was a long pause before David replied, "Instead of being worried about me and my team, maybe you should start looking at *why* that factory was raided. You could start with a Chinese businessman at the top of the conglomerate who bought the business, then maybe work your way on down to the seller's next-of-kin listing that bears a strange resemblance to the intel I found in Syria."

For once, Duchess thought, she and David were in agreement—and while she was mildly impressed that he'd made the connection with Wei Zhao, she wasn't about to tell him that Zhao's yacht had already been raided, and was now under exceptionally discreet FBI surveillance as it remained docked at the World Ocean Superyacht Marina in Jacksonville. By now, the boat had been ruled out as a threat; its owner hadn't, however, and the agents hadn't seen Zhao for a long enough span of time that Duchess feared he'd somehow slipped their best surveillance efforts.

She said, "My people have scrubbed every hard drive in the factory with the full knowledge and support of the Charlottesville PD. Who are, incidentally, awaiting a location to pick up your team. This is a lawful order, David. If you weren't involved, then you have nothing to worry about."

"I denied involvement, Duchess," David said, "I never said I had nothing to worry about. But I'll happily reverse course on proclaiming my innocence the second I find something that requires your vast resources to interdict."

"Stand down, David. There are protocols in place to stop this thing now that it's reached our shores. Those protocols don't include you or your team. So be a good little soldier and turn yourself in while you still have the chance. The second this call ends, any leniency I have for your well-intentioned actions is going to fade away, and once it does, I'm going to be severely pissed off."

There was a moment of silence before David responded, "Well as the wise man said, 'This too shall pass.'"

Then he hung up, and Duchess's face turned to stone.

Leaving the phone beside her ear, she tapped a button. A man replied, "Go ahead, ma'am."

"Notify the Charlottesville PD, Virginia State Police, and FBI. I want an APB out on David and his team for suspicion of involvement with last night's factory raid as per a classified informant. Once they're in custody, the Agency will take control."

55

Now alone at the helm of his team house workstation, Ian continued his search for further intelligence.

The team had been staged in Fredericksburg for seven hours now, waiting for his word. And as he continued to analyze every scrap of intelligence at his disposal, it occurred to Ian that no team of shooters could ever truly understand the lonely vigil of the intelligence operative endeavoring to support them from behind a computer. There was no glory in it, no glamour, no war stories for future grandchildren.

And while it wasn't manual labor per se, the essence of it was much the same: you report to your place of duty, and continue the rote work until your shift was done and often long beyond.

You could argue there was an artistic process behind it, too, because as the work progressed, a canvas was indeed painted, a sculpture crafted where there was only clay before. Like the artist, the more pains Ian undertook, the more his customers appreciated the finished work.

Except at the moment, he wasn't making any fucking progress at all.

It wasn't just that his resources were limited, it was that Duchess and some windowless office full of analysts had infinitely more to work with, the full resources of the CIA and NSA and God-knew-who-else toiling away at the same data he was, and probably much more. It was a Catch-22 of sorts—even if he miraculously uncovered some vital location, Duchess would have found it first, and have forces arriving not only to stop an attack but arrest his team.

And once that happened, Ian's own incarceration would follow in short order.

Still, what choice did he have? The bond with his team exceeded rationality, and was every bit as strong as that of family with the added bonus of a complete and total willingness to die for one another. Ian would never betray his team just as they'd never betray him; but right now, he seemed to be the only one who understood the lunacy of their situation.

For Cancer, Reilly, and Worthy, there seemed to be an almost autopilot response to follow David's guidance into oblivion. They were used to split-second tactical calls that couldn't be questioned without endangering everyone involved, combined with an unspoken addiction to both adrenaline and the teamwork aspect of what they did.

Only Ian seemed to retain a grounding in logic and a bigger picture that indicated the obvious: their team had hours of freedom remaining. It was one thing to stretch the rules when you had a tenuous satellite radio link to higher command and no UAV coverage contradicting your official version of events. It was completely another, he thought, to murder a couple people in the continental United States, then violate an official order to turn yourselves in. There was no coming back from that, no conceivable return to legitimacy. This would end with either the grave or jail for all of them, and yet he continued to toil away regardless. If his team was going down, then Ian would support them until the moment the cuffs were slapped on his wrists.

So his present obstacle wasn't a matter of willpower.

It was a simple matter of *data*.

He'd scrubbed the hard drives forward and backward, seeking any connection to his Fredericksburg clue and finding none. For the past hour he'd resorted to speculation, spinning every possible version of events in his head and trying to find evidence that supported it.

Ultimately, though, he came to the grave realization that he was chasing ghosts, looking for links that simply weren't there. The possibility that an elaborate relay was used to ping the outgoing calls to a cell tower in Fredericksburg as a mere decoy was very real, and growing larger with every second that Ian didn't uncover some new evidence.

Falling back in his seat, he leaned against the headrest and stared at the ceiling, then spun his rolling chair in a circle. His team was counting on him as their last line of support, and Ian recalled his team leader's haunted face when he returned to the team house after a night of evading the Charlottesville PD. How David had stared at him with hollow eyes, delivering his final guidance in the moments before Duchess called.

I'm sure you'll figure it out. Just ask yourself what your dad would do.

Recalling those words made Ian question exactly what his dad *would* do in this situation—and with nowhere else to turn, he reached for his phone and dialed.

A man answered, "You a telemarketer?"

"It's me," Ian said. "Is this a bad time?"

"Hell no. Smoking a cigar and looking at the lake. Though I'm guessing since you dialed me from an unlisted number, this isn't a social call."

Swallowing, Ian replied, "No, Dad, it isn't."

Ian hadn't been the best son, but it wasn't easy to grow up in his father's shadow, to have every professional associate he met distill his existence down to an association with his family lineage the second he mentioned his last name. Particularly when Ian wasn't some gun-slinging legend, but an intel man whose every effort fell short of his father's legacy.

"Well," his father replied, "out with it, then. What sage advice can I impart?"

"I'm looking for something important. There's a mountain of data, I only have one clue and a hunch to go off, and I'm not even sure it's right."

"What does your gut tell you?"

"My gut tells me that my hunch is correct."

"If there's one thing I taught you, it's not to second-guess your intuition. So why are you?"

"Why am I?" Ian asked, feeling irrationally angry at the question. "Because I've been looking for hours and I haven't made any forward progress."

"Hell, son, if that's the case, there's only one thing to do."

"What's that?"

"There's a rule about military retreat that applies just as well to intelligence, as far as I'm concerned."

"Which is?"

There was a pause before his father continued.

"If you absolutely can't move forward, then move back."

Ian felt a cool, tingling sensation race down his spine. His mouth went dry, an eyelid twitching in response to some mental connection spurred by his father's statement.

"Dad, I have to go."

His father sounded like he was smiling as he replied, "Happy hunting, son."

Ian hung up, pulling his chair close to the desk as he reoriented himself at the keyboard with a renewed sense of determination.

He assumed the launch assembly had been constructed in Charlottesville, and his gut instinct about the phone clue told him it had since been transported to Fredericksburg. And if it was still there, it was for one of three reasons: because it was being welded to the mobile platform from which the launch would occur, because the rockets hadn't yet arrived, or a combination of both.

The only other alternative was if the mobile platform had already departed toward its final target, and if that was the case, he was already too late.

So he focused on the only vector he could, doing what his father said and moving backward.

Ian went back in time with his intelligence picture, trying to determine how the rockets had made landfall in America. If he could figure out how they'd arrived, he could potentially figure out where in Fredericksburg they'd been sent to.

And a trans-Atlantic crossing from Syria to the US had only two options: by air or sea.

Ian doubted the former; few possibilities short of a privately-owned jet would allow for air travel of such a large cargo load, and even then, the somewhat insane classified security measures of airports in the post-9/11 world made such a smuggling effort almost inconceivable. Zhao could have sent a private jet into Syria, of course, but Ian doubted that would have gone unnoticed by the massive Agency efforts to interdict the rockets.

The sea, by contrast, was a different story altogether.

International waters were the maritime equivalent of the Wild West, a space so vast that any regulatory enforcement became a virtual guessing game of ship locations and cargoes. Even on legitimate freighters coming into major US ports, customs agents could only inspect a tiny fraction of containers. The rest passed through with the aid of little more than thin, serial-numbered metal bands routed through the lock assembly along with the padlock itself. Those bands were replicated easily enough, or bypassed altogether—enterprising smugglers could simply remove the hinge bolts on the container doors, lay them down without disturbing the seal, and load whatever cargo they pleased before reassembling the unit intact.

The end result was a thriving trade for drug transit along international trade corridors, with an untold volume of narcotics reaching their destination among the millions of sea containers transiting the ocean every hour of every day. Hundreds of tons of cocaine were seized each year, and even the most optimistic of law enforcement leadership estimated that massive volume represented less than ten percent of the total.

But they'd last seen the rockets five days ago in Syria, and a quick search told Ian that such freighters took between ten to twenty days to cross the Atlantic.

That wasn't to say that numerous other vessels weren't capable of making that voyage in a fraction of that time; and it was those faster ships Ian directed his attention to, accessing maritime transit records and customs reports in what quickly devolved into a bottomless pit of information.

So Ian changed tack and went with a more granular approach: he hacked the US Coast Guard.

Well, he thought, "hacked" was perhaps a strong word for what he did. Many of the records were accessible with an easily penetrated login, owing to the unclassified nature of their exhaustive documentation of all US-flagged vessels, to say nothing of incoming reporting from civilian vessels. There was an open line of communication between any vessel off the US coast and the Coast Guard emergency frequency, and Ian scanned that line of communication for anything amiss.

Most of the reports were banal: engine trouble at sea, victims of heart attacks or divers with decompression sickness who required aerial transport to land-based medical facilities. But another record caught his eye: a joint Coast Guard and DEA raid of the *Scyllis*, a yacht belonging to one Wei Zhao.

Rather than being excited about this development, Ian felt dismayed—Duchess had already investigated the possibility, which was troubling on two fronts. First, she made the connection before he did. And second, she'd exploited it without any apparent results.

So he went back to scouring the banal Coast Guard reports, scanning the data and hoping something would trigger his intuition. It took Ian another six minutes to find it, and when he did, he zeroed in on it with a laser-like intensity.

On the morning of July second, the offshore fishing vessel *Amelia* filed a report of a man overboard. The captain's account, corroborated by the rest of the crew, was that a rookie crew member named Robert Swanson had gone out for night watch and never returned. They ostensibly reported his absence as soon as they noticed the next morning, and Coast Guard investigators had boarded the ship to take sworn memorandums. The event was ruled an open-and-shut accident—an inexperienced man had either fallen asleep, lost his footing as a wave struck, or been stumbling drunk when he'd gone over the side. His cries would have gone unheard over the sounds of the boat engine and sea, and he'd never be seen again.

Except for Ian, the report stood out among a long list of others far too unremarkable to invoke suspicion. He did the math on the boat's course, and its return to port—there was at least a theoretical possibility that it had recovered some cargo deposited into the sea by the *Scyllis*, and the timing of its return was consistent with transfer of its catch to a Virginia-bound truck prior to the team's raid at the metalworking factory.

Then he dug deeper, penetrating the transfer records for fishing boats returning to the *Amelia's* last port. The collective catch was transferred to trucks owned by three separate companies, each taking possession of cargo categorized by tons of fish. One of the names looked inexplicably familiar to him: Blackwood Seafood Company.

And upon tracing the business's corporate lineage, he realized why he'd recognized it.

Ian had seen that name once before, when researching the ownership of Steno, LLC, the company that had purchased the metalworking factory from Laila's mother and stepfather. Six other businesses fell under the corporate umbrella beneath the multinational conglomerate Palvita International, owned and chaired by Chinese billionaire Wei Zhao.

He knew what he'd find even as he hammered keystrokes into the computer with all the speed he could manage. Ian's suspicions were confirmed as the screen flashed to the logistical records of Blackwood Seafood Company—a single truck had departed the port for a distribution facility in Fredericksburg, Virginia, and now he had an address.

56

The hotel room in Fredericksburg was average in size, but under the circumstances, Worthy felt like it was claustrophobically small.

He was seated on the lone armchair, surveying the team in their current resting places—Reilly stretched out on one of the twin beds, Cancer on the other, both men looking like reflections of one another with their arms folded behind their heads as they stared at the ceiling.

David should have been sleeping, recovering from his long night on the run from the police.

But he'd refused not only to sleep but even to sit—so far, he'd been passing the time by pacing the room, making everyone nervous, his hollow stare becoming more so with each hour spent awake.

"We should get tacos for dinner," Reilly said to no one in particular. "And what the hell is Ian doing?"

"Well," David responded, "he's either searching through intel at the team house or he's halfway to Mexico and laughing his ass off. Either way, you're right. Tacos would really hit the spot."

Cancer gave a long sigh. "If Ian doesn't have something for us soon, I might just drive back to Charlottesville and wring his scrawny neck. Hard to imagine that kid swam out of his dad's enormous balls."

Sitting up to take a seat at the edge of the mattress, Reilly replied, "You're still pissed about having to ditch your knife, aren't you?"

"'Course I am. Know how many people I killed with that thing? I was going to pass it down to my son one day."

"Well I lost two guns, including my grandfather's 1911," Reilly pointed out. "And you don't even have a son. Or a wife or, to my knowledge, even an ex-wife."

Cancer looked hurt to his core, the first time Worthy had seen an indication of humanity in the team's second-in-command.

He responded, "That's just...fuckin' hurtful, man. Why would you say that?"

David walked to the bedside and set a comforting hand atop Cancer's shoulder.

"Cheer up, buddy," he said. "If Ian delivers, you'll have another chance to kill people again in no time. Just means you'll be using bullets this time, is all."

Some measure of hope returned to Cancer's eyes.

"Thanks, David."

Worthy wasn't sure what to make of the scene before him. Now that the team had gone rogue in direct violation of Duchess's orders, and faced incarceration in the best-case scenario, it seemed everyone's maturity had regressed by a decade or two. They'd spent nearly eight hours in the hotel room, eating delivery food, watching movies, and shit-talking one another over the most minute trivialities, waiting for a no-notice raid on an objective that Ian had yet to find, without anyone mentioning the obvious—the world had shifted on its axis the second David had, in as many words, told Duchess to go fuck herself.

They were disavowed, roving fugitives with a dwindling shelf life.

And there was nothing they could say in their own defense. Their Agency-issued weapons, ammo, and equipment were stockpiled in the two vehicles outside, and that infraction alone brought with it any amount of jail time that Duchess cared to threaten them with. Add in a couple dead bodies in the metalworking factory and the fact that they'd driven an hour and a half in the hopes of some further lead to follow, and the sky was the limit with regard to how this Independence Day would end.

But no one was discussing any of that, nor the somewhat glaring possibility that Ian's theory about a cell tower in Fredericksburg was wrong, and had simply been a call relay like they used on their own phones. If that was the case, their time would be better spent trying to flee the country.

When David's phone rang, it felt as if all the oxygen were sucked out of the room. Cancer and Reilly bolted upright, and Worthy followed them to surround their team leader in a semicircle.

David put the phone on speaker mode as he said, "Tell me you have some good news."

Ian responded, "That depends on your definition of 'good.' It wasn't easy, but I found a lead. The key was identifying a suspicious man-overboard report from an offshore fishing boat—"

"Ian," David interrupted, "the clock is ticking. We just want breakfast—no one cares how the sausage was made."

There was a pause then, and Worthy suspected it involved a moment of Ian fuming on the other end of the line.

Finally he said, "It's a seafood distribution facility, twelve thousand square feet, and from what I can see, a lot of that is refrigerated processing and freezer space. The address is 204 Southern Avenue, fifteen minutes away from your location."

"We were going to get tacos for Reilly, but I suppose we could head there instead. Push us all the imagery you can—we'll plan our raid on the move."

"At this point, I think we need to consider roping in Duchess."

David shook his head.

"We get shot up and killed, you call her and sing your heart out."

"Concur," Cancer said. "We tell Duchess, she's gonna send cops. Cops are bound by laws. We ain't."

Reilly shrugged. "But if she sends cops, we have time for tacos."

David looked over and said, "Racegun, what do you think?"

With a half-smile, Worthy said, "What are we doing, taking votes?"

"No. Tell me anyway."

"If I'm going to spend the rest of my life in a prison cell or a non-extradition-treaty country, I want to go out with a bang. We've been hunting BK for too long to give up now. This isn't about who gets the kill—but out of everyone in the world, the only guys I trust to get the job done no matter what are in this room."

"And me," Ian said, "back at the team house."

"Sure. Whatever. Point is, I think there's a sufficient sense of urgency to justify anything and everything we can do, that we'll get more mileage out of extra-legal measures than the feds would with all their oversight. We're already off the reservation. Let's make it count."

Ian said, "You guys need to take it easy with the killing this time. The best thing you could do is capture some living detainees, especially BK. Finding out who put this operation together is as valuable as recovering the rockets."

It was David who responded.

"Ian, I love you. You're my brother. But there's a hard truth you still haven't learned about this business."

"What's that?"

David gave a patient smile before replying, his final response as the team made their way to the door.

"Some people just need to get shot in the fucking face."

57

Ian's computer screens were filled with the live feed of every surveillance camera he could find around the seafood distribution center's perimeter.

The internet was a magical thing—by penetrating the online networks of the adjacent businesses, he could view their live surveillance camera footage with only slightly less effort than it would have taken him to hijack a traffic camera in Tehran.

But the pitfalls of his current position were many: the available cameras presented an incomplete view of the business park surrounding the objective building, and there was precious little he'd be able to tell the team that they couldn't see themselves in the next minute or two.

Then came the matter of their communications.

Ian was piping into the team frequency via a tenuous FM relay system that was already on the fritz, and he could only hear his teammates communicating between long garbled bursts of static. They'd only received his return traffic intermittently, so their backup connection of cellular phones was going to be required sooner rather than later.

And finally there was Ian's own reservations about the mission at hand.

He suspected the rockets were stockpiled in that building, awaiting departure the moment their launch system was ready to be loaded. It didn't make sense for the enemy to put all their eggs in one basket by combining the projectiles and launcher before they had to—that way, even if the launch system was interdicted by cops, they could relocate the rockets and await their next opportunity. Hell, they could lean the rockets against a rock and fire them whenever they pleased—insurgents in the Middle East had been doing just that with varying degrees of success for years—but precision-engineered launch tubes would provide Bari Khan with near-pinpoint accuracy, and Ian doubted the terrorist would waste an opportunity like that. Whatever his target, Bari Khan was going to hit it with everything at his disposal.

Ian felt a knot forming in the pit of his stomach, which could have been attributed to a bad feeling or simply his unease at not being physically present with his team. As unsuited as he was for purely tactical situations, the reality here was much worse—he was relegated to watching from afar, with an incomplete view assembled by a patchwork of adjacent surveillance cameras and without adequate communications. He wanted to *be there*, felt a deep, undeniable drive to speed to Fredericksburg and join his team.

But his position in Charlottesville was simply too valuable. He was the last remaining line of support for the team, the only one who could sift any intelligence they found since the Agency was formally out of the picture.

There was another reason, too, and it was one of insurance.

Should the team be wiped out to a man in the operation ahead, Ian was the only one who could report their findings to Duchess in a last-ditch effort to stop Bari Khan. If he made that call too soon, she would flood the distribution center with police in an attempt to arrest his teammates; if he made the call too late, Bari Khan could slip through their fingers yet again.

Ian shook his head. As if a second domestic assault operation weren't bad enough, he now had the legal ramifications of CIA blowback to consider.

He caught a flash of movement on one of the screens, focusing in on it to see the unthinkable: a medium duty delivery truck speeding into view from the distribution center's south side.

Ian sensed at once that it was suspect, driving too quickly for the surroundings, running a stop sign between buildings as it careened down a side street and out of view. Even at the video screen's oblique angle, he made out the Blackwood Seafood Company logo on the driver's side door panel.

Jesus, he thought, was that the attack platform? He didn't have time to perform the mental math in determining if a delivery truck of that size could fit the launch tubes for every rocket currently at large—but if it could, it would be *brilliant*. That delivery truck could fit on any road accessible to the average American sedan, and probably half of those were too narrow for a semi to traverse.

Grabbing the hand mic, he transmitted over the team frequency through the relay.

"Stop movement, stop movement. One-by delivery truck leaving objective to the north, prepare for vehicle interdiction, how copy?"

The only response was a squelch of static, and Ian had no way of knowing if his transmission had been received short of watching the screen before him.

Then he saw that he was too late—two figures raced forward to initiate the assault.

Ian's hand flew to the phone beside him and, hesitating for a split second of consideration, he picked it up and began to dial.

58

Cancer led the way to his designated breach point, with Reilly following a few steps behind.

He heard a burst of static over his earpiece, and knew at once that it was Ian's dumb ass on the ineffective FM relay.

David transmitted back, "*Angel, you're coming in broken. Clear the net.*"

Cancer smiled at the response, thinking it was one of several oddities playing out in the current situation.

For one thing, they were in full combat gear, night vision devices flipped upward on their mounts as they slipped past the security lights ringing the building. The sounds of traffic reached them from adjacent side streets as they moved with weapons at the ready, slipping toward their target amid a completely unsuspecting civilian population.

Then came the matter of their plan, which could be briefly summarized as follows: there was no plan. How could there be? With a time-sensitive target and no interior layout, precious little planning was required.

The distribution facility shared one border with a larger building containing an auto repair facility and—go figure—a seafood restaurant.

Out of the facility's remaining three sides, all contained multiple loading docks, some for delivery trucks but most large enough to accommodate eighteen-wheelers.

Without sufficient personnel to isolate the objective, they'd have to rely on Ian to notify them of any "squirters" fleeing the building. And given the FM relay going to shit every five seconds, Cancer wrote that possibility off from the start.

So the solution was simple: the team was going to take their chances. Do what they'd always done, and play it fast and loose.

Accordingly, the northeast wall would remain unguarded, while the southeast had a solid wall with the adjacent facilities. Cancer and Reilly would enter through the southeast side of the building, while David and Worthy breached through the northwest. Once inside, both split team elements would clear in a clockwise direction until they found the rockets or were killed.

Like he thought at the outset: simple.

Cancer darted up a set of concrete exterior stairs to a closed metal door, giving the handle a single short pull to confirm it was locked. The action was little more than a rote formality; no one was leaving the building unsecured, and as quickly as he registered the handle's resistance, Cancer took a sidestep and spun outward, scanning for targets in the parking lot as Reilly moved in to apply the explosive charge to the door hinges.

Taking in the sight before him, Cancer was both thrilled and mildly surprised to see that life was proceeding as normal in Fredericksburg: parked cars and vehicle headlights proceeded up the roads in his line of sight, even a few distant civilians made their way to the seafood restaurant at the far side of the building.

No one looked up to see the two men in full tactical kit preparing to demolish a door before raiding the distribution facility, and even if they did, they'd likely have no idea what to make of it.

It didn't matter, he thought. They'd become aware of what he could conservatively term a minor disturbance soon enough.

"We're set," Reilly whispered beside him.

Cancer transmitted, "Team Two ready."

David's response was near-immediate.

"*Stand by—three, two, one. Execute, execute—*"

The concussion of Reilly detonating his door charge washed over Cancer in a single explosive shockwave that was followed by car alarms ringing to life in the parking lot, headlights and turn signals flashing in quick succession as his vision cleared from the blast.

Then Cancer spun toward the now-open doorway, raising his rifle as he darted inside and cut right to clear his first corner.

59

Duchess held the phone to her ear, feeling her lips slide into a smile—or was it a smirk?—at the sound of the panicked voice on the other end of the call.

Christmas had come early, she thought.

Here she was trying to track down David's team with the help of multiple local law enforcement organizations on top of the FBI, and the intelligence operative from her wayward assassination element had just personally dialed her office phone.

With Gossweiler breathing down her neck over the previous night's raid in Charlottesville, Duchess wasn't just going to have these men arrested.

She was going to crucify them.

"Where are you?" she asked. "I want a location in the next five seconds, and if you're thinking about lying to me, know that you'll live to regret it."

Ian replied, "Duchess. You've worked for the Agency for a long time, and I respect your opinion."

"Thank you."

Ian continued, "Now stop talking and listen to what I'm telling you. There's a delivery truck with the Blackwood Seafood Company logo in Fredericksburg, Virginia, currently traveling northbound on US Highway One and passing the Route 17 interchange. The odds of the rockets *not* being aboard are about two percent. Forget about arresting us for the time being and interdict this goddamn thing before it kicks off an attack we can't stop."

The call ended then, a hollow *click* followed by the sound of a man stating, "He ended the call, ma'am."

"Yeah," Duchess said, "I got that."

"Any updates?" the man asked.

He wasn't inquiring about the content of the conversation—after all, he'd heard the exchange as clearly as she had, to say nothing of recording it for posterity. Rather, he was asking whether she took the conversation seriously enough to provide updated guidance to the law enforcement entities currently awaiting further orders.

And that was a great goddamn question, she thought.

David's team had strung her along quite enough in the past four days, starting with their illegal transport of Agency equipment and ending with their current fugitive status. She knew good and well that this call could easily be the latest in a long line of diversions and half-truths.

But the bottom line was that 633 rockets were at large, along with Bari Khan, and Duchess couldn't afford to take any chances.

She replied, "Get me the Fredericksburg PD first and the State Police second. Tell them we have an emergency update requiring immediate response."

60

Worthy cleared his third doorway and cut left, sensing David entering the room behind him as both men scanned for threats and found none.

While Worthy had never been inside a seafood distribution plant or anything close to it, his surroundings were about what he'd expect.

Blue-painted metal staircases led to the second floor, rolling assembly lines with power cords descended from the ceiling, stainless steel tables and giant weighing scales interspersed with floor pallets were stacked high with boxes. The entire place was freezing cold, Worthy's thin Georgia blood feeling frigid in his veins despite the effort of moving continuously under the weight of his full kit. Trolleys and hand carts were tucked against the little remaining wall space, obstacles he had to be careful not to trip over.

Above all, the space smelled like ice and dead sea creatures, the scent filling his nostrils every angle he turned. They may as well have been clearing the interior of a giant lobster.

There had been no trace of the rockets or even defensive measures in place to safeguard them, either from his element or the other split team; by all appearances, they'd just raided an empty building with the added complication of cops arriving at any second in response to what must have been numerous calls from concerned citizens reporting simultaneous explosions.

Abandoned building and law enforcement response aside, Worthy had another concern.

He was well enough versed in close quarters battle to know his teammates' spoken and unspoken cues, and since he was paired with David yet again, he caught the sloppiness of motion indicative of lapses in alertness or worse, judgment.

Worthy could do nothing at present to correct either, and so he cleared his corners with all the rapidity that his experience endowed before hurriedly checking David's sectors, pulling double-duty for lack of trust in his partner.

Following David's lead, Worthy flowed into the next room—and it, like all the rest, was empty. Aside from the facility's lights being on, there were no indications of human presence whatsoever. As they closed on the next doorway, he whispered to David.

"What do you make of this?"

David replied, "Either Ian was wrong and sent us to a dry hole, or it's a trap."

As if someone was trying to clarify the situation, a man began moving beyond the doorway to the next room.

The first footfalls Worthy heard sounded distant, echoing against the cavernous walls as they approached and increasing in speed. Within a second the noise of feet slapping the floor escalated to a run, not away but *toward them*.

Worthy flowed inside the next doorway, panning sideways to identify the runner, wondering if he was about to intercept some terrified factory worker sent fleeing by the other split team element.

But the man he saw running at them from across a wide seafood processing room didn't look scared. He had Arab features and an athlete's focus, moving in a bulky cold weather jacket as Worthy scanned him for weapons. His hands were balled into fists, with no visible firearm or even a knife.

Worthy absorbed the sight within a fraction of a second, the only time he'd have to make a decision that could turn out to be the best one he'd ever made—or the worst.

Aligning his sights on the man's face, Worthy fired a single suppressed gunshot that passed through the bridge of the man's nose, sending a spray of brain matter out the back of his skull as he tumbled forward. The unzipped seam of his jacket flew open to reveal a neatly aligned row of rectangular blocks, visible for a fleeting moment before the man struck the ground chest-first.

Ducking behind a metal rolling cabinet, Worthy transmitted in a feverishly urgent voice.

"S-vest! S-vest!"

He caught sight of David crouched behind a stack of boxes against the far wall, his transmission following Worthy's own by a fraction of a second.

"Exfil, exfil, exfil."

Cancer replied, "*Team Two copies.*"

Steadying his footing, Worthy prepared to cover his team leader's withdrawal and watched for David to make the first move back out the way they'd come.

But against all logic, running wasn't on David's agenda at the moment—he was taking aim deeper into the processing room, firing his first shots of the mission.

Keeping his body behind cover, Worthy angled his rifle around the side of the rolling cabinet to scan for a target—if another man was sprinting toward them, they may have only a moment to kill him before disintegrating in a jihadist fireball.

But Worthy's next glance across the room didn't reveal a single target; it revealed at least a half-dozen of them.

As David fired beside him, Worthy drilled two rounds into the nearest man, sweeping his barrel right to engage a partially visible head emerging from behind a parked forklift. Worthy managed to fire two rounds in less than a second, a pink mist confirming his accuracy before he continued his sweep with a mounting sense of panic.

The enemy fighters who suddenly appeared behind every possible object in the room may or may not have had suicide vests—but what they did have were firearms, and they began returning fire with deafening blasts as Worthy and David gunned them down as quickly as they appeared.

But even with Worthy's uncanny reflexes, he feared it wouldn't be enough—these men weren't restrained to any logic of fire and maneuver, instead scrambling toward him across abundant covered positions provided by the processing equipment. They appeared to be a mix of Caucasians, Chinese, and Arabs—some were wild-eyed, others calm and shouting to one another, and a few sounded the shrill battle cries of men who'd long since resigned themselves to dying inside this building.

Worthy and David couldn't make a move for the door without getting shot, and while Cancer and Reilly were surely moving toward the sound of gunfire as quickly as they could, he intuitively knew they couldn't possibly make it in time to alter the outcome of what was now occurring.

David's voice transmitted over his earpiece.

"*Cancer, Team One pinned down and in need of support. Racegun, assault forward.*"

Worthy realized what his team leader meant—David was trapped behind the wall-mounted conveyor belt, unable to move against the sprays of sparking metal as bullets impacted his covered position.

Worthy, by contrast, could dart out from either side of the rolling cabinet he was braced behind, and he had a good idea for his next covered firing position.

He laid down some suppressing fire first, barely registering Cancer's transmission of "*Team Two moving.*" Worthy utilized one side of the cabinet as cover to unleash blasts of gunfire against every known and suspected enemy position. Emptying his magazine, he tucked himself behind the cabinet for the last time and conducted a reload.

Then he spun out from the opposite side, crouching low as he took five charging steps that sent him slamming against the side of the forklift.

Taking aim from one side, he saw a new universe of firing angles, the now-exposed flanks of two men who'd previously been hidden from view. Worthy decimated them both with a ten-round volley, their bodies dropping as he ducked behind the forklift, then popped out the other side to sling lead at a partially visible man trying to locate him.

David exploited the surprise to maneuver forward, his figure a flash of movement in Worthy's peripheral vision. By the time the first bullets began clanging against the forklift, David was behind cover, engaging the shooter with two suppressed bursts.

The incoming fire against the forklift ended, though he could still hear pop shots from a single shooter coming from deeper in the room. Unable to locate the man, Worthy decided to do something that would either prove very brilliant or very dumb within the next three seconds.

He climbed atop the forklift, squeezing his body against the seat to gain an elevated vantage point with the faith that his reflexes would outpace the enemy's.

The next milliseconds unfolded with excruciating slowness—he saw the last visible fighter braced behind a stacked pallet, a white man who swung his rifle from David toward the new flash of movement.

Worthy tried to align his sights, the effort ending as his suppressor struck a metal roof bracket on the forklift. He leaned back to clear the obstruction, then thrust the buttstock back against his shoulder as he took aim in time to see a single muzzle flash from his opponent.

Firing at the same instant, Worthy saw the man's throat explode in a burst of red as he fell out of sight. The enemy had missed his shot, and Worthy hadn't—though the victory seemed of precious little consolation at present.

David transmitted, "*Team Two, wave off—we're good. Exfil, exfil, exfil.*"

The response came in the form of a deep, thundering blast that shook the entire building.

The overhead lights flickered, and David was transmitting as the echo receded.

"*Team Two, status?*"

He got his answer not in the form of a transmitted response—there was none—but in the sounds of unsuppressed gunfire that followed from deeper in the building.

No words needed to be spoken after that—David and Worthy were sprinting past the enemy bodies, hoping none had survived with the wherewithal to take aim as they made their way toward a new gunfight.

Unaware of his orientation in time and space, Reilly fought through a fog of consciousness to try and determine what in the hell had just happened.

The last thing he remembered was advancing through the building with Cancer, trying to make their way to the gunfight that had obviously ensnared David and Worthy. He had one second, maybe two, of trying to determine the source of a new noise, one that he concluded to be running footsteps—and by the time he and Cancer were opening fire on a man in the doorway, the explosion had erased the world from view.

The facility seemed to vanish in a cloud of plaster dust and smoke, a stinking mist of high explosives and human flesh that sent hundreds of steel ball bearings into flight and turning the room into a pinball machine of destruction.

Now that he was regaining his vision, Reilly saw the industrial ceiling lined with snaking pipes and ultraviolet bulbs that flickered with flashes of light that sent spikes of pain to the back of his skull.

He was flat on his back, unable to summon the requisite strength and coordination to move his limbs. Glancing down, he saw a row of bloody dots stitching his left arm—ball bearings from the suicide vest embedded in his flesh—though that was the least of his worries.

The blasts of automatic gunfire sounded distant through his ringing head, growing louder and clearer as he regained his wits. The incoming gunfire and ricochets created a hailstorm of bullets that zipped and spun through the air around him, an angry hornet swarm of metal clanging off every hard surface.

Groggily looking sideways, Reilly felt for the rifle slung across his shoulders, detecting it through the gloved palm of his numb right hand. He struggled to lift it across his chest, the effort requiring the sum total of all his focus and strength.

The enemy was moving into the room, trying to find him and Cancer through the smoke, shouting to each other and firing indiscriminately.

This wasn't going to end well, Reilly knew at once, though he couldn't seem to make his body move fast enough to respond. Hell of a way to go, he thought—after all the physical and tactical training, all the deployments and gunfights, he was powerless to intervene in his fate thanks to some asshole clacking off a suicide vest.

As he struggled to lift his assault rifle to defend himself, Reilly caught a flash of movement from a doorway to his side. He wanted to shoot, couldn't orient his weapon—and then saw that the man now entering wasn't an enemy fighter but his salvation.

David sped through the door, cutting right and out of Reilly's view before a second man entered.

Thank God, Reilly thought. The figure blazing through the doorway at the speed of light was Worthy, descending from on high and shooting with a speed that Reilly had never witnessed before, on the range or otherwise.

Worthy's rifle went empty, and rather than spend the second it took him to reload his magazine, he dropped his rifle and drew his pistol instead, taking aim and resuming fire by the time his primary weapon had fallen on its sling.

But then his pistol went empty too, slide locking to the rear as a wounded Chinese fighter fell to the floor in Reilly's view. The downed fighter locked eyes with him, then shifted his rifle for a final kill shot against the disoriented medic.

Before he could pull the trigger, a spray of bullet impacts stitched across the man's side and he collapsed dead, David appearing over his body a second later and shouting, "Clear!"

Then it was over—no more gunfire, no enemy shouts, just the ringing in Reilly's ears from the blast before David moved to help, straining to lift him to his feet. Reilly aided the effort as best he could, feeling strength return to his legs as he stood shakily, looking for Cancer in the room's smoldering interior.

He located his teammate a second later. Cancer had apparently fared better in the blast and was already standing under his own power, though bleeding from his right thigh in what appeared to be a wound from the suicide vest.

"Exfil," David announced. "Let's get the fuck out of here."

61

In the seconds before David called, Ian committed fully to his plan.

He was the only team member with any semblance of rationality remaining, untainted by the overwhelming exhilaration of combat and the most emotionally distanced from the situation at hand.

The rest were biased not only by sheer virtue of experience with near-death scenarios, but by following a single leader who was quickly turning into a madman, if he hadn't already.

After a full night of running from the cops, David was deliriously sleep deprived and running off fumes of rage and hatred. Ian considered his response to a request for living detainees—*Some people just need to get shot in the fucking face*—and then allowed that his team leader may have been losing his mind as well. Ian had increasingly gotten the sense that David's marital situation had grown more tenuous, and that wasn't a recipe for mental health when his primary inputs were combat action and fighting for his life.

All that added up to Ian's second greatest concern at present, landing just shy of a successful terrorist attack: David was a charismatic young leader intent on accomplishing his personal mission at all costs, and he'd take his entire team—and the Agency's long-overdue reincarnation of a targeted killing program—off the cliff edge along with himself.

When David finally called, Ian answered on the first ring.

His team leader's voice was contemptuous.

"Your brilliant idea was one giant trap. We barely made it out. Two of us are wounded, we're low on ammo, and down to one car. So thanks for that."

"I tried calling you off," Ian shot back. "A delivery truck left the objective as you guys were closing in."

"You have eyes-on?"

"I have an idea, based on intermittent surveillance footage. Get going northbound on US Highway One."

"We're on the move," David confirmed, "and you better not lose sight of the truck before Duchess finds out."

"She knows," Ian replied at once.

"She...what? How?"

"I called her."

"Why would you do that, Ian?"

"I couldn't call you off, and the rockets have to be onboard that truck. Don't be an asshole."

"It's my *nature!*" David almost shouted, the sound of a car accelerating audible on the other end. "So I suppose our route is crawling with cops, isn't it?"

"Yeah. Probably."

"Wonderful. Thanks a lot, Ian."

"Don't blame me for the comms relay going down," Ian said. "If you want to get your head out of your ass for one second, there's more."

"Yeah? What's that?"

"My last visual on the delivery truck was at a traffic cam on Olive Chapel Road. It should have passed my next camera angle of the road at Alden Bridge—but it hasn't."

"Great. So what's in between the two?"

"That's my point—there's a single paved eastbound route called Portofino. So the truck must have taken it, but all it leads to are a few neighborhoods and businesses that I can't find any connection between. No suspicious sideroads, tunnel entrances, nothing. The truck didn't break brush to drive into the river, so there must be a concealed trail or enemy facility. Maybe a cache. We've got precious little to lose by searching that road for anything suspicious."

"Except our lives."

"Well, yeah," Ian said, "except for that. Get moving and search for some vehicle outlet constructed since the satellite imagery was updated. You've got a one-minute head start."

"A one-minute head start to find a needle in a haystack. You're just full of good fucking news, aren't you?"

"Well, I have to tell you—"

David cut him off.

"Head start against what? And do I want to know why I only have one minute?"

Ian swallowed.

"Because that's how long it will take me to reach Duchess."

"Don't you dare."

"Make no mistake, David," Ian said, "I *absolutely* dare. Stopping this attack is more important than who gets the credit. The only reason I'm calling you first is that the cops are tied up at the seafood distribution facility, and if you can find the truck before they do, then maybe—just maybe—we'll score enough credibility not to rot in jail for the rest of our natural lives. So don't fuck this up."

62

Riding in the passenger seat, I braced myself as subtly as I could, cringing in mild anticipation of a crash as the trees whipped past the glow of our headlights on either side of the road. I said nothing, however, trying not to project any weakness to Worthy, who was negotiating the winding forest curves as quickly as our vehicle and his reflexes would allow.

Which, considering it was Worthy, turned out to be pretty fucking fast.

From the backseat, Reilly said, "Two miles of road remaining before the dead end. Next street to our left is a subdivision."

Holding a phone in his right hand, Reilly was ticking off road junctures on the satellite imagery that Ian had sent us as we searched for some vehicle pathway that had been constructed in the interim. His left arm was out of action, wrapped in pressure dressings and hastily tied in a field sling.

"Pass," I said. "Let the cops search it. We're looking for a Hail Mary."

The neighborhood entrance passed in a blur outside the window, and Worthy whipped the vehicle at near-minimum traction around another bend in the road.

From the seat behind me, Cancer said, "We ain't catching a Hail Mary if you roll us into the trees at fifty miles per hour." Cancer had absorbed four ball bearings from the suicide bomber, and wore a pressure dressing on his right thigh as a result. I could hear the pain in his voice as he added, "And try to remember this is our last car."

"Last car," Worthy asked, "or last chance?"

"Either. Both."

He was right on both counts, of course—we'd used two cars in our hasty raid of the seafood distribution plant, though since we'd been required to exit the premises in a considerably more rushed fashion than we'd entered, one of those cars remained parked outside the building.

Worthy responded, "Never thought the mission would end like this. Clown car of hellbent men barreling toward a target that might not be there."

Reilly added, "Decent band name, though. 'Clown Car of Hellbent Men.' We'll have to start that up when we get back."

"*If* we get back," I corrected him. Because not even Ian knew what he was sending us to, and it was quite possible that he was *wrong*—that he'd simply missed some camera angle showing the delivery truck escaping from some alternate path. But at this point there was nothing else to go on, nothing of value on this stretch of road that was quickly ending.

Worthy offered, "Maybe they saw us coming, and our raid flushed the truck out."

"Not a chance," I said. "Whatever Bari Khan is doing, it's part of the plan he's had since Syria. We're the ones improvising, not him."

But at this point, what did it matter?

The abandoned team car outside the seafood facility was full of our fingerprints, with stray hair for the police to cross-check with DNA samples that Duchess was probably providing them at that very moment. Reilly's injury had effectively removed a quarter of our already small team from the fight, leaving the three of us with limited ammunition—Worthy and I had expended much of our supply shooting it out with enemy forces.

This was a total shitshow, four men in disarray with no choices and no time: the story of my team's entire short history, whose final chapter was being written tonight.

"Slow down," I called, then, feeling Worthy braking the vehicle, continued, "Reilly, fifty meters ahead on the right—is there a trail on the imagery?"

My heart thudded as I waited for his response, my eyes riveted on a barely perceptible break in the trees.

"No," Reilly answered, and Cancer spoke immediately after.

"That's got to be it, boss."

I caught a glimpse of a crude path with tire tracks cutting into the woods, just wide enough to fit a single vehicle. The odds weren't great; it looked like a logging trail, and one that we could have very nearly passed by without noticing.

I said, "We're taking it. Kill the lights and transition to NVGs."

Worthy extinguished the headlights, and my view of the whitewashed road turned to darkness, re-illuminating in green shadows as I donned my night vision. Worthy wheeled our car into a slow right-hand turn, aligning our tires within the tracks as our car rumbled forward on a bed of dirt and tree roots.

Worthy rolled down all four windows, and we oriented our weapons into the warm night air. I had no idea whether to expect incoming gunfire or a dead end, both equally plausible.

The chanting of frogs and insects poured from the woods, an irritatingly loud symphony that prevented us from discerning any human activity. Shit, I thought, they could have had a full team digging a rocket cache by pickax and we wouldn't hear it until we were virtually on top of them.

Reilly said, "The river is about two hundred meters ahead."

"Stop the car," Cancer said as we slowed to a halt. "David, we need to proceed on foot, look for visual."

I said, "You're right. Dismount and we'll parallel the trail."

Then I reflexively reached for the door handle until Cancer spoke.

"No doors—they'll activate the interior lights."

Gritting my teeth, I thought, why not? Let's add another indignity to the growing list that defined our every action since the first time we'd missed killing Bari Khan in our first Syrian ambush.

We began clambering out of the open vehicle windows with varying degrees of gracefulness. I managed to pull my upper body outside the car, sitting on the windowsill before adjusting my rifle and sliding my legs out. From the sound of it, Reilly was having the toughest time both on account of his size and having one arm in a sling. Though judging by

Cancer's pained grunts, he didn't have a much easier effort with his injured leg.

No words were spoken then—Worthy assumed his position as point man and moved into the trees to our right, turning to parallel the trail on its path forward. Cancer fell into the left flank position and I took the right, with Reilly trailing to my right rear as the last man.

We moved through the forest in a four-man fire team wedge, the most fundamental building block of infantry operations. Gone was the notion of any Agency status as elite contractors; we were going through motions taught in every military basic training around the world, our advanced weapons and equipment offset by injuries, our depleted ammo supply, and our complete and total lack of any semblance of a plan.

Worthy turned back to me abruptly, pointing to the side of his head and then shaking it to indicate his comms were down.

I transmitted in a whisper, "Radio check."

No response, and a quick scan of my teammates mirroring Worthy's hand signal told me that our radios had shit the bed along with everything else.

Then Worthy gave another signal, extending an arm to his front.

I made out what he was pointing to, but just barely—the slightest hints of glowing light that originated from further down the trail, casting a dim, shifting green glow through the trees.

With the extreme amplification under night vision, the real source was probably no more than a flashlight or two, their proximity difficult to determine through the woods. Still, we had no way of knowing who or what we were seeing—they could be enemy or civilians, riverside Fourth of July spectators or terrorists.

There was no time to troubleshoot communications—I waved a hand forward, telling him to continue our patrol. We were going old-school, a Vietnam-style foot patrol with the aid of night vision and not much else. At the same time, I was cognizant that my team was following me into hell—literally or metaphorically, take your pick—and I felt a deep surging gratitude, regardless of what was about to occur. I was a foster kid, an orphan with some distant memories of my father; but these three men were friends and brothers, along with Ian, though I cringed to credit him at present. He was putting us in a difficult position by notifying Duchess, but his heart was in the right place, and when I asked myself if I'd do anything different in his situation, my mind was silent.

Worthy continued slipping through the forest, leading the way until he abruptly took a knee and extended an arm to our left.

Scanning the trail beyond the trees, I saw what he was pointing to: a cluster of five men on the trail, facing the direction we'd approached from.

They were loosely arrayed, though I could tell from their posture that they were all likely armed. I could easily determine from context that this was an enemy observation post, meant to buy time in the event anyone followed the trail to their location.

Looking forward, I saw Worthy staring at me for guidance. He wanted to know whether to reorient our small formation to assault the men.

I gave an exaggerated shake of my head, knowing that at this distance Worthy probably couldn't make out much more than my night vision device swinging from side to side. Sure, we could assault the observation post, but to what end? Whatever we sought was down the trail, an unknown target marked by the flashlights, and we no longer had the manpower to take on all comers.

Worthy obeyed, rising and continuing to advance amidst the chanting crickets and croaking treefrogs that covered the sounds of our movement.

As we advanced, I half wondered if Bari Khan was simply displacing the rockets far enough from the seafood processing plant to launch them into Fredericksburg proper. That course of action seemed too subtle, however, too low-profile for him.

But if that was his plan, all the better: it meant he was waiting in the trees ahead.

In that sense our team was an asset to Duchess whether she accepted it or not. She'd tasked us with killing Bari Khan, and we were about to. Sure, it was on the wrong continent and in violation of every classified national charter governing our existence even when we were a team, much less while operating as criminal fugitives. But a mission was a mission, and no matter the ultimate outcome, we were about to complete ours.

The question of whether we'd stop the attack before it was too late to do so, of course, remained up for debate.

We'd have our answer soon enough, I thought as we closed with the source of light through the trees. And amid the shifting glow, I was gradually able to discern the box-like shadow of what could only be Bari Khan's delivery truck, parked at the end of the trail with its headlights off. The dark forms of men swarmed around it, probably moving the rockets into the launch assembly.

Then I discovered something far more concerning: the phosphorescent green hues of my night vision were too clear, revealing too much night sky to represent anything so hopeful as a rocket cache site or even a launch platform installed in a clearing.

Instead I was looking toward the river itself; they weren't offloading the rockets onto land, they were offloading them onto the water. In that regard, I intuitively knew what I was looking at before I could visually confirm the structure.

A low, black swath of shadow too symmetrical to be of nature's doing resided past the truck, and there was no possible explanation besides the one my mind was screaming in that moment: Ian had been right. But where the intelligence operative was expecting a semi-trailer, Bari Khan had used a boat—and it was about to sail up the Potomac as a floating artillery barge, its 633 rockets poised to fire on Washington, DC.

I charged forward to Worthy, waving one hand in an overhead circle to signal Cancer and Reilly to consolidate. Our mission was over—I no longer cared about incarceration or even death. Depending on the boat's speed, they were twenty minutes or less from firing upon our nation's capital, and regardless of what happened in the next sliver of time, we had to notify every possible responder, from Duchess on down, of what was about to occur.

I'd gladly offer my wrists to handcuffs, happily surrender my freedom along with my team's whether they were compliant or not, to stop that ship from proceeding north up the Potomac River. Because if we were all killed in some heinous crossfire, what good would our lives have served? What purpose was there behind the collective agonies we'd suffered around the world first as mercenaries, then as CIA contractors?

But there was another reason, too, this one more selfish than the rest.

My wife and daughter were sitting on the National Mall at this very second, and if I lost them, then nothing else that the world had to offer would ever keep me from self-destruction in the ensuing anguish. Whether I wanted to admit it or not, this was no longer about the survival of untold civilians—it was about my family, plain and simple, and every one of the myriad factors external to that faded to irrelevance in that second.

I slapped Worthy on the shoulder, kneeling beside him as Cancer and Reilly rushed to our side in a huddle.

Whispering just loud enough for them to hear me above the night creatures, I said, "Rockets are headed up the Potomac for DC. I'm sending up the SOS."

"Do it," Cancer agreed, and without the benefit of functional radios, I withdrew my cell phone to contact Ian.

But in addition to numerous missed calls and texts from Laila, the screen showed no signal.

There was no way we were far enough removed from civilization to justify this discrepancy. Instead, I knew in a fleeting second that our radios hadn't malfunctioned after all.

I whispered, "No signal. The boat must be running a cellular and FM jammer to prevent civilians from reporting anything suspicious."

Reilly replied, "Want me to evade back to the road, try to get a signal and call the cops?"

An outside observer could have regarded this inquiry as an act of cowardice, though I knew it to be the exact opposite: any of us would have been loath to abandon our team, to opt out of the proceedings, however catastrophic.

But Reilly was the most injured among us, useful for little beyond operating a pistol with his one good hand, and he'd volunteered to assist from the worst possible position out of a heartfelt commitment to stop the attack at all costs. If we were all killed, he'd spend the rest of his waking hours contemplating his survival; in that regard, death was a small price to pay.

I shook my head.

"We haven't had comms since we left the car. They've got land-based units jamming radio and cell communication—that's what I'd do if I were BK. So let's use that to our advantage."

Worthy replied, "How are we supposed to do that?"

"Whoever's on that boat is reliant on audible gunshots to sound the alarm. We kill them off silently until we're compromised, then hold our own until the cops arrive. At this point they've got to be a few minutes behind us at most."

Rather than issue a verbal response, Cancer held up his fist to the center of our circle, and the rest of us tapped it with our knuckles as he whispered, "Fast and loose."

Reilly advanced with his pistol gripped tightly in his right hand, painfully aware that if he fired a shot, his team would be done before they began their interdiction attempt.

So he reserved the handgun for a last-resort engagement of someone threatening the life of one of his teammates. It was unlikely they'd need any help from him anyway—with his left arm slung to his side, he couldn't effectively operate a rifle and was relegated to the role of rear security at best and last-resort shooter at worst.

Which was just as well, he supposed, because the ball bearings in his left arm were fucking killing him.

Each step brought with it a new wave of pain, the metal spheres jostling for position among muscle mass that was surely infected. Even if he had painkillers to gobble, he needed his full wits for the effort ahead, whatever that might entail. Nothing was more detrimental to a team than a wounded medic, and Reilly's only consolation was that the suicide bomber hadn't advanced a few more paces into the room before detonating himself. If that were the case, David and Worthy would be alone.

He caught his first clear sight of the boat a moment later—it was a large river cruise vessel, with three levels of interior decks bordered by tall observation windows. But the real prize would be on the rooftop lounge, where the launch assembly had probably been soldered into place over the course of the previous week.

For Bari Khan, it was a smart play: the three-level boat would place the launch assembly out of view from any other vessels, and the elevation would give the rockets the maximum possible range.

The delivery truck was parked at the edge of a makeshift dock, two men positioned off the side, apparently waiting for the boat to depart.

As Reilly trailed his team toward the delivery truck, it looked like he wouldn't need to shoot. Worthy advanced toward the trail, David and Cancer falling on-line at either side until he halted movement.

The three men began firing almost simultaneously, a whispered chorus of suppressed gunshots that dropped the two men in a hail of subsonic rounds.

Exalted at the silent kills, Reilly felt his hope give way to fear as a sound rose through the trees around him—the boat's engines spooling to full power, sending the massive craft lurching slowly upstream.

Holstering his pistol, Reilly broke into a run in an attempt to catch up with his team, who were now emerging onto the trail and turning down a short wooden dock as the ship gradually slid away.

Reilly saw a single man appear on the middle deck, leaning over the rail as Worthy stopped in place, taking aim as the luminescent streak of his infrared laser intersected with the man's head.

There was no way to hear the suppressed shot over the sound of the boat engine; instead, the man's body tilted forward, over the rail, becoming a black shadow in freefall until it impacted the water's surface amid the churning wake.

Cancer and David were sprinting down the dock then, leaping aboard the rail of the moving ship and hauling themselves over the side. Worthy was only a second behind them, clambering aboard as Reilly realized with muted horror that he'd be too late; if anything, he'd be lucky to place a single good hand on the final second of railing before the boat cleared the dock.

He ran forward anyway, struggling through the pain of his lacerated arm shifting in its sling. Charging the final steps toward the edge of the dock, Reilly leapt with his lone functioning arm outstretched.

His leap ended when he collided with the ship's side, hand slipping from the top railing rung and catching hold of the one below. Reilly held tight with all the force he could muster, feet struggling for purchase on the slick hull.

But he was too heavy, his grasp too tenuous to hold on; he was bracing himself to plunge into the water when he felt hands across his back, saw the dark forms of David and Cancer bracing against the rail as they struggled to hold him in place.

Worthy arrived a moment later, deftly straddling the rail and grabbing the back of Reilly's tactical belt to hoist him upward.

Together, the three men struggled to lift Reilly's immense weight as he did what he could to walk his feet up the ship's sidewall toward them. He felt himself shifting upward, hands scrambling across his body as his torso cleared the top rail, and finally he swung over it in a pendulum before slamming onto the deck with an explosion of pain in his left arm that immobilized his entire body as he fought not to scream.

Reilly panted for breath, rolling to his back and looking up at his teammates.

But they were gone.

Clambering to his feet, Reilly saw the three men moving away from him, advancing toward the nearest doorway with their weapons raised.

Drawing his pistol, Reilly made a move to follow them but registered a new sound over the groaning engines and rippling water—police sirens screaming down the trail, far too late as the boat surged upstream, churning a frothy wake across the Potomac.

63

I followed Cancer through the first door, clearing a foothold for our team on the interior deck.

The room was a long corridor with life vests mounted on the walls from floor to ceiling. But it was otherwise empty, and that much proved to be a small mercy—after our desperate scramble to board the ship, we needed to get out of sight and determine our plan of action. Worthy had already shot one man off the second deck, and it was a matter of time before his absence was noted, if it hadn't been already.

As soon as Worthy and Reilly entered the room behind us, Cancer directed them to pull security and then approached me for a quick huddle.

He whispered, "You thinking we sabotage the boat?"

I shook my head. "We don't have any munitions big enough to put a dent in the hull or the engines. And we could take over the control room, but BK would just fire the rockets as soon as the boat stopped moving. Right now, the only thing in our favor is the element of surprise—we need to get topside, take down the launch assembly."

Pulling out my phone to check for reception, I saw that it still had no signal—and then, for the first time, I looked at my last missed text from Laila.

Cancer asked, "You think he's gunning for the White House?"

"Not the White House," I said, feeling my neck flush with heat. "The National Mall."

I showed him my phone screen.

One million Americans celebrating freedom. Wish you were here. I love you, babe.

The picture was what I wanted him to see—a selfie of Laila and Langley, both smiling.

But it was the "one million Americans" comment that the picture conveyed more than anything else: spectators were packed nearly shoulder-to-shoulder around them, the silhouette of a child sitting atop his dad's shoulders standing out in relief against the Lincoln Memorial in the background.

Cancer nodded, sounding almost reverent. "Shit, this guy is good—with 633 rockets he'll be able to turn the National Mall into a kill box from the Lincoln Memorial to the Capitol Building, and destroy everything in between. Vietnam and World War II memorials, Washington Monument..."

"And the people," I replied, putting my phone away.

"Yeah," he said, "and the people. What about DC's air defenses?"

"That's why BK is doing it now. Any low-altitude countermeasures will be disabled for the duration of the fireworks display."

Cancer muttered two words.

"Well...shit."

Then, before I could speak, he addressed Worthy and Reilly, both pulling security on their respective doors.

"Party's on the roof, fellas. Racegun, take us to the stairs."

Worthy began moving at once, following the arrow beneath a sign labeled STAIRWAY TO DECK 2. I took up the second-man position behind him, with Cancer and Reilly following at a jog.

In that moment I didn't care about the million bystanders on the National Mall, or the immeasurable heritage of the priceless monuments about to be destroyed on what was the national sacred ground of my country.

Every ounce of my concern, my rage, my anguish, was centered around protecting two people: Laila and Langley, my wife and daughter stranded in a crossfire that had yet to commence. I didn't care about my life or anyone else's, would have done anything and killed anyone to protect those two people from harm. Bari Khan suddenly didn't seem any more savage than I felt in that moment; only our root cause differed.

Entering the stairwell behind Worthy, I followed him to the central deck.

Worthy emerged onto the middle deck interior, cutting left near a long dining hall packed with tables and chairs, a set of four long buffet tables sitting empty. It was a ghostly sight, the lights of buildings on both shores sliding past through twin observation windows. This ship was moving fast, and as he cleared forward with his team behind him, Worthy considered that was both a good and bad thing.

On the plus side, the enormous volume of the boat's engines concealed his movement, augmented by the rush of wind and lapping water of the Potomac.

But that was where the good news ended.

The same roaring engines that would cover their movement were likewise speeding the boat north toward DC, and if his team didn't stop the attack before then, no one else would.

He ran toward the next section of stairwell marking the far wall to his front, his infrared laser swinging from side to side as he moved, prepared to engage any emerging threats. But before he reached the door to the stairs, he slowed to observe an item on the floor that he nearly tripped over—at first he thought it was a body, but then he realized it was too symmetrical, with squared corners marking the dark shape.

The duffel bag was a long rectangular block, like something used to store hockey equipment. Its placement on the floor was too haphazard to be a boobytrap, and yet too out of place to be a holdover from the ship's previous crew, whoever they were.

He nudged the bag with the toe of his boot, felt the clanking of heavy metal cylinders—and didn't need to open it to know that it contained a bundle of rockets.

However many enemy fighters were aboard the ship, they must have been ferrying the bags up to the top deck. Worthy suspected that the majority of them would be busy loading the tubes—and with over six hundred rockets, that was going to take a considerable amount of time. Bari Khan didn't have unlimited manpower in the States; after all, this wasn't Syria, and he'd already committed two assault teams with suicide vests to the seafood processing plant in addition to the five-man blocking position he'd seen on the trail.

How many men could he possibly have aboard the boat?

He received a partial answer a few seconds later, halting in place to take aim at the doorway to the stairs, silhouetted with the brightening glow of a flashlight descending from the top deck.

It wasn't one man who appeared then, but two—and the first fell dead amid the sparking flashes of ricochets that erupted in the stairwell as Worthy opened fire along with two other members of the team.

But the second man darted out of sight, headed up the stairs as Worthy broke into a run. If the jammer was forcing his team to operate without radios, then it had the same effect on the enemy—so he could be racing headlong into an ambush, but what choice did he have? If the escaping fighter got word out to the main enemy element, Worthy's team could be overrun by a massing force of terrorists who could then proceed to fire the rockets anyway.

Worthy ascended the stairs three at a time, vaguely registering dark splashes of blood in the stairwell—this fucker was wounded, but that alone wasn't enough to help the team. He needed a definitive kill to know that their clearance was proceeding undetected for the time being, and as this thought crossed his mind, he emerged onto the carpeted surfaces of the highest enclosed deck. An open lounge with a full bar was positioned against one wall, and the far end of the room held a doorway leading to the final short stairwell separating them from the ship's open roof with its launch assembly.

A shadowy figure was loping toward those stairs, the wounded enemy calling out as Worthy opened fire on him from behind.

It was sloppy shooting by anyone's standards, the first rounds lacing into his thighs and buttocks as he sprawled headlong to the ground, rolling onto his back. Worthy raced forward, stopping just as the man's head became visible at the end of his infrared laser beam to deliver the kill shots.

But the man was rolling over below him, shielding his face with a hand amid groans of agony. Worthy opened fire, seeing his rounds tear open the man's throat—at this close range, the top-mounted laser offset caused his bullets to impact below his point of aim—and Worthy quickly adjusted his barrel to send four rounds tearing through the man's palms and into his head before he finally went still.

The team flowed past him as he reloaded, Cancer whispering over his shoulder,

"Nice shooting, hotshot."

Cancer strode past Worthy, assuming position as the lead man as he closed with the stairwell to his front.

Each step brought with it searing pain from the quartet of steel ball bearings in his right thigh, and he pushed through the discomfort with the knowledge that speed was their only remaining ally—Worthy's suppressed gunshots had been quiet, but the enemy had already tried to call out, and subsonic rounds did little to aid in stealth once they punched through wood and tumbled off metal surfaces.

At any rate, the next flight of stairs was the final one before the rooftop deck, and Cancer intended to be the first one atop it.

He was about to cross the open doorway when a man leapt down the stairs, so close that they almost collided with one another—whether he'd heard the sound of bullet impacts or come to search for his comrades was anyone's guess, and Cancer cracked off three shots in the time it took him to register the figure before him.

The man grunted in pain and grabbed Cancer's rifle, driving him forward out of the doorway as more fighters came charging down the steps.

Cancer vaguely registered the men moving to his left and right, the two ranks now mingled with one another.

His own wounded opponent was still struggling to keep Cancer's rifle down, and after a moment of crippling pain in his leg as he resisted the effort, he let his barrel dip toward the ground and fired a bullet into the man's shin.

Then Cancer body-checked the man as hard as he could, shouldering him backward as the enemy fighter stumbled in a failed attempt to stay upright on his injured leg. Driving his suppressor into the man's chest, Cancer fired a double tap and watched the flashes momentarily illuminate his target before he collapsed dead.

Turning to assist his teammates, Cancer saw them engaged in a fight marked by the suppressed gunshots at near-point-blank range before finding a sight that struck him as somewhere between absurd and comical —Reilly, wisely choosing not to fire his unsuppressed pistol at risk of warning additional enemy overhead, now held a man in a headlock, wheeling him sideways to prevent him from being able to effectively grasp his slung rifle.

Cancer closed on Reilly with two quick steps, and delivered a hard punch to the man's head.

Reilly held his opponent in a crushing headlock, squeezing his throat in a viselike grip as Cancer's first blow impacted against his skull.

Ordinarily Cancer would be Johnny-on-the-spot with his fighting knife, but he'd had to ditch that particular tool after the metalworking factory raid—and now he resorted to pummeling the man's face with a fist.

But physical strength was Reilly's area of expertise, not Cancer's.

After three blows failed to knock the man unconscious, Reilly was fed up.

"Hold this," he said, releasing his headlock and shoving the man toward his teammate.

Cancer struggled to grasp the disoriented man, turning him just in time for Reilly to deliver a savage blow that cracked across the man's face and sent him and Cancer flying backward into the wall.

Then Reilly drew his pistol, ducking into the stairwell to provide security for his teammates currently dispatching the remaining enemy fighters behind him.

He held his aim toward the closed door atop the final stretch of stairs, waiting for the suppressed gunfire to abate and hearing the last subsonic bullet impact the floor without a follow-up.

The stairwell was too tight to fit two men across, and the seconds it would have taken him to descend and allow his teammates to go first were apparently deemed too long by David, who whispered sharply behind him. "Go!"

So Reilly did, his left arm throbbing in agony, mind keenly aware that the pistol in his right hand was no match for whatever enemy were waiting on the top deck, prepared to launch their rocket attack against his nation's capital.

He charged upward nonetheless, closing on the rooftop deck with the single thought that he'd have to clear the doorway as quickly as possible, then get the hell out of the way so his three teammates could put their rifles to good use.

But as if in a dream, Reilly reached for the handle only to feel it turning of its own volition. Then the door was pulled outward by a single man whose face was lit by a shifting cascade of light under his night vision.

The face-to-face encounter lasted a fraction of a second.

Reilly's thoughts were remarkably clear and linear. He was unsure if one of his teammates could take a suppressed shot from their angled position on the stairs, and briefly considered ducking out of the way to let them try and thus preserve the element of surprise.

But this man held a submachine gun in one hand, and a single burst from that could wound or kill Reilly's entire team in the time it took them to hear it opening fire.

There was only one thing to do, and Reilly did it with astonishing speed —canting his pistol upward, he fired a single shot that passed through the man's lower jaw, propelling through his brain and killing him in place.

Then Reilly plunged forward to tackle the man out of the doorway, slamming him onto the top deck to clear the way for his teammates and struggling to aim his pistol forward as he registered a dazzling display of neon color illuminating the night sky.

I vaulted Reilly's body in a single long stride, cutting left to clear the doorway as I took in the incomprehensible sight beyond.

The rooftop deck was almost completely filled by metal tubes angled upward in neat rows, linked by daisy-chained wires that would fire them in a near-simultaneous succession.

But that was only the second most stunning feature of the view atop the ship—to my front right, the Washington, DC skyline was stark against the deep, booming explosions of fireworks, a brilliant and blinding cycle of colored sparks that turned the night into a shifting sky of radiant color.

I registered the incoming and outgoing gunfire from my team battling an unknown number of fleeting shadows darting amid the network of rocket tubes, the vast majority of which held a payload whose lethality was going to be sent screaming into the capital within the next twenty seconds.

I visually traced the cords as they snaked between rows of metal tubes, seeing that they descended on a single point at the front-right edge of the deck. I took off at a sprint, running toward the spot with a speed beyond anything my exhausted condition should have allowed.

Then I saw another figure doing the same, running five long paces ahead of me.

I knew at once this was Bari Khan. He was going to fire the rockets himself, and whatever device waited to initiate that process, he was making his way toward it now.

To my right, I saw a shifting view of the Washington Monument reaching skyward, its vertical height coming abreast of the ship as we fought to overtake the enemy.

The boat began slowing then, at what had to be the designated stopping point on the river, a calculated position that every rocket tube had been aligned off of to send their deadly cargo screaming toward the National Mall.

The entire crux of my team's efforts since targeting this man across two continents now fell upon me amid the fireworks exploding overhead.

I fired on the run, blasting imprecise shots toward Bari Khan's fleeing figure until my rifle bolt locked backward on an empty chamber—but at least one bullet had found its mark.

He lurched forward, stumbling as he struggled to regain his footing.

Still running at full speed, I closed the distance between us and, with a final leap, tackled him from behind.

We crashed to the ground, him on his side with me on top of him. I sat up on my knees, taking hold of his head in both hands and jerking it upward.

Before I could smash his skull against the deck, every muscle in my body went rigid with blinding pain.

A cold metal blade was sliding into my abdomen, the soundtrack of firework blasts fading into a vague white noise as the air rushed out of my lungs. I instinctively braced my hands against his right arm, forcing it down to the deck as the blade withdrew from my stomach.

My strength began fading then, vision registering the knife in Bari Khan's right hand as I looked to his opposite side, searching for a firing device.

I found it clutched in his left hand, with the handle pulled to extension —the time fuse was already burning, and it was too late to stop the launch.

My eyes followed a thin wire toward the first metal tube in an array of hundreds linked by a single snaking wire, and while pinning Bari Khan down with my full body weight, I searched for someone who could help.

The only figure I saw was Reilly, running toward me with a pistol in one hand.

My breaths were constricted, each gasp of air shallower than the last. I used my remaining breath to cry out, "Doc! *Break the chain!*"

Reilly's gaze followed the wires to the first tube. He flung his pistol to the deck, drawing a grenade and slowing to a halt in three stuttering steps as he used his injured arm to yank the pin free.

Beneath me, Bari Khan was struggling to bring the knife back into my side, the point breaking skin as another searing torrent of blood spilled out. The pain brought with it a momentary surge of adrenaline, and I wrested his right hand for control of the knife before the rest of my strength gave out.

I fell atop him, feeling hard metal against my sternum—the knife's handle.

The blade plunged inside Bari Khan's chest, penetrating his breastbone under my weight. He gasped as a bloody froth formed at his lips, bubbling and spewing across the side of his face as he said with impossible calmness, "This is just the beginning."

He was mortally wounded, and used his final breath to rasp the words, "*Meryem, Patime...wǒ yào huí jiāle.*"

Then he went still, my vision beginning to narrow as blackness closed on the periphery. I tried to focus, looking up to see Reilly heaving his grenade, its spinning black orb crossing a sky of dazzling color on its flight to the first rocket tube.

It descended to its final point of impact, one that I desperately hoped would destroy the daisy chain before it began.

I watched in horror as it fell short, detonating in a fireball between the second and third tubes. Shards of metal flew outward from the blast, hissing through the air as the grenade's echo faded to a second explosion—this one a deep popping sound that originated from the first tube.

The next seconds proceeded as if in slow motion, a terrible progression lit by the nightmarish red and blue glow of fireworks blasting in the sky.

I was moments from blacking out, struggling to focus as I saw a single rocket launch. It appeared as little more than a flashing shadow that sailed twenty meters out of the tube before its motor ignited. Then a sparkling orange glow appeared at the tail, marking the rocket's progress until it streaked out of sight, arcing through the night on a flight path toward the National Mall.

Then a jet-black veil overtook my view, and I passed out atop my enemy's corpse.

64

Laila Rivers watched the fireworks burst overhead, casting flares of brightly colored light across the Lincoln Memorial.

She squeezed Langley's tiny palm in her own, looking down to see her awestruck daughter staring skyward, completely absorbed with the blazing glow overhead.

This should have been an utterly perfect moment, and it was, save one glaring inconsistency: David wasn't there to share it with them. Even her parents had bowed out with head colds, leaving her and Langley to attend alone. Laila had used her last text to David—unanswered, like all the rest she'd sent that day—to tell him that she loved him.

And it was true, she knew in her heart. She loved David unconditionally, knew that despite his many shortcomings he meant well as a husband and served as the best father that Langley could ask for.

But the harmonious interludes of domestic bliss had become less frequent, and more often than not marked by the incessant lies that rolled off his tongue as seamlessly as he breathed. Laila had never caught him in the act, though judging by the nature of his work it remained unlikely she ever would.

Instead, she registered his words with the distant recognition that their marriage was second place behind some great secret, the ultimate lie whose source she was unable to determine. David didn't strike her as the type of serial adulterer who'd deceive her for years. By all appearances he loved her and Langley, and he loved his country, though Laila questioned which had the foremost place in his heart.

Ordinarily, moments like this would make her proud of her husband's patriotism. Here she was in Washington, DC, the focal point for the ideal of human freedom if not always the perfect implementation. She got goosebumps as the national anthem played before the start of the fireworks, felt a very real sense of pride at the sight of these great monuments that embodied the principles on which her country was founded.

But the dazzling display meant little when weighed against the deceptive farce that her marriage had become, the late-night returns home by a husband who'd been gone too long, and offered far too little information in response to her own career updates if and when they had a chance to reconnect.

In the end, Laila knew one thing for certain. She didn't just *need* David; she *wanted* him as well, and in return she'd received not so much as a call after he failed to show up today.

And as she watched the radiant fireworks in the night sky over DC, she wondered not only where David was at that moment, but what his thoughts were about the state of their family. Because Laila could toe the line for her child, to an extent—but beyond that she was only one woman, and she hadn't signed onto a marital contract to be the one upholding the only true end of commitment in the years or decades ahead.

But her thoughts halted abruptly with an imminent sense of danger, and Laila perceived an odd noise penetrating the cracking fireworks. It was a thin, whistling howl, crescendoing to a deafening level as she pulled Langley into her breast. She fell forward onto their picnic blanket, shielding her daughter from danger as horrified screams erupted among the crowd.

The whistling howl reached a deathly wail a split second before impact, and then her body was jolted by a deafening explosion that rocked the ground with such violence that she thought she was dead.

A searing flash of heat roared over her backside, and amidst the flare she felt a tiny razor shard of debris slice into her left shoulder. The fragment came to rest at the front of her deltoid, radiating a smoldering burn that spread through her entire body as she held tight over Langley, anticipating another explosion.

But the sound of the blast echoed across the monuments, leaving in its wake a horrible chorus of agonized cries from the wounded.

Sitting up, she took Langley's face in her hands and asked, "Are you okay?"

Her daughter nodded, eyes wide. "Are you?"

Laila didn't answer, looking instead to the sight around her—panicked masses of civilians, screaming and trampling one another to get away from a fresh crater in the earth. The site was ringed by motionless bodies, and an outer circumference of writhing people covered in blood.

"Come on, sweetie," Laila said, taking her daughter's hand and heading for the impact sight.

She saw that she was not alone—other figures emerged through the fleeing crowd, racing toward the casualties to help.

Arriving at the outer ring of bodies, Laila recognized the scope of carnage that awaited not only her but her daughter—half-charred people who were quite clearly dead, their sides and skulls torn open in an explosion whose source she couldn't attribute to an errant firework.

The damage was simply too severe, too all-encompassing to be the result of a random mishap, and Laila realized in one savage second that she'd been unwittingly thrust to the front lines of a terrorist attack. It could have been a suicide vest, or a grenade, or some bomb whose origin she didn't have the background to identify—but as a medical professional, she knew at once that the shrapnel wounds that had decimated the dead and survivors alike were no accident.

Groans from the wounded permeated the high-pitched wails of panic, and Laila looked across those obviously dead, horrific as the sight was, to focus on the grievously injured, looking for someone who was in danger of imminent death within the minutes it would take the first medics to arrive.

She didn't have to look far.

65

The hospital room was as stark as those she worked at on a daily basis, though instead of administering to her child subjects, Laila was currently the patient.

Langley was curled up beside her on the hospital bed, half-watching the television screen as it flashed between on-the-scene reporters and newsroom hosts discussing the tragedy of an errant firework that had detonated amid the crowd of spectators on the National Mall, killing twenty-three and injuring fifty-seven.

Laila felt her head shaking without conscious intent, knowing that the official reports were, to put it lightly, complete and total bullshit. A doctor had removed a tiny, twisted metal shard from her left deltoid. She felt the gauze dressing now covering the wound, thinking that no firework could have possibly flung such a swath of destruction during a carefully planned national display. There was no explanation of an accident that would account for what she and her child had seen in the aftermath—least of all the casualty they treated.

The teenage girl had been splayed out, unconscious, bleeding from a shrapnel wound at the top of her thigh. Laila had seen at once this was an arterial bleed, the dark fluid spurting with each beat of the girl's heart, and she knew the wound was too high on her leg for a belt tourniquet.

Scanning the debris around her, Laila had seen an insulated water bottle—which, at her word, Langley quickly retrieved. Pressing the cylinder into her casualty's pelvic V-line, Laila used her knee to hold the bottle and apply pressure to stem the flow of blood from a severed iliac artery. After unbuttoning the shirt she wore over a tank top, Laila slid it off and routed one sleeve beneath the small of the girl's back. But she couldn't reach far enough to pull it out the opposite side, and before she could so much as adjust her position, Langley had reached her slender arm under the patient, pulling out the other end of the shirt.

Together, the two shimmied it beneath the girl's buttocks, retrieving the cloth from between her legs and tying a knot over the bottle. Even with Laila's knee applying her full bodyweight, the flow of blood had reduced but not stopped entirely. She needed more pressure and swept her eyes across the debris, trying to locate a stick of some kind before Langley asked what she needed.

And once Laila told her, Langley had darted off the way they'd come, returning moments later with a half-charred American flag attached to a three-foot-long metal pole.

Then Laila slid the pole through the shirtsleeve knot, using both hands to twist it in a circle as the tension drove the bottle further into the teenager's thigh. When the pole began to bend under the effort, Laila used one hand to hold it in place while sliding the other beneath the girl's knee to feel for a popliteal pulse but finding none.

There was precious little celebration at the time; the first wave of EMTs arrived moments later, one of them assuming control of the hasty tourniquet. Laila had tried to find another casualty she could help, but it was impossible. Instead she'd nearly been bowled over by EMTs racing to the scene from medical checkpoints scattered across the National Mall, and DC Metro cops cleared the scene of all bystanders still capable of walking.

And now she was in the hospital along with everyone else who'd been in close proximity to the blast, the least injured currently awaiting release.

Pulling Langley closer to her side, Laila said, "You saved that girl's life, you know."

Langley shook her head against Laila's shoulder.

"We."

"What?"

"You said I saved that girl, but it was us. *We* saved her life."

A female doctor entered a moment later, holding a clipboard for her hourly checkup of the many patients who had been admitted in the past two hours.

Laila nodded to the television screen. "They're wrong. I don't know how I know, but I'm telling you—they're wrong."

The doctor replied patiently in a response that, Laila was sure, she'd delivered many times over the course of that evening.

"You're in shock, Mrs. Rivers. A firework fell into the crowd and exploded."

Laila shook her head resolutely. "I know this doesn't mean anything, but I'm an MD, and that was no firework. It was a bomb, or a missile, or—I don't know." She sighed, exasperated. "But it wasn't a firework."

The doctor gave a sad smile as she checked her and Langley's pupils for dilation. "From one MD to another, you're in shock, sweetie. And if your next two check-ups don't show signs of a concussion, you'll be cleared for release. Until then, try and get some rest."

But as she departed the hospital room, Laila realized that rest wasn't on the agenda for tonight.

The three men who entered the room could be best described as *suits*—an African American, a Hispanic, and a white man—and they were quickly intercepted by a male RN telling them that the patient was being monitored for a concussion and not yet cleared for release.

A single flash of a badge from the Hispanic man served to quiet the nurse's objections at once and in full. Then he turned to Laila and said, "You need to come with us, ma'am."

She pulled Langley tight beside her on the hospital bed. "I'm not going anywhere without my daughter."

The man nodded as if that much was obvious.

"That's not a problem. Langley has to come with us, too."

Laila struggled to understand her situation, the night's events growing more surreal by the minute as the SUV she rode in whisked her further into the depths of DC and, ultimately, into the brightly lit tunnel of an underground parking garage.

The driver's response to her inquiries was little more than the doctor's had been: she was in shock, he said, and everything would be explained in short order.

The man beside him in the passenger seat had little more to say, transmitting indecipherable short code into his lapel as the vehicle made its way to a parking spot amid a swarm of other cars.

And for the second time that night, Laila noted with increasing concern that her daughter Langley seemed strangely more composed than she herself did.

Squeezing Laila's hand in her own, Langley actually said the words, "It's okay, Mom," as if she had any clue what was going on. Laila found herself wondering about the exact nature of her relationship with David, despite the official story of their meeting at the hands of a failed wedding engagement to an alcoholic mother.

But these thoughts were soon swept from her mind as the SUV braked to a halt, the suits in the driver and passenger seats dismounting to escort Laila and Langley through the throngs of people clustered under bright ultraviolet lights. Laila didn't know who they were or what she was looking at, save the fact that she knew what *wasn't* present: there were no media cameras or reporters amid the business-suited men and women clustered in the underground garage, alternately speaking to one another and texting into Blackberry devices.

Instead she followed without objection, clutching Langley's hand, until she reached the center of the storm.

And at the midpoint of that maelstrom of people, she saw a few individuals who stood out by virtue of their incongruity to the scene around her: a silver-haired man with medical dressings on his thigh, a hulking bodybuilder-type with one arm in a sling, and a short, squat man with a distinguished air who watched her with reserved detachment.

A slight African American woman in her fifties stood beside the final man, ending her sentence abruptly to appraise Laila and Langley with an expression of curiosity and, unless Laila was reading the situation wrong, a flashing smile that quickly faded.

They all surrounded a single figure seated in a foldout chair, his clothes bloodied, face flushed, looking on the brink of total exhaustion.

David.

Without thinking, Laila plunged through the crowd toward him.

He saw her and smiled, struggling to rise from the chair as she collided with him in an embrace that was joined by their daughter.

Laila heard David grunt, and she looked up to see his face turn ghostly white with pain. He clutched at his stomach, and Laila saw the bulge of a medical dressing beneath his shirt.

"Oh, I'm—I'm sorry, David."

But he forced a smile and kissed her cheek, pulling her in again and reaching for Langley with his other arm.

"It's okay," he said.

Then, with his breath hot against the side of her face, he whispered, "I think it's time I tell you what I actually do for a living."

Laila felt hot tears spilling down her cheeks, and she began to sob.

66

Charlottesville, Virginia, USA

I finished pouring my second cup of coffee and returned to the dining table where Laila and Langley were finishing breakfast.

Easing myself into the chair across from them, I felt the nagging abdominal pain that had been getting less prominent with each passing day. I'd almost completed my final round of antibiotics, and the wounds were healing nicely with puffy white scar tissue, a reminder of a terrorist attack that could have been much worse. A two-digit death toll among civilians at the National Mall was no small matter, but it just as easily could have reached five figures or worse—and very nearly had.

"How's it feeling today?" Laila asked, sensing my discomfort no matter how much I tried to conceal it. That's what made her a good doctor, I supposed—she saw right through the stubborn assholes like myself who tried to hide all signs of weakness.

"It's good," I replied. "I've never felt better."

The statement wasn't an exaggeration. Ever since returning to Charlottesville two weeks earlier, I regarded both my family and my home with a deep and abiding sense of gratitude more profound than anything I'd ever felt. I'd entered that house thousands of times, but ever since the attack it bore a strange newness, seemed to breathe with a life of its own that was endowed in part by my recognition that I'd nearly lost it forever, along with my wife and daughter.

Langley set down her fork and asked, "Can I go play?"

"Sure," I said, checking my watch. "We don't have to leave for another hour."

Sliding back her chair, she took off for the living room and its attendant smattering of toys.

Today was reserved for our Saturday rituals: a stroll down Charlottesville's Downtown Mall—which felt considerably safer than the National Mall at present—complete with ice cream for Langley, beers for Dad, and shopping for Mom. Just a normal American family out for the day. The following weekend, we'd be heading to a campsite in the Shenandoah National Park for a couple days of hiking, continuing Langley's quest to see a wild black bear.

Laila looked calm, at peace for the first time in months. She'd finished her pediatric residency, and that had certainly helped. But we both knew it wasn't the main source of her stress, a distinction which belonged solely to me.

And while our day-to-day routines remained largely the same, things had forever changed between us.

I no longer lied to her about what my job had entailed, and like me she bore a physical reminder of the attack: a thin scar across her shoulder from a shard of rocket shrapnel. And like my own scars, it seemed to bear witness to the importance of my team's work for the Agency.

That was, if we still *had* jobs with the Agency—that much remained for Duchess to determine, though as long as my team remained free citizens, I had no cause for complaint either way.

The important thing was that Laila was happy, still in love with me and Langley. She just needed a scrap of truth, and I'd finally given it to her—and now, having restored her trust, I would never lie to her again.

"So," Laila asked, "want to see what our daughter is up to?"

I nodded, rising from the table and bringing my mug.

We'd been keeping a close eye on Langley since the attack, watching for any signs of trauma.

But Langley had been remarkably composed about the entire ordeal, as if nearly dying in a terrorist attack were just a small hitch in her summer break.

At first Laila and I had thought she was in an extended state of shock and denial. Laila had told me how our daughter had seen dead bodies at the blast site and aided her in treating the teenage casualty. So, we took her to three rounds of therapy with a child psychiatrist to determine her state of mind—only to have the doctor admit she was remarkably well adjusted about the whole thing. I considered that this could have been a result of her life experience before I met her, and possibly as a result of her lineage.

I stopped at the entrance to our living room. Laila approached behind me, sliding her hands around my waist as I draped an arm over her shoulder.

Together we sipped coffee and watched our daughter directing her Barbies in an elaborate plan to rescue a prince held captive on the top floor of a dollhouse serving as a castle. The role of dragon had been assigned to the gift I brought home after my first return from Syria, the stuffed pink rabbit currently positioned ominously before the castle-slash-dollhouse.

As we watched her play, Laila asked, "What do you think she's going to be when she grows up?"

I shook my head softly.

"I was wondering the same thing."

Laila and Langley went upstairs to get dressed as I restored the kitchen to order following breakfast.

I'd barely finished cleaning the bacon grease from the pan—the ultimate act of domestic servitude—when my phone rang.

The ringtone was a quiet chirp, one I hadn't heard in some time.

I answered it quickly.

"Wasn't sure I'd hear from you again."

"I wasn't sure I wanted to call you again. Don't make me regret it."

Duchess had been understandably busy as of late, least of all with the small matter of cleaning up after my team. After the FBI seized all relevant evidence of my team's activities leading up to our final raid on the boat, all that remained was negotiating an unconditional pardon—and that turned out to be the easy part.

The president and his family had occupied a fireworks viewing stand on the Capitol Building steps, and if his armored glass could survive a rocket strike, it wouldn't have lasted for two. He still refused to meet us, of course, which annoyed Reilly to no end. But I regarded it as a minor inconvenience when weighed against the prospect of lifelong incarceration.

I asked, "Any word on Wei Zhao?"

"Still at large, and probably the richest subject to ever evade an INTERPOL manhunt. Given his resources and the fact he planned on hiding in advance, I'd be surprised if we find him anytime soon."

Frowning, I said, "I couldn't help but notice a certain coverup of this event in the news."

"And for good reason."

"Really?" I asked. "I seem to remember some democratic ideals speaking out against the suppression of information. As I recall, that kind of government action and worse are what drove Bari Khan to do what he did."

Duchess sighed.

"As usual, David, you're both right and wrong. That ship your team raided bore a multitude of evidence pointing to Chinese state sponsorship of the attack."

"And that information isn't reaching the public why, exactly?"

"Because after somewhat exhaustive analysis, we found it all to be fabricated."

I found myself nodding. "So he wanted to start a war between the US and China."

"He did," she said. "And in his defense, it was the smartest play Bari Khan made. No amount of damage he could have inflicted on China would compare with what the United States is capable of in the wake of a terrorist attack. But that's not the least of it."

"What else is there—and what about the words he spoke in Chinese? Did they make sense?"

"Yes, but they don't help us."

"How so?"

"The first two words were names—Merym, his wife, and Patime, his daughter. Both killed in a Chinese concentration camp."

I felt my chest tighten with the recognition of what this man had lost...would I be any more civil if our roles were reversed?

Or would I be worse?

I managed an unemotional tone as I continued, "And the rest?"

"*Wǒ yào huí jiāle* translates as, 'I'm coming home.'"

Swallowing hard, I asked, "Has our birdie begun to sing?"

I was referring, of course, to the lone surviving terrorist, presently in CIA custody—the man Reilly had knocked out with a haymaker blow before we ascended to the top deck. Not even the ship's captain had made it out alive; my team had found him in the control room, dead from a self-inflicted gunshot wound.

Duchess replied, "Oh, he's singing a song you won't believe. But we'll have to save that for a conversation in person."

"In person?" I asked, suddenly intrigued. "It sounds like you're saying I still have a team."

"For now, and only because you thwarted the attack. Though this was your last chance to color outside the lines of authority. You had one alibi before being disbanded. But you used about seventeen, and if you're expecting any more latitude in operational authorities, I'll have to disappoint you in stating that you're severely mistaken. This entire program—and my leadership of it—is now under more political and military oversight than ever before."

"Understood," I said. "Thank you."

"I'll get in touch when we have something for you to move on. Goodbye, Suicide."

"Goodbye, Duchess."

Ending the call, I hurried to finish the dishes, my mind racing.

There was much I didn't know—who had handpicked Bari Khan to lead the attack, or why. After all, he'd demonstrated remarkable tradecraft and sophistication, complete with financing and logistical support from a now-fugitive billionaire. There was simply no way that Bari Khan got that lucky on what was ostensibly his first terrorist operation, and Ian felt the same way.

Someone had to be pulling the strings, and until we figured out who, I'd remain troubled by Bari Khan's words: *This is just the beginning*.

I brushed the thoughts from my mind. Whatever additional information Duchess had about the origin of the attack or her living detainee's information, it could wait. At the moment, I had far more important things to attend to.

Starting the dishwasher in my perfectly ordinary suburban home, I went upstairs to join my family as we got ready for the day.